Tendril Hearts

By

LJ Vickery

Published by Weir River Press—USA—
Hingham, Massachusetts
Original Copyright 2018 by LJ Vickery
Cover Art by Taria A. Reed

Vickery,LJ/Tendril Hearts
ISBN-10 1-7329088-2-6
ISBN-13 978-1-7329088-2-6

PUBLISHER'S NOTE:
This book is a work of fiction. Names, characters, places and incidents either are the product of the author's imagination or are used fictitiously, and any resemblance to actual persons, living or dead, business establishments, event, or locales, is entirely coincidental.

To my Readers

Thank you for loving all the Blue Hills gods as much as I do! For those of you who have kept up with the series, this book (book eleven) is a continuation of the peril that was uncovered in book ten. Although the final four books have individual love stories seen to completion (like the first nine), the situation for the gods is reaching a crescendo and won't resolve completely until book fourteen.

I hope that won't deter you from continuing to follow these intrepid Mesopotamians as they complete their journey!

How to find what's new:

If I ever stop writing long enough to produce a newsletter, I'll let you know, but for now, follow me on Amazon. https://www.amazon.com/default/e/B014HW MBEO

Or see my website: www.ljvickery.com

Again, thank you for all your support!

Chapter One

"Archie. Knock it off…" Dumuzi swiped at the side of his face as he slowly came awake. His ears tuned instantly to the night peepers chirping in chorus all around him. *Dammit.* He wasn't at home in bed. He'd had another episode and was outside, somewhere in the Blue Hills. He paused. He tensed. That wasn't all. Something else was off.

The god of vegetation was used to being licked awake by his dog, but… A shiver ran down his spine as a cool breeze wafted across his wet cheek. *Shit.* He could feel the actual dog slobber, not just the vague sensation of a tongue's touch. Was he imagining things? Could he feel the wind stirring? Dumuzi cautiously raised his head. He moaned deep in his throat. It was no illusion. The late spring dampness of the dark forest blanketed him.

He attempted to swallow around his dry tongue and forced his eyes to open. Archie was a few feet away, watching him with head tilted, holding an air of expectancy. Dumuzi didn't like it. He slowly sat up and brought his gaze to his feet. *Holy hell. Visible.* A whoosh of air left his lungs, and he dropped his hands to the ground for support.

His fingers flexed in the moist layer of last year's leaves where they covered the ground next to his body.

1

Dumuzi grasped handfuls to anchor himself...then couldn't resist. He brought full palms up to his nose and inhaled deeply. *Oh, gods.* Plant matter. His senses tingled. He, the god of vegetation, was touching and smelling composting leaves for the first time in nearly four hundred years. His eyes filled with tears...which quickly dried in panic. The only reason for his visibility weaved its tendrils into his brain.

No. Push it away. Don't think. Stay grounded.

"Come here, Archie." The border collie's tail wagged violently, and the dog's mouth, full of white teeth, split into a wide grin. He bounded to Dumuzi's lap and nearly toppled the god with his enthusiasm.

"Yeah, boy. I'm real again." Dumuzi wrapped his arms solidly around the wriggling bundle of fur and hugged for all he was worth, trying to keep his trepidation at bay. "Gods, you're warm, and...whew. Archie, you need a bath." The smell of dank dog fur was, unfortunately, only a temporary distraction. Trembling, the god reluctantly put the dog aside and rose to his feet. Dumuzi let the implications of his sudden turn to the physical wash over him. Dammit, he wasn't ready for this.

Fuck. Fuck. Fuck. He spun and punched a tree to his left. *Ouch.* The pain felt good, and the blood that seeped up from the broken skin had a mesmerizing effect as he attempted to come to grips with the facts of his visibility. *Right. Facts. Deep breath.* Somewhere nearby, gods be cursed, was his *Chosen*—the woman with whom he would mate for the rest of eternity. It was the only explanation.

Of course, it had been proven among the gods they could become visible in the presence of someone whose bloodlines they'd contributed to back in colonial times—when they'd last been corporeal—but Dumuzi had only fucked one woman in Merrymount. It had been a brief, anonymous fling that had ended nearly a year before fate had overtaken the group and rendered them bodiless. He hadn't left behind any children from his loins. He was sure of it. Therefore, the woman he was about to set eyes on was certain to be his gods-damned destiny.

Dumuzi had known it would happen sooner or later, but he wasn't ready for it...would never actually be ready for it. Not with the big-ass problem he'd bring into a relationship. In the past, he'd spurned most personal interactions by keeping a mantle of vagueness wrapped around himself. His Blue Hills god-buddies teasingly called him the stoner-god for his lazy, don't-care-about anything attitude...and in his early years, they would have been correct. He'd spent decades well-acquainted with alcohol and opiates before he realized they weren't of any use battling his problem. Once he came to terms with that, he'd perfected his "out-of-it" demeanor which kept people from prying into his fucked-upedness. Better to look like he didn't care at all than to let folks know how ruined he was on the inside.

The Blue Hills gods were a great bunch, putting up with him and always including him in their more important quests and battles, but the rest of the time? They left him alone to mellow out by himself. They were no fools. All of them were aware of Dumuzi's problem and had made sure to let him chill when duty didn't call.

When the veg-god had found Archie—or more accurately when Archie had found him—he'd tried to push the dog away, but the canine would have none of that. The intrepid collie stuck by him, especially during Dumuzi's worst moments, and it seemed, surprisingly, to work out okay…so far.

Hanging with Archie was one thing, but hitching his troubles to a human female would be completely insane. Not only that, he didn't *want* to become mate, keeper, and/or nursemaid to a *Chosen.* He'd seen how it altered the lives of his fellow gods…and yes, they all seemed supremely happy, but that's because they had great communication with their forever spouses…and great sex. Dumuzi could look forward to neither.

The immortal sighed. His feet dragged. It was time to get a look at the hapless woman. She wasn't aware of it, but she was doomed to mate with him for the salvation of every god and goddess in the compound. An Underworld decree had made it clear, all thirteen gods in his group had to be mated by September fifteenth—a mere four months away—or every one of them would be pulled back into hell, fighting demons for eternity. He would never be selfish enough to relegate his friends to that fate, so he would do his duty and get mated. But his *Chosen* would have to be selfless enough to also sacrifice herself for the good of the group. It was a huge thing to ask, but he had to make sure it would happen.

Dumuzi tuned his acute hearing to a sound not far off in the dense trees. A group of humans of course.

"We need to be quiet, Archie," he told his companion. "No noise and no sudden moves." The black and white border collie lowered into a herding stance and crept forward with his master.

The idiots they approached had started a fire and done nothing to lower their voices. That boded ill. It probably meant they were all young and stupid or…Dumuzi peered through a screen of new leaves. *Right.* Stoned and drunk. There were beer bottles strewn about and an open bag of weed next to one of the boys who was happily rolling a joint. *Idiots.* There was clearly more than an ounce in the bag. If they got caught, they'd go to jail instead of getting a ticket. *Shit.* Been there, done that. Hell, Dumuzi was an expert…but why were these kids self-medicating and self-destructing? And gods-dammit, which one was making him visible? He looked around the group, growing more and more displeased as his gaze hopped from one face to another.

There were three boys and two girls, and not one of them looked old enough to be legal. Dismissing the males, Dumuzi studied the female faces. One girl had large, stunning brown eyes and straight dark hair that hung down to her ass. The other was a pixy looking little thing with a gamine face surrounded by copper red waves. If he hadn't been so sure of his non-parenthood status, he would have said the second girl could pass as his own. Their hair color was identical, and even at this distance, he could see pecan-hued eyes that mimicked his. *Shit.* Could he have…? *No.* Impossible. But the only other option was that one of these two young, untouchable-aged women was his *Chosen.* And that totally sucked.

He felt a gut-wrenching twist of guilt. These girls had barely begun to live, and now, one of them would be sacrificed to him for the good of all his friends. But which one…?

Before he could get his mind to settle on his next course of action, he heard the unmistakable sound of crunching boots tromping through the woods toward the group. He'd know those footfalls anywhere. The state police had either been alerted there was a fire in the woods or had seen it on satellite. Either way, the authorities had come to take a look. Dumuzi groaned. The party was about to get busted, but his potential mate and her friends were oblivious. Should he intervene? Warn them? He thought quickly. *No.* A quick plan formed in his head, and he stayed back to watch and hope things unfolded the way he wanted.

"State Police. Don't move." The order came out of the darkness, and three flashlights clicked on. As Dumuzi assumed, instead of staying put as commanded, the kids scattered. Boys to the left of him, girls to the right. The three cops went after the boys, and Dumuzi fell into step silently behind the fast-moving girls.

"Riley, you head for the road, and I'll go deeper into the woods." The red-headed one pushed her friend in a northerly direction. "I'll make a bunch of noise until I think you're safe, then I'll hide." Dumuzi figured it was as good a plan as any, but he'd seen the troopers in action. They'd round up every one of the kids before the night was over. He'd bet money on it.

"Stay safe, Sienna," the raven-haired one named Riley called back over her shoulder as she sprinted away into the dark. The girls couldn't be too intoxicated, they were still able-bodied as they high-tailed it through the woods.

Dumuzi chose to stay with the girl named Sienna. He watched Riley as she ran away because in one hundred yards—he needed to be within that proximity of his *Chosen* to stay visible—he'd either disappear or not. Dumuzi counted off as Riley absconded. *Ninety-eight, ninety-nine…* He looked down. Yup. Still visible. *Tag.* Sienna was it. Now he could only hope she was eighteen. Not that it would make any difference to the gods…or him, for that matter. The mating ceremony would still have to be performed. Afterward, however, he wouldn't get anywhere near the chit for sex. He'd be mating in name only.

Still, she couldn't just disappear off the map. That wouldn't be fair to her loved ones. And underage meant her parents would have to give permission for Sienna to be "married." He'd have to seek their approval while somehow assuring them there would be no consummation of the relationship.

An authoritative voice echoed across the forest. "Riley Jonnell. Sienna Dixinson. We have your friends, and we know who you are. Turn yourselves in now, or we'll come to your houses and add 'resisting arrest' to your charges."

"Fuck. Morons." Dumuzi heard Sienna curse, and a muffled sound indicated she'd probably kicked something in her anger. "They couldn't keep their mouths shut? I'm going to kill them. Assholes."

He and Archie dodged back into the cover of some holly bushes as Sienna stomped past.

"I'm coming," she groused loudly. "…and I'm totally screwed," she added quietly to the heavens. "My father is going to be so pissed."

Dumuzi followed and watched as the girl named Riley entered the clearing at the same time as Sienna. He shifted, foot to foot and kept a hand on Archie's back as the entire group sat sullenly while the police gathered up empties, fulls, marijuana, and papers, then kicked dirt over the fire until only embers remained. "I'll come back with water and make sure it's out," one of the officers said. "You kids are lucky it's been a wet spring. You could have started a forest fire, and you'd be in worse trouble than you are now."

Not one of the youngsters answered, but the god saw an eye roll from Sienna—bold girl. Dumuzi guessed the kids were thinking about what awaited once they were herded back to the police barracks. The god could commiserate. It might have been several thousand years since he'd been in the same position, but one never forgot what getting caught felt like. That Sienna could still affect sarcasm was a testament to her ballsiness. He didn't know if that boded well...or ill.

Dumuzi left the group and walked back toward the compound, misting out of physical existence as he reached a one-hundred-yard separation. He knew what he needed to do now, but for his plan to work, he'd need to employ Shamash's help. He hoped the god wasn't too wrapped up in his new bride.

Chapter Two

"Dad. Really?" The phone conversation was relayed to Dumuzi by an invisible Shamash who stood next to Sienna in the state police barracks while Muze stayed outside, unseen. He could hear her father giving her hell and telling her he was tired of bailing her ass out of trouble.

"Sienna, I'm sick of this. It's late, and I have to work early in the morning. I'm not bailing you out. Maybe if you stay in jail for a night, it will make an impression on you. Or you can call your mother. Let her deal with you." Dumuzi heard a click as the man hung up.

Wow. Sienna's dad was cold. Of course, Dumuzi had no idea how many messes Sienna had gotten herself into in her short, seventeen-year-old life. He groaned. *Yes.* Sienna was seventeen. And wasn't that just a ball buster? It looked like her mother or father would have to do some kind of a consent thing for her to disappear into the Blue Hills. Having her go missing without a word was not an option.

Shamash, what's going on now? Dumuzi wanted this whole thing over with so he could go back to his innocuous existence.

Your girl is attempting to call her mother who currently resides in Denver, Colorado. I will let you

9

hear what is said. In order for Sienna's conversation to be broadcast, Shamash had to be standing practically on top of the girl, but oddly it didn't bother Dumuzi in the least. And from what he'd witnessed in his band of brothers, every male would be fit to kill if their woman's space was invaded so closely. Dumuzi shrugged, not surprised. It proved he wasn't cut out for mating.

"Hi, Mom, it's Sienna." The words came out of the girl's mouth in a mumbled mess.

"Hi, sweetie. Since I only have one child, you had me at 'hi mom,'" the woman joked. Her voice sounded warm and soothing. This was more like it, thought Dumuzi. At least the kid had someone who cared for her.

"Mom, me and Riley are in jail. Dad won't come bail me out, and Riley's Gram isn't answering her phone." The bomb was dropped quickly, and there was a long pause on the other end of the line.

"Well...your father is...uncompromising as we both know. What have you done this time?" An audible sigh sped to satellite, then back to earth.

"We were...you know...smoking pot in the woods." The words were barely comprehensible to Dumuzi, but the mother clearly understood the teenage sotto voce. She snapped to alert and became all business.

"Okay, I'll get the next plane out. Just don't worry about anything. I'll keep trying Gramma Frank, so she could get to you first. I know it might not be easy but try to get a good night's sleep. Oh, and where are you?"

"I'm in the Blue Hills, at the..." Dumuzi imagined Sienna must have looked around, wondering how to direct her mother to the State Police Barracks, but her savvy parent took charge again.

"Put me on the phone with one of the officers, and I'll make arrangements with them. I'll see you soon, sweetheart. Don't fret. We'll figure this out. I promise." She paused before adding, "You know, you can always come live with me."

"We've talked about that, Mom. I want to stay here in this high school with my friends."

Dumuzi pictured the ubiquitous eye-roll again, but the cool sounding Mom refused to be flustered.

"You're already a junior. In another year, everyone will be going off to college."

Silence met her assertion.

"Fine. We'll talk about making a change then. But right now, let's deal with our current problem."

Dumuzi heard Shamash's voice next. *Sienna is giving the phone to the desk sergeant, and a hot looking lady cop is escorting her back to her cell.*

What hot looking lady cop? Quinn's voice popped in. Shamash's new wife had been listening in—along with what Muze assumed would be most of the other gods and goddesses. She sounded put out at Sham's description.

Damn. I mean, yes, there's a good-looking policewoman, but you know there's nobody more beautiful than you, my lovely wife. Don't worry, this cat isn't about to stray.

No prowling for you, or they'll be no treats when you get home.

Dumuzi knew Quinn was just busting Sham's balls. There was so much love between the golden leopard god and his *Chosen,* if it weren't so much fun

11

listening to them, he might be tempted to gag from an overdose of saccharine.

Had that been a growled response from Shamash? Highly likely. Great. Now his buddy couldn't wait to get home for some hot kitty sex.

Hey, asshole, stop thinking about the tail at home and get back to tailing *my Chosen.* Dumuzi heard a chorus of "nice ones" from the other gods, but Sham took it with good humor.

You'd better watch out, Muze. Sienna's tail right now is underage, so even if you do the ceremony with her, there'll be no touching until she's out of the cub's den.

Fuck you, he said to be heard, then taking a page out of Sienna's book, rolled his eyes. The last thing Dumuzi wanted was a relationship. He purposely changed the subject. *What's happening now?* It was frustrating not to be in the police barracks, but Shamash, being a mated god, had the bonus-ability to mist in and out at will. He needed to depend on the cat-man right now.

We're heading back to the cell where her friend Riley is waiting.

Good. At least they have each other for comfort. It was something Dumuzi had never enjoyed. He'd always pushed people away in his younger years, unwilling to risk friendships.

Lahar's voice from the compound cut into the conversation.

FYI, the mother won't be able to get a flight out until the red-eye at 12:55 Denver time. With a layover, that puts her in Boston at 7:05 tomorrow morning. The computer-geek god had been busy. *So if you're going to put your plan into action, Muze, any time before morning will be good.*

Well, there's no time like the present. The vegetation god misted in from the woods where he'd stayed, invisible, to become solid as soon as he hit the barracks parking lot. He let his ears in the building off the hook. *I can take it from here, Sham. Thank you. Go back to your bride.*

Excellent. You don't have to tell me twice. Good luck.

Dumuzi took a deep breath and entered the station. He knew the easy part would be compelling all the officers into going along with his agenda, the hard part would be Sienna. If she was like any of the other *Chosen,* she would not be subject to mind-manipulation, and he'd have to rely on her innate curiosity and boldness to get her to go along with him. Alternately, she might resist and scream bloody murder at her offered extrication. He hated to resort to caveman technique, but if it came down to it, he was prepared. It was what gods did. He walked up to the window where an officer sat on duty.

"Hi. I'm here to bail out Sienna Dixinson," Dumuzi said with all the authority he could muster. He knew he looked like the ultimate stoner, a visage he'd worked hard to perfect for thousands of years, but he attempted to open his eyes wide and ditch the uber-relaxed body language just this once. It must have worked.

"Are you her father?" The officer asked. *Ouch.* That one hurt. Did he look like he was old enough to be the kid's dad? *Fuck that.* Of course, he was really two thousand, four hundred and thirteen years old, but he always fancied he looked twenty-five...or even younger. The damned cop needed glasses.

"No, I'm her cousin," Dumuzi lied, trying to keep the snark out of his voice. "Her father couldn't come, and he called me to make bail."

"That's fine. I'll get the officer in charge to bring you back to take care of business. There's some paperwork to fill out, then you can see your cousin and take her home."

"Thank you." Dumuzi bit his tongue and remained polite, but silently hoped the young cop went prematurely bald.

Posting bail and the accompanying paperwork didn't take long. The woman cop Sham had designated as "hot" had been more than happy to take care of him. If he'd let her, she would have frisked him from top to bottom...stopping somewhere in the middle, for sure. The female attention diverted him, and he shamelessly flirted back. Muze figured why not after being invisible for so long. He justified his actions as sharpening his "charm" skills before trying them on Sienna.

Dumuzi signed his first name, using Dixinson as his last. Claiming to be family was the easiest ruse. And when he held up a blank piece of paper—a la Dr. Who—he compelled the lady-officer to think it was his driver's license, and that a second piece of paper was a notarized authorization from dear old dad, remanding Sienna into Dumuzi's custody. Very tidy.

"I almost didn't need the license, your family resemblance is so pronounced, but we have a certain protocol. You understand." She eyed him like candy again. "Everything seems to be in good order." *Fuck.* Was she actually checking out the front of his jeans when she said that? Dumuzi felt color rush up into his face—the curse of being a redhead. He'd hoped she wouldn't notice the uncomfortably large bulge in his pants. With his newly acquired visibility, he found he had very little control over his dick. It kept popping in and out of "happy" of its own free will. *Well, damn.* He guessed he should be glad some part of him was getting a kick out of this clusterfuck.

"Let me bring you back to Sienna. I'm sure she'll be pleased to see you."

Dumuzi certainly hoped so. He followed her sashaying ass down the hallway, aware the officer was putting a little extra swing in her hips. And yup, there went his cock again. He certainly was destined to make a good first impression on his bride-to-be.

"Sienna?" The hot-officer called out quietly as both girls lay on their cots. "Your cousin has come and posted bail."

"My who?" Sienna slowly propped herself up into a sitting position, wrinkling her nose in Dumuzi's direction as she took him in head to toe. The god began talking before she could say any more.

"You know," he quipped. "Your good old cousin Muze, here to take care of business 'cause your dad's such an ass." He'd let the stoner look drop back over him like a blanket and waited to see what Sienna would say. Her eyes narrowed, and Dumuzi watched as Riley switched cots and scooted over as close to Sienna as she could get.

"The guys already got bailed," she whispered, unaware that Dumuzi—with his god hearing—was privy to everything she said. "Maybe they sent their connection to get us. He kind of looks like a dealer or something, don't you think?"

"Yeah. You might be right. Check out his eyes," Sienna whispered back.

"Screw that," Riley replied, "Check out the action in his jeans. That is one smokin' dude. He's frigging huge."

Dumuzi wanted to poke his fingers in his ears and chant. No way were two underage girls talking about his package. He could only be grateful when Sienna refused to play Riley's crotch game but acquiesced to his ruse.

"So…Muze. Are you here to get Riley, too?"

Damn. This was something Dumuzi hadn't thought about. He figured to spring his bride, fill her in on the details of the rest of her life, get her mother's permission, and ignore her for eternity. He hadn't thought about the friend.

"Cuz, I'm not going anywhere without Riles."

Dumuzi caught the look in Sienna's eye that said she might just go along with his game if he complied with her demand. And if he didn't, there was no way in hell she'd follow him out of here. Dumuzi huffed. If he wanted her, he was going to have to take the friend as well.

"Well, your dad didn't say anything about your friend, and I'm not her relative, so considering that she's underage…"

"Nope, hot stuff," Riley cut in. "It's your lucky day. I was eighteen two weeks ago. Anybody can post my bail." She hit him with the force of her big dark eyes, and Dumuzi knew he was sunk. Riley was the queen-pin between the friends, and what she wanted, she obviously got.

"Back to the paperwork room?" Officer Libido smiled broadly and gestured toward the door. She was clearly pleased he wasn't leaving yet. Dumuzi sighed and turned his steps in that direction, heading out first, but not before he heard another whisper.

"Look at cop-lady checking out your 'cousin's' ass," he heard Riley snicker. "Bet she wouldn't mind getting a piece of that."

Could this night get any worse?

Twenty minutes and a thousand dollars lighter, Dumuzi made his way back to the cell. Both girls were sitting up expectantly, and he was quite certain they'd plotted and come up with a course of action that would take him out of the picture as soon as they left the police barracks. What they didn't know was Huxley and Jake were standing at the ready outside to help run interference. Muze was certain, between them, they could thwart any escape attempt. Three gods against two little girls. What could go wrong?

"So are you ready to go?" Dumuzi watched hips sway to unlock the cell. *Damn.* His prick was active again. Who knew an ass could look better with a gun strapped in close proximity? The door swung open, and both girls emerged. Sienna ignored him, but the cheeky Riley didn't miss a beat.

"Looks like you're *ready to go*, too. Should we leave and give you some alone time with officer-luscious?" she whispered as she gave him an elbow.

Dumuzi held in a growl. "Go. Now. Or I'll be tempted to lock you back up."

Riley smirked and linked her arm with Sienna's. "Lead the way." Her gaze dropped, ready to check out his ass.

"Oh no," Dumuzi shook his head. "After you." There was no way he'd walk the length of the hall, knowing his posterior was being perused and graded. Sienna laughed and pulled Riley out of the holding area—smart girl. Once in the parking lot, Dumuzi could tell the girls held off putting their plan into action out of sheer curiosity.

"So who are you?" Sienna stood a good six feet from where he paused, arm still linked with Riley's. "My dad and mom are only children, so I have no cousins." She looked pointedly at his head.

Dumuzi smirked. "I know, the hair color was a lucky break. It made me think I could use a family connection to spring you. You *wanted* to get out, didn't you?" he asked lazily.

"Yeah, but not to be raped and killed in the forest." Sienna's eyes took on a sharp cast. "So, why don't you start explaining what's up while we're still near enough for cop help."

"Okay." Now Dumuzi would have to go slowly. Every word needed to count so Sienna wouldn't try to bolt and make everything more difficult. "I saw you get caught out in the woods, and I've been through enough similar shit on my own to feel for you." Now it got tricky. "I have a friend inside the station who overheard that your dad wouldn't post bail, so I decided to do it instead. I'm not sure why. I just didn't want you to have to spend the night in a cell."

"Right." She pulled out the eye-roll again and made him feel like an ass. It did sound pretty lame. So, if that didn't fly, how the hell was he supposed to convince them to come back to the compound?

"Umm, I wondered if you needed a place to crash for the night...since you can't go home to dad's." Dumuzi held his breath.

"Nope. We can go to Riley's place. Her grandmother works nights, but Riles has a key. We'll be fine."

Shit. What was it the guys all said? A *Chosen* couldn't resist the god she was meant for. Maybe he'd have to try pouring on the charm. Dumuzi stepped one foot closer and gazed deep into Sienna's eyes. "I'd really like it if you came back to my place for the night." He tried to inject all the right emotions into his request, but it still came out feeling lecherous—even to him.

"Not even close, buddy." She pointed to a police cruiser bumper sticker—*Stranger Danger*, then fished around in her back pocket. "Going to call a cab, now. It's been nice."

Dumuzi didn't know what else to do. Despite the ruckus about to be raised, he called on his friends. *Lahar, can you disable the parking lot surveillance and kill the lights? Hux, Jake, I could use a little help here.*

The lights went out, and his two god friends materialized behind the girls. "What the fuck?" Riley spun and put her back to Sienna's, facing the two large men. She looked even more freaked out than Dumuzi expected. "Listen assholes, try anything, and we'll scream the fucking Blue Hills down," she warned.

"Wait," Sienna got a canny look on her face and sent back a hand to calm her friend. "They've gone to a lot of trouble to get us out. I can't imagine this is about some weird booty call." She pointed a jaded look at Dumuzi. "Tell me, what is it you want from us?"

Dumuzi sucked in a sharp breath. He needed to disclose everything, but if he did, instead of being labeled a rapist, he'd position himself as a lunatic. Jake, gods-bless-him, saved the day.

"The name is Jake Marsthall," he said, flipping open his badge folder. "I'm with the DEA, and we've been trying to break into a local drug ring without any success. We have reason to believe your friends got their weed from one of the kingpin's dealers in the area. We're hoping to work our way up the chain...with your help."

"What?" This was Riley again, who was clearly not happy at the request. Unfortunately, that attitude was mirrored on Sienna's face. "Yeah right. You want us to narc out our friends? Uh, uh. You've got the wrong girls. Come on, Sienna." Riley grabbed her friend's hand and tugged, but Sienna didn't budge.

"Could you guys give us a minute?" she asked, narrowing her eyes speculatively.

"Sure. Take your time," Jake acquiesced.

The pair walked a short distance away for privacy, but Dumuzi and the two other immortals could easily hear everything.

"Listen, Riles. I'm not sure what's going on here, but there's something happening I can't explain." She shook her head as if to clear it. "You know my...problem?" Sienna looked around as if to make sure she still had privacy.

"Yeah, yeah. That's what got us into this mess to begin with. What about it?"

"Well," Sienna licked her lips. "Ever since that guy Muze showed up, it's been stepped up about a gazillion."

"You're shitting me?" Riley's eyes shifted disturbingly, and she cleared her throat. "So…do you want to hear something else that's freaking weird?"

Sienna nodded with a grimace.

"When the hunk showed up, some strange-ass things started happening in my head, too."

Dumuzi was stumped. What the hell were they talking about?

"No biggie, though." Riley grabbed Sienna's arm. "Try not to panic. It was probably the fucking drugs," she finished up.

Sienna looked at her friend, warily. "Okay, I don't buy that but keep me in the loop. I don't want any of my shit slopping over onto you." She laid her hand over her friend's grasp. "Riles…I can't even begin to tell you…if these guys somehow have the answer to what's been happening…if I can tap into it… What I'm trying to say is, I'm so desperate, I'm ready to go anyplace with them." She flexed her shoulders. "Will you stay with me?"

Dumuzi almost heard the deep swallow that the outwardly bold girl took before speaking again.

"If you think by hanging with them you can figure things out, I'll stay with you, Si." Her bluster came back. "But if you get us torn up into little pieces, I'll never speak to you again. Have you seen the biceps on these freaks? Shit. It will be 'death by big guy.' No weapons necessary."

"Now you're reaching." Eye roll.

Well, here was something that finally pointed to Sienna being connected to him. She was scared and intimidated, but willing to risk everything for some unknown reason. At least it looked like the girls would comply and come with him of their own volition if only to find out what his connection was to Sienna's "thing." He watched as the girls walked back to them.

"Okay. We're going with you…but just for tonight," Sienna agreed. "And the rules are, we get to keep our phones, and the two of us don't get separated." The girls held hands as if their lives depended on it.

"Good." Dumuzi felt relieved this might go easily. He was halfway to mated. "Come on then." He walked toward the woods and felt the hesitation behind him.

"Wait. Where's your car?" Riley's dark eyes were big and questioning.

"We don't have one," Dumuzi supplied, puzzled. "Our house is only a mile away…into the woods."

"Oh, no." Sienna shook her head, backing up a step and tugging her friend with her. "We've partied here enough times. There are no houses out there. What are you trying to pull?"

Hux spoke from behind them, in the way that always sent women swooning to their knees. "We have a lovely home we hope you'll want to see. It's very private and not many people know about it, but Muze is correct. You can't drive to it from here. We need to walk."

The girls looked anything but comforted despite the fact Huxley could usually melt panties with a mere twitch of his chin.

"Maybe this isn't such a good idea," Riley spoke for them both. "I think I'll get one of the cops to give us a ride home, then you can email us or something if you still want to be BFF's." Riley was beyond twitchy now, and the pair inched back toward the barracks.

Dumuzi had an idea.

Tess? Lenore? Holly? Are any of you still up?

Yo, happy man, Tiamet's teething so neither of us is getting any sleep, Lenore answered.

Girin, too, came Tess's voice. He didn't hear from Holly, but Charlie chimed in.

Maity had a bad dream, so we've been walking it off. What can we do for you?

Dumuzi suddenly had hope. The goddesses with their adorable children could surely assuage Sienna and Riley's worries.

Can you guys pop down to the police barracks and help me talk my future Chosen and her friend into coming back to the compound with us? I'm afraid me, Jake, and Hux are a little too scary for them.

Before he could even blink, the three women, two babies, and sweet little three-year-old Maity were heading out from the tree-line. *Thank gods.* Reinforcements.

"Look, girls, here are some of the ladies who live in our house with us. They have babies. What could be more innocent than that?" Dumuzi expected instant relief and capitulation, but there was anything but...especially from Riley, who was rendered speechless and gaping.

Sienna, however, was more vocal after giving the whole group a suspicious once-over. "You're not a cult of some kind?" She turned to the ladies. "And you guys aren't sister-wives, are you?"

Tess started laughing so hard, she nearly dropped a startled Girin. She barely got herself under control to apologize to her infant son. "Sorry, sweetheart. Mommy got silly all of a sudden." She stepped forward and freeing one hand from her baby, swept it down her body and twirled around. "Ever hear of a sister-wife wearing sleepwear from Victoria's Secret?" she asked cheekily.

"Or any whose favorite color is hot pink?" Lenore added her two cents worth, fluffing at her fuchsia baby-dolls.

"You have a point," Riley admitted sullenly, still looking overwhelmingly unhappy. She deferred to Sienna. "What do you think?"

It didn't take Sienna more than a few seconds to answer. "I think we need to find out what's going on. I'm willing to risk it if you are."

Riley nodded gravely, and Sienna turned to Dumuzi.

"Okay, lay on, MacDuff."

Smart girl. Dumuzi actually grinned. She knew the oft-misquoted line didn't mean he should lead, and she would blindly follow. Sienna was actually issuing a challenge—may the best man win.

Chapter Three

Veronica threw the last of her hastily assembled toiletries into a carry-on bag. She had no clue what she was allowed to take on the plane, and she had no time to look it up. There was a mere hour and a half until her flight took off, and most of that would be spent getting to the airport. Verrie could have kicked back a notch and caught a morning flight, but as appealing as that was to her personally, she didn't want Sienna to languish in jail any longer than necessary.

Jail…and Sienna's father wouldn't get her out. Her ex-husband, Dwight Dick-head was an ass. Okay. His last name was Dixinson, but since the acrimonious divorce and custody battle fifteen years ago, Verrie had only been able to think of him as "Dick-head," and who could blame her? He'd taken her daughter from her, using Verrie's mental instability to make a case Sienna would be in danger with her mother—an accusation that was so far from the truth, it still made her ache with the memory—but Dick-head had somehow convinced the judge of its probability, and because of that, Verrie had only enjoyed supervised visits with her toddler.

When Sienna was seven, Verrie had taken a trip to Colorado to visit a friend and been floored to find out the problems that had plagued her for so many years on the east coast became nothing more than a distant echo when in the mountains. And it wasn't an anomaly. When she returned home to Boston, her difficulties started up again. Screw that. She decided to move. It broke her heart, but she figured if she could maintain a clean bill of health with doctors in Colorado, she might...just might get partial custody of Sienna.

She'd made the move, explaining her decision to her daughter, citing her hopes for the future. Sienna had taken it well, and at least with the advent of Skype, they kept in touch and talked every night. They never missed. The separation was heart-wrenching, but the health benefits were huge. After three episode-free years and with multiple doctor affidavits, Verrie was the person she'd been before her devastating condition had manifested.

She had applied once more for joint custody of her daughter, and this time, she'd won her battle. Ten-year-old Sienna had been allowed to come to Colorado and spend summers in the mountains. Their relationship had reestablished and blossomed. The time spent together had been glorious for both of them...but bittersweet when every August, Sienna had to leave for Boston and school.

Verrie was so out of the loop right now—it being mid-June and not having seen Sienna for ten months—she had no idea what had been going on between her daughter and Dick-head. Obviously, on their nightly Skype sessions, Sienna hadn't been telling her the truth when giving her assurances that home and school were going well.

Now, Verrie had to guess what this all meant—her daughter being in jail, her ex not bailing her out—it had to be bad. A shiver of apprehension sped up and down

Verrie's spine. Her own troubles had started in her late teens, becoming fully manifested in her early twenties. She sent up a fervent prayer Sienna wasn't headed down her own dark path.

Besides those bleak things to ponder, Veronica had trepidation for her own well-being. She hadn't been back to the coast in nine years. What would happen once the plane landed? Would her troubles return? Her doctors assured her after a nine-year hiatus, her symptoms were most likely gone for life. But still, she worried. If her debilitating condition reared its ugly head again, would she have the strength to help Sienna?

The drive out of Boulder was quiet with the advent of night. Still, the trip to Denver International would take the better part of an hour. Verrie lived in an apartment on Arapahoe Drive and had to make her way through the city before skirting Denver to get to the airport. Which would give her way too much time to think, and that wasn't good. She tried to shut her brain down and concentrate on the crisp, dark night outside her small compact car, but memories began to seep in.

Mother…father…together. Wrapped so tightly around each other, even at a very young age, she wondered if there had ever been any room in their lives for her. She was with them, but she wasn't. More often, Verrie was dropped off at her loving Aunt Frank's house. Whether that had to do with the number of hours her parents worked or the fact they craved being alone together when not working, she never knew.

The pair had been kids when Verrie was born, her mother barely twenty. She'd been told they'd been in love since grade school. She never heard them disagree or raise their voices toward each other until the year she started school. Being a quiet, observant child, Verrie knew somehow their happy lives had derailed, that things weren't right. The worry in Aunt Frank's eyes was proof enough and only added to her fears.

In retrospect, Verrie knew exactly what had happened because, God help her, history had repeated itself when she was still in her teens. If only they'd sought help. If only they'd found another way to solve things…like she had by going to Colorado.

Bitterness twisted at her gut. At least they'd stuck by one another. Dwight the dick-head had gone the selfish route. Clearly, he hadn't been in love with Verrie like her father had been with her mother, so instead of making a suicide pact as her parents did—when she'd been barely six—ending things, hand in hand, Dwight had kicked her out.

In the long run, it had been better for Sienna that way, but still, Verrie hadn't given up. Even when Dick-head crushed her to her lowest point, she never would have taken her own life. She loved her daughter too much…and wasn't that saying something about her dead parents.

If ever she was certain about her decision to live, it was right now. If what Verrie suspected about her daughter was now coming to pass, Sienna would need her more than she ever had before.

Veronica shook herself. She let her mind skip from the discomforting memories of her parents to linger on the more pleasant recollections of her childhood under the wing of Francis-Ann—Frank— Dewalters.

Aunt Frank was not her real aunt, she wasn't even a blood relative. But she'd been her mother's best friend since baby-hood…as had been *their* mothers and their mothers before them. If the women involved were to be believed, the familial friendships stretched back hundreds of years, always between only daughters of only daughters.

She had been thrown into Aunt Frank's life early, a place where attention was paid to her needs. Verrie never questioned why. At the express directives of a long, hand-scrawled will scribbled by Verrie's parents before they'd pulled off their final exit from earth, they put her into the hands of a woman whose life as a single mother had already been difficult enough. But Francis-Ann had never resented Verrie's presence. She'd thanked God every day for giving her another daughter—a best friend for her own child, Nancy, and somehow, she'd managed to raise them together with love to spare.

Verrie shook her head, wondering how Aunt Frank had managed. The woman had kept food on the table, and joy in their lives, and not once had she resented working multiple jobs to keep the two girls housed and clothed.

During Verrie's first few years in Boulder, trying to keep her head above water, she'd had a look into that life, and it had proven difficult even without children to nurture. Balancing school with waitressing, she'd supported herself while attending college. There were many times she thought to give up, but that would have given Dwight Dick-head too much satisfaction, so she'd persevered.

It was only in the last few years—having earned her advanced degree—she'd been blessed to find a job as a guidance counselor at the local high school, and things had become much easier. Now, she was going to have to take a leave of absence to deal with her own teenager's difficulties. She only prayed they were normal problems adolescents faced, the kind she was used to dealing with in her job, rather than something more dire.

Verrie snorted, letting her sense of humor take over for a bit. It didn't surprise her in the least that whatever trouble her daughter was in, Riley was right beside her. She remembered fondly her own teen years spent running wild with Riley's mother, Nancy. Her heart contracted, wishing she could have the brash, comforting words of her old friend now, but Nancy—wild, loyal Nancy—had disappeared the year her daughter Riley was born, and once again, Aunt Frank had found herself with the care of yet another child.

Thoughts of Frank had Verrie scrambling in her purse for her cell phone. She hit Frank's number, but after one ring it went right to voicemail. She left what she hoped was an upbeat message, citing it had taken the girls getting jailed to bring her back to Boston, but Frank would see right through the bluster and be worried for her. Verrie sighed. They'd deal with that when her feet hit pavement at Logan Airport.

An hour later, Veronica stood in the procession to take her turn through the body scanner when her phone rang. When she looked at caller ID and saw Frank's name, she stepped out of line.

"Aunt Frank, thank goodness. I didn't know if something happened to you."

"I'm good, Verrie," the woman whispered, "but I can't talk. I'm on a case, waitin' fah authorities." Frank had gone on to become a social worker…and a damned good one, but it often meant staying long hours at some of her cases' houses. If there was a domestic situation, she was always first on the scene, holding down the fort until DSS could send reinforcements which many times had her pulling an all-nighter. "The girls called, but they didn't leave a message to tell me what was wrong. It must be wicked bad if yeh on yeh way heah." Veronica could hear the worry oozing from Frank's voice. The woman's Boston accent always got thicker when she felt pressured.

Verrie tried to stifle her sigh. "They're actually pretty safe right now since they were locked up for smoking weed in the Blue Hills."

Frank gave a gasp on the other end of the line. "Crud. I thought I'd finished with all-a-that when you and Nance made it through teenage-hell." The pain in her voice was unmistakable as it always was when she talked about her daughter. Verrie could hear her push it away. "So they called yeh ex ta bail 'em out?"

"They did," Verrie snorted, "and yeah, you probably guessed, Dwight-daddy-dearest wouldn't post bail. With you unavailable, Sienna didn't know who else to call, so I'm in line at the airport, hoping there won't be a cavity search."

Verrie heard a smothered grunt. "Huh. It could be the best action yeh've had in yeahs, sweetie."

"Not funny, Frank." It was, but Verrie was eyeballing the screening line that grew smaller and smaller and had to cut her conversation short. "Listen, it's time to find out if the TSA guy's hands are warm or cold." She attempted to keep the mood light. "Will you be able to meet me at the airport in the morning?" She gave Frank her arrival time.

31

"I should be through this job by then," Frank assured. "Would you rathah I went ahead and gut the girls?"

"Why don't you wait." Verrie tucked the phone up under her ear and dug through her purse for her boarding pass. She wanted the first "face to face" with the kids and didn't want to bother Frank on the phone with what she believed to be the real problem. "We'll drive out of the city together. They didn't sound too distressed unless you count Sienna's mood toward her father."

"Sienna's been fully awauh of her fathah's dick status for quite some time now, so don't worry too much on that scoah. I'll see you in the mornin'. We'll both be lookin' really good by seven a.m.," Frank joked.

"Right," Verrie chuckled. It wouldn't be the first sleepless night for either of them. She gave her de facto aunt all her flight information, signed off, and put herself at the end of the line.

Five minutes later, she tugged her coat back into place, situated her feet back in her black leather short boots, and made quick work of the jetway. *Yup.* Warm hands that would probably prove to be the best part of her entire trip.

Chapter Four

Sienna and Riley lay close in the dark. Despite the two queen-sized beds in the room they'd been given, they'd chosen to curl up next to each other instead. Dumuzi knew because, as creepy as it appeared, he'd sent Candy into their room to spy, and she had relayed that little gem.

Just like two peas in a pod, Muze. They're done for the night. I think it's sleepy time for me too. I wouldn't mind hitting the hay and 'podding' with my husband for a while. Am I free to go?

Yeah. Sure Candy. I don't think there'll be any big revelations tonight. You can take off.

Wait. I spoke too soon. The sassy one is rolling over. I'll plug you back in to their conversation.

"Sienna?" Riley's voice cut through the hush that hung over the house.

"Yeah, Riles?" Sienna also sounded wide awake. Dumuzi shouldn't be surprised. Some unusual shit had gone down for those girls tonight—not that the entire contingent of gods had come forward to be introduced yet—but there had been enough intrigue to make even the least suspicious of characters take notice.

It had been decided before they got home, Dumuzi, Jake, Huxley, Tess, Lenore, and Charlie had been more than enough immortals to throw at the girls until the

33

pair had enjoyed a good night's sleep. Now, it looked like snoozing was the last thing on the agenda.

"About your problem…"

Dammit. There they go talking about Sienna's problem again, Dumuzi groused to Candy. *We need to figure out what the hell they're talking about.*

"Uh-huh." Sienna voice remained oddly neutral, almost like she was being extra careful.

"Well, I don't want to sound freaky or anything, but I've definitely and completely been down from my buzz for hours now, and umm…my version of your shit has been getting worse ever since we arrived in Casa-del-giant-guys," her voice dropped to a whisper, "and now it's just scaring the piss out of me."

According to the quick play-by-play from Candy, Sienna zinged into a sitting position. "You're shitting me, right?" she asked with wide, tormented eyes. "Don't mess with me about this, Riles. You know it's not funny."

"I'm so not messing with you, Si. I swear to God it's happening…like right now. You don't suppose whatever you've got is catching, do you?"

Candy described the look on Sienna's face as partially gob-smacked but mostly pissed off.

Muze, your girl just stood up on the bed in what I'd call a defiant stance, and she's spinning around pointing her finger in every direction. Candy sounded as puzzled as he felt. Then Dumuzi got an ear-full he wasn't expecting.

"Okay, you fuckers. Stop screwing with Riley," she yelled, jabbing her digits in the air. "Isn't it enough you're fucking up my life? Now you have to pick on her too? Cut the crap."

"Uh, Sienna? Do you think you ought to rile them up?" her friend asked tentatively. "Right now at least, the voices don't sound especially nasty."

The voices. Dammit. Dumuzi's stomach dropped. *Candy, they're talking about our voices. They can hear us.*

"Damn straight I can hear you," Sienna hissed out in one long breath, "and if you don't tell us what you want in like, two seconds, we're going to scream the fucking house down."

Dumuzi had heard that exact tone of voice from the goddesses in the house when they were good and ticked off. Sienna wasn't messing around. He choked on a distressed chuckle. Her attitude certainly gave veracity to the assumption she was a deity in the making.

Okay, okay, he attempted to placate her. *I'm coming in the door now, and Candy will make herself be seen.* The god opened the door slowly from where he'd been standing in the hallway and poked his head inside.

"Chill out and let me explain," he began, but Sienna's posture didn't relax one iota as he continued. "We were hoping to spare you all of this until morning, but we had no idea you could hear our voices." If he had thought ahead—if any of them had—they might have been suspicious. The majority of pre-*Chosens* and even some of their offspring like Maity had been able to hear god-talk. It had been a seriously bad oversight.

Candy had opted to waft out the door, become embodied, then walk back in. Apparently, she figured it might be too much for the teens if she just popped from invisibility without first laying in some adequate mind-fuck protection.

"Hi, girls. Don't freak out, okay?" she began. Her cocky smile and assured nature already made Dumuzi feel less adrift in the uncharted waters in which they swam. "You're right. You have been hearing voices…ours and everyone else's in the house, I'll be guessing. So for that reason, we need to get all our residents together before we start filling you in on what's happening." Candy switched to head communication.

Sorry to wake you all up, but our guests have been eavesdropping on our private channel, and they don't feel very warm and fuzzy about it. We need damage control. Stat. And do them a solid, she punned, *Make it a walk-in, not a pop-in.*

Damn. Candy was good at this. Dumuzi was going to have to start paying stricter attention to protocol if he was going to hitch himself to a human. He really didn't have the first clue how to act.

Riley looked excited—not at all stormy-faced like Sienna remained.

"You're not kidding, are you. Wow, I can hear everything you're saying. That is so cool. Isn't it cool, Si?" She turned to look up at her friend and her exuberance shut down. "…or not," she trailed off and immediately changed to a concerned tone. "So, is this what you've been hearing all this time, Sienna?"

The color had risen in Sienna's face, and she still stood on the bed, chest heaving and hands twitching. She was clearly unsure what her next move should be but shook her head.

"No. It's not." Her mouth settled into a flat line. "But it's too much like the other to be a coincidence." Her face darkened even more. "These have to be the

36

guys who ruined my mother's life, and now they're trying to get started on you and me." She jerked her chin at Riley. "Grab your purse. We're getting out of here—right now." She attempted to move, but Dumuzi put up his hand like a stop sign.

"Wait now, whoa." Dumuzi was all for his sullen little bride having some god-skills, but what was this about ruining lives? He was in over his head, but she was going nowhere. He didn't want to have to physically restrain her, but he would if necessary. That would slap some hurt on trust issues for their future.

He was never happier to see Marduk, the leader of their deposed group, walk through the door.

"Thank the gods," he muttered and pointed to the girls on the bed. "Marduk, this is Sienna, my...uh...guest and her friend Riley."

"Sienna. Riley," Marduk inclined his head regally. Muze could see both girls were awed at the enormous newcomer. Marduk tended to have that effect on people. Dumuzi figured it should have ticked him off that Sienna seemed more impressed with the thunder god than with him, but he really couldn't work up one ounce of indignation. Maybe that's what he got for forcing himself to remain mellow for the past few thousand years. It was possible he didn't have any strong emotions left...even where his *Chosen* was concerned. He'd zoned out on what Marduk was saying but quickly caught up.

"...so if I can apologize for our lack of foresight, I'm sure we can ease your worries about everything else."

Sienna's stomach took that moment to complain loudly.

LJ Vickery

"It seems like filling you in on secret voices isn't the only thing we've neglected." Marduk sent a silent yet pointed reprimand at Dumuzi. "I suggest we all reconvene in the kitchen where Absu will whip up some food."

I will be honored to assuage the hunger of two such fine young damsels. The proper god hadn't shown up yet, so he most likely segued to fire up the oven at Marduk's suggestion. Dumuzi caught a slight smirk on Riley's face.

"You've got some marquis making us chow?" she quipped.

Oooh, baby, Riley just called you a marquis. How did we miss playing that game? It was Charlie's head-voice taunting her ever so proper husband. *Marquis de Sade. It's going to be my new favorite.*

Female giggles rent the air in response, and males cleared their throats. Dumuzi nearly choked, but he wasn't about to explain to the two perhaps-clueless mortals that Charlie and Absu had a decided Dom/Sub relationship—TMI.

"So shall we...uh, head to the kitchen?" Dumuzi not-so-deftly changed the subject and raised his hand up to Sienna. She reluctantly took it and allowed herself to be lowered from the bed. He noticed, however, she yanked her hand away as quickly as possible, preferring to stand mashed against her friend as if to ward him off. Dumuzi sighed. Her power to make him visible was extremely puzzling. Not a single spark had shot up his arm at their contact. What the fuck had everyone been talking about? There were no special fireworks between him and his mate. Muze didn't know whether to feel ripped off or relieved.

Kitchen meetings were always so much more comfortable and informal than Marduk's office conferences. The only problem was the number of Blue Hills inhabitants had begun to overflow the available space. Still, they crowded in. Dumuzi listened with half an ear while Tess introduced the girls to the entire household.

"You've met me, Lenore, Charlie, our children, and the two guys who were with us at the police barracks, Jake and Hux." Both men nodded their heads while shoving little squares of steaming hot zucchini quiche into their mouths. Absu had taken the small tidbits from the freezer where he kept home-made food for emergencies such as this. It hadn't taken but a few minutes for him to heat them up.

Dumuzi grabbed one—his first bite of food in nearly four hundred years—and groaned as the flavors ricocheted inside his suddenly saliva-filled mouth. "Oh my gods, Absu. This is unbelievable. And you used my zucchini."

"This vegetation had nothing to do with you," Absu teased, and Dumuzi braced for the punchline. "It was procured from the grocery store."

Dumuzi rolled his eyes, gave Absu the finger, and popped the rest of the square in his mouth. "It's all mine, no matter what shitty chemicals they dump on it," he smirked.

"Well, you can have your fill of shitty chemicals tonight. I've planned an all vegetarian meal for your first supper."

The carnivores in the group groaned good-naturedly while Dumuzi ignored the puzzling glance from his future mate. Time enough to explain all that later.

Tess ignored the interruption and continued, "Dumuzi you know," —she skipped by him rather rapidly, considering his importance in Sienna's future— "and my husband, Marduk is next to him. He's the unofficial boss here. To Marduk's left is Lenore's husband, Anshar, and at the stove is Charlie's husband, Absu."

The girls gave small, half-hearted smiles while looking warily toward a raft of new people just entering the kitchen.

"You'll never remember everybody's names, so I'll just throw them at you as they come through the door." Tess paused for a breath and began making a list. "My sister, Holly, and her husband, Dagon. Candy, who you've met, and her man, Enlil. Here's Emesh and Douglas, then Hux's wife, our good doctor, Dani-Lee. The single guys are Ninurta, Ishkur, and Lahar…

Shit. Dumuzi cringed. Tess had just introduced Ninurta, who was the only god still one hundred percent invisible-one hundred percent of the time, but taking a worried glance at the girls, he let out his breath. Thankfully they seemed too overwhelmed to have caught the mistake.

"Then back to the couples, we have Kulla and Obedience, Shamash and Quinn, Enten and Glory. Jake's wife Anna is my birth mom," she said this with a special smile, "and speaking of Mom's, Angie—with that big guy, Tiny—is Obedience's mother, and Kate is Glory's." She looked at the girls, sporting a wry grin. "I know your heads are spinning but bear with me. We're almost through."

"Next is my dad, Greg Abelard, and after him are husband and wife, Ken and Vesca. Addie-May and Dorian are just over there, bringing up the rear. There," she said satisfactorily. "Did I forget anyone?"

"Hell yeah," was the reply, as five more very buff males pushed their way past the big, dark warlock, not intimidated in the least by his low growl.

"Oh, geez." Tess slapped her forehead. "I forgot you guys were here." She turned to the girls once more. "This intrepid group of five are all DEA agents from California who are trying to decide if they're staying here permanently. Ken and Jake are actually DEA, too. I'll give you their nicknames because nobody ever calls them by what their mamas christened them. We have Gramps, Cubby, Flick, Z, and JP."

Flick spoke up fast before Tess could get any further. "We told our uh, German friends to keep themselves scarce until the young ladies were brought up to speed if that's okay."

Dumuzi knew he spoke of the six blue guys in residence. They were Lauernley from the Rhine Valley, and their colorful skin would have sent both girls right over the edge. The jury was out on whether or not that would happen even without the advent of the pigmentally diverse beings arriving on scene.

Tess nodded her agreement. "Good call." She turned to the girls. "So are you guys good? Any questions?"

Despite the fear and mistrust that lurked behind Sienna's eyes, the girl spoke right up.

"Yeah. Who the fuck are you people?" She didn't wait for an answer but spewed what had probably been in her brain since coming onto the property. "Why have

I been in the Blue Hills, like a million times, and never seen any of you or this humongous house before? Why are we here, and how come you're all talking in your heads in English when it's never been that way before?" She stuck her chin up belligerently, obviously waiting to see how many of her questions would get answered.

Absu stepped forward and shoved a plate into her hand and one into Riley's, ordering them to eat. "No information will be forthcoming until you have partaken of sustenance. I believe a blood sugar low may hasten a swoon if what you hear is disagreeable to your ears."

"He means eat up if you want the scoop," Candy supplied.

"We get it," Riley shoved a square into her mouth. "Between British Studies and AP English, we've read plenty of Shakespeare."

"*From the two parties, forsooth,*" Absu came back.

"Merry Wives of Windsor," Sienna whipped off without hesitation, and Dumuzi's brain stuttered. Wow. The chit was damned bright.

"Well, yes," Marduk interjected, also clearly surprised. "But now, it's time we get down to the business of your questions. Dumuzi will have a go at explaining everything."

Since he was not used to paying attention, the vegetation god had already mentally misplaced the list Sienna had made, and in true stoner fashion gave a blank-faced, "What?"

"Oh, for the gods' sake, Muze." Candy loved him like a brother but hated putting up with his shit. "I'll give you the list, one by one." Dumuzi arranged his face into thoughtfulness.

"First, they'd like to know who the fuck we are." Candy was clearly going to do this verbatim.

"Okay, then," he advised the humans, "maybe you should sit down." When neither girl moved, he amended, "Or not." This wasn't going to be as easy as he'd imagined. How had the other guys done the big reveal for their women?

"We, uh, at least most of us here," he waved his arm in his fellow god's vicinities, "are from Mesopotamia." There. That was a good beginning.

He was immediately shot down.

"An archaic term for the area between the Euphrates and Tigris rivers—Syria, Iran, Turkey. You expect us to believe that? But go on." Sienna wasn't going to give him a single break, so he jumped back in.

"Right. That's true. But *when* we're from, it was all called Mesopotamia."

"*When* you're from?" Riley wrinkled her nose.

"Yup. Like for instance, I was born in 299 BCE. Marduk—the oldest guy here— dates back to Hammurabi's code times, and the rest fall into similar time periods."

"Wait." Now Sienna's bright brain was cooking. "Your weird-ass names. They're all god names from mythology."

"I resemble that remark," Anshar joked, but it didn't derail Sienna's thought process.

"So, if I've got this right, you've either all drunk the Kool-Aid and are delusional, or you're playing at trick-or-treat year-round."

"No. Neither. Although we've been accused of worse." Dumuzi tried not to grin. She was cheeky, this one, and although he wasn't attracted to her in the least, he could still appreciate some good sarcasm. "We are, indeed, the gods you've read about, hence the reason nobody is aware of us in the Blue Hills…"

"…which is the answer to question two. Nobody gets to know because nobody would believe it, and the house is made invisible to outsiders," Candy finished Dumuzi's sentence.

The vegetation god chose to ignore her. "We will prove everything to you with feats of godliness." He looked around. "Who wants to do the honors?"

As he expected, Anshar was always up for a good mind-blowing.

"Behold, ladies." The all-sky god bowed and disappeared, then did a little un-solid conversing. *I am invisible but standing right next to you. Hold out a quiche square, please.*

Riley did as she was told, albeit with a trembling hand, and the food disappeared. *We call it 'acquiring,'* he informed them. *We can take things,* the quiche reappeared in Riley's hand, *and give them back.*

"Oh my God, Si. Did you see that?" Her face was a study in confusion. "Do we believe this?"

Oddly enough, Sienna had a look on her face that was part smirk but mostly relief. "Yes," she gave a small chuff. "Yes. At least I do. Because Riles," Sienna turned and gripped her friend by the arm, "if I choose to believe this, then I'm not crazy…and my mother's not crazy, and all the worry and the fucked-upedness gets to go away. Do you not get it?" Her eyes lit up, and for the first time, Dumuzi saw a real smile from the girl, not the jaded one that made her face look too old for her years. "If what they say is true, the voices haven't been schizophrenia at all. They've been fucking invisible gods."

Riley grinned back. "Wow, Sienna. I get it. That is so cool. We need to call your mother right now," she delivered enthusiastically.

"Yeah. No. Wait." Sienna was trying to get her mind and her priorities straight. "What about my other questions? Why did you bring us here?" She looked questioningly at Dumuzi, but without the rancor that had previously veiled her heart.

Dumuzi frowned. He turned to Marduk who was scowling too and shaking his head slightly. Without the option of private head-talk—which Muze doubted he would have with his *Chosen*-to-be within range—the vegetation god could only imagine Marduk didn't want the girls to have that answer yet. He sighed, letting them down in what he hoped was a gentle way.

"That question can only be answered when your mother gets here. Since you are not of legal age yet…for anything contractual…we need her to bear witness and give permission for your purpose in the compound." Then Dumuzi remembered her last question.

"As for that English language thing you were asking about…" Now he forced his face to take on a perplexing air. "I think I can say we're all in the dark about that one," he lied. "You say your mother suffers from the same mental intrusions?"

"Uh-huh. Far worse than me and Riles. It wrecked her life."

45

"Then maybe we should let her tell us about it when she arrives." Muze looked to Marduk who gave a satisfied nod.

"If you guys can figure this out…fix my mom's life, I promise you, I'll do anything you want. Really. Just say the word." Sincerity shown from Sienna's eyes, and Dumuzi breathed a sigh of relief. The girl might not want to mate with him, but she would do it if they could stop what was going on with her mother. And yeah, he knew what that was as did every other god in the kitchen. They just didn't want to say anything yet, lest it scare the bejeezus out of the girls. He focused on the practical for now.

"Lahar says her plane will land in just under an hour. I think our DEA guys should meet her at the airport."

"Okay," Sienna agreed, "but if you don't mind, I'm going to call her and tell her to look out for them." Sienna was proving she had a logical head on her shoulders. "If you try to stuff her in a car without my heads-up, you'll have a hell of a fight on your hands."

Looking at Sienna, knowing what a handful she was, Dumuzi believed it.

There was only one other problem eating at him besides his non-attraction to his adolescent bride-to-be. He slipped out the open sliders onto the stone terrace and sent a look toward Marduk. He needed to air his fears. The god of thunder—and the best boss a guy could have—got the signal and moved smoothly away from the group, joining Dumuzi in the just breaking, morning light.

"Something on your mind, Muze?" Marduk gave him a knowing stare. Dumuzi snorted. Of course, the savvy god would already have figured out what was bothering him.

"You're way ahead of me, aren't you?" Dumuzi stuck his hands in his jeans pockets and shrugged uncomfortably when Marduk gave him a nod. But he still felt the need to verbalize.

"You know what I am," he began and got another quick nod from Marduk. "And you remember how it was when I was young." He didn't have to wait for another affirmative. "You're also aware when we were in Merrymount, there wasn't a lot of…activity from me, but when there was, it was easy to get far away and lose myself in all the undeveloped countryside." Dumuzi looked at his friend and mentor and was relieved when Marduk took over.

"And now that you're corporeal again, you're worried because the Blue Hills is such a busy place, and you won't be able to hide."

Dumuzi propped his elbows on the stone wall and dropped his head into his hands. "You've got it, boss-man. If it was a few years ago, I might not be so worried because my condition had all but gone away, but it's ramping up again. I know you're aware of that." He swore bitterly. "Fuck. After a nine-year moratorium, why is this shit happening again?"

"I don't know, man, but we'll find out." At the skeptical look Dumuzi shot at him, he bristled. "We *will* find out, Muze. I promise."

Not one to belabor the point, Marduk continued, "In the meantime, we'll do some intervention. The guys won't mind getting involved and following you when it happens. You know how we all like a challenge. We'll get you secured, put you in the osmium cell in the basement."

"With Matthew?" Dumuzi raised a brow.

Marduk smirked. "It will serve the bastard right, getting the crap scared out of him." He got serious again. "We'll take care of you, Muze. Don't doubt that."

Dumuzi stood up straight and let Marduk see the relief in his face. "Thanks," he breathed out, "and if we're lucky, no blood will be shed. Archie is aware when it's going to happen and can give me a few minutes warning like a real service dog."

Marduk grunted out a laugh. "The same way dogs can predict an earthquake or a tornado, huh?"

"Something like that." Dumuzi actually gave a smile. "As soon as he starts nuzzling me to let me know, I'll put out a distress call, and you guys can come get me and put me safely away before it starts. That'll take a huge weight off my mind."

Marduk came to him and clasped his hand, pulling him into a bro-hug, the likes of which he hadn't felt in hundreds of years. Tears threatened, but he pushed them back.

"We've got your back, Muze. Count on it." He pulled away with a light punch to Dumuzi's chest. "But right now, you have to go win the interest of your *Chosen,*" he reminded the vegetation god with an imperious scowl. "I'm not feeling the love, but I expect you to step it up. Our lives depend on it."

Dumuzi didn't have to be reminded. As unappealing as he found the prospect, he knew his duty.

Chapter Five

Veronica got off the plane and walked blearily into the well-lit Logan Airport lobby. She blinked a few times before she spotted the smiling face of Aunt Frank and strode toward her, only to be intercepted and surrounded by six big guys in suits.

"Excuse me." She tried to push past them, but they were having none of it.

"Sienna Dixinson's mother?"

She bristled at the stranger with the self-assured posture intoning her daughter's name. "Yes. I'm Veronica Foxey," she responded coldly. "Who wants to know?"

The albino guy with the chiseled chin gave her a look that was surprisingly warm and reassuring. "We're here to take you to your daughter. Didn't you get her message?"

Verrie scowled, dropped her overnight bag at her feet to fish around in her pocketbook. Coming out with her cell phone, she punched it on. Not. "Damn. Dead battery," she groused, then saw Aunt Frank out of the corner of her eye, approaching like a tornado. *Oh-oh.* Whoever these guys were, they were about to get new assholes ripped.

"Who the hell ah yeh, and why ah yeh stoppin' my baby?" A pissed off frown marred what otherwise was a stunningly beautiful, sixty-year-old face.

Verrie wanted to grin at the black-suit posse. They were about to get a front-row seat to the dichotomy that was her long-time aunt—tough talker, aggressive in action, wrapped up in the visage of a freakin' angel.

All five foot two of Francis-Ann elbowed into the group of men, sending sparks flying from her large blue eyes toward anyone who had the audacity to look back. Her blonde hair, flying in a wispy halo around her head had turned even more platinum looking with an addition of gray Verrie had never seen before. *Man.* Who knew gray hair could make someone even more gorgeous?

"Ma'am."

Speaking of gray hair, the man who sported a total white crop of it dared to face Frank.

"I'm Agent Pelwick," he informed her, whipping out an ID for inspection. "These are my fellow agents from the DEA. If you'd just step back and have a seat, this is agency business. We'll speak to you when we're through here."

Oh my God. Wrong thing to say. Now there would be some fireworks.

But Aunt Frank surprised her by dropping the aggression and going all pretend-sweet on their asses. "This wouldn't have ta do with Verrie's daughta Sienna bein' in jail, would it? Verrie called and told me Si was in trouble."

"Yes, ma'am." A luscious-looking black guy stepped forward, obviously trying to be more forthcoming than Agent Pelwick. He looked apologetic and offered up a bit more information. "We've taken the liberty of removing her daughter from jail and are holding her in a new location."

"Okay," Frank still played. "Which means yeh eithah abandoned my kid, or yeh have Riley, too." Now her eyes narrowed, showing her true colors. "Which one is it?"

"Yo. Chill out. I'm Flick." A dark-eyed, dark-skinned beauty stepped out from the group and took over, bending down to get right in Frank's face. "I can tell you're just dying to ramp up and make a scene, so I'm going to cut the crap and get us all the hell out of here without creating paperwork for Logan security. Okay?" Not waiting for her acquiescence, he continued, "Here's the skinny. We sprung Sienna and Riley from the state police barracks last night, and they are right now at our headquarters, waiting for your friend Verrie…uh…Ms. Foxey?" Flick turned slowly and raised his eyebrows. He tried hard to keep the twitch from his lips.

Verrie shrugged disgustedly. He'd just figured it out. Wait for it…wait for it…

"Veronica Foxey. Verrie Foxey. Oh man. That's sick wizz," he grinned. "You could be…"

"A stripper. I know," Verrie said the words for what was probably the quadrillionth time in her life. To give him his due, Flick quickly tucked his smirk back in and turned to re-engage Frank.

"And you. Are you Riley's mother?"

"Grandmothah, but I have total custody." She brushed past him to take Verrie's arm, picked up her carry-on and hefted it over her shoulder. "And you can take us ta them right now."

"Wait a minute, Aunt Frank." Verrie was all for getting to the girls, but really? They were just going to plop into a vehicle with these six Neanderthals? "Before we go, I want to see ID from all of you," she told them, purposely planting a suspicious look on her face, "then I want to borrow a phone and call my daughter to verify your story."

"Cool," said the one called Flick. "Guys. Ante-up the ID." He handed his to Verrie first.

"Emiliano Santavera." She nodded, trying to come up with something to get him back for figuring out the 'Verrie Foxey' so soon. "I can see why you shortened it." Lame, but she was sleep deprived. She passed the little leather folder along to Frank, then one by one perused all the rest. "Mike Pelwick."

"Gramps," he said a little sheepishly, and Verrie thrust her hand forward for a shake. She often had feelings about people when she touched them, and Gramps' hand slipped into hers with a nice comforting grasp. So far, so good.

She let go, briefly read his credentials, and moved around the circle. The albino was Coby Leopold, who introduced himself as 'Cub.' The lovely black man was Zion Blanell, known as 'Z,' and the Asian hunk was Jett Pahuyama, initials JP. Handshakes all around gave off positive energy, and she was almost satisfied. There was one who hung back, giving off some kind of odd vibe Verrie tried hard to zero in on but was somehow missing. He introduced himself as Dunsky, or "Dunce," and his reticent handshake told her he was distracted and hiding something. He pulled back.

We have her, Marduk, and we also have Riley's grandmother. Make sure Sienna answers her phone.

Her mom's going to call her on Flick's line to find out we're legit.

Verrie's face turned to stone. *Shit.* She could fucking hear him in her head. Her body swayed. She needed to sit down…or fall down. She quickly began listing excuses in her head. It had been a long night, and she was overwrought. Her innate fears had her imagining things. She had been expecting brain-intrusion, and so she made up the voices. *Yeah.* The third one had to be it. She breathed slowly in through her nose and out through her mouth. *Be sensible, Verrie,* she admonished herself. Keep it together. Don't let anyone see weakness. She'd schooled herself in years past to ignore the voices without a twitch of betrayal on her face. She could do it again. It was all pretend.

Her reasoning began slowly to return, and she enumerated the ways this was not like her experiences in the past. Number one, she'd never seen someone whose voice she'd heard, they were always disembodied. Number two, none of the voices had ever spoken in English. It had always been some dark, hodge-podge of grunted syllables that invaded her brain. And number three…well…shit. There was no number three. Didn't lists always have three things? She was so nervous, she almost giggled. Number three or not, hearing voices again wasn't good. She needed to get Frank off to the ladies room for a crazy-check.

"Um…guys? Ladies room first, phone after. If I don't pee right now, I won't be responsible for what happens to your car seats." She turned and grabbed her aunt's hand. "C'mon Frankie." Verrie heard a decided snicker and turned back to see all the men elbowing each other. She shot them a look and couldn't find "nice" as she hissed. "What?"

"Oldest line in the book," Flick laughed. "Let's hit the ladies room. That's when our 'guests' try to disappear." He waved a hand at her burgeoning protest. "It's fine," he dismissed. "Talk things over with your Aunt and come to some decision that will make you feel better as long as you stay put and accompany us willingly." He looked at his watch. "Just make it fast, will you? I don't want to miss Ellen."

Verrie's humorous side awoke briefly. She couldn't help the twitch of her lip at the thought of the big, tough dude watching daytime TV. The whole situation would be so much easier if she wasn't afraid she was going bat-shit nuts again.

Frank took charge. "You pretty guys stay right theah. We're gonna powdah some noses."

Yeah, thought Verrie. *We're going to powder our noses.*

The men surrounded them and moved smoothly across the lobby toward the ladies room door. So much for staying put. But seriously? Both she and Frank had known they'd stick close. They pushed into the restroom, and the door swung shut behind them. Verrie collapsed into her aunt's arms.

"What-sa-mattah, sweetpea?" Frank soothed. "These guys seem like theah fa real. We'll have ah girls back in no time, and the foah of us will figya things out."

"That's not what I'm worried about." Verrie pulled back from her aunt's arms and wiped a shaky hand over her cheeks where a few tears had escaped. She looked right into Frank's concerned eyes. "I have a bigger problem than that. After the one named Ken introduced himself, I thought I heard him keep talking…in my head."

"Ah, fuck."

The expletive came from outside the bathroom, and Verrie started. *What the hell?* There was no way any of those guys could have heard her whispers.

"Well, hell, Verrie. Was it the same kind of gibberish like befoah? You think these guys are some kinda aliens or somethin'?"

"Nope, Aunt Frank. This was straight up English, and he was telling someone named Marduk you were coming with us too, and they needed to make sure Si answered her phone when I call."

"Did he get an ansuh from whoevah he was talkin' to?"

No, I did not. The guy named Ken's voice butted right into the conversation, and Verrie gasped for breath, swaying. She held up a hand to stop Frank from saying anything more.

And if I'd known you were going to be able to hear us, I would have been more polite and used my phone. It's just that head talk is easier.

For some reason, rather than being completely freaked out by the new words in her head, after processing for a minute, Verrie actually felt better. She became pragmatic. Instead of random noises, this was actually conversation…certainly a first. Okay. So, if she could understand him, maybe he could understand her. Verrie allowed herself to "think" at Ken—something she hadn't done with the voices since the very beginning. Back then it had only served to make them escalate.

This is Ken, right?

Yes, it is.

Wow. An actual answer.

And who else out there can talk like this?

None of the other guys here.

His answer surprised Verrie, but he was quick to explain.

These guys are all just DEA, with no…uh…otherworldly skills. But most of the folks back at our headquarters have mind-speak capabilities. Would you like to hear them?

Verrie wasn't sure. It had been a long time since she'd had to face—up close and personal—the voices in her head. What the hell. She might as well bite the bullet and get it over with. *Yeah, okay. Go ahead.*

Ladies and gentlemen of the compound. Please say a big hello to Sienna's mom, who it turns out has the same mad skills as her daughter.

And that answered *that* question. Sienna was hearing things too.

Welcome to Boston.

Hello from all of us.

Can't wait to meet you.

A flurry of voices hit her head, both male and female. Here was something else that had never happened. The tones she'd heard before had always been deep moans and grunts, indistinguishable from one to another. These were all separate and very different.

Mom?

Now Verrie was freaked. Her knees gave out, and she slipped to the floor. Frank crouched down beside her, but Verrie managed another silencing look in her aunt's direction before trembling out her daughter's name.

Sienna? Is that you?

Yeah, Mom. It is. Wow. Who knew this stuff could be cool as well as scary? Hey. How come we've never done this before?

Another voice cut in. *It's because we have harnessed the ability to make our voices travel farther than is normally attributed to immor…uh, our people.*

That's Marduk, Mom. He's the leader of these guys.

You mean the head of the DEA?

Nope. That's Jake. Verrie heard her daughter mumble as she asked somebody. *That's right, isn't it? Jake?*

Yes, that's correct. Another male voice chimed in.

Then the guy Marduk's tonal intonation was back. *But introductions can wait. Why don't we get your mother back here before we let you all know what's happening? We don't want her…or you…to be too overwhelmed.*

She heard her daughter agree in a very grown-up way and decided if Sienna could digest what was going on, she owed it to her daughter to do the same.

Hey, Mrs. F. The cheerful head voice nearly sent her spinning again. It was most definitely Riley, and Verrie swallowed her incredulity before answering.

Riley? You can talk like this too?

Yeah. Cool, right? I don't know what you guys have been bitching about because this is totally dope. Hey, say hi to Grams for me, will you?

Yeah. Okay. I will. But seriously? Right now I have to pee worse than ever because you all have scared the piss right out of me...so sign off...or whatever you do. I don't need anybody in my brain while I'm urinating, okay?

Yeah, Mom. We'll leave you alone, her daughter replied. Was that a whole lot of snickering? *Can't wait to see you. Love you.*

Love you, too, peach. Uh, bye for now. Ken? Frankie and I will be out in a couple of minutes. Feel free to listen in if you're feeling pervy, she snarked.

Now there was definite laughter. *If I wanted to, you couldn't stop me,* he chortled. *But you'll learn to keep us out in time. I promise.*

Well. That was something.

"Yah wanna fill me in?" Aunt Frank was still sitting beside her on the questionably clean bathroom floor, looking calmly expectant. Verrie uncurled her body upward, and Frank followed.

"Well, the voices have turned friendly, and they've been joined by my daughter...and Riley."

"Riles?" Now Francis-Ann got flustered. Apparently, the first bit she could take, but her granddaughter having mind-skills? Maybe not so much.

"Yup, and I'm happy to say she's enjoying the hell out of it and says 'hi,' by the way."

"Well, holy shit." Frank sat back down on the floor, blinking in a stunned fashion. "So what's next?"

"Dammit. Next, I wet my pants if we don't pause the big fucking reveals. Give me a minute here."

As soon as Verrie closed the stall door, pulled down her jeans, and sat on the toilet, she allowed her head to drop. Cradling it in her hands, she tried to lose the tension in her body as she relieved herself. Breathe deeply. Relax the muscles. There was no need to worry.

Her daughter sounded fine. Riley was ecstatic, and the group of men waiting outside to escort them to what they called "headquarters" were some of the finest looking pieces of beefcake she'd seen in a long time. That was a plus, wasn't it? She might be nearing forty, but she wasn't dead to a nice view. She could appreciate a hot, young physique, couldn't she? It had been so long since she'd had a man, maybe she could hope they had some older friends at home. *Yeah, right.* Like she'd ever allow herself a relationship again. Hurt and betrayal—that's all a so-called partnership was good for.

Verrie pulled up her pants. Besides, this was all about Sienna. Why had her mind even wandered in the direction of men? She'd been celibate since Dwight Dick-head had kicked her out, and she'd be a god-damned nun 'til the day she died. That was a fact.

Time to get on with business.

Explanations would soon be forthcoming, arrangements would be made, and hopefully, by this time tomorrow, she and Sienna would be headed back to Colorado. *Hopefully.*

Chapter Six

Dumuzi remained quiet during the conversations flowing back and forth from the airport. He wasn't sure why. He didn't open his mouth to welcome Sienna's mother to Boston. He told himself it was because being introduced to the parent of his bride-to-be was going to be weird, but if he was honest, it was something else.

Her voice made him nervous...actually jittery. His stomach had clenched, and his cheeks had gone rigid. There was an undercurrent to her tone that bothered him...a lot. He brought a hand up to rub his eyes. He hated not being able to explain the feeling in his gut, but there it was. Dammit. This was one meeting he wasn't looking forward to.

Dumuzi whistled for Archie. He needed to walk off his trepidation, and the forest vegetation and spring swamps called to him. *Going out for a while,* he called to nobody in particular. He was used to making his whereabouts common knowledge with his buddies, and now that he was embodied, it was even more important. He was going to have to be ever so careful.

Stepping through the trees, the morning sun beat down on his shoulders, the warmth penetrating his thin white t-shirt. Damn, it felt good. He walked a path his invisible feet had trod a million times over the past hundreds of years, but this time, he was able to touch every tree, every leaf, every vine sprouting from the newly awakened earth. June had always been one of his favorite months, and having his senses back, this was the best one he could ever remember. He plucked a young sassafras leaf from a tree and popped it into his mouth. The flavor burst on his tongue, and he let out a wild, happy whoop that had Archie dancing and dodging in front of him, more than willing to play this new game whatever it was.

Laughing, Dumuzi picked up a stick and threw it with all his god strength. Archie went bounding away, his excited barks disappearing into the trees. Muze didn't follow because once he got one hundred yards from Sienna, he'd be invisible again.

The god watched his dog for a moment, then sighed. Dumuzi's burst of exuberance slowly diminished, and as much as he tried to avoid analyzing anything, he couldn't help but mentally chastise himself.

Instead of being in the woods, he should be using this time to get to know Sienna. Any other god confronted with their *Chosen* would have done so. But to be honest, the prospect held no great appeal…and it wouldn't make any difference to the outcome of their union. Familiar with each other or not, all the proper steps would be taken to join them together. They'd go through the amulet ceremony, they'd mate. *Okay. Stop.* There was a big "eww" in his brain contemplating that one. Mate with Sienna? Not on anyone's life. Just because he was the baby of the gods and looked twenty-five, didn't mean he was close to her age. Hell, he'd been around for over twenty-four hundred years, and Sienna was a mere child. The prospect of getting physical with her left him cold. And what did he know about virgins? *Argh.* Just the thought of that word made him want to poke his eyes out.

He'd have to see her naked. Again, his gorge rose.

When all was accomplished, Sienna would probably end up hating him and distancing herself—separate bedrooms, separate lives. That was the way it had to be, and considering his non-existent attraction to the girl, he could only illicit half-hearted regret for their disassociated futures.

Dumuzi looked up to see if he could locate Archie but stumbled and went suddenly dizzy. *Crap.* He needed to watch out for roots now that they could actually get in his way. He shook his head, but the spinning wouldn't stop. He forced himself to stop and think. Fear gripped his bones. He remembered these physical signs. He hadn't experienced them with an actual body in hundreds of years, but if he was correct, he was about to turn. Archie hadn't been around to warn him.

"Archie," he called. "Gods-dammit." He toed off his sneakers and began to shuck down his jeans. "Archie."

Marduk. Mayday, he called out in a panic.

Muze. We've got a situation of our own, here. Do you need help?

Changing, Marduk. Dangerous. Send...help. His world spiraled into blackness.

****

"Breathe deeply, Sienna." Tess turned a worried face up to her husband who felt like he was being assaulted from all sides. He knew his face looked fierce as his wife kept after him. "Do you think it's a panic

62

attack?" When Marduk didn't answer right away, his wife looked pissed and about to rip him up and down but was thankfully interrupted by the other human in the room.

"Hell, no." Riley cried. She'd been busy raiding the refrigerator but slid rapidly across the kitchen floor on her slippery socks and threw herself down beside her best friend who'd sunk to the flagstone surface. "She's having one of those schizophrenic episodes where she hears the weird-ass voices."

"Dammit, Marduk. Call Nergal." Tess supported Sienna's back as the girl moaned horribly, holding her head.

Before Marduk could answer, Riley spoke again.

"Isn't there something you guys can do? She hears your voices, too."

Marduk quickly formulated a plan of action but got blindsided again.

Marduk, Sienna's mother is down. We were just about to get into the car when she dropped like a rock. I can't get anything out of her but garbled noises, and her aunt says these are the attacks she used to have all the time before she left Boston.

Marduk received the evil eye from Tess. She had no idea all the shit he was being hit with, and he needed everyone to know. He opened an all-god channel.

Dumuzi is 'down' in the woods—all the gods would know what that meant. *Sienna's mother is having the same thing happen as Sienna, and we need to split up to take care of it all.* He gestured to the gods he knew could handle Dumuzi—Enlil who could turn into a bull, Anshar and Dagon who were both serpents, Enten, the polar bear although they teasingly called him the Yeti, and Shamash the golden leopard. *Go find Muze and contain him.* The group had the presence of mind to walk from the kitchen before changing skins, then quickly misted outside.

Ladies, form a circle around Sienna and divert the external energies from her while the rest of us go to the aid of her mother. He turned to Riley, still speaking in his head. *How long do these episodes usually last?*

"A couple of hours, uh…" *A couple of hours,* she amended, so everyone could hear her.

Right. As soon as Sienna is under control, get her up to her room. We'll have her mother back here as fast as possible. He was pointing at gods, preparing to leave when…*Shit.* The roaring outside brought his head up and everyone else's. The fracas in the woods shook the house. *Holy hell,* Marduk spewed. *This is one serious cluster-fuck.*

As evidenced by his declaration, King Waylon and his five Lauernley guards burst into the kitchen at a run. Marduk tried to ignore Riley's horrified expression—it would take far too long to explain the blue pigment right now—and focused on another helpful faction.

"What would you have us do?" Waylon asked Marduk without preamble. The need for expediency cutting through any bullshit.

"Do you have anything up your sleeves that will mute the noise filling the area? It's going to attract a lot of outside attention, and that's the last thing we need."

"You know it. We'll throw up a water barrier," the blue King assured Marduk. "The liquid will deaden the noise, and it should be sufficient to keep gawkers away."

"Gawkers. Yeah. Right." Riley's own mouth had been hanging open, and her voice came out small as she repeated the words, her nostrils flaring. Lenore took charge.

"Don't lose it on us now, girl. You've faced jail, the land of the giants, and voices in your head. You can't let a few errant roars and a bunch of blue guys ruin your record."

Riley's head bounced up and down in an exaggerated affirmative.

Great, thought Marduk. She looks like she's going down for the count. More damage control. Before dealing with her, he instructed, *Dorian, take a handful of guys and get to the airport. Fix things with Sienna's mother as fast as possible and get back here.*

Marduk felt impotent staying put, but it couldn't be helped. He had to get to the root of the problem and dig up answers.

Nergal. If the thunder god could have screamed, he would have, but it was hard to regulate volume with head talk. He had to suffice with making the call as imperative sounding as possible, and it wouldn't hurt to embellish. *Get your ass up here, pronto.* That should light a fire under the king…and probably earn Marduk a beat-down for his insolence. Marduk realized, a little late, he should have warned their guest.

"Riley. Don't freak out," Candy had the presence of mind to squeak out. "The largest guy you've ever seen is about to pop in—" The explanation stopped there due to the sudden rent in the air.

Shit, yeah. Cluster-fuck.

Nergal, King of the Underworld, appeared in the kitchen with a pissed off look on his flushed face and a roar of anger. Riley scrambled backward, placing her ass firmly up against the dishwasher, shrieking in surprise.

"What the fuck." Tears made quick tracks down her face as she tore her eyes away from the enormously pissed off king. "Please. You guys," she appealed to Tess and Candy. "Make this all stop…" she moaned.

"You bet, sister." Candy's face twisted angrily. She raised herself up, strode straight to Nergal and poked him in the chest.

"Stop looking so bloody…kingly," she seethed. "You're scaring our guest." The royal head of the Underworld looked momentarily nonplussed, but with a fast perusal of the kitchen, took in Riley's ashen face and Sienna's downed body before grabbing Candy's hand and gently bringing it down to her side.

"I'm sorry for the attitude. I can see things are tense here. But to understand, I was just about to start interrogation of Nedu when you called." Heads nodded all around.

Nedu was a traitor who had been working with the gods' longtime nemesis, Beletseri, and the king was trying to get to the bottom of some very bad and very ancient shit. The outcome of that shit would either have them going to the rescue of Beletseri—who had been captured by an egotistical shape-shifting madman—or leaving her to languish in the Malaysian climes, eating bugs for the rest of her eternal life—kind of a big deal.

"So, fill me in on what was so important, I had to be summoned abruptly?"

"This…" Marduk—not apologizing—pointed to the twitching, fetal bundle on the floor that was Sienna.

"…is Dumuzi's *Chosen*." Sienna wouldn't know what that meant, but the king stepped a little closer.

Brave soul and good friend that she was, Riley moved swiftly and protectively to Sienna's side while Marduk continued. "She, and her mother who is en route, suffer from hearing evil voices in their heads, and we have a good idea where they might be coming from."

While Marduk was talking, Glory, Charlie, Quinn, Obedience, and Dani-Lee went elbow to elbow with the goddesses already on the floor, surrounding Sienna and sending protective energies inward from their circle. It worked like a charm—Sienna's body unclenched at once. Her eyes popped open and her refocused gaze targeted Nergal who had moved to kneel by the group. She blinked twice.

"Tell me what the voices sound like." Nergal's voice was soothing, compelling. "Can you recall any of their words?"

Sienna stared at the stunning, seven-foot-tall god with the chestnut-hued ponytail and bronzed jewelry. Marduk wondered if she'd freak out again, but her speech, though strained, didn't collapse.

"The voices are always low…guttural," she whimpered, remembering. "They hurt, and you can't get rid of them until they decide they're finished." She blinked and looked around at the circle of women. "Except you guys made it stop."

Hadn't he and the gods experienced the same thing in Hell? Marduk grimaced.

"The loudest one…the voice that seems to be in charge chants the same thing over and over."

"Can you repeat it?" Nergal's aura was all soft and tender. He could obviously feel how close to the edge Sienna remained.

"I can because it's always the same...it's saying something that sounds like 'ugly doll.'" She managed to screw up her mouth. "But it's more like 'uggla dwall.' Does that mean anything to you? Does it make any sense?" Sienna pulled herself up now, with the help of Tess, and accepted a glass of juice being thrust into her hand by Absu who had also remained behind.

Nergal and Marduk exchanged worried looks.

Nergal translated. "Goddess, mine. What the fuck?"

Marduk was equally confused. "That's nothing we've run across before." He blew out a long breath. "And it's my understanding this has been going on for quite some time." He pointed to Sienna. "She says her mother has dealt with it for years. And speaking of which, when her mother gets here, we need to make a timeline of events. I have a very strong feeling Dumuzi's episodes might be tied into this somehow."

Huxley's voice cut into his train of thought.

Sienna's mom is under control, he confirmed. *We're headed home.*

Thanks, Hux. Marduk turned his attention back to Nergal. "We'll have a general assembly in my meeting room to hash this out. At some point, Sienna and her mother will have to be brought up to speed and told...about Dumuzi."

"She doesn't know yet?" Nergal sent an incredulous look from the recovering girl to Marduk.

"We thought it would be best to wait for her mother's arrival, and things have been spinning out of control ever since."

"Whoa. Yeah. Like totes cray-cray," Riley piped up, clearly having recovered her equilibrium. "I feel like I just dropped some really heavy-duty acid," she admitted, and Marduk had a feeling they'd caught the girls just in time. If there had been any more unsupervised episodes to "numb," especially with substances stronger than marijuana, there could have been some really bad long-term consequences.

Riley wasn't finished with her tirade. "And I don't know who you are," she pointed accusingly at the king, "but you have to stop being so hot. Do you know you're in danger of ruining my whole future sex life? None of the guys at school can come close to you on a scale of one to smokin'." She crossed her arms belligerently across her chest.

Nergal let out a deep chuckle that resonated around the room and had Marduk groaning. The king's vocal vibrations would ramp up the damp panties in the room. The thunder god didn't want to remember, but Tess, his own darling wife had told him if he didn't exist, Nergal would be the one her wet dreams would revolve around. Fucking king.

"Okay. Enough." Marduk reached his limit. "His liege doesn't need his ego stroked any more than it already is. Ladies, it's time for you to take Sienna off for some rest."

"Uh-uh, not even close." The girl in question struggled to her feet and stood glassy-eyed and swaying, but there was no mistaking the set of her mouth. "I'm not going anywhere until my mother arrives, then we're going to be attending this meeting you've called. I have a feeling most of it will be about us, so don't even think I'm going to miss it." She dug her feet in, and all of a sudden, Marduk saw goddess written all over the girl's visage. Not only that, but her eyes became flecked with the same kind of gold as Sham's. Marduk would not be the least bit surprised to find out—when a DNA test was performed—Sienna and her mother were descendants of the big cat man. That would also make them distant relatives to Candy. His head spun. Damned fun with genetics.

Marduk noticed, almost as an aside, the roaring in the forest had stopped. He didn't know if it was due to the Lauernley's containment field, or if Dumuzi was back under control. He attempted to connect privately with Enlil.

Status report, Enlil?

Muze is back to normal or as normal as he ever gets. There was a chuckle. *And he returned to us rather abruptly, I might add, which is more than I can say for the serpent boys.* Now Enlil sounded exasperated with Anshar and Dagon. *They've gone off together somewhere to raise holy hell. I told them to be back at the compound in half an hour. I think they understood me.*

Marduk ran a hand back through his long dark hair. Sometimes being in charge really sucked. He shook his head, squared his shoulders, and indicated the kitchen doorway to Nergal. The king took the hint and began the exodus to Marduk's office.

Okay. We're giving it a half an hour. Meeting. My office. Everyone shows up. This is not a request.

Chapter Seven

Dumuzi came awake slowly and looked up. The sun was still low in the morning sky, so he hadn't been out for very long. Maybe he'd behaved himself. The god turned his head and looked into the eyes of a bloody, pissed off golden leopard—or not.

There was a loud snarl, but then the huge cat was yanked back by a firm, unrelenting hand. "Cut the crap, Sham." Enlil's voice came from behind the big feline's tensed body, and Dumuzi relaxed onto the forest floor. "Don't mind him, Muze. He's just being a pussy because you beat down his ass."

Dumuzi forced himself to sit up, running a hand through his spiky, disheveled hair. "Fuck, Sham. I'm really sorry, man."

The cat gave what looked to be a shrug, sat back on his haunches, and proceeded to morph back to god. Muze heaved a sigh of relief. "Is everybody else okay?" He looked around and saw only Enten, who was also slowly sucking polar-bear fur back into his pores. Dumuzi's mouth fell open. "You're shitting me, right? Marduk only sent you three to deal with me?"

"Hell, no," Enlil grinned, his horns still thrusting up from his skull, making no effort to hide his bullish nature. "Anshar and Dagon were here too, but you snapped back to yourself so quickly, they had to go amuse themselves elsewhere. You know how it is when the serpents are on a roll."

Dumuzi's eyebrows went up. Enlil shrugged. "Yup. My guess is George's Bank." The god named an underwater ridge off the coast of Cape Cod, renowned as a productive fishery. "Hopefully, they'll come back stuffed and happy."

There was a smothered expletive from the now morphed leopard, and Dumuzi stood up, moving to where Shamash sat with a hand pressed to his face to staunch the blood flow. The vegetation god's voice came out gruffly.

"I really am sorry, Sham." He looked at the deep gouge, running from the corner of Shamash's lip up to his temple. "But thanks for getting in my way." He peered closer. "I think we need to get you back to Dr. Dani. That gash is definitely stitch-worthy."

Enlil agreed, "Yeah, let's get you transported, cat-man." He turned amused eyes to Dumuzi. "And it'll suck to be you, Muze. When Quinn sees what you've done to her pretty man's face, she's going to strangle your stamen and pulverize your pistil."

A strange, warm feeling passed through Dumuzi's chest, and he gasped out a laugh. Leave it to Enlil. It had been years since any of the guys had poked at him with a vegetation or swamp jokes. They used to do it all the time…but not since he'd become so introspective and secluded. It felt strange…and good to be teased again. He hoped it would continue, he kind of missed it.

"Right. It's lucky for you there'll be no permanent scar," Shamash growled, hamming it up. "But you'd better watch your ass next time we face off—Leopards never forget."

"I thought that was elephants," Dumuzi handed him the straight line and lent a hand to pull his cat friend to his feet.

"Shit. You're right. I forgot." Shamash came up and punched Dumuzi in the arm. "Just like I'm going to forget this ever happened." He touched his bloody face and allayed Muze's fears. "Don't worry. We're good."

"Okay, you two. Finish the kissing-and-making-up shit so we can get back to the compound. Or do you need to find a room?" Enlil got two bird-salutes before the pair turned, arms around each other's shoulders to begin the brisk walk back to the compound. Even though all of them but Dumuzi could mist out, it was unspoken they weren't going to leave the god alone in case he had another episode.

Ten minutes later, Dumuzi found himself laughing out loud watching Quinn's antics, amazed he could feel this good so soon after he'd wigged out so badly.

The gamine goddess was all lit up, watching Dani stitch up her god, darting in and out around the doctor, poking her husband's arms, legs and—if Dumuzi wasn't mistaken—sneaking a quick pinch to his nipples and his ass on every other turn.

This is completely cool, Spot.

Dumuzi choked back a laugh at Quinn's nickname for her big cat. And rather than being angry Dumuzi had caused the slash, Quinn had thanked him. *It makes you look all rough and tough. Are you sure we can't keep it?* Her tongue came out of its own volition, aimed at the top of her mate's boo-boo. She was just able to pop it back in before contact, and Muze was surprised she suppressed the instincts that compelled her to lap Shamash "all better."

73

It will only stay if we rip it open again seven or eight times in the exact same place. So, no, we won't, Sham said patiently. *It hurts like a son-of-a-bitch.*

Quinn gave a pout at the pronouncement while Dani stepped back and snipped the sutures. Her pout quickly changed to a satisfied smirk. *All finished, babe,* she proclaimed to her husband.

Shamash blinked, and Muze stifled another laugh. Damned if Quinn's sexy posturing hadn't done its job. Dani had been able to finish stitching without Shamash going all cat-aclysmic at the doc's ministrations—sweet.

"Just in time," Dani declared. "We're due in Marduk's office in..." She looked at her watch. "...three minutes. Huxley says the airport group is just coming up the driveway with Sienna's mom and Riley's grandmother. Time to roll."

Dumuzi got to his feet and experienced a strange feeling in the pit of his stomach again. He reached a shaking hand out to rest on Archie's warm head, but the dog gave him no sign of impending doom. *Okay.* He let out a relieved breath. It was not the kind of "bad feeling" that preceded a change, but still, the disquieting flutter invading his insides was very un-him.

Muze had made it a point throughout his entire life to let drama and angst roll past, keep his emotions tamped down so he wouldn't turn into his beast. So, what the fuck was happening now? What disturbed him? All signs pointed to Sienna, but being in her actual presence hadn't made him feel agitated, just regretful. *Fuck.* Here was the second time today he'd had this...unsettledness. What the hell was going on?

He warily followed Sham, Quinn, and Dani from the infirmary, not looking forward to what was about to unfold. Something bad was making his stomach clench. He thought for a moment. *Duh.* Of course, he was about to meet Sienna's mother, and shortly thereafter, fill her head with the compound's godly credentials before convincing the woman she had to let her underage daughter mate with him. *Yeah.* That was enough to send him scurrying for the peppermint, chamomile, and ginger...or Pepto-Bismol for anyone else who wasn't the god of all growing things.

Dumuzi's feet hit the landing twenty feet above the front hallway at the same time the front door swung inward, and his whole body froze. His angst instantly reached epic proportions. *Warning! Warning*! He wanted to tell everyone to get down and protect themselves. Potent energy surged into the house, energy of an unexplained kind with an invisible source. Were they under attack? Had the enemy somehow infiltrated?

Dumuzi looked around, his tongue paralyzed. Not one of the other gods looked worried. Nobody else felt it? *Hell.* They all continued laughing and talking as if nothing was happening. Even Archie seemed unaffected.

He found himself in a partial crouch, eyes moving over the banister to take in the group below, more on edge than he'd ever been in his life. His gaze moved past the relaxed-looking agent's faces, past the pretty older woman behind them, and into the middle of a protective ring of gods. Here was the source of the distressing energy, and Dumuzi was powerless to stop it.

Invisible tendrils only he could see began climbing their way towards him. They streamed straight at him, taking on color and life as they neared. *Holy shit.* Dumuzi knew.

He clutched the wooden railing in front of him as his body became surrounded and wrapped tightly in a cocoon of...warmth. *Dammit.* He was so screwed.

Sienna wasn't his *Chosen.* Her mother was.

Mine, mine, mine, his brain chanted as his muscles worshiped the feeling of being enveloped. His silent, repetitive words must have skipped right over everyone's heads, penetrating the only gray matter that...mattered. The nondescript, dishwater blonde at the center of the agent's circle turned and looked upward. Her mouth dropped open, and she too became immobile. They locked eyes for an indescribable moment, but she must have been impacted in a different way than Dumuzi. Either that or the tendrils he'd inadvertently sent back down in return for hers girdled her too tightly. The woman's lids fluttered, and she crumpled to the ground.

"No," Dumuzi's voice reverberated from the marble floor to the domed, stained glass ceiling. Every eye in the house focused on him except for Doctor Dani's. She popped out and wafted in next to the downed woman, already busy checking her vitals.

"What the..." Marduk looked up, then down. "Oh."

"She's fine," Dani-Lee announced loudly, interrupting. "It must have been all the excitement."

"Hah. Any more excitement around here and we'll all be dead," Marduk continued, his mouth quirked in a knowing smile. He pinpointed Dumuzi with a stare.

"Looks like we had that one all wrong, hey, Muze?" Marduk's words affirmed that the vines wrapped around Dumuzi's heart were real...and there to stay. *Yes. No. Shit. Shit. Fuck.*

"What's going on, Marduk?" Tess and her entourage herded Sienna into the room. They'd missed the excitement. Sienna's mother was still down, but coming around, and Dumuzi was aware the minute Sienna spotted her.

"Mom." She flew out from the protective entourage of women. The agents and gods quickly parted and allowed the girl to rush to her mom's side before closing up ranks again.

Marduk's voice, answering his wife, blocked out the low, soothing words passing between mother and daughter. "It turns out Sienna is not Dumuzi's *Chosen...*" he paused for effect. "...but her mother is."

Marduk grinned and spoke to the vegetation god again. "Nice going, causing her to pass out when she got a look at your ugly cabbage," he teased. "I do believe that's a first. None of us has ever caused our intended to wilt."

"Intended?" The voice came up, surprisingly strong from the midst of the group on the floor. "What the hell? Are you all batshit crazy?"

With help from Dani and a stunned-looking Sienna, the woman got to her feet, all—instantly—no-nonsense. "I came here to get my daughter, nothing more." She looked around the packed front entry, clearly witness to all the hands covering up smug smiles. Her brows drew together even more sharply. "Do I make myself clear?"

Heads nodded, but Dumuzi was a few mental steps behind. Most of his brain hadn't heard her question. He needed to hit play-back to be certain of what she'd said, but it didn't matter. There was only one thing on his mind, and he gave voice to it. His uncharacteristically imperative tone carried downward.

"Your name?" he rasped out, his voice ringing with urgency. "What is your name?"

The woman refused to look up at him. She clearly would not meet his eyes again. Dumuzi felt empty, but he got it. If Sienna's mother had been hit as hard as he had, she'd be scared shitless, however, she surprised him.

"Veronica Foxey," she called out, her eyes fixed on a far wall, her answer strong.

"Verrie, for short," Flick's impish voice cut in, then paused for dramatic effect. "Verrie. Get it?" he repeated. "She's Verrie Foxey," he snickered.

"Flick. Not good." Anger crept up Dumuzi's spine as he growled. "You need to shut up. Now." His hands could easily slip around the agent's throat if he were closer—damn lucky for the irreverent human they were a floor apart. The god managed a deep breath and swore to himself. So, this was the jealousy thing all the guys talked about; the feeling of totally owning and being owned, to the point of violence. He didn't like it, too much emotion flooding his drought-dulled cells like an irrigation system suddenly thrust open. It was wonderful. It was awful.

Shut down...shut down. Dumuzi slowly regained control. *Dammit.* The sooner he could go back into dormancy, the better off everyone would be.

In the aftermath of the deluge of emotion, Muze saw Hux grab Flick and say something low to the agent he didn't catch. By the color that drained from Flick's face, it was probably something along the lines of "screw with a god's *Chosen,* especially this one, and die a slow and painful death."

Yup. Dumuzi was feeling all that and didn't it just suck.

He tried to shake himself free from the fucked-up grip, but an instant splicing had already taken place between him and his mate, and it was all too real. She had, with a single look, insinuated herself into every cell in his body, and he already felt her growing there. *Dammit.* He needed to stop the progression. She could not become a part of him.

The situation had to remain as before…as he'd assumed it would be with Sienna. Just because the faces had changed—and he now resembled walking wood—didn't mean the parameters of his imminent relationship should change. He needed to stay strong, stick to the course he'd self-prescribed. In order to follow those rules, he brought up faces from his past.

There. A deep breath out. There was his path back to becoming remote and detached. All he needed to do was remember how he'd failed everyone he'd ever loved. The faces, easily recalled, were a cautionary litany.

Now he'd be able to keep Veronica—he couldn't think of her as Verrie—from passing his boundaries. He would not repeat history's mistakes.

Dumuzi looked down at his legs, willing them to move. Once he got them going, a less than graceful descent of the staircase ensued. *Shit.* His knees still felt partially petrified. But fuck it. He'd get over it. The god reached the main floor, and brushed by Marduk, ignoring his future mate to head for the thunder god's office.

"Don't we have a meeting to attend?" he snarled over his shoulder. "We need to get everything explained and out in the open so we can move things along."

"Smooth, Dumuzi," Marduk elbowed in beside him and growled into his ear. "The least you could do is greet your woman."

"Not interested, Marduk," he lied. "Let's just get this over with, okay?" He pushed the meeting room door open but tuned in to what went on behind him.

"Verrie, hon," —it had to be the older woman's voice— "I know you wah on yeh ass, but have yeh taken a good look around? I think we've fallen into Chippendale heaven." She dropped her voice. "And that redhead who just walked through the doah is tryin' like hell to keep yoah dollah bills from endin' up in his g-string."

There was a lot of tense laughter from his friends following that ridiculous bit of nonsense, and Dumuzi wished he could scoop his ears out so he wouldn't have to hear any more.

"Whatevah it is that shot between the two a yeh was awesome."

Dead silence met that statement. Good. Veronica was sticking with denial, too.

"Cat got yeh tongue, V?" the woman questioned, not getting a response.

"Nope, I don't," Sham answered into the void without thinking, and his buddies cracked up for real this time. Dumuzi huffed. At least the leopard had broken the god-awful tension which helped slap Muze back to reality.

Damn. He was going to have to try harder not to be such a complete asshole as things progressed. He and his friends needed Veronica to undergo the amulet ceremony with him, and he needed to join with her—just once—to consummate their union. If she thought he was a prick, they'd never get all that accomplished.

He needed to be a little charming, a little complimentary, but not enough she had any expectations they would have a future together. It was going to take some delicate pruning for Muze to know how many of their intertwining branches he should allow to grow…and which ones needed to be bluntly severed.

Chapter Eight

The silence in the meeting room was broken by Verrie's attention-getting cough. *Strange.* Dumuzi expected her to settle down in her chair and take a back seat at the proceedings to see what would unfold, but apparently, she had something to say.

"You know, I hear all of you in my head..." she began, standing up.

Dumuzi took the time to really look at her now that she was close and paying no attention to him. She looked young despite the fact she had to be in her late thirties because of Sienna's age. Her figure—in a form-fitting, white t-shirt and skinny jeans—showed off average sized breasts and a trim double-hand-full ass. Not his normal type, but certainly nice. Her hair, shoulder-length and a blonde too plain for description, was neither straight nor curly, simply framing her face in a non-intrusive way.

Dumuzi honestly felt he would never have given her a second look back in the day if not for two stunning features—Veronica's vivid blue eyes flecked with shards of gold, the exact colors of a Pipevine Swallowtail butterfly, and her lush, bow-shaped lips. Succulent lips he could already imagine nipping and sucking into the warm cavity of his mouth. His cock stirred. *Yeah.* Those lips were unbelievable, but he needed to cut the crap and shut down his dick's attempt at show and tell.

Dumuzi forced his gaze back to the whole package. Otherwise prim and authoritative, he found nothing else that would make him stir. He keyed back in to her voice—provocative, smooth—it flowed like cool rain on a parched field. *Damn*. Interested again. He didn't need that complication. Why were there so many things about her to like even when trying to discredit her attributes?

"…which is very disconcerting in itself," she continued. Veronica gazed around the circle at the sitting and standing crowd. "But what I'm finding most disturbing, other than the fact my daughter, my friends, and I are reluctant '*guests*' in your home,"—yeah, she'd put a lot of emphasis on guests,— "is the fact that you have someone in your '*dungeon*'"—more emphasis— "in a '*jail cell*'"—one more time— "and nobody's paying any heed to his loud ranting."

Sienna and Riley broke in with a quick, "We're hearing it, too."

Veronica nodded and continued her sexy little speech.

"Is that where we're going to end up?" She tried not to show any fear, but Dumuzi, already so in tune with her, saw the corner of her right eye twitch. He almost spoke, but Marduk beat him to it.

"Hell, no." The thunder god quickly squashed that train of thought. "Matthew is a…a… he's a…" He stumbled over his choice of words, but luckily, King Nergal took over.

"Matthew is a traitor who, despite his criminal acts, may be given a chance to redeem himself. That is the reason he is here, in a clean and well cared for area of the lower floors, and not in the bowels of my realm where he could, eventually, end up."

"The bowels of your realm?" Veronica's eyebrows couldn't have raised any higher. "What are you talking about? Who are you people?"

"Nergal, your grace," Marduk placated the king who bristled at being questioned, "we've yet to fill Sienna's mother or her friend in on our background. If we could just take this slowly…"

"Screw slowly," the woman named Frank interjected, and before she could take her poor choice of words back, laughs and elbows flew. Dumuzi got the same instant picture in his mind all the smut-loving individuals in the room conjured. Frank was a damned fine-looking woman even if she was a human getting up in years. Any one of them—if not mated—would pleasure her in a heartbeat.

As a point of interest, Dumuzi shot a glance to Ishkur, their gray-haired god. Funny, he was the only one not laughing and was looking anywhere but at Frank. Not a *Chosen* kind of chemistry between the two, but a possible hook-up? Dumuzi made a mental note to keep an eye on that one.

"Ha-ha," Frankie, also studiously avoiding the side of the room where Ishkur stood, joined in sarcastically. "Foh the recuhd, I nohmally like it fast and hahd." Her bright green eyes flashed around, selectively. "But none of you guys could handle me, so no use gettin' yuhselves worked up." She got back on track. "But enough bullshit. Verrie has a damned good question. Who and what the hell *ah* you guys, anyway?"

"They're gods, Gram," Riley couldn't keep her mouth shut. "From ancient Mesopotamia." Both Frank and Veronica looked like they were about to speak when Sienna pre-empted them, getting up to walk toward her mother.

"It's true, Mom." She gripped Veronica's arm. "They showed us some neat stuff only gods could do. And Mom, don't you get it?" She paused and looked her mother right in the eye. "We can hear their voices in our heads. Doesn't that tell you anything? Doesn't that make you feel just the teensiest bit curious to know…with our problems…we can hear gods? Like maybe we're not fucked up in the head?"

"Language, Si," her mother cautioned, looking a little like she might fall to the floor at any moment. Dumuzi unconsciously moved closer. If anyone was picking Veronica up off the hardwood, it would be him.

"But," Veronica glanced around as if unsure whether to say more, then went for broke. "Their voices are human, honey. English. The ones I've been hearing," she narrowed her eyes at her daughter and shook her head, "and the ones you've apparently been hearing as well, speak some rough, odd, garbled language." She was obviously pained and couldn't help herself from asking. "Why didn't you tell me it was happening to you too, Sienna?"

"Because I knew you got better when you moved to Colorado," her daughter explained. "And I wanted to finish high school here. I figured I could handle it for one more year. Then I could come live with you."

Veronica moved to wrap her daughter in a smothering hug. "You should have told me, anyway. I would have preferred that over you and Riley resorting to drugs." It was pretty clear to Dumuzi that Sienna's friend had gone along with the partying to show solidarity. Neither one of them fit the profile of bad-kids-smoking-and-drinking-in-the-woods. Hell, they'd been quoting Shakespeare and knew about Mesopotamia. No way were they total stoners, these were a couple of smart, motivated girls.

"You would have worried too much and probably messed up your life by coming to be with me...like now." Sienna's voice was accusing, but her look was pure love. She backed down. "So, now what?" She wrinkled up her nose.

"Now, we help you get rid of the evil voices, for good." Enlil ground a fist into his palm. The wind god was always up for a good fight.

"Evil voices?" Frank picked up on that one. "How do you know what Verrie and Si ah hearin'?" She was looking protective and pissed.

"If everyone could just settle down, I'm going to try to explain," Marduk groused, clearly exasperated at all the chatter. He barely managed to be polite while telling everyone to shut the fuck up.

The room quieted.

"Thank you," he acknowledged. "Now, I'll begin by giving you a brief history of our group." He looked around while everyone settled. "We are—thirteen of us here in the room—ancient Mesopotamian gods who were sent to hell thousands of years ago for various trumped-up charges," he dared to sneer at the king. "When it was decided we'd suffered enough in the Underworld, we were given a second chance. We were sent to earth, to Merrymount, which is now Quincy, Massachusetts, in the year 1624 to perform a task. The problem was, within four years of being here, we screwed up on our assigned duty. But instead of going back to hell, we were left to wander the Blue Hills, invisible for all time, or so we figured."

The stunned expressions on the women's faces told it all.

"Thankfully, we were wrong." He sent a blazing hot surge of energy toward his wife, Tess. Thunder rolled outside.

Yeah, yeah. Get on with it, Muze smirked. Everyone knew the two were inseparable.

"We discovered—last year in April—we could regain our bodies. It took a while to find out why, but eventually, we discovered it would happen by one of two methods…uh, actually three." Marduk looked from Dumuzi to Sienna knowingly. "We either found the person who was destined to become our eternal mate, or a semi-mortal whose bloodlines we had contributed to…"

"Meaning we'd gotten ourselves…uh, busy in Merrymount," Anshar sent waggling eyebrows in Frank's direction for her previous comment, "and planted a few seeds." This one was aimed at Dumuzi who barely held back a snarl.

"I get the pitchah," Frank smirked and turned her attention back to Marduk. "So, keep going."

"Thank you," he nodded. "We've since found out sometimes a child of a *Chosen* even a mother or a sibling can make the happy event of embodiment happen."

"So, let me get this straight. If there are three ways for you to become visible," Veronica repeated, "when you meet someone who has the power, how do you know which category they fall into?"

She was now more than studiously avoiding Dumuzi.

"With a descendant or a periphery relative, we get no strong feelings of possessiveness or…"

"Horniness?" Sienna was quick on the uptake. She turned to Dumuzi who wanted to duck under the conference table and hide. "Now I get it. You were totally uncomfortable with me because I made you visible," she pondered, "but I didn't make you want to screw…"

"Sienna," Her mother's nearly hysterical voice tried to stop where things headed.

"Let me finish, Mom." Sienna never took her eyes off the vegetation god. "I didn't cause any lust in you, and that's why you were all pouty and shit. You thought I was your eternal…whatever. But I wasn't. And," she added cannily, "as soon as my mother walked in the door, I ceased to exist." A sly grin grew on her face.

"I'm right, aren't I? It's my mother who does it for you. She's the one you want." Sienna's excitement bubbled over, and she addressed Veronica again. "That means you have no choice, Mom. You're going to be a freaking goddess like these other guy's wives. That is so wicked cool."

"Oh, no." Veronica held out her hands, rose from her chair, and backed up a few steps, shaking her head. "No way. That is not going to happen."

"Verrie, calm down." Glory moved in behind the wide-eyed woman. "We're getting ahead of ourselves," she used a calming tone. "Let Marduk tell you everything before you freak out."

Veronica looked like she wanted nothing more than to flee but let herself be led back to her chair where she sat heavily.

Dumuzi wished she'd look at him again, just once. Since their original connection in the hallway, she'd done a great job of shutting him out…and it bothered him. Somewhere deep inside his chest was the need to let her know everything would be okay…even when she looked like she wanted nothing from him. But shouldn't he be happy she was shutting him out? Isn't that what he hoped for?

"Thanks, Glory," Marduk picked up where he left off. "Fortunately, or unfortunately," Marduk gave an apologetic shrug toward Veronica, "the *Chosen* of a god—which is what we call his eventual mate—is inexplicably drawn to her fated immortal, so no matter how she thinks she feels, she will relent to a mating in the end."

Now there was no mistaking the gasp from Veronica as she dropped her head and cradled it in her hands.

"And that's good for us," Marduk held his hands up and gestured all around. "Because if all of us don't join with our *Chosen* by September fifteenth of this year, we'll be pulled back to the Underworld…forever." He let that one drop, and the room went dead silent for a full minute as he let the newcomers digest this shit piece of news.

"I have a question," Frank piped up. "Which ones a you ah gods, and which ones ah…" Her mouth fell open in a large, shocked "O."

Dumuzi turned. Perfect timing, the blue guys had just slipped into the room.

"Ignore them for a few minutes," Marduk ordered and addressed his long-time companions. "Original thirteen gods, please join me, front and center." Anshar, Dagon, Enten, Enlil, Lahar, Emesh, Dumuzi, Shamash, Ishkur, Ninurta, Kulla, and Absu came to stand next to Marduk. Once they lined up, the thunder god spoke again.

"Before you are the original thirteen," he explained. "You can only see twelve of us because Ninurta hasn't been turned visible by any mate or relatives yet."

Dumuzi looked at the woman named Frank who seemed to be counting...then counting again. "Well I'm not shooah if I'm the one ta point this out, but yoah wrong. I'm countin' thirteen." She tipped her head adorably to one side and chewed on her bottom lip. Did Ishkur just groan?

Marduk pointed to Ninurta.

"Shit. You see him?"

Dumuzi flinched. You knew when the boss's voice cracked, something was pretty weird.

"Yeah. Kinda grumpy lookin' fella with spiky dahk haiya and gray eyes?"

"Okay," Marduk thrust a hand into his own thick, dark *"haiya"* and shook himself like a big dog. "One question, then we'll leave it for now. Gods-dammit, we need to focus on one issue at a time." He ran his eyes knowingly down the line of gods. "Gentlemen?" The single word posed a question. They all knew what the thunder god asked. Was anybody else feeling a *"Chosen*-like" attraction to any of the females? The boss got a negative head-shake from each god, and Dumuzi was pretty sure, despite Ishkur's horniness, they were being honest.

"Alright, fine." Marduk was willing to put that to a temporary rest. "Do any of you other ladies see Ninurta?" When all of them nodded yes, he grimaced. "Fine. But believe me when I say, to the public in general, he's still invisible. Right Flick?"

"Yeah. I still can't see his ugly ass," the agent confirmed.

"Good. Back to business." He pointed a finger at Veronica. "You, for better or for worse, are Dumuzi's eternal mate, and that means one of a few things."

Marduk enumerated, "First, we're going to solve the mystery of the voices which we immortals have already ascertained come from some form of Underworld demon." He ignored the look of shock that passed over the women's faces.

"Secondly, we're going to attempt to tie all of your hearing-voices episodes to those of Dumuzi's…events. It is my belief he, in a really fucked up way, has been preparing himself for this moment all his life."

Now Dumuzi felt stunned. What was Marduk getting at?

"And third." There was no mistaking the edict from Marduk. This was not a request. It was a demand. "Dumuzi, you will get to know Verrie in the next few days. You can fill her in on all your glorified titles— god of vegetation, god of swamps and marshes, dominion over wild creatures, etc.— then the two of you will mate." He turned softer eyes to Veronica. "I'm sorry, but that's the way it has to be."

Chapter Nine

Verrie's head spun by the time Marduk dismissed everyone except her party of four and a handful of...gods—if that were to be believed. She had to assume they were telling the truth. They'd convinced her daughter, and Sienna was no fool. Some fairly compelling evidence must have been presented. Either that or Si had grasped on to the spoon-fed explanation for the invading voices, seeing it as a less painful route than being diagnosed as schizophrenic. Verrie didn't want to capitulate that easily, but it sure did seem like a nice get-out-of-jail-free-card, an easier route. And speaking of easy...

Verrie's eyes slid across the room. Dumuzi sure was one easy-on-the-eyes male. She tried not to fixate on the man, uh, god, but she couldn't seem to keep her eyes off him. At the moment, Dumuzi was gazing over his friend Dagon's shoulder, pointing at some dates they were writing on a timeline similar to the one Marduk was preparing in front of her. She sighed. The guy was fucking gorgeous...no...luscious. That was the right word.

Verrie had been celibate for so long, she wondered if drool oozed from the corner of her mouth. *Right.* She'd need to get that under control. Even if things happened the way Marduk said, no way she and

Dumuzi would be sexually compatible. *Hell no.* Who was she kidding? Honestly, Dwight Dick-head hadn't just left her because of the voices—that had only been the final straw. No, the predominant reason for their separation was he'd finally tired of the way their sex life played out. And there was every reason to believe she and Dumuzi would reach that same insurmountable impasse.

The man—she still couldn't use the word god even mentally without flinching—was six-foot-two or -three with massive shoulders tapering down to a broad chest, flat stomach, and...damn, she couldn't go there. She swept her gaze back up to the mop of copper-colored hair that curled around his ears and ran riot, down past the collar of his forest green t-shirt. She couldn't possibly know for sure—her one look at his face had given rise to her ridiculously feminine swoon earlier in the front hallway—but she swore his eyes were deep earth brown, flecked with verdant mossy hues. *Major sigh.*

God of what? Verrie couldn't remember Marduk's exact words.

She tried to pull her eyes away, but the angle of his body had his ass pointed directly at her. And what an ass—Verrie stood mesmerized, her palms crimped—the guy filled out his jeans in all the right places. The material hugged his lean hips and transitioned smoothly to delineate two taut globes she knew would flex delectably under her fingertips. The thought of what lay further south had her hands curling even more. If she transitioned from his ass to between his legs, his balls would be—in contrast—the softest of orbs that would tighten up into his septum when she teased...

LJ Vickery

"Mom?" An elbow to her side brought Verrie out of her stupor. "Marduk just asked you a question, like three times." She dropped her voice to a whisper, "Stop looking at his butt."

Great, she was an embarrassment to her seventeen-year-old daughter. What did that say for the state of her sanity? And Sienna was right. She should have finished lusting after nice asses years ago. Shit, she *had* finished with all that. What was it Marduk had said about an undeniable attraction? Could that be the reason her libido ran riot?

"Not to worry, Sienna." Marduk's eyes had clearly followed Verrie's to Dumuzi. "Your mother has a lot on her mind."

Was that a smirk the big guy was trying to hide? Verrie gathered her best, stern guidance counselor demeanor and wrapped it around herself like a shield, determined to ignore the man who would be her...mate? Holy hell. What had Sienna gotten them into?

"Yes, Mr. Marduk. What was the question again?" Verrie became all business.

"You can drop the Mr., Verrie, it's just Marduk." He turned back to the drawing in front of him that showed a timeline from the sixteen hundreds to present day. "I'd like to work backward and try to get a good idea of when you, Sienna, and your mother may have been episodic. Perhaps you even remember a grandmother?" Marduk looked up, expectantly, but her negative shake dashed those hopes. She'd never known her grandmother...or anything about her. Aunt Frank shuffled her feet as Verrie studied the paper.

94

It already had her birth date and Sienna's and her mother's year of death. Now, if she could focus, Marduk wanted the time periods when the voices had invaded and when they'd gone dormant. It seemed important to him, and if it helped Sienna, Verrie would do her best to remember.

"Well, certainly I heard them today upon landing. But I've been living in Colorado for the past nine years and haven't heard a peep since I moved there." She looked up at her daughter. "When did the voices start for you, honey?"

"It was during the third week of school, last fall. I wrote it down. September nineteenth." Verrie saw Sienna's body tremble and moved to hug her around the waist. "I was in gym class, of all places, and the voices just came out of nowhere." She gave a wry smile. "I must have zombied out because I got a volleyball to the head, and everyone said I went down like a sack of rocks." Sienna looked knowingly at her mother. "I remembered what you had gone through, so I didn't say anything about the invasion in my head to anybody but Riles."

"Yeah, and it freaked me out," Riley conjectured, "because we'd always talked about it with Gram. She kinda knew from family history, it was only a matter of time until it got to Si."

"Why didn't you girls tell anybody?" Frank's voice was troubled. "Whydya try to deal with it on yeh own?"

"Well, like I said before, I wanted to finish high school here with my friends. I figured if I could keep it a secret, Dad wouldn't send me to a mental hospital, and eventually, I'd join Mom after graduation." Sienna shrugged as if her plan made a lot of sense.

"So we started doing a few things…"

"Like smokin' pot?" Frank cut in.

"Well, yeah, Gram. Sienna found it cut the voices down to a low growl…and I knew you'd want me to help her out, so we did it together." Riley's defiant stance dared anyone to argue.

"And your father?" Verrie asked.

Sienna dropped her head.

"He found my stash one night, then a pipe after he'd told me to smarten up. I guess getting thrown in jail was the last straw for him. Who knew he wouldn't come bail me out?" she pouted.

Verrie would have known.

"It seems like *that* all worked out for the best," Marduk's insightful comment brought them back to present. "Now we can work to find out when and how the voices come and how we can stop them." He paused. "Give me a moment, will you?" The silence didn't last long before the god explained.

"I've got Lahar and Shamash on genealogy duty. They've found some interesting stuff and will join us as soon as they're finished. Apparently, someone did a good job tracing your family history, so they've been able to find quite a bit."

"Ah, shit, I could'a told ya that," Frank stated. "I was just waitin' ta see how much we could trust ya, but since yeh at tha computah, yeh gonna find out anyway." She squared her petite shoulders. "Verrie's mom and I spent a long time diggin' through old stuff in my attic and lookin' in the Boston Library ahchives researchin' ah family lines. We thought it was cool that ah muthahs and grandmuthahs wuh friends, and that we'd been told it had been that way foh-evah." She looked toward

Verrie now. "I'm sorry I nevah told ya about yeh grandmuthah, but I didn't want ya to think you wa cursed to become crazy. She heard the voices too. It was easiah not ta let on about that…oah that I knew about her."

"So you ended up putting it up on one of those genealogical sites because…?" Marduk left the question hanging.

"Cuz if anything happened to me, I wanted Verrie or Si or whoevah came aftah them to be able to trace ah connection…without all tha crazy-ass stuff gettin' in the way."

Verrie thought she might want to sit down. "So, Aunt Frank, you knew my grandmother?"

"I knew yeh grandmuthah and yeh great-grandmuthah. They both had tha…demons, too." She narrowed her eyes at Marduk, still clearly not willing to trust him one hundred percent. "They were just a lot stronga than yeh mum, God rest her soul."

"So, to get back to this," Marduk reminded them. He'd filled in the date for the nineteenth of September, and with the ladies help, got at least four other episodes of Sienna's on the timeline. They subsequently went back nine years to map some of Verrie's.

She recalled exactly when she'd heard them first and remembered a few that had fallen on significant dates—a homecoming football game, the day of her first ultrasound while carrying Sienna, and one on her ex's birthday which ended up as a huge fight that led to their acrimonious divorce.

Frank was even more help, pinpointing a few of Verrie's mom's worst moments. The woman's first episode had occurred on Halloween day when she was eighteen, and there had been a really bad one the day before her marriage to Verrie's father. Marduk nodded his head, satisfied.

"That should do it." He looked over at Dumuzi with Dagon. "They're still working on theirs, so let's see what Lahar and Shamash have come up with, shall we?"

This time he let Verrie hear him.

Lahar, Sham, we're ready for you to show us what you've got.

The one named Shamash popped in out of thin air, and the one named Lahar subsequently walked through the door. At Verrie's raised eyebrows at the two different modes of entry, Marduk gave her the reason.

"Shamash has gone through the amulet ceremony with his *Chosen,* so he can mist in and out of places at will. Lahar has yet to meet his significant other, so he is tied to his body within one hundred yards of his descendants—Glory, Douglas, and Quinn—and completely invisible if they're not around. Hence, Sham materialized, and Lahar had to use his own two feet."

"Sucks to be you, man." Shamash clapped Lahar on the back. The big golden cat god had only gained total control of his body a few weeks back, so his teasing was mild and from the heart.

"No problem. You're just jealous I'm so good looking, I don't need to hide with invisibility like you." He made a fake grimace at the golden-curled god, but Verrie knew it was all for show. She looked the two gods up and down. They were, without a doubt, both very good looking. One might even say "smoking."

Not.

What? The word sprung out of nowhere....well, not nowhere. She turned narrowed eyes to the red-head still bending over the table. A slight tinge of crimson stained his cheeks. Oh yeah? He'd sent her that terse, one-word command? Was he reading her mind now?

Well, read this, buddy.

Verrie screwed up her face and thought back to the ass and ball fantasy she'd had before. She had nothing to lose. If she and hunky green-man were destined to be mates, she wanted...no, *needed* to see if he'd be any fun in the sack. God or not, it would suck to go from no sex to boring sex again.

Dumuzi's mild redness became a hot glow. *Hah.* The huge god liked it. *Score.* Verrie wanted to do a high five with someone.

Score? Really Mom? It was Sienna's voice that came back to her, not the deep growly one she'd expected. *Do you have any idea you've just transmitted your very inappropriate picture to everyone who can do this mind-thingy?*

Oh shit. It was Verrie's turn to color up. She'd only wanted to poke Dumuzi a little, but instead ended up embarrassing the crap out of herself...and him too if his dropped head was any indication.

Apparently, the Blue Hills population didn't find any of it inappropriate.

Lucky man, Muze, the periphery voices began.

Hopefully, veggie-man, you can grow some big ones to keep her happy.

Full hands are happy hands.

I love me some ass time.

The last one was Lenore.

Verrie wanted to disappear into the floor.

"Listen…I'm sorry. Uh," *Listen, I'm sorry,* she said it both ways, waiting to get a reaction from the only one who really mattered.

Dumuzi didn't turn around, but *my Lord.* Did he actually just wiggle his tush at her?

First things first. His strong but amused voice made her squirm in more ways than one. *I'm teaching you how to talk selectively which is what I'm doing right now. Until then, no more outbursts. Do you feel me?*

His words threw her provocative pictures right back into her head…in full color.

Verrie gasped as she swallowed which sent her into a paroxysm of coughing. Her eyes watered. But oh, the big devil. Verrie's toes wiggled in delight. He was someone who could take shit and dish it back.

Her lifelong crap-o-meter just nudged a little toward the positive direction.

Chapter Ten

"Listen, why don't you two kids go play?" Marduk looked from Verrie to Dumuzi, having picked up on their interaction. "We have enough to go on we can finish up here. I'll call another meeting when we've analyzed all our data."

"What if…" Dumuzi didn't want to even speak the possibility out loud.

Marduk knew what he asked, and so did the other immortals in the room. But the thunder god played it as if it was only Verrie they had to worry about. "We have Sienna with us. She'll let us know if the voices start up."

Sienna nodded vigorously.

"And I'm assuming Archie will give you advanced warning," he finished.

"What?" Verrie shook her head. "How can your dog possibly know when my voices are about to appear?" She looked suitably confused, and Dumuzi figured it was time he gave her an answer that would gently ease her into his fucked-up-ed-ness. He prevaricated, but only a little.

"I have something that happens to me, sort of like you, that Archie senses coming on. We think it may be related to your episodes. It's the reason we're making these charts. We want to see if my…thing…happens at the same time as yours." He turned to look fully at Veronica for the first time since the hallway.

His mouth slammed shut. Damn it all to hell, he'd been right—she was fucking spectacular. Not only that, but at his partial revelation he might share her curse, empathy began to shine from her very expressive butterfly-blue eyes, digging a hole right down into his parched heart.

He squared his shoulders. He needed to get a grip, train his reaction in a different direction, no letting his heart get involved. He had nothing to offer Veronica—a mated life with him would resemble a fucking horror flick. How fair would that be? Because unlike all of his god buddies, his transformations had nothing to do with being agitated. If that were the case, he'd be in the clear and zip-a-dee-doo-dah, incident free, since he'd been self-medicating one way or another from childhood. But for him, his nightmare came without provocation, and most likely would for the rest of his eternal life. How could he pin that on Veronica, too?

"You don't have to feel sorry for me," Dumuzi dropped his eyes and groused. *Shit.* If he kept looking at her, all bets were off on what he'd want to do. They needed to keep things between them strictly business. He shouldn't for a minute bring back to mind the little fantasy scene where she'd been fondling his nads…oh yeah, he did. *Shit.* Dumuzi stifled a groan.

"I've been fucked up a lot longer than you have." He saw her grimace at his choice of words, but there they were, reality on the table. "So don't lament my life. I've had time to get used to it." Or not, Dumuzi thought.

She walked over and reached for his hand, ignoring his edict while clearly attempting to diffuse the tense moment. "Why don't you show me around?"

That fucking voice came out of her again as smooth as a leaf of Lambs Ear. He was suddenly very scared. The way she made him feel, he might be able to deny her nothing. He fumbled for words.

"Sure," he said, letting her tug him out of the room and away from everyone's watchful gaze. "Do you want to start at the top or at the bottom?" he questioned. Seeing Verrie suddenly bite her full lower lip and stifle a giggle, he mentally kicked himself. *Geeze.* Were they going straight to double entendres?

"That's not what I meant," he sputtered. Holy crap. He was used to playing the innuendo game with his buddies, but he'd never played it with a woman before…if you could discount Candy and Lenore, who were completely raunchy all the time and practiced their craft arbitrarily.

"Why don't we start at the top and work our way down?" she finally answered, letting him off the hook…and great, he felt the color creep up his cheeks again. Now he was thinking of alternate meanings.

"Listen," She turned to Dumuzi and stopped him with a hand to his chest. "I have a better idea. What's through that door?" Veronica pointed to the vast coat closet that had rarely been used before gods had become visible and taken mates.

"It's just a closet. A big closet," he answered, puzzled. "Why?"

"Come with me." Veronica jerked on the hand she still held, leading him to the portal.

Was she cold? Did she want a jacket?

She pulled open the door, giving a quick look behind them to make sure no one watched, and scooted inside, yanking him in behind her.

"Veronica? What are we doing?" Dumuzi watched her close the door behind them, and the small room plunged into darkness. She moved toward him with sure steps. He could see in the dark, but could she? Perhaps. Some of the *Chosen* could before they had been mated.

"Getting something out of the way," she told him, her voice no-nonsense as she backed him into a corner. "I'm not leaving until you've thoroughly been kissed, and I know for sure this whole thing is going to work out."

She couldn't have shocked Dumuzi more if she'd told him all plant life was purple. Until *he'd* been thoroughly kissed? The stunned god grabbed both of her wrists as she moved them toward his chest.

"I repeat, what are you doing, Veronica? Taking matters into your own hands?" It made sense she'd want some control over their future together. He just hadn't figured she'd jump on it so fast.

A seductive smile came to her plump little mouth. "Maybe that and seeing how well matched we are," she murmured with a sigh, pressing her body forward despite her restrained arms.

Fuck it. It had been far too long. Dumuzi let go of her hands and scooped up under her ass, lifting her higher against him. She found and tweaked both of his nipples on the way up, causing his grip to tighten and his head to seize. *Wow.* He'd never had his nipples pinched before. It made him nearly limbless and he

104

paused, waiting breathlessly to see what else Veronica might do.

She didn't take long to show him.

His delicate flower skimmed his mouth lightly, moving soundlessly from right to left, and when her butterfly lips finally settled, it was all about soft and seductive. He made a noise low in his throat, and she must have liked it because she gave him the same delicate brush two, three more times before he opened his mouth under her explorations and allowed her tongue to taste him. He tasted back. *Divine,* like ripe, forbidden fruit.

With a groan and one thrust, he went deep.

Things went from calm to frenzied in seconds.

She sucked his tongue into her mouth, climbing him higher and clinging to him like a vine. Her hands and feet—oddly devoid of shoes now—were everywhere at once, wrapped around him. He barely had to hold her up, so strongly had she entwined with his body. And her hot core—my gods, her hot core even through their jeans—slammed into the thickness of his cock, giving it the sustenance it needed to grow thicker and longer. Dumuzi could barely breathe.

This is what it felt like to be with a *Chosen.* He got it now.

Dumuzi was ready to strip her naked right now and get the mating underway. But in the fucking hall closet? Not the most romantic place to get to know your eternal partner. He forced his brain to re-engage. What did it mean that Veronica had practically attacked him? And which did he want first, sex or answers? His woman made room between them and stroked his turgid pistil through his pants.

Okay. Decision made. Sex first.

He reached for her breast, but Veronica jumped down and backed up.

Or not.

He bit his tongue in frustration. Had she changed her mind?

"I need to see you...naked," she breathed out, nestled among the hanging jackets.

Shit. She *was* able to see in the dark...and *hell, yeah.* There was no god alive who was ashamed of his body, and Dumuzi was no exception. Confidently well-built and overly endowed, Veronica would surely love what he had to offer. His hands went to his belt buckle.

"Wait." That silky voice again.

Dumuzi licked his lips.

"Let me," she implored.

He moved his fingers away, more than willing, and hers got busy. He wanted badly to touch her back, but he was letting her call the shots. To keep himself from temptation, he linked his digits behind his head.

Veronica looked up, and her eyes blazed. "Oh, yeah, baby. I love that position." Could her tone get any smokier?

Dumuzi felt his jeans hit the floor, the boxers underneath all that covered him. His root rubbed against their confines, struggling to seek air.

"Tell me you want them off," Veronica crooned. "Beg me to let your cock loose."

Dumuzi didn't know what game they played, but he liked it. "Strip off my shorts, Veronica."

She purred out loud before slowly, painfully, and in long, drawn-out increments, obliging. She lowered the rear of the material first, exposing the tops of his butt cheeks, running her fingertips back and forth across the expanse of his skin, teasing the twin dimples he knew lay at the top of his cheeks. Another small tug to the seat and the still air in the closet warmed his backside, helped by her palms which enveloped the top few inches now revealed.

Dumuzi impatiently moved to help, but Veronica stepped back and dropped her hands. He gave her a questioning look.

"Do you want me to continue?" Her small tongue poked out and licked across the swollen pinkness of her bottom lip.

"I'd like nothing better." Was that his voice? All dark, low, and...engaged? What was she doing to him? His normally inattentive self had fled the closet along with his good sense.

"Then stay still and keep your hands up," she ordered.

"Yes ma'am." And why not? This whole scene was beyond hot.

She moved closer, and reaching around, tugged the back of Dumuzi's boxers to sit beneath the rim of his ass. This time when her hands found his flanks, she moved her palms inward and dipped deliberately between his globes, causing him to clench.

Uh, maybe not. Nobody had ever touched him there, and he wasn't sure how he felt about it.

"Loosen up, immortal," she hissed against his chest, making sure not to rub against the part of him that wanted all the attention.

Dumuzi bit the inside of his cheek. She obviously wouldn't get to the good stuff until he complied with her wishes. The god forced himself to relax.

Veronica moved a finger down through his cleft but thankfully, didn't delve any deeper. He let out a pent-up breath.

"More fun for another time," she taunted seductively, giving his rear-bud a tap.

Damn. He tensed right up again. He'd see about that.

"Now, what about this lovely, hard cock of yours?" She stepped away when what he wanted was more forward motion. "It's straining for release."

Veronica was right about that. And not just the release she was talking about. His balls, if they got any tighter, were going to punch a hole up into his abdomen before sending ejaculate to the closet ceiling.

"Ahh." One finger breached the elastic top of his boxers and brushed whisperingly over his cock.

He refrained from crying out as she spread the teardrop of moisture around the turgid tip but vocalized when she removed the inquisitive digit. "Shit. More, Veronica," he growled.

"Quiet now, immortal. We wouldn't want anyone to hear us, would we?" She took the questing finger, stuck it between her lush lips, and sucked. "Mmm. You taste delicious. Earthy."

Dumuzi breathed deeply through his nose. Veronica was something else…and speaking of earthy. He could smell the dampness that oozed from between her legs, swamping her pussy. He pictured her glistening nether lips, and his prick grew inexplicably larger. There was nothing he'd like more than to lap up all that moisture. He sent her a picture of his head nestled between her legs and felt her deep, satisfied sigh.

"We'll get there. Don't worry. Right now, I'd like to see all you have to offer." She stopped her slow torturous method of clothing removal, and in one smooth move, tugged his boxers down to his knees. When she finished, his cock stood directly in front of her face.

"Oh my," she whispered. "I'm not sure if I can…"

Dumuzi wheezed out when instead of continuing, she ran her tongue up the length of his pulsing flesh before engulfing him in one swallow. *Damn*. It was the most intense suction he'd ever felt, so good, his spine tingled with a release imminent.

He moaned as she slid her lips up, and his prick popped free.

She chuckled, low in her throat. "What would you do if I sucked you like that again?"

He wasn't even close to embarrassed when he answered. "I'd come in about three seconds."

"Well, we can't have that." And in another move he hadn't expected, she wrapped her hot little hand around him instead of her mouth and held firmly. "Listen carefully." She tightened her grip. "You don't have my permission to come yet."

What the…what? Did Veronica just say what he thought she said? Did she have any idea who she was talking to...and, hell, what she was doing to him? By telling him not to come, she'd just driven him close to the edge. She was playing in dangerous territory, and he growled. Time to change things up.

He grabbed her hand so both of them held his cock. "No more games, Veronica." He couldn't help but move their entwined fingers up and down his considerable length, shuddering at the pressure.

"You're letting go of my cock, and as soon as you do, your pants are coming down. You'll face the wall, and bend over. Then I'll fuck you so hard you'll…"

Hey? Where are you two? Marduk's voice sliced through the thick tension like an edging tool. *It's time to get back to business. I'll give you two more minutes.*

"You heard the man." Veronica's eyes sparkled up at him with a potent mixture of unrequited lust and mischief. She removed her hand and quickly lifted his boxers, tucking him back in with bitter-sweet efficiency. "Two minutes won't finish this, and," she lowered her voice and mocked Marduk's tone, "we're wanted in the ready room."

Dumuzi growled again. "And here I thought this was the ready room." Dumuzi was going to kill Marduk. Dead.

When Veronica shrugged and turned to go, he reached out and grabbed her arm, voicing what he'd wanted to ask before being distracted by sex.

"What's this all about?" He floated the question between them. "Is this some *Chosen* thing, a compulsion you had to act on it?" He pulled his pants up and fastened his belt buckle, seeking out Veronica's beautiful eyes. She warred with herself. He could tell the minute her mind latched onto what she'd say. He was pretty sure it would be the truth…but not the whole truth.

"It was a test." She bent and put her shoes back on, not meeting his eyes again.

"And?" He raised an eyebrow.

"And you'll be happy to know you passed." She turned and opened the door, losing the opportunity for more questions.

Dumuzi wasn't upset. *Hell no,* he was elated. Veronica had set the sexual bar high with their closet interlude. He'd damn well make sure to exceed her expectations during their next encounter…and that encounter couldn't come soon enough.

Chapter Eleven

"Sorry Muze, if I…uh…interrupted anything." Marduk kept his chin down when he said it—that was good. If Dumuzi saw so much as a smirk on the thunder god's face, he'd happily engage in knocking it off. *Damn.* All his unreleased, backed-up testosterone had every cell in his structure full to bursting, and he was fucking uncomfortable.

Not only that, Dumuzi was aware—as everyone trooped into the large office once again—the smell of his and Veronica's sexual arousal would permeate the air. Every god and goddess in attendance would know what they'd—almost—been up to. It burned his ass.

"Get comfortable," Marduk began. "We may be here for a while. We have a lot of stuff to cover, but top on the agenda are the correlations we've made between Muze and Verrie's family. Here's what we already know. Dumuzi's episodes, sporadically spaced throughout the years, come in clusters and correspond to the few days around the full moon."

Dumuzi wondered where Marduk was taking this.

"Without leading the witnesses," he glanced to the four human women sitting together, "we found Verrie and Sienna's voices have all come near the full moon as well."

"I never realized…" Veronica's eyes went wide. "I guess I was always so consumed with pain, I never thought about timing."

"Sienna," the thunder god turned. "The night the police picked you up in the Blue Hills, you had an incident with the voices just previous, did you not?"

"Yeah, I did." Sienna looked thoughtful.

"Dumuzi had an episode at the very same time," Marduk stated, but before they could ask what that episode might be, he kept on. "As a matter of fact, we've been able to definitively match up nearly a dozen concurrent events without a doubt having paired the exact time periods for the clusters. For instance…" he tapped the button to activate the computer white-board on the wall. "…the latest cluster began last September which had been puzzling to us because, before that, Muze hadn't had a relapse in…" he pointed his indicator backward on the timeline. "…nine years."

There was a gasp from Veronica. "No." She put a fluttering hand to her throat. "Th…that's when I left Boston for Colorado."

She looked shaken. The self-assured woman who attacked Dumuzi in the closet had disappeared. He couldn't help himself. The vegetation god rose from his seat and walked purposely to stand behind Veronica, putting a comforting hand on each of her shoulders, leaned down, and whispered.

"It's okay. We'll figure it out. That's what we're here for." He gave her a quick squeeze and was gratified when one shaking hand came up to cover his own. Something he couldn't name swelled in Dumuzi's chest. *Mine.* The word taunted him.

Marduk continued, "That band of activity lasted for twelve years, having started in 1993, and again matches up with the duration of Verrie's voice invasions." He flipped to another chart.

"Oddly, one would think Muze's problems should have started with Verrie's because she's his *Chosen*, but we know his phases have occurred off and on since he was very young."

Which was a fucking long time ago.

"So with Frank's help," Marduk plodded on, "we've matched his problems with not only Verrie's but her mother's and grandmother's."

This just got hella disturbing. Dumuzi's head started to pound which was damned strange because gods didn't get headaches. Marduk was still talking? There was more?

"Thanks again to Frank and to the computer skills of Lahar and Sham, we have a very complete genealogy, going back to...not Merrymount in 1624 as you might have imagined, but to Mesopotamia in that same year." This raised a lot of god's heads. Here was something new. All the *Chosen* so far had god related bloodlines that had begun in Merrymount. Could it be that Verrie's god connection had emanated from a much earlier time?

"In Sumer to be exact," Marduk inclined his head to the humans, "which is what you call Iraq." He paused to take note of the written chart again. "We have a continuation of the family line upon leaving Sumer. In England, commencing in 1647 which for those of you who are history buffs will recall is the heyday of the HEIC—the Honorable East India Company—when the exodus from the area between the rivers was rife.

Verrie, your family made the trek from Sumer to England and settled in London for a couple of centuries before finally migrating to Boston in 1820."

Wow, it was a lot to take in, but as Marduk spoke, Dumuzi had been thinking dates. "So, even though you only traced her family lines to 1624, her ancestors were most likely in Mesopotamia from the time I was young until I got, uh, booted out in 17 AD," he pondered.

"That's what we figure," Marduk agreed. "And you had your episodes from 239 BC until you…left, so that would tend to confirm it."

Dumuzi had, that year, joined the gods in hell, but he wasn't going to mention that in front of Verrie.

"And I didn't have any more occurrences until well after Merrymount. Until after I was invisible," Dumuzi swallowed hard, "beginning in 1820."

"At the exact time when Verrie's ancestors moved from England to Boston." Marduk sat back and crossed his arms over his chest.

"And I've had them ever since…"

"Yes, in time periods that correspond directly to the lives of the American-born women on our timeline, beginning with their late adolescence and continuing until their deaths." Marduk looked satisfied everyone was up to speed with what he knew.

"So what the fuck?" Anshar spoke up, looking thoroughly confused.

Dorian, their resident warlock took the first stab at putting things together.

"It seems these demons have been following Verrie's family for centuries. But for what reason?" he pondered. "Perhaps they've been waiting for something…like the two of you to come together?"

115

Dorian looked from Veronica to Dumuzi, pinning the god with a dark stare. "It seems your unconscious self has been aware when one of these family members lives near, and has reacted in a…" he tapped his upper lip, "…protective fashion?"

"I agree," interjected Marduk. "But why?"

Dagon put forth another question. "And what about the demons' words?" the serpent god pondered. "Uggla dwall. What could they possibly mean by saying 'Goddess, mine'?"

This was news to Dumuzi who bristled. Nobody had told him they knew what the demons had been saying. How dare the vile creatures call Verrie or even Sienna theirs? His fingers tightened unconsciously, and he felt Veronica shiver under his touch. Dumuzi couldn't help it. He wanted to rant. The demons had no right. He bit back his denial with difficulty. Now was not the time. He'd only impede the stream of consciousness that was currently happening among the fine minds in the room.

It was Enlil's turn to speculate. "Maybe it would be smarter if we took Muze out of the equation for a moment. Wouldn't we be better served to know who began the family bloodlines back in ancient times?"

There was agreement from his wife. "And, of course, what Verrie's family has to do with Frank's?" Candy supplied. "Doesn't anyone else think it odd, putting their genealogies side by side, they've been together at least since immediately prior to their immigration to England?" The records only reached back one generation before London. It would be difficult to find anything older unless the family had lived in a prominent city like Babylon. Dumuzi was suddenly sure Marduk would put some of the guys on that possibility.

"And then there's the fact Riley can hear us speak," Enten's voice chilled the air, "and even though Frank can't hear us, she can see invisible Ninurta. I think that also deserves looking into."

"Okay, so here's the plan." Marduk pointed to Dr. Dani-Lee. "You take the ladies up to the infirmary for some blood tests and DNA swabs. Verrie, after you're through since we're still in the full moon window, I want you to try a controlled reaching out to those demon voices."

Dumuzi growled. "Hell no." He felt a shimmer of unease roll down his spine. *Shit.* Was he going to lose it right here, right now? He looked down at Archie who'd come to his feet but wasn't tugging on him in the way that preceded an event.

"We'll be with her at all times, Muze. We'll tap into the voices through her and see what we can find out. It's the only way to get to them, and you know it."

Dumuzi felt the pain ramp up in his head again, and he looked down to see his *Chosen* rubbing at her temples. He wanted to laugh at his sudden understanding. The headache he was feeling was hers. That was fucked up. They were already sharing feelings before the amulet ceremony? But he had to address an even bigger potential headache.

"What about me?" Dumuzi and everyone else knew when Verrie had her head invaded, he would become an instant danger.

"Sorry, buddy, but you'll be rooming in the cell next to Matthew's until we're through."

That's just what he thought Marduk would say. And it didn't make him happy. Being separated from his *Chosen* with someone else responsible for her well-being made every one of his hackles rise. "Fine. I get it. But make it quick, okay?" he snapped. "I don't like any of this."

"Can I ask a question?" Veronica's hand shot up, quaking though it was.

"Of course, Verrie. And you don't have to raise your hand," Marduk smiled kindly. Veronica twisted in her seat to look at Dumuzi.

"What happens to you when the voices talk to me?" Her eyes were big, and her lips trembled. Dumuzi figured he knew what she was thinking. She'd just made out with him in the coat closet and wondered if she'd been kissing some kind of freak. Well...yeah. He didn't know what to say. Luckily, Shamash came to his rescue.

"Let's leave Muze out of it for now because he's not in control of his 'change' the way we are. But we'll give you a quick demonstration of the various creatures we become. Gentlemen?" The blond god stood up and started taking off his clothes.

"What are you doing?" Verrie squeaked. "Sienna, Riley. Turn around. Close your eyes."

"Screw that, Ms. F," Riley trilled. "If these guys are going to take off their clothes, I'm watching." She turned, arching her brows, pleading her case. "When will I ever, in my entire life, get to see guys like these in the buff again? I'll probably end up married to some hundred-pound weakling geek...so, please?" Her eyes and words beseeched.

Dumuzi could see Frank wavering.

Riley pressed her point, "Pretty please, Gram? It's not like we don't have HBO. Besides, if we leave, shouldn't you have to go too?"

The last one did it. "Awright." She turned her attention to the hands-at-buttons-and-zippers gods. "But asses only guys. I don't want these girls seein' any dangly bits. Ya got me? Jewels ta the wall."

"Yes, ma'am," Shamash grinned, and Dumuzi set himself to watch the female faces…all the female faces while the men faced away. Even the goddesses were unconsciously licking lips. Married to serious booty or not, they weren't impervious to some impressive, additional immortal flank. Anshar, Dagon, Enlil, Enten, Lahar, and Shamash all turned their backs and stripped down.

"Anybuddy gut any dollah bills?" Aunt Frank breathed out, causing a room-wide chuckle that broke the tension. Her pretty pale skin had gone a lovely shade of pink. "Nothin' like this at Centahfolds." Dumuzi assumed that was some kind of male strip club and bit back a few of the choicer things *he* wanted to throw at his naked buddies. Because, *shit*, they were trying to do him a favor.

"Ladies." Sham looked back over his shoulder. "Please don't be afraid. The six of us are going to morph into creatures that, for some reason," he gave a low growl over his shoulder toward his wife, Quinn, "completely 'do it' for our mates."

The transformations began, and Dumuzi saw eyes darting in all directions. The women didn't know who to look at first. Large dorsal fins and scales appeared from the backs of Dagon and Anshar. Horns sprouted from the heads of Enlil and Lahar, and fur emerged from the pores of Shamash and Enten, one golden, the other white. As their human skins disappeared, each one slowly turned to give the audience a good look at their changed bodies. Snouts replaced noses, and long, sharp fangs were de rigueur. Snarls, brays, and hisses cut through the room.

"Holy shit." Frank's whispered comment just about summed it up.

Dumuzi quirked one side of his mouth. This was the god-squad who had taken him down earlier in the woods. What a fucking bunch of freaks, he grinned. But who was he to talk? He was the freakiest of them all. He looked at Veronica's face to gauge her reaction.

At first, he saw shock, that was certain, but to give Verrie her due, the shock was quickly replaced with curiosity. After curiosity—when the menagerie began to make noise—humor became the predominant reaction, and Dumuzi relaxed his gut.

"Mom? Can we have one, please?" Sienna's teasing voice sounded above the cacophony. "This is better than Twilight," she grinned. "Who needs vampires when you can have gods?"

The goddess-ladies in the room whooped and did high-fives—it was clear they agreed with Sienna.

"And since we wouldn't want to waste a good morphing…" Candy strolled up to her husband Enlil—currently the bull—and reached up to stroke a horn. "What do you say, stud-man?"

He snorted through his bovine nostrils and scooped Candy up as if she weighed nothing.

"See you guys later," she smirked and gave a pinkie wave back as he carried her out the door. The room quickly cleared of all creatures, except Lahar's ram, in under thirty seconds.

"Don't tell me they're all going to…?" Sienna's voice trailed off. "Oh my god, Mom. Can't you just wait to find out what your god turns into?" She looked at Dumuzi and back at her mother like she'd just discovered ice-cream.

"Sienna," her mother warned. "Don't even go there. I can wait." Veronica gave Dumuzi a negative shake of her head. He got it. She didn't want to know what he turned into while there was an audience around to witness her reaction. He was glad. The vegetation god wasn't ready to let his *Chosen* know there could be no happy endings with his alter-ego.

Although…his brow creased…he couldn't be sure of that. All the guys had been certain they'd harm their *Chosen* while transformed, and that had proven to be far from the reality if the noises echoing throughout the house at the moment were any indication. Could it possibly be the same for him? For them? *Shit.* One thing was certain. He wasn't going to try it out without lots of extra security on tap.

Marduk looked amused at the going's on but focused on Lahar who began to suck the curled horns back into his head. The ram-man remembered to turn back to face the wall just in time.

"That is so cool." Riley came out of her stupor. Before anyone could react, she was hurrying around the table, making her way toward Lahar. "Can I feel one of your horns?"

As she reached, a distressed growl emanated from the being who was half god/half beast.

"Don't touch," Marduk yelled like thunder.

Riley stopped dead in her tracks. At the look of terror on her face, the god tried to soften his tone "Sorry, but uh, back off, okay?" He looked sheepishly at Frank while Riley retreated. "Could you do me a favor and explain erogenous zones to the young ladies?"

"Oh, puh-leeze," Sienna stepped in and rolled her eyes. "Give us a break." She turned to her friend. "Riles, don't touch the man's stickie-outie parts, or you might get more than you bargained for."

There was a lot of coughing in the room, and some decidedly feminine snickering while Lahar came fully back to god form.

Marduk's face looked a little flushed, but to give him props, he didn't wait for equilibrium to return before getting on with business. "Uh, Lahar? As soon as you're able, I want you and Sham to make the trip to Iraq. See if you can find any census or birth records for Verrie and Frank's family in any of the museums. Make it quick and make it clandestine." Marduk didn't have to say "invisible." It was implied. The boss reached out in his head to the golden leopard who was in his room with his wife.

Shamash? As soon as you're through, see me. I have a road trip for you and Lahar.

A loud, imperative snarl shook the compound.

Yeah, yeah. We get it.

Chapter Twelve

Verrie didn't know what she was thinking. As Dr. Dani led them up to her infirmary, so many things were going round and round in her brain. Foremost, of course, was Dumuzi. Because…*damn.* Hormones buzzed that had been dormant for at least a decade. She'd attacked him in the closet. A closet, in retrospect, that was not normal. Verrie hadn't had a chance to ask Muze—they'd been kinda busy—but a few things around them had been sort of…ghostly? Shining? Odd, but of course not the oddest thing she'd encountered since entering the god's household, so she dismissed it for the time being.

The apparitions, or whatever they were, certainly hadn't stopped her crazed need for Dumuzi. Now, there's something she *couldn't* stop thinking about. She'd boldly let out her natural, sexual assertiveness. And, *score*, instead of being repulsed by her hyperactive libido, the god had seemed to enjoy it. Verrie could still feel the dampness between her legs from the encounter, and although her head spun with periphery questions—about ancestry, gods turning into creatures, and the fucked-up voices in her head—her predominant thought was, *When can I get back to the delectable Dumuzi*? Cripes. Was she sick or what? Sex should not be the first thing on her mind.

Her illness…her long-term illness, and that of her daughter was possibly on the verge of being solved, and all she could think of was the hot male and how hard he'd been under her questing tongue. Dammit. She should have given in to temptation and sucked him to orgasm. She might have climaxed from that alone without ever being touched. It would at least have scratched the desperate itch that now consumed her. As for coming from sucking him? That would have been a first. Verrie licked her lips.

"I know what yoah thinkin'," Frank whispered and elbowed her in the ribs. "It shows all ovah ya wicked face." She bit her lip to stop grinning. "Just wheah were the two of ya that ya both came back with crooked clothes and messed up haiah?"

"The hall closet," Verrie whispered back, still reliving the entire experience. "And Aunt Frank…I attacked him." She could hear the near-hysteria in her voice.

"And that's bad becuz….?" Her aunt/mentor's eyes held even more humor which calmed her a little. Frank continued. "Just ta let ya know, yoah not alone in your lustful thoughts. Theah's one-a-them gods I coulda taken to a closet if he'd given me the time-a-day. Damned thing was, he didn't glance at me once. I guess I'm too old faw him even though he looked about my age. I suppose he's picky. When yoah a god, maybe ya can get young things even if you've aged outta the mahket."

Verrie was nearly knocked off her pins. "Don't be ridiculous, Frankie." They now scurried to keep up with Dani and the two girls moving away from the stairs and disappearing fast down a hallway. "You're stunning, and any of these immortals would be more than lucky to have you."

"Well, maybe it isn't me. Maybe they ahn't foolin' around due to theah deadline to find these *Chosen.* Mistah grayin' at the temples can't be wastin' time screwin' off with just anybuddy if it means headin' back to hell." She'd regained her quick smile, but Verrie could tell Frank was still bothered—or more accurately, conflicted. She almost sounded pissed the god hadn't looked at her. That was unusual. Frank wasn't celibate, by any means, but Verrie had never known her to be *interested*-interested in any guy. She'd always been a bang-em and leave-em kind of girl as far as Veronica knew. Hell, she'd never, ever, even talked about her daughter's father—Verrie was aware Frank never married and assumed the pregnancy had been a slip-up on her aunt's part.

Frank clammed up, so Verrie didn't pursue it any further, but she filed it away for conversation at a later date. She wasn't about to let her aunt off the hook.

"Come in, ladies. Come in." Dani hit the light switch and illuminated a room that would have made any high-tech clinician envious. As far as Verrie could tell, it was equipped with every machine and every amenity she'd ever seen during her long history of doctor office visits. She forced down a shiver of apprehension. Medical intervention had never been a plus for her, but she had to remember this was different. Instead of thinking she was crazy, these people…uh, immortals…were trying to get to the root of her problem. She forced herself to swallow back the bile that had risen in her throat. She needed to buck up and grow a pair.

Why are you distraught?

Verrie almost fell down. Dumuzi's voice imperiously thrust itself into her head without warning. She was momentarily stunned. When she didn't answer, he continued.

I sense great discomfort. Are you in need of my assistance? His deep voice growled which was an incredible turn-on. Or did her clenching insides have more to do with the fact that rather than think she was a nut-job, someone actually attempted to comfort her?

Nope. Verrie swallowed. *Nope, I'm good. Just doctor's office anxiety. That's all.* She'd forgotten all the gods and goddesses could hear her when she spoke into the ether, and she got Dani's quick response.

Nothing to worry about, Verrie. A quick blood test which Enlil has said he will be gracious enough to analyze and a swab back-up which will be sent to a very confidential lab where I have friends. Then we'll be done.

Mom. Chill. It'll be fine. Sienna chose to do the head-thing too, and Riley wasn't far behind.

Yeah, I'm with you on needles, Riles misunderstood. *But in the interest of you and Sienna getting well, I can take it.*

Okay. Okay. Everybody, out of my head. Veronica couldn't help herself. She needed this over with. "Dani, here." She sat at the chair with the little arm appendage thingy and rolled up her sleeve. "Do me first."

Dani was quick and efficient, and Verrie shouldn't have worried. Riley also proved herself to be a champ, and despite looking a little green during the stick, had weathered the needle just fine.

Enlil appeared in the room just as the doctor finished up with Frank, and Verrie's attention was drawn to a rack of blood-filled test tubes.

"Enlil, I'm going to get a little scientific on you and do a blind test. I've set out several vials of blood, some from gods, some have come from our agent friends, and the rest have been drawn from our four visitors." She indicated the rack, quickly adding Frank's vial, shuffling a few others around in the process with notations made on her hand-held clipboard.

"Now, if you will proceed and tell me if they have a marker for a particular god, I'll make note. When you're finished, I'll let everyone know what we find."

Verrie watched, confused as Enlil moved forward and picked up the first vial. What was he going to do?

He raised it to his nose and sniffed.

"Phew." He screwed up his face in mock disgust. "This one is Dagon, all over," he gagged.

Geeze. The god could smell things in the samples.

Dani tried to hide her laugh while writing on her clipboard. "I told you I was using some of our banked blood," she snickered. She followed Enlil's progress down the line. He didn't hesitate as he lifted them in order.

"This one is human, no god-traces. This one is…it has a faint essence of Sham. Not much, but distinctly him." He picked up the next tube. "Candy with a dash of Sham sprinkled in," he smirked, licking his lips at his wife's blood. "…another with a small element of Sham, and…another?" Clearly, this confused him and Dani too, by the look.

Verrie cocked her head, trying to ascertain the cause of their consternation. They weren't saying.

Enlil carefully replaced that tube and extracted another. "Completely human," he intoned, but this time without the mischievous edge he'd shown before. "Emesh. Huxley with a dash of Marduk, and…" Here, he paused again. "…another of those faint Shamash samples." Verrie could see the two communicating and shaking their heads.

"Okay, we're finished." Dani wrote something quickly on her chart and Verrie could tell—by the attitude in which the doctor held her head—she quickly tuned Enlil out and conversed privately with a different god, most likely Marduk.

Shit. Something was wrong. *Goddammit.* Nothing good ever came of her being in a doctor's office…Sienna's birth, excluded. She'd known that this was a bad idea. Verrie felt like hiding, and she *didn't* want to know what they'd discovered.

"Tell us what ya found?" Frank had no such qualms. "You look like ya just swallowed a big friggin' goose egg. Yawr all bulgey-eyed and shit," she shot at Enlil.

"I'm not at liberty to say, but please," he'd obviously noted Veronica was also freaked, "I'm certain the news will be very welcome to you."

Wait a minute. Verrie replayed Enlil's blood game of hide and seek, going over his succinct answers…and one and one suddenly made…four.

"Oh my God." She reached for her daughter, then scrabbled with her other hand to touch Riley's arm. "They found four samples of human blood touched with some of Shamash's. That can only mean one thing.

We're not just friends..." She let that dangle a split second before Frank picked up the thread.

"Hell, no." Her aunt's face lit up. "It means we'ah related. Fah real." She grinned from ear to ear. "All these yeahs and all these generations, it hasn't been friends stickin' togethah, it's been friggin' sistah's or cousins...or some such shit? Family," she smiled. She turned to regard Dr. Dani. "How do we find out ouah exact connection?"

Dani sighed. She and Marduk had probably wanted to find the answer to that themselves before the cats got out of the bag. Verrie snickered. Cats. Out of the bag. She, Sienna, Riley, and Frank all had cat-god blood. *Meow.*

"That's where a search of ancient records will have to come in," the doctor confirmed. "As well as an interrogation of Shamash who will have to try to remember what...and who...he was doing in ancient times before he got sent to hell."

All parties, back to my office. Right now. Marduk's voice brooked no argument.

"It looks like summoning your demon voices will have to wait," Enlil told Verrie, herding them all out of the infirmary. "Sham's about to undergo a shakedown—god style." He said it with more than passing glee, and Veronica could only imagine what that meant. *Hell*, these guys liked to tease the life out of each other.

Back inside the vast meeting area, Verrie was aware all eyes now greedily fixed on Frank. Her aunt hadn't missed it either.

"Okay, guys. What the fuck?" Frankie wasn't one to mess around.

Marduk cleared his throat. "Um. Since you've been shown to have Sham's blood,"—the god of justice looked inordinately proud of the link that had been found— "like Verrie does, it's possible you're also a candidate to become a *Chosen*." He looked at the three—as yet unmated—gods. "Lahar, Ishkur, Ninurta?" the thunder god questioned. "You need to think again. Have any of you felt…twinges of attraction for the lovely Frank?"

Hell, Marduk, Ninurta groused. *It can't be me. I'm not visible yet.*

"True," Marduk allowed. "Alright then. Lahar, Ishkur? Either of you feeling it? And be honest. If you don't fess up, all we have to do is clear the house out of your descendants who are making you physical, and we'll have our answer, one way or another."

Lahar spoke first. "As much as I'd love to f…ahh, find out that Frank is mine," —his eyes danced over her taut, petite form— "I don't have any god-tosterone screaming *Mine* which I know is how all the other gods feel…including Dumuzi who right now has sidled up so close to Verrie, it's probably getting tough for her to breathe."

Yeah, Verrie noticed that too. His body had moved practically on top of hers while Marduk spoke, heat permeating her every pore. She tucked her tongue between clenched teeth. *Don't purr, don't purr, don't purr,* she chanted to herself, but Dumuzi must have heard because he sent back.

You'll be doing more than purring by the time I'm through with you, he growled.

Dammit. Soaked again. Her panties had just dried out from their first go-round.

"That leaves you, Ishkur," Marduk stated thoughtfully. Verrie noticed that, just like Frankie said earlier, the hunky older god's gaze landed anyplace but on her aunt.

"Not interested," he mumbled, raising curiosity in the room. "Well, sort of interested," he huffed. "But not in the way that means she's my *Chosen*, so I'm not going there. Been there, done that." His voice turned to a snarl.

Before Marduk could comment, Frankie's snarky voice entered the fray.

"And a good thing, too," she hissed. "Because I'm not interested in addin' yoah sorry old ass ta my list of willing and satisfied lovahs." Then under her breath, but so everybody would hear, she added, "Some people just think theah too good for regulah folks."

Everyone shifted uncomfortably before Dumuzi called things back to order.

"Okay. Fine. Marduk? Frank's not a mate. Can we figure things out for me and Verrie? It's only the beginning of June, and we have until September for Ishkur to get his head out of his ass and find his real *Chosen*."

"Muze is right," Enten added. "Let's solve this one, first."

"Agreed." Marduk raised his brows as the normally equitable Ishkur stormed from the room. "We'll leave him be, for now."

"And ah'll leave him be fohevah," Frank stated assuredly. "At this point, he'd have ta beg me on bended knee befoah I'd have anything ta do with him." Despite her own predicament, Verrie couldn't wait to witness a showdown between the two. There'd be fireworks over Boston, for sure.

"Shamash, please step forward." Marduk moved on with business. "I'm sorry to tell you I've called Nergal back to do this interrogation. He'll be able to suck the memories out of you better than I can. He's an expert, after all."

"I thought you wanted me to head to Iraq. Shouldn't I get going?" Sham shuddered.

"That can wait. This is important."

Verrie, who only knew Nergal as the king in the Underworld, wondered if unlucky souls relegated to the lower depths had to undergo a mind-suck of sorts by the enormous deity?

Nergal appeared, and she looked over his stern visage and bronzed body. A mind suck wasn't sounding so good, but another kind of sucking maybe…

Dumuzi's arm came up around her middle and squeezed possessively. *Shit.* Was she never going to be able to have a private thought again? She cleared her mind and settled her body into his. And…*major sigh*…why was she thinking about Nergal? Muze felt better than good.

The god, Shamash didn't look happy about his fate. He sat down heavily, and he'd lost his natural golden glow. Not only that, if Verrie wasn't mistaken, long, sharp claws extended from the ends of his fingers and gripped the arms of his chair. His lovely petite wife, Quinn, stood behind him scratching the backs of his ears, trying to ease some of his tension—without success.

"I'll try to be gentle," Nergal attempted to calm the cat god. "Normally, I'm pulling information from reluctant…guests. You'll be more of an open book." He screwed up one side of his face. "Which reminds me." The king looked at Marduk. "I need to tell you what I've finished extracting from Nedu." He looked agitated before getting back to the cat god.

"So, Sham, if you don't fight me, and you let me wander through your archives freely, I should be able to complete this quickly…if not quite painlessly."

Shamash blanched further and nodded his head. "Let's just get it over with."

"Fine," the king agreed, before confirming with Marduk. "I'm looking for a list of the women Shamash slept with before he was brought to hell in…240 BC. Is that correct?"

Shamash was the one to answer. "Unless I'm a complete idiot, I'd say you were looking for some of the last women I slept with." He looked back at his wife and apologized with. *Sorry, honey, but I did some serious catting around in my younger days. Even though Aya was my consort, she was not my only bed-partner nor I hers. We had what people now refer to as an open relationship.*

It was clear to Verrie, Quinn would forgive him anything as she squeezed his shoulder in solidarity before he continued. "But whoever I fu..ah, slept with had to have gotten pregnant right before I left because if I'd made some women pregnant well before I was banished, you can bet I would have been called on it. There was no way any father back in ancient Babylon would have passed up an opportunity for his daughter to marry a god, especially one of justice and salvation."

"Also," he pinned Dumuzi with a compassionate stare, "according to Muze, his episodes began in 239 BC., the year I got sent to hell."

"Okay, so the last year of your ancient life on earth, it is." Nergal placed his hands on Shamash's skull and everyone, including Veronica, held their breath.

Chapter Thirteen

Verrie watched carefully.

Shamash's body went rigid, and his face took on a blankness that was scary…for everybody. The cat-god's friends had ceased their teasing banter and wasn't that just an indicator of how serious this operation was?

No one made a sound as Nergal's jaw twitched and clenched. It was as if he devoured the information coming from Sham's brain and found it not to his taste. When the king's visage finally cleared, everyone took a deep breath. Dumuzi sent Verrie a private, brief explanation.

Nergal wound his way back through Sham's memories and must have seen all the shit we went through in hell…shit that was mostly Nergal's fault. I guess he didn't like seeing his own handiwork which fucking serves him right.

There was a pause.

He's past that now, Muze continued. *See how his eyes are doing a REM-like movement, processing information? Oh. There. A grin. He must be on earth for Sham's last year in Babylon. Seems like Nergal could be getting an eyeful. I'll bet our god of justice is meting out something extremely x-rated for the king to be so amused.*

And just like that, it was all over. Nergal came back into the present, sporting a huge smile. Sham, drained and shaken in the aftermath, at least hadn't fallen out of his chair. That had to be a good sign, but everyone looked worried nonetheless.

It's very dangerous to do a mind-suck, Dumuzi told her. *If handled incorrectly, one can be left as nothing but a shell.* He didn't sound too worried, though, and Verrie gained some comfort from that. *Nergal and Dagon are two of the best at it I've ever seen. Sham will be fine.*

Marduk stalked over to the rousing god. "Sham. Can you speak? Do you know who I am?" Marduk placed a hand on the god's shoulder, gripping tightly and looking concerned.

Shamash raised his eyes from under a suffusion of golden curls which had dropped into a face covered with sweat. "Yeah." His voice was weak and raspy. "You're the asshole who let Nergal plunder my brain. Fuck you, Marduk."

"Now, now, Shamash," Nergal chuckled, and Marduk broke into a big smile. "My trip through your gray matter was worth every minute of your pain." The king looked extremely satisfied with himself, and as Shamash regained his equilibrium, his need to ask showed foremost on his face.

"Okay, so who was it?" he asked, grabbing the hand of his mate and holding on tightly.

"Not who, singular," Nergal smirked. "Who—*plural.*"

"Huh?" Shamash looked suitably confused as did every other being in the room. Nergal savored the moment.

"Do you remember a lovely pair of dark-haired twins, by any chance?" The king of the Underworld looked to be enjoying himself immensely. "Mmm. Olive skin, upturned breasts…" he cleared his throat. "Do the names Abi and Arwi ring any kind of bell?"

Shamash screwed up his face but obviously, came up blank.

"Ah, I thought not," the royal drawled. "I'm not surprised. You were exceedingly drunk in my voyeuristic journey."

Verrie bit back a laugh. It was clear to her Nergal loved to "watch."

He continued teasing, "I must say you showed a strong talent even while in a compromised state. You were able to…uh…sustain activities for a good portion of the night."

Shamash looked suitably uncomfortable. Exhibitionism clearly wasn't on his Christmas list.

"The girls, on the other hand, were magnificent. They were totally without boundaries and completely into celebrating."

"Celebrating?" Shamash squeaked out.

"Oh, did I forget to mention? You were all high on a big score you had in court where you cleared Abi and Arwi's dearest uncle of a murder charge."

"Uselli, the butcher?" Sham's vocal cords twanged. "Him, I remember." He blinked twice. "His trial occurred in the fall of my final year in Babylon. It was the last time I was successful at court. I was framed with Aya's death and sent to hell not two months later." He stroked his chin. "I've always speculated I was set up as retribution for having cleared Uselli's name." His voice became bitter before he paused as if to clear his head of the trial.

Verrie figured he succeeded as his tongue swept out of his mouth and his eyes went wide.

"Did I…do his nieces? *Those* twins?" Everyone watched Sham swallow hard. "Shit. How could I not remember that? Those two were so hot…" He'd averted his lips so his deaf wife couldn't see what he said, but he trailed off anyway. "Damn, I'm such an asshole."

"Well," Nergal continued his needling, "it wasn't as if you had a choice. The uncle held a grand banquet in your behalf, plied you with drought after drought of some very fine mead, then sent his nieces off to 'put you to bed.'"

Shamash groaned and dropped his head into his hands. "See, I told you. The local populace had been trying to get me to procreate for centuries…and I was always so careful. It wasn't like Merrymount where we were completely anonymous and screwed around without thinking. Back in ancient days, everyone knew we were gods. It was almost a game to try to tie us to a mortal." He raised resigned eyes to Nergal again. "So I…" he trailed off.

"Oh, you did," the king confirmed. "Over and over, in all positions, and with great gusto…"

"Enough," Shamash's voice regained its strength, and he'd clearly had it with the sexual revelations in front of his wife. He switched his focus to Marduk. "So where do we go from here?"

Marduk rubbed a hand down his face, thinking. "Dumuzi's timeline shows his episodes began sixteen or eighteen years after you were banished which would correspond with the adolescence of a child you might have spawned. Those episodes continued, off and on, until he joined us in hell in 17AD. I'd say it's time for you and Lahar to take yourselves off to the Middle East and do some digging."

"Right," Lahar agreed. "We'll see if we can find birth records for a child…or children from your twins."

"Not my twins," Sham grumbled.

Lahar ignored him. "We'll see if we can follow that line forward to not only Sienna and Verrie but to Frank and Riley. I'd say it's pretty much a done deal what we'll uncover."

"You're also looking for any unusual occurrence of demon activity during the first two hundred and fifty-six years of Muze's life," Marduk reminded him. "He doesn't remember exact dates, but he was tormented on and off during that entire period. I trust you to dig up everything you can."

There were snickers in the room. Sometimes with ancient cuneiform, digging up was exactly what had to happen.

"Okay, we're off." Sham got up, turned, and kissed his wife goodbye, then popped from the room.

"Bloody hell," Lahar groused, wanting to follow, but walking to the door instead. "I can't wait to get a *Chosen* if just for the ability to mist out again at will."

Complain, complain, Ninurta's invisible self cut in. *At least you can smell, taste, and feel again. Try being the only one left without a body.*

"Yeah, okay, Galahad," Lahar replied sarcastically. "That's your own, celibate fault." The ram-god's boots sounded down the hallway until they too disappeared.

"Now." Marduk rubbed his hands together, expectantly. "I suggest some demon hunting, do you all agree?" He looked around the room at his fellow gods with eager eyes.

"I wholly concur," Nergal answered. "Especially, since I found from interrogating Nedu, he's been in league with a rogue bunch of demons for centuries…dating back to ancient times."

"You're shitting me?" Marduk barked in surprise. "Fuck," he continued. "I'd forgotten all about you grilling the god with all the crap going on here. Demons? Nedu? I had my suspicions he was a moron, and now we know. What idiot god would get involved with demons?" Marduk ground his teeth and turned to Dagon, mumbling. "Sorry, man. Present company excluded." He turned back to Nergal with a little less enthusiasm. "What else did you find out?"

"I pulled a number of interesting and disturbing things from his brain." The king shook his head. "Confirming facts which Matthew proposed, including those regarding my infant son. Beletseri had nothing to do with the death of Girin. Not only that, but for years our dear Underworld secretary has been used as a pawn by Nedu and this group of demons…for the sole purpose of gaining control over *your* group of gods— with a decided ramp up after you began to regain your bodies here on earth."

"What?" Marduk grunted questioningly, and every god sat up straighter in their chairs.

"That's right. The demons, led by someone higher up the food chain, who our interrogated god cannot name, has been pulling Nedu's strings, orchestrating his actions for years. He, in turn, was manipulating Bel."

"Gods. Who could be behind it?" Enlil had his arms crossed over his chest and looked ready to kill.

"Unfortunately, I don't know. That's where Nedu's brain totally broke down." Nergal looked disgusted. "The god of the gate was a lot weaker than I imagined, and his cranium—trying to hide things from me—couldn't take my deeper probing. All I know before his synapses collapsed in on themselves, he was still absolutely certain he'd be the right-hand man to someone who verged on great importance if their mission to enslave you all succeeded."

Marduk turned to Dagon who had been sitting very quietly throughout the afternoon. "Dagon. You know more about demons than anyone but Nergal." If Marduk was stroking the god's ego to make up for his previous comment, it wasn't mentioned. Dumuzi filled Verrie in again.

At one time, Dagon aligned himself against the gods and recruited demons for his own ends. Meeting his Chosen, Holly and mending fences with his cousin, Anshar shifted his allegiance firmly back with the gods.

The thunder god still pontificated, "You speak several of their languages fluently and understand even more dialects. Are you aware of a group of demons more scurrilous than most?"

Dagon looked sharply at his friends and tented his fingers. "I've heard rumors there are some highly intelligent factions down below. We came across some roughly organized bands ourselves." He reached for his wife, Holly's hand. Once again Dumuzi brought Verrie up to speed.

She braved hell to bring him back to earth, and with the help of a group of Underworld good-guys we call the glowies, they battled many different species.

"The ones who come to mind, most specifically, are the ones who can become invisible and spew poisonous gas, but I'm pretty sure we know where all that group is located." Dagon deferred to Nergal.

"Dagon's correct. I have a modicum of control over the creatures living within my immediate jurisdiction, and all of them are accounted for. I've checked." He turned thoughtful. "I believe we must be dealing with a different sector of hell altogether. One that is not under my direct scrutiny. I may need to call together all my minor kings to initiate a demon counting census."

"It sounds like a rational approach," Dagon nodded. "Both uggla and dwall are cross-species words, so they don't help us at all with our search."

"Okay, then the time for speculation is over," Marduk stated. "Muze. You're off to the dungeons. Jake, Candy, will you take him down and make sure he's secure?"

"Sure thing, boss man." Candy gave him a fresh little salute. Verrie could tell there was a teasing thing the two engaged in, but as cute as it was, it didn't take her mind off the fact she was about to raise some demons. She'd let her mind flow with all that had been said by Nergal and the others, but the bottom line, it was her head the creatures had been invading—hers and Sienna's—and the next bit of business wasn't going to be fun at all. Still, her heart went out to Dumuzi.

"Will you be all right?" she asked, afraid her sudden and unexplained feelings for him showed in her eyes, but she couldn't seem to do anything about it.

"I'll be fine." Dumuzi reached out and stroked her cheek. It was comforting and electrifying all at the same time. "Unlike the other guys, I don't remember a single thing when I'm…turned," he revealed before putting a scowl on his face. "I just don't like the idea you're contacting those cretins."

"Look on the bright side, Muze," Anshar put in. "As soon as we find out where they hide, you can let your inner beast loose, track them down, and destroy them all."

Verrie could see the pulse in the side of Dumuzi's neck beat harder—the thought excited him.

"You're right, Anshar. We can all put our bad-hats on and kick some demon ass," he said excitedly. "After all the torment they've put Verrie's family through and the fucked-up number they've done on me, I think we'll make short work of them."

"That's the spirit," Absu said, rousingly. "First blood to the avenging gods, I say."

Verrie would have laughed at the proper English gent if she hadn't been so anxious.

"Okay. Get moving." Marduk tipped his head to the door. "And Jake, let me know when he's under lock and key so Verrie can begin."

"Sure thing." Jake and Candy followed Dumuzi through the door, and Marduk turned to the remaining goddesses in the room.

"If you wouldn't mind, ladies," he began, "since none of you speak demon, and all the gods have a rudimentary understanding, I'd like you to form that protective energy circle around Sienna again while Verrie attempts contact. There is no reason for both ladies to suffer."

"Thank you, Marduk." Verrie let out half of her tension. She was nervous enough about this without having to worry about her daughter's well-being. She watched Lenore herd Tess, Holly, Quinn, Obedience, and Charlie into place around Sienna. While Lenore, Vesca, Anna, Dani-Lee, Addie-May, and Glory made a second barrier around that group. Once in place, Verrie felt the humming energy crank up. That was one powerful bunch of women.

Jake's voice from the cellar hit their heads all at once. *Muze is secure. Matthew is bitching like a pussy about being in the cell next to him, but Candy thinks it'll be good entertainment, so let her rip.*

Thanks, Jake, Marduk sent back, then turned to her. "Are you ready, Verrie?"

There wasn't any way she'd ever be ready for this. But she succeeded in convincing herself at least this attempt was being made in a controlled environment with gods, humans, and blue guys—all bigger than life—around her to help if things got out of hand.

She took a deep breath and went deep. She'd never tried being the one to initiate contact, but she didn't think it would be difficult.

Chapter Fourteen

The first thing that alerted Verrie she was about to be successful was the screaming from the basement, drowned out by the loudest, most guttural roaring she had ever heard. It almost derailed her already tentative probing to contact the demons. Verrie's mouth went dry. Clearly, it was Dumuzi making the more hideous of the two noises, and…

"Matthew's getting an eyeful," Anshar snickered quietly, confirming her thoughts that the as-yet-unmet Matthew voiced the hysterical outbursts.

"Shh," Marduk quieted Anshar with a stern look, and Verrie straightened up too. It wouldn't do to get distracted. She attempted to concentrate again.

Let's see… *Demons. Where are you?* She dared poke harder and felt her self-imposed brain restrictions drop away. *Let me hear you, demon-boys,* Verrie postured. She could do this. She let out a deep breath and reached for her dominant self, the one she hardly ever dared pull out but had now used twice in the same afternoon. *Come on, you bastards. Are you afraid? Afraid because I'm seeking you out instead of the other way around? Let me hear you,* she taunted. *Come play under my rules now.*

Verrie was fully aware on one side of her, Nergal had plugged into her head in such a way he could hear everything she would hear. Dagon on the other side had made the same connection. They, in turn, would broadcast the things that came through her to the other gods in the room and to Dorian. If she understood correctly, the dark warlock was a member of some other-worldly governing board and held legal jurisdiction in all realms, including that of Nergal. Kind of like an uber-policeman…and he looked the part.

Uggla.

Damn, her mind had wandered, and she hadn't been prepared for the cutting pain accompanying the one-word greeting that came back. Verrie now knew the word meant goddess. Which she wasn't…yet.

How do you say 'not a goddess' in demon? Verrie gritted out to Nergal. She kept a good hold on her composure despite the discomfort.

"Try '*Nugt a Uggla*,'" Nergal told her. "If they speak any of the languages with which we're familiar, they'll understand."

Verrie repeated the words strongly to the demons and received a small tirade in answer.

Glah bah uggla. Glah bah dwigg gul.

Shit. That hurt. Verrie grabbed her head and attempted to keep her stomach from lurching.

Got it. Dagon crowed, either ignoring her discomfort or completely unaware her protoplasm was under fire. *They say you are the goddess, and you're the one they seek. We should try to draw from them the reason they seek you, so let's get them riled enough, they'll drop their guard. Call them cowardly bastards for daring to bother you and your family.*

Dagon gave her the words, and with a dredging of fortitude, she repeated them in what she hoped was an aggressive tone.

There followed a bunch of indistinct babble that sounded highly irate and had Verrie moaning and gripping the seat of her chair as each torturous syllable flew back at her. On top of that, a voice from the basement that was Dumu—but not Dumuzi—suddenly joined in.

Leave her, he spat. Then loosed what must have been a repeat of those words in demon-ese. *Gralt geh,* adding, *Continue to torment her and I will kill you all.* As those words were duplicated, Verrie could almost see venom dripping from some kind of fangs. A visual? Was she getting a look at the demons…or Dumuzi?

Degga gunt? A rasping voice asked a question, and Nergal laughed.

Ahh, so they haven't come across Dumuzi before. The king sounded happy. *They want to know who he is.*

There was a lot of growling from the demons and worried snuffling sounds. Apparently, Dumuzi was a wild card they'd never been able to hear before—even though they affected him—and they didn't like the outside involvement.

Glah gralt, the demons hissed.

Verrie had been paying attention to the words previously spoken, and despite her level of pain, she knew the beings had said, "leave her."

You bastards are the ones who will leave, Dumuzi spewed. *If you don't, I will rip you apart with my claws and devour your stinking flesh.* This was reiterated, even more vehemently—if that was possible—in the demon tongue.

Now Verrie wondered who was more terrifying? The spawn from hell she'd experienced all her adult life or her nascent—gulp—mate? He sounded scary as shit.

While all of this went on, Verrie vaguely registered gods popping in and out of the room. She could tell Marduk was getting excited.

This is good, Verrie. Keep them talking a little longer. We've ruled out Nergal's realm below the Mariana Trench.

If Verrie hadn't felt like the top of her head was about to explode, she would have giggled. His orders made the situation sound like a bad cop show. Keep them on the line a little longer...one ringy-dingy, two ringy-dingy, call for Ms. Foxie from the depths of hell. *Geez.* Was she losing it?

Gaddawah gralt uggla.

Okay. There was a new one, and it sounded like the speaker was having a hissy fit.

Translation please, your royal hotness? Verrie snickered, and her head spun. *Ooh.* She was beginning to feel very...floaty. With a detached curiosity, she recognized her body had taken over and was injecting natural morphine into her bloodstream to combat the pain. This was something she'd never had to do consciously, it had been a side-effect of the voices that developed over time. She'd forgotten how loopy she got...or was this more fucked up than usual?

Uh...monster leave goddess, Nergal answered with a quirked eyebrow, looking at her with suspicion. Verrie was squinting from the headache, but she was still able to see the king glance questioningly at Marduk. *What's happening to Verrie?*

Not to worry, Verrie stood up, did a quick twirl, and patted his shoulder. *Verrie is feeling just fine.* She put a finger to his lips and shushed him, sending her voice back to the nether-fiends. *Demons. Old buddies, old pals. Gotta go now. Uggla dwigg gaddawah. Wheee. I got that one, didn't I. It means I'm gonna go find me a monster. Grrrr.*

She vaguely heard her daughter's voice. "Is Mom drunk?"

"Not that we know of," Marduk barked. "Verrie. Stay focused. We can't lose them now, we're so close."

She didn't' care what Marduk wanted. She knew what *she* wanted

"How do I say, 'bye-bye demons?'" Verrie asked Dagon, getting inches from his face and tugging so hard on a lock of his blue-black hair, it made him yelp.

"Ooh, I think my boy liked that," Holly's voice came from somewhere within the women's circle and was filled with heat. "He can be a very bad beast, Ms. Foxie. If you ever want to join us…"

"No, no, Holly." Verrie stuck up a stop-sign hand. "Not in front of my young ladies." She waggled a finger toward the female group. "Si and Riles don't need to know about ménage a…ménage a…uh, threesomes. Even with delectable, lickable…" She came even closer to Dagon who looked like he was having trouble keeping his hands on the table. Verrie stood up abruptly. "Damn. Did I say that?" She spun around again. "Where's my big man? Oh, yeah. Gotta go." She gave a quick flash of her fingers and skipped out the door.

"Shit. They're gone." She heard Marduk's pissed off voice follow her as she bounced down the hall and laughed when he added, "Emesh, Douglas, go keep an eye on her." He then switched to head-speak. *Jake. Has Dumuzi changed back yet?*

Negative Marduk. He's still deep into angry-time.

Well, Verrie is coming down, so don't let her out of the elevator. That's all she needs, to see Muze in his fucked-up state.

Ah. Elevator. Verrie's mind seized on that with glee. She'd have to thank Mr. Marduk for pointing her in the right direction.

Dumuzi, my sweet, I'm coming, she trilled. Spotting the elevator across the expanse of the enormous front entry, she ran quickly to it and pushed the call button. She sensed bodies crowding in behind her and turning to lean on the wall for support, she willed her eyes to focus up close.

"Emesh," she gushed. "Douglas." She shook a finger under one of their noses…which one she couldn't be sure. "You two aren't going to try to stop me, are you?"

"What do you think, Douglas? Should we just let her rip off the band-aid?" Emesh's warm voice washed over her like a honeyed balm. She hoped he would keep talking. "I think the sooner she sees what Dumuzi becomes, the better. And in her…" he waved a hand around airily, "…state," he cutely rolled his eyes, "she might take it a little easier."

"I say we go for it," the beautiful mocha-brown Douglas agreed.

Yippee. They weren't pulling the brake on her happy little train.

"Hell, I haven't seen Dumuzi's other side. I'm damned curious what the fuss is all about." Douglas flashed her a smile.

"Okay," Emesh sniffed, holding the door to the elevator that had just arrived. "But both of you be warned. Unlike a lot of the other guys, Muze is not an appealing sight."

Verrie poked Emesh in the chest on the way into the lift. "Hey, that's my man you're talking about, and I'll thank you to keep your lip buttoned. Haven't you ever heard of beauty and the beast?" she quipped. "Fairy tales do come true, buster, and this beauty is going after *her* beast." The doors closed behind them as Verrie silently dared Emesh to disagree. He smartly buttoned his twitching, upturned lips.

Elevator. Elevator. Verrie stood, tapping her foot impatiently. What was the damned thing doing? Going to China? Would that she could poof in and out like the gods. *Wait.* Would she be able to do that if she mated with Dumuzi? *Cool.* Now that was the way to move.

When the doors finally slid apart, Candy stood, splayed across the opening like some kind of starfish.

"Okay, okay, okay," Verrie snarked, attempting…and failing to duck under Candy's arm. She shot back up to a full five-foot-five height—one inch taller than Candy. "I get it. He's not pretty like Enlil—who's fucking sexy as hell with those horns—but if anyone tried to keep you from your man, what would you tell them?" Verrie might be feeling deliciously giddy, but she wasn't stupid. The goddesses all loved themselves some gods, and nobody got betwixt them.

"I'd tell them to stuff it up their keister."

"Right. Up their keister."

Candy grinned and stood back with a sweep of her arm, letting the elevator group pass.

Well, how about that? Keister must have been the magic word, Verrie smirked.

"Oh, Candy, you didn't."

Jake was her next obstacle. He might be a little more difficult. The big DEA dude—all crewcut, square-jaw, bad-ass of him—didn't look like he was about to move anytime soon. She once again fished out her lady "dom" chops.

"Move it before my friends and I slap you in a cell." Her eyes slid to the left and noticed the door to a very interesting room named "Sub-space"….with a sign-up sheet outside showing the times of day and a whole lot of names filling in the spots. Well, what do you know? The gods enjoyed some kink. Here was a game she knew how to play. She turned back to Jake. "Once I've turned goddess, you don't want me teaming up with your wife to put you in *that* particular lock-up," Verrie purred. "Because I'll tell you right now, you'll give the term 'bottom' a whole new look."

"Shit, no." Jake's face drained of color, and Verrie couldn't keep track of who was laughing hardest—the gay couple who had the right of "bottom" and "top," or Candy, who probably just envisioned her straight-laced boss trussed and mussed. Verrie didn't care. It had gotten her what she wanted—a hallway pass.

I'm coming, my big, protective monster, Verrie threw out into the air, and her steps didn't hesitate even when a large roar came from the far end of the long corridor. *Don't be shy,* she admonished. *There's something lovely in all of us.*

Before she reached her destination, her gaze was drawn to a sullen individual sitting dejectedly on a bench in a cell to her left.

"And you must be the esteemed bastard, Matthew," Verrie chimed. "Although I have yet to hear all of your transgressions, I delight in informing you our very own King Nergal has decreed your Bel… Hey, there it is again." Verrie lost herself for a moment. "Isn't that the name of the Beauty and the Beast chick? I am so loving this whole metaphor thing."

Matthew was at the bars now, his eyes growing wide. "What was it the king said?" he asked in a shaky voice that had some nice tonal qualities. *My.* He'd be a good-looking man if his eyes weren't so close together.

"Huh? What?" Verrie tried to focus because to give the guy his due, he wasn't yelling or anything despite his anxiousness.

"You said something about King Nergal and Bel," he prompted.

"Oh, yeah." Verrie brightened. "He said she didn't kill any babies, and she's only a pawn in someone's game."

As she saw Matthew's face blanch, she tried to figure out what she'd said wrong and attempted to add a few assurances. "I'm sure she's a very good pawn…since she's not a baby killer, and Nergal's trying to get to the bottom of whose pawn she is. Don't worry."

His face remained blank, despite her affirmations, so she felt it was a good time to move on. "Have a nice day." She waved and skipped the next ten feet to the last cell on the right.

"Come out, come out, wherever you are," Verrie chanted and saw movement in the far end of a very large, enclosed space.

"Dumuzi, I've come to liberate you." She wrinkled up the corners of her eyes in satisfaction at her joyous double entendre. *Yes.* She was coming to release him from his confines, but she was also going to free him from thinking he was an ugly monster.

"Now, come over here where I can see you," she coaxed. "There's absolutely nothing you can look like that will scare me. I promise."

When he didn't move, Verrie sighed. *Really?* He was going to make her be bossy again? Why was it all the males here who she'd given a glimpse of her assertive side seemed to like it? Was it a god thing? They were all so powerful, maybe it was kind of fun for someone else to take charge for a bit? She'd have to feel that one out—later with the other gods, right now with hers.

"Okay, I've had it, Dumuzi. You're being a very bad boy," she growled, "and I can think up all kinds of punishment for a monster as disobedient as you. Now, I want you to march over here, this very minute, and don't think about giving me any sass. You got that?" Verrie demanded an answer.

A disconcerted grunt came from an enormous, dark shape in the corner, but she saw it unwind from its crouched position.

She crossed her arms over her suddenly heaving chest as the Dumuzi-thing stood to full height. *Okay.* Seven feet? Eight?

This was Dumuzi, Verrie reminded herself. Dumuzi of the delicious cock and the rock-hard abs. Dumuzi who wanted to protect her from demons.

Her heart started beating harder under her ribcage as large…feet came a stride closer.

He stepped into the light.

Holy Mother-of-God, Jesus, Joseph, and Mary. She'd never seen anything like him in her entire life.

Was there anybody else she could pray to?

Chapter Fifteen

Okay. So they'd been right. Dumuzi wasn't cute. Verrie abruptly lost all her daffy sizzle. She didn't know what she'd expected, but it hadn't been this. Her feet wanted, in the worst way, to move backward, away from him as he approached the bars of his cage, but her gut said "no."

Douglas, who had been curious and right with her all the way, had no such qualms. She felt him back off.

Shit. What should she do? Verrie took a deep breath, and it helped. At least the…pile of vegetation moving toward her didn't smell. *No.* Quite the opposite. It…he…smelled exactly like Dumuzi, only more so. Okay, that was a positive. His earthy scent filled her nostrils, and it had turned her on earlier, in the closet. She could use that.

"Dumuzi," she said, in her best, most prim schoolmarm tone. "As you can see, I am no longer tormented by the demons' voices, so you can calm down."

The seven-plus foot mountain of muck and vines stalked closer. He still hadn't raised his head so she could see his eyes—that might or might not mirror those of Dumuzi.

"Did you hear me…mate?" Verrie figured what the hell. She might as well remind him of who she was supposed to be. "Everything is a-okay. My head is once again my own."

His face rose slowly out of the swampy mass of his body, bringing his shoulders to even greater height.

Yikes. His head scraped the ceiling. Once again, Verrie fought the urge to move back, and instead, connected with his now visible eyes. She grew hopeful, but upon further scrutiny, she shivered. They were the same color she was familiar with, brown with flecks of mossy green, but there was no indication in their depths he knew who she was.

She was captivated by their blank coldness and almost, but not quite, missed the casual lifting of his arm. His arm? *Yeah, sure.* If that was what you could call it. The limb—she almost laughed at the pun—was more like a twist of green tendrils, each individually curling, stretching out to dart at odd angles, searching, prodding. The tangle as a whole moved toward the bars in her direction—she was transfixed.

Verrie let out a squeak of fear when she was grabbed from behind and yanked backward. "What the—"

The roaring reaction to her forcible withdrawal cut into her surprised words. It was unlike anything she'd ever heard. The air around her pulsed as the muddy green monster vibrated with anger.

Jake, maintaining a commanding arm around her waist, spoke into her ear. "He could have been the one who grabbed you with those innocent looking little vines," the agent hissed. "He's faster than he looks and extremely dangerous." Jake raised his voice to be heard over the bellowing rage coming from inside the cage.

"Those tendrils can extend several feet, and once they hook on to you, they pull you in."

Verrie tried to calm her breathing to take a closer look at the Dumuzi-monster now that he was pissed and showing all his true colors…lots of colors. The beast mimicked every swampy forest she'd ever seen—greens, golds, and blues, all bound together by wet, muddy browns.

His legs mimicked his arms with the bright green vine-y filaments constantly twining and reaching. His torso more resembled the thick, taut ropes of old growth. Verrie avoided his face, hoping he would calm down before she had to confront him again, and concentrated instead on the glorious appendages now extending from his back.

Wings. Holy shit. His wingspan had to be at least fifteen feet, and it was probably larger when not impeded by cell walls. Verrie noted, unlike his other extremities, these were not creeping and crawling. They were made up of the softest-looking verdant moss she had ever seen—pliable, delicate, smooth. Her mind instantly wondered what it would feel like to be wrapped in that cushiony fleece.

Dumuzi's roaring had not abated, and Verrie quickly figured out what was wrong.

"Jake, let go of me," she spoke loudly over the din. "He's freaked because you grabbed me. Remember, from what we've been able to figure, he thinks he's my protector." Verrie swallowed. Which would mean if he got his little…tendrils…on her, he wouldn't hurt her. Would he?

Jake let go.

The bellowing diminished, and Verrie finally allowed herself a look at Dumuzi's face. Her mouth hung open for a moment before she snapped it shut.

Copper coloring still covered his head, but instead of his long, spiraling locks, his topping had the consistency of fall leaves artfully arranged. It dipped down over a strong, chiseled forehead made from packed, dried mud? His eyes glittered dangerously above a surprisingly cute, green button nose. And his mouth? *Oh.* His mouth. Looking there, the little moisture left on her own tongue completely dried up.

Four long, dangerous fangs emerged from between lush, sage-colored lips, two from the bottom and two from the top, and they looked so sharp, a small swipe from any one of them might completely remove a hand…or slit a throat. They were white, stark white, in contrast with the forest colors covering the rest of him.

As if sensing her terror, Dumuzi opened his mouth wide and sucked the fangs back up into his gums where they became little more than pin-point protrusions. His tongue, which still looked very similar to the one she'd been sucking on earlier, swiped lazily across the tips. *What?* If Verrie didn't know better, she'd swear he just executed a deliberately sexy move. *Huh.*

She took two steps closer and pushed a hand behind her to keep both Jake and Candy at bay. The agents were twitchy as hell and right on her heels. Emesh, on the other hand, had positioned himself across the way, nearer to Matthew's cell but was concentrating on giving off a subtle warmth that had Dumuzi's little green whorls taking note. It was as if the bits couldn't help themselves, gravitating toward the god of summer in a happy dance. It was helping take the edge off of Dumuzi.

Verrie moved another few inches. "Do you know who I am?" she asked, and his button nose twitched. His wings, in the process of folding up, fluttered briefly.

"I think you do," she told him. "And you're not going to hurt me, are you?" Verrie suddenly became positive he wouldn't. Her rational brain told her Dumuzi had suffered right along with not only *her* during her episodes but with every one of her ancestors throughout the years who had been subjected to the same torture. Every time the demons had fucked with someone in her family, Dumuzi had turned into this monster. What better reason could there be than he had been attempting to render protection, but until now, had been unable to reach whoever he was trying to safeguard?

Boldly, she approached the cell. This was either life or death—Marduk had assured her she belonged to Dumuzi, so she was counting on living.

Faster than her head could get around it, two supple vines on his right arm separated from the rest and shot toward her, one twining around her neck, the other around her waist, dragging her toward him to rest up against the bars of his cage. With great effort, Verrie kept her muscles lax and her breathing regular.

"Drop her, Muze," Jake's voice challenged behind her. "I'm not fooling around." There was a dangerous edge to his voice.

"Jake, please." The vine around Verrie's throat wasn't tight enough to choke. She allowed rational thought to tamp down her fear and realized the creeper around her middle was more caressing than confining. "He's just trying to get to know me. Please." She turned her eyes away for a second from the brown ones that drilled into hers. "Give him a few minutes. If it looks like it's going all wrong, you can intervene." Verrie knew she was supposed to spend the rest of eternity with Dumuzi, so she'd better get used to his dark side.

An actual semi-amused smile touched her lips as she wondered what Sienna would think of Dumuzi's swamp-guy. And speaking of her captor, she heard him emit a small, annoyed grunt at her little grin. Sienna, always logical, would find some way to rationalize his looks and focus on the positive. Verrie needed to do the same.

Dumuzi didn't move, so she needed to find things to talk about. Verrie told him what had struck her funny. "I was just remembering Sienna couldn't wait to find out what hotly sexy creature you turned into. I think she was imagining something along the lines of buff and fuzzy." She drew back her head and looked at the moist, sludgy substance that clung between the sharp-hued vines of his chest. "I'm not sure she had a walking mud-bath in mind."

His brow creased and a sound of unease moved up through his chest.

Verrie backpedaled. "Oh, don't think you're chopped liver, here," she placated. "As monsters go, I believe you have most everything she's ever seen on TV beat, hands down."

Now that she looked closely at the ropey thicket that was his chest—and everything lower—his vines actually emulated some pretty serious muscle groups.

She'd heard of rock hard, but wood hard? *Oh.* Okay, that got her laughing again.

She hadn't let her eyes fall to her monster-man's privates, but the possibilities of tendril vs. stump had her imagination running riot. Verrie shook her head. *Criminy.* She'd been without a man so long, even swamp-thing was looking good to her. Of course, knowing Dumuzi was underneath somewhere didn't hurt.

"So, where do we go from here?" she asked, cocking her head to one side, giving his face another once over. Not expecting an answer, she also wasn't expecting his lightning fast motion. A long coil of green whipped past her head and without hesitation, returned to the cell just as quickly. At the jingling noise, Verrie understood he'd just snagged the cell door's keys from the hook across the room.

"Well, what the fuck, Muze?" Candy's voice was equal parts humor and incredulousness. "You've been fucking with us? You could have grabbed those keys whenever you wanted, you bad-ass monster." She struggled to bring herself back under control. "Shit, Jake, we've been totally had."

Jake was clearly reluctant to join the swamp-thing-good fest. "It doesn't make any difference. He's still dangerous. Did you see the gash he put in Sham earlier?" His scowling face returned to the action at the cage. "We're staying right here, Muze. Just so you know, I have a tranque gun filled with herbicide, so don't piss me off."

Dumuzi ignored the agent, and Verrie watched as his smart little tendril placed the purloined key into the lock and turned. It snicked open, and the monster, once the cell door swung open, sent new greenery out to surround Verrie. The fresh foliage drew her into the cage.

It had been fairly easy to maintain a degree of calm while bars separated her from swamp-god, but Verrie found herself shaking anew as she was quickly pulled inside, and the barred door closed behind her. Another grunt and she was towed across the cell to the corner where Dumuzi had been hunkering earlier. He settled back on…haunches and pulled Verrie onto his lap. The impact didn't jar. He instead rocked like a waterbed—not bad. On another note, she did feel her clothes were becoming mud-soaked, so yup, he was as wet as he looked.

Verrie began to relax again. With the absence of any aggressive moves on her mate's part, she thought she could handle this. As long as Emesh kept up with his impression of the sun and she didn't catch a chill from all the damp, she could hold out.

How long does Dumuzi normally stay in this form? She sent her words upward, hoping to get a response from Marduk.

He's usually out for a good two hours. Sometimes three.

Verrie nodded to herself after receiving the answer. It was about twice the amount of time her demon induced torment sessions. That made sense. If what he was experiencing was protective-mode, he'd want to make good and sure she was over the assault before he changed back. Verrie allowed herself to pat one of the branches that held her in place. She might have another hour or two to wait. What could she do to get to know him better?

When several verdant curlicues began to move, conducting a wiggling search of her person, Verrie knew the swamp monster must have been asking himself the same question. *Okay,* so he wanted to explore a little. That was fine. It was all very innocent...until one green tendril began working its way down the front of her shirt. She gave it a sharp smack.

"Hey, buddy. You can stop right there." She narrowed her eyes and lifted her chin to look him full in the face, up close and personal. "While I might be interested in playing games with Dumuzi later, I'm certainly not going to give you first dibs on what I have to offer. Got it? Now back off."

The spiral withdrew hastily and hid back amongst the other sprouts in the thick, braided arm. Huh. That had gone well. Maybe she should turn the tables?

"Not that I'm averse to exploring a little more of you." Verrie watched him thoughtfully to see what his reaction would be. Was that a flicker of interest in his big brown pools?

Remembering how much Dumuzi had enjoyed her dominant tendencies in the closet, she speculated that swamp-guy might be open to the same thing. When, if ever, had anyone dared to stand up to him while he was in this guise? Oh sure, they'd fought him, subdued him, but had anyone ever tried ordering him around? Attempting to get inside the psyche of a monster, Verrie ruminated that perhaps a big-ass-being would get tired of always making the hard choices to terrorize or...kill. *Okay.* Not so much that one, but didn't everyone need a break sometimes from being alpha? It wouldn't hurt to try...Verrie hoped.

"Okay, mud-monster. Let me go, and get on your feet," she rapped out a no-nonsense command.

Holy shit. He snapped to it. This could be good.

"Hands at your sides, and no sneaky little guys poking out, you got me?" Dumuzi did as she asked with alacrity, and Verrie heard Candy snicker from outside the cell.

You go girl. Enlil loves it when I play boss, too, she sent. *But don't tell anybody, he likes to pretend he's always in charge.*

Verrie cut back a smirk. She really liked the kick-ass women in this household. If she stayed, they would all be great role models for Sienna.

She got back to business with her swamp-partner. "I'm going to run my hands over your arms to see how you're put together," Verrie told him. "But you will hold completely still. Grunt once if you understand."

He gave a deep snuffle. *Good.*

She laid her palms on his shoulders.

For someone who was wet and in a basement, Dumuzi was surprisingly warm. Emesh's doing? She didn't know. Her fingers trailed down her swamp man's arms, between hills and valleys that completely resembled the muscle and tendon structure of that which lay beneath everyone's skin. *Funny.* That's exactly what it looked like. Muze's insides were on the outside…and brown and green, she chuckled to herself. When she was satisfied with his arms, she went to his pecs.

"I'm going to explore your chest now," she lowered her lashes, "and if you're a good boy, I'll go further south." In reality, she had no intention of going for his man-parts, but it would keep him on his toes if he thought otherwise. His whole body tightened up in front of her, proving her point.

Verrie's hands ran across the thick, ropey lengths of hardness that laid striated across his upper torso. She located a small knot and gave it a tweaking tease, pleased to see his startled jump. *Yup.* She'd found a nipple.

Biting her tongue against a "hell, yeah," she dipped lower, bypassing what she thought might be his bellybutton, and moved her hand right to left, then left to right from muddy hip to muddy hip. There was a hard to ignore, impressive piece of wood that stuck up between them, trying its darndest to get in her way, but she deftly avoided it. She finally removed her fingers from his hips and stepped back to an accompanying unhappy chuff from her new friend. He started to reach for her hand.

"Uh-uh." She gave him a slight slap on the wrist. "I'm in charge, here," she reminded the monster. "Now stretch out your wings."

Verrie held her breath in anticipation. Of all the interesting places on her swamp-man's body, his wings had most intrigued her. They looked so moss-like and soft. She couldn't wait to caress them. He extended them from his body with a small whoosh.

"Lovely," she murmured, taking in the fine network of viridian growth that flourished over an argillaceous base. She smoothed her palms across the lush surface and preened to see the big beast shiver at the contact. "Ahh, you like that." She deepened her touch and received...not a purr...not a hum, but certainly a rumble of some sort that gave voice to his pleasure.

The call of his softness had her putting her hand explorations on hold to rest her head against one cradling appendage. *Mmm*. It was so cushy. She let out a huge yawn. It had been a damned long day, and the combination of coming off a drunken whirl, an adrenaline high, *and* a power play had done Verrie in.

"What do you say we curl up for a nap?" she asked, and without a word, her new beau scooped her into his arms and settled her once again on his lap. Only this time, he stretched his long legs out in front of him and wrapped both of them up in his wings.

Verrie smiled over the top edge of his aileron, wiggling her hand free and giving a thumbs up to Jake, Candy, Emesh, and Douglas, who were all looking at her with varying degrees of astonishment.

"Lights out, immortals?"

She didn't get an answer from any of the deities who looked resigned they would be settling down for a long wait. The comment instead came unexpectedly from Matthew in the cell across the way.

"Now I know why you guys always win. You're all fucking nuts."

Chapter Sixteen

Dumuzi came slowly awake, and without opening his eyes, he sniffed. Wet dog? *Nope.* He shifted his weight. *Shit.* It wasn't Archie snuggled up to him. The god lifted a hand to the warmth smashed up against him, and his fingers curled around...fuck. Was that the underside of a breast? Gods-dammit, this wasn't his dog. It was...shit and fucking no way. It was Verrie. Was she crazy? Had she confronted his swamp-side? Did she have a death wish?

He tore his eyes open and found himself staring into her bright, swallowtail-blue depths which at the moment held more than just a hint of...amusement? *What?* Was she frigging kidding him? He had to be hallucinating. She hadn't really entered his cell and confronted his alter-self, had she? Dumuzi blinked, then groaned when she flashed her teeth in a wide smile. *Hell yeah, she had.* And that pissed him off. He pushed her angrily off his, *ah shit,* naked lap.

"What the fuck were you thinking?" He stood up and backed away from his future mate, reaching for the jeans he'd shed the previous night before morphing, tugging them up his legs. He gave Verrie what he hoped was a hard, cold stare.

"Well good morning to you too, sunshine." She moved gracefully from the floor and without meeting

his word challenge, brushed dried mud off her shirt—
his dried mud. Dumuzi groaned.

"Is it?" He found his volume rising. "Is it really a
good morning? Did you ever consider last night you
might not be around to see one?" He picked up his t-
shirt and pulled it over his head.

"Don't be silly," she began, but Dumuzi was on a
roll.

"I won't have this, Veronica. I won't. You have no
idea the kind of danger I pose. Mate or not, you will
never again sleep in the same room with me. And the
advent of you entering my life will not make me give
up the calm personality I've worked so hard to
achieve."

"Calm personality?" Her voice rose an octave to
match his tone. "Calm personality?" she repeated. "Oh,
do you mean your *detached* personality?" Verrie's eyes
sparked up at him. If she were taller, she would have
damned well tested him nose-to-nose, completely
unintimidated. "It seems since the moment you saw me,
you've had a hard time holding on to *that* threadbare
old security blanket, haven't you?"

Before he could respond, Emesh spoke up from
outside the cell, yawning. "She has a point, Muze. I've
certainly never seen you this jazzed even back in the
day when we were constantly being dismembered in
Hell. I mean, shit man, the rest of us always craved
what you'd been smoking to help take the edge off.
Sucked for us that it was just your own natural-
avoidance-high. Where's all that non-attitude now,
swamp-boy? Funny how it seems to have gone bye-
bye."

Dumuzi glowered. His fists opened and closed. Emesh's sunshiny face was about to get pulverized and…argh. There it was again. *Feelings. Anger.* He looked down at a body suddenly clenched. His dick was hard again. *Lust.* He turned and gripped the bars of his cell, attempting to slow his racing heart.

"Why don't you just go fuck her and get it out of your system?" Matthew's face moved between the bars of the nearby cage to taunt him. "Then maybe you can get back to stoner-central where you belong."

Dumuzi's vines appeared again from his very human-looking arms, shot through the osmium bars and across the narrow hall to grab the god by his throat. He felt the tips of his fangs punch down, positioning themselves to tear flesh. Matthew's silent laugh taunted him.

Go ahead. Bite me, you freak. I'm a god, so I'll heal, but what about you? Will you ever get back to the way you were?

Oh, Matthew was really good at head games, Muze glowered.

Will you ever heal from whatever's had you running and hiding like a baby for thousands of years?

Dumuzi dropped his tendrils as though they'd been burned and backed away. Without turning to look at Veronica, he wrenched open the door to the cell and bolted down the hallway. He couldn't get away quickly enough.

"Well, hell. He was a lot nicer when he was the swamp-beast," Veronica's whispered words followed him to the elevator, and Muze groaned in pain.

Why? Why did he have to sense emotion again? He wanted nothing more than to escape to his room, to go

170

back to being calm. This roller-coaster of feelings his mate provoked in him wasn't good. It was just as Matthew said, he *had* been hiding for years, and it had served him well, better than anything else ever had. But now, there intruded the titillating words and soft body of his woman, his *Chosen. No. Stop letting her in.* He needed to get back to his happy place, his haze of existence. And dammit, he would. Nobody would stop him. He hit the button, and the doors opened, then closed silently behind him. *Done.*

The elevator came to the main floor. Dumuzi exited the lift and strode determinedly across the large foyer, ignoring the call from Huxley who had come in through the front door, juggling three large bags of bagels. He took the grand staircase two treads at a time. He'd do his duty. He'd undergo the amulet ceremony with Veronica—the sooner, the better. He'd even complete the gods-damned ritual with a mating—a *single* mating. Then he'd be done. He had every faith Marduk would figure things out for Veronica and Sienna, and Lahar and Shamash would come back from the Middle East with answers. They just wouldn't involve him. *No way. No how.*

By the time he hit his room, Archie had joined him, and the happy pup danced in circles, hoping for a walk in the woods. "Sorry, Arch," Dumuzi reached down and scratched the dog's head. "I need to get my calm on which means a whole lot of doing nothing." He shut the door behind him with a firm click.

****

"Well that wasn't very helpful," Verrie wrinkled her nose and stepped out of the cell to join the group of four who looked at her worriedly.

171

"Crap, I thought you had him eating out of your hand until he freaked," Candy shrugged her shoulders, looking as puzzled as everyone else.

Emesh draped an arm over Verrie's shoulders. "First of all, don't despair," he advised. "We all had problems we couldn't face until our *Chosen* came along to help us." He reached his free hand toward Douglas who took it and squeezed.

"That's right," Candy agreed. "And some, like my husband, only let go of shit after kicking and screaming to the bitter end." She joined Emesh and gave Verrie a big hug. "Don't give up on him. As soon as the two of you are mated, he'll be fine, and he won't know what hit him."

Verrie looked at the well-meaning group and instantly made up her mind. "You know what? I don't want to have things resolve because of some magic, hocus-pocus chemistry thing. I want him to mate me with joy in his heart and his eyes wide open."

"Not easy when you're pretending to be stoned." The voice of Matthew cut into the love fest, and Verrie actually laughed. As much as her hosts didn't like this character, he'd jabbed a few home truths at Dumuzi, and she appreciated his candor. Making up her mind, she determined her secondary task while in residence was to see if she could help mend fences between the upper-story gods and their dungeon guest. That should give her mind something to dwell on when she got sick of beating her head against Dumuzi's deep, dark, impenetrable forest of a brain.

"Matthew, if you stop being such an asshole for a second, you might get a little more positive attention," Verrie shot over at him. "Listen, as soon as I go kick

Dumuzi's ass, I'll be back to hear the story of your life. And don't think you can pull anything over on me. I'm used to dealing with the worst of the worst—high-schoolers."

The prisoner's bark of laughter warmed her heart as she and her immortal entourage left the basement. Her session with the prisoner would probably be the high point of her day. Because she knew, at least for the immediate future, her interactions with Dumuzi would mostly suck.

The group rode in silence to the surface.

"What was that all about?" Marduk—along with a large backup group, all stuffing bagels into their mouths—stood with arms folded across his massive chest to confront them as soon as they cleared the lift. "Muze wouldn't even look in our direction when he stormed upstairs." Using the term "stormed," Verrie knew, didn't come lightly to the thunder god's tongue.

"He was agitated," Jake stated, grabbing breakfast from a nearby bag. When Marduk just looked at him, he qualified. "Yeah, agitated. That's all."

Candy filled in the gaps. "He woke up this morning to find he'd spent the night in his cell with Verrie, and it made him furious. Then he was completely pissed off to find himself furious. Apparently, the man hasn't allowed a true emotion to seep into his viscera in thousands of years. Now with his intended in residence, he's got more than he can handle." She helped herself to food when she finished.

"And I plan on needling him as much as possible," Verrie stated. If she had sleeves to roll up, she would have done so. "I know what he's up to. He's planning on mating with me, then ditching me so he can go back

173

to being Mr. Apathetic. Well, I've got news for him—it isn't going to happen. I've been married once, then jettisoned because I had voices visiting my head. Now this one thinks mating with me might get *rid* of the voices and will subsequently attempt to ignore me once we've been joined in unholy matrimony." She looked around to make sure her daughter wasn't in the room.

"Well, I say, fuck that," she spit. "I want a husband who is man enough to stick by me no matter what, and if you guys say Dumuzi is it, then he sure as shit won't be burying his head in a swamp while I'm around." She looked at the god-audience who had amassed and ignored the bagels to concentrate on more important issues. "Now, who's going to show me which room is his?"

Lenore danced forward. "Me, me," she chortled, licking cream cheese off her lip. "But before we go up, if it hasn't happened already, may I be the first to welcome you to Casa-del-immortals. And let me add, you are going to make one kick-ass addition to the Goddess League."

"Goddess League?" Verrie raised her eyebrows.

Charlie, the demure little blonde spoke up. "Sometimes, when our husbands get out of hand and start throwing their weight around a little too much, we women have to step in and head them off at the pass," she giggled. "So we created a group that intervenes. It's not healthy if they get to make *all* the decisions around here."

"Unless it's in the bedroom," Addie-May poked Charlie in the ribs.

It took Verrie a split second to connect that comment with the "special" room she'd seen in the basement. *Huh.* A nice couple of subbies? Wouldn't they be surprised to find she was just the opposite? Some definite fun to be had in the future…but only if their husbands were up for some group playtime—not necessary but diverting to contemplate.

"I'd be honored to join your Goddess League once I've been properly accepted as a mate. For that," she looked upward toward the doorways leading away from the staircase, "I'll need to set things straight with my intended. So, if you'll excuse me?" She looked to Lenore who didn't hesitate to raise her palm for a high five before turning and leading her up the stairs.

Halfway down the hall, Lenore paused in front of a door and flourished a hand at its closed surface. "Your reluctant groom's suite, M'lady," she smirked. Before Verrie could make a move, Lenore raised her fist and knocked.

"Muze? You have company."

A sleepy voice, completely devoid of emotion answered her query. "Go away, Lenore. I'm resting."

Oh, so it was going to be like that. Minutes out of her company and he'd already wrapped his protective thicket around himself again. *Well, screw that.*

"Dumuzi, open the door. It's Verrie."

"Go away." His voice acquired a bit of an edge. That was good.

"I'm not leaving," Verrie replied. "Now unlock the door and let me in."

"No."

She almost laughed at the one-word reply. He was trying to maintain a hold on his impassivity, but it wouldn't last long. She looked at Lenore.

"May I?" the platinum blonde offered.

Verrie didn't know what the goddess had in mind, but she gave an affirmative nod, and *damn,* she wished she'd had her phone ready. Sienna would have loved this snap-chat. The five-foot-two spitfire, dressed in a hot pink micro-skirt and six-inch silver heels, raised one sparkly shoe, and let loose at the door with a resounding thud, smashing it in with one, well-placed kick. Executing a sweep of her arm, she smirked, "He's all yours."

"Thank you, Lenore," Verrie couldn't keep the shit-eating grin off her face as she crossed the threshold. *Damn.* She was going to get herself some of those awesome strong-lady powers…and a pair of those killer shoes. She closed the broken door as best she could.

One glance to where Dumuzi lay on the bed and Verrie saw he'd somehow managed to ignore the wood-bashing incident. She snorted. Before she was finished with him, it was the only thing he'd be able to ignore.

"Dumuzi?" She let the full purr of the inner kitty—she now knew she had one from long-ago Sham—vibrate across her vocal cords.

"What?" He had one arm flung over his face, and he wasn't budging.

"Are we still on track to get married?" She saw him flinch. Ah-ha, not the question he'd been expecting.

"Mated. But, yes, we are," he grumbled lazily.

"Well, then," she licked her lips. It was a shame his eyes were closed, and he hadn't seen that. "Are we still going to…get naked together?"

Okay. A decided stirring in Mr. Swamp-master's jeans.

"Yeah, I guess that's going to happen too." He kept his voice nicely devoid of emotion, but his pants were still busy tenting and wasn't that a good "tell."

She let the silence draw on for several minutes until he gave up his pretense of muteness. "Why are you asking?" The question barely trickled through his pursed lips.

"No reason, except…" She moved forward quietly and sat on the side of the bed. She felt him tense up at the mattress's movement. "I think we ought to get the sex thing out of the way. Especially if you plan on ignoring me after the ceremony. I've been warned. The ladies say sex performed after the formal rite is almost unavoidable. And since you want to remain aloof, you can't want that." She shrugged, so the bed moved. "So, that being the case, you'll be leaving me completely horny…which will make me want to jump your friends…or your friend's wives. However, if we take the edge off now, perhaps I can behave myself."

Was that a growl she heard from her aloof man? Just what she'd hoped for. If it was one thing she'd picked up on, the gods were very possessive of "their" women and couldn't sanction intercourse with another male…*or* female.

"You won't be having sex. Period," he grated, and Verrie laughed, a light, trilling sound.

"Is that so?" she mocked. "I'll have you know, I've got a healthy libido that has gone far too long without gratification, and if the ceremony gets me all ramped up, I'll probably go on a tear."

His twitchy cock looked mighty tempting. Verrie wished the maddening god would just give in already.

"So, you think it'll help if you do it...now?" He tried to keep his voice cool, but Verrie heard the underlying heat. She let out a pent-up breath. *Yes!* He was going to comply.

"I do." She reached for the button on his jeans, only to have his hand come down and clamp over hers to keep it from moving.

Now what? Hadn't he just given things the green light?

"What are you doing?" his hitherto even voice broke like an adolescent's.

Really? He was asking that? Never into head games, she had enough of his vacillation.

"Fine then. If you didn't want to, all you had to do was say so," she snapped. Verrie yanked her hand out from underneath his, scooted to the side of the bed and jumped up. "I need to use the bathroom if you'll excuse me." There, let him stew for a few minutes. It wouldn't hurt.

Verrie washed her face, found a toothbrush under the sink, and brushed her teeth before allowing herself a few extra minutes to relax on the toilet. Getting up, she straightened her clothes determinedly and walked back into the bedroom to stand over her reluctant mate.

"No more bullshit. If you want this, and I'm not allowed to touch your pants, you do it," she ordered. "Unfasten your jeans. Right now." She rocked her schoolmarmish tone and...bingo. Just as she surmised. Her poor Dumuzi looked almost relieved to have her making the decisions.

Without a fight, he popped the button to his pants and lowered his zipper. She already knew he was flying commando, and that worked to her advantage. She got a tantalizing peek at a lush, fiery trail that led southward, the material still shielding her eyes from his entire glorious nether-mane. *Damn.* She couldn't wait to see her real redhead in all his glory. Their closet tryst had been too dark for a real look.

"Now, get off the bed and stand in front of me."

The god moved quickly for someone who was supposedly disinterested, and when he stood no more than a foot away with his penis still hidden, she issued her next order. "Take your dick out of your jeans and hold it toward me." Verrie was exciting herself, mouth watering with anticipation. She could hardly wait. She'd already tasted his salty sweetness once, and her panties were wet thinking about doing it again.

His shoulders finally relaxed, and he gave a reluctant but sultry grin.

Thank the gods, he was going to join in to play the game in earnest. He drew forth his turgid shaft with languorous agony, the bulbous head of his beautiful pink cock finally slipping free. *Luscious.* He stroked it competently.

"Lovely," she breathed. "I see you're really good at handling yourself, but can you handle this?" she taunted, dropping to her knees at his feet.

"Feed that big prick into my mouth. I haven't had breakfast," she teased. A groan escaped him and he moved closer. Holding his prick at an angle, he ran his rod of velvety soft steel back and forth across her lips. She opened for him, and he slowly pushed in. Verrie sucked hard, just once, then abruptly drew away. His dissatisfaction was demonstrated with a growl. She had him now.

"Put your hand on the back of my head and fuck my mouth," Verrie demanded in her naughtiest voice, and the god moaned his approval.

She swallowed his exquisite length as he thrust, opening her throat, and taking him deep. He fisted a hand in her hair, first pushing, then pulling. On his withdrawals, she tickled her tongue up the underside of his solid shaft, teasing the long vein that ran from the base to just under the smooth head. She swiped at his creamy slit, then followed his drive back down, inhaling him again and again as he found his rhythm.

Somewhere along the way, she cupped his balls, and it didn't take long before she felt them draw up into his body.

"I'm going to come, Veronica," he hissed, attempting to pull away. She grabbed his solid ass with both hands, digging her nails into his flanks, forcing him to stay in her hot mouth. No way he'd deprive her.

Verrie closed her eyes, waiting, and relished the first spurts of his release deep in her throat. She moaned around him, sucking and listening to his now strident cries as he emptied himself, and she savored the taste and texture of his release. God, there was nothing better.

She drew away slowly, giving him some final licks and relishing his aftershocks. She'd been so excited, she'd probably marked his smooth ass with half-moons, but she didn't regret it. And being a god, he'd get over it. She briefly allowed her eyes to close and inhaled his earthy scent. Okay. Marduk had been right. She'd certainly found her happy place with Dumuzi. There was something to be said about fate. She slowly began to work her mouth from his cock.

"Are we done here?" Dumuzi's voice cut through her fog.

Her first thought was, "What the fuck?" He could dismiss her when he'd been sucked to satisfaction? *Oh, hell no.* They were absolutely one hundred percent *not* finished, and she was going to let him know it. "We are so far from…" He thrust his still hard dick between her protesting lips, effectively silencing her.

"Let me rephrase that," he interrupted, his voice sounding not indifferent as she'd feared, but, well… pleased. "I meant that as a statement to say *you're* done here." He pulled his cock out and lifted her up from the floor in one swift motion. Her face was suddenly even with his intense, growling visage. "I've played this your way, and it was fun, but I like being in charge."

Her pussy clenched, and wetness bloomed. *Wow.* She should have figured from what happened in the closet, Dumuzi wasn't going to let her have total charge. Something new for Verrie. She'd been the sexual dominant with Dwight Dickhead, her one and only lover, until he'd booted her out because of her "freakishness" not only in the head but in the bedroom. *Yeah.* It was on him that in the end, he couldn't own up to liking his natural submissiveness.

She'd always wondered how it would be… Verrie looked deep into Dumuzi's firm and assertive eyes. *Yup.* He meant business, and *she* was going to have to submit. The thought actually thrilled her. The only question was, how was she going to "top" from the bottom?

Chapter Seventeen

Everybody, to me.

"Are you shitting me?" Dumuzi blinked, mere inches from Veronica's incredulous eyes. He knew she'd heard it too. "He wants us back in that freaking meeting room, *now*?"

Dumuzi had remained a peaceful, laid-back soul for years and years, but all that hard-won placidity had disappeared in the last twenty-four hours, culminating in this moment. And he wasn't about to waste it. He was ready to rip Marduk's head from his shoulders. Seriously? Another cock-block? How many did this make for the thunder god who was going to regret he had a tongue...or a mind with which to speak? This was *so* not happening.

Dumuzi needed—right now...not hours from now—to be buried deep within Veronica's welcoming pussy, pushing his way into her wet core. *Not* pushing around policy with his fellow gods. Surely, Marduk and company could solve whatever they needed to without him? Had he ever, in the past two thousand years, rocked the boat and gone against the tide? Hell, no. He'd always just let them flap their jaws and complacently gone along with whatever they decided. That record was about to be broken, right the hell now. Enough was enough with the interruptions.

Busy here, Marduk, Muze sent out, nipping his intended's chin and receiving a delicious shiver in return.

Not giving you a choice, Marduk barked back. *We have visitors. This can't wait.*

Marduk threw up a mental wall, so it would do no good to argue further, the boss god wouldn't even hear him. *Fuck.* A quick decapitation or a slow evisceration? Muze would have to think on it. Marduk had however long it took him to get downstairs to remain intact.

Dumuzi gently placed Veronica's feet on the floor. Exhaling a pained sigh, he quickly zipped his pants.

"Don't think this resets your opportunity to 'lead,'" he warned, sending a quick hand around to grasp her sweet little ass and give it a predatory squeeze. He wanted to roar. She'd had his cock in her mouth twice already, and he had yet to get her out of a single piece of clothing. That would change the very next instant they were alone.

"Wouldn't think of it," she breathed, and it sounded sincere.

"Fine." He was satisfied he'd be in charge when the next private opportunity arose. He didn't mind her dominance…as long as he had equal time. "Then let's go see Marduk," he huffed, every inch of his body on edge, crying out for hers. "And he better make it fast."

He took Veronica's hand, pulling her to the door. Halfway there, her stomach gave a deep rumble. Dumuzi stopped. He laughed. Sexual tension broken.

"Okay, with a quick stop in the kitchen so you don't pass out from hunger when Marduk gets long-winded…because I've decided not to kill him." His sudden need to provide for her, protect her shouldn't have surprised him considering her *Chosen* status, but he was nonplussed nonetheless.

"I've just had my protein for the morning," Veronica teased with a satisfied purr. "It's you who're going to need the calories...for later." She dropped his hand and exited the room with an exaggerated sway of her hips.

Damn. Hard again. The sexy, bossy woman made his whole being come alive with her innuendo. Dumuzi couldn't remember the last time he'd felt so aware, mentally or physically. Way back in ancient times, he'd successfully shut himself down, never again over the centuries seeing the world in color. And now? Not only had colors suffused his existence since Veronica's arrival, they were accompanied by bloody fireworks.

When the whole "find your Chosen" thing had first been unveiled, he'd assumed he could remain aloof from whomever he was supposed to partner. Dumuzi shook his head. What a fucking dolt. None of his mated brothers had been successful with that during their mating frenzies, so why had he thought to be any different? Maybe because he hadn't really been paying much attention...but now? Well, now his eyes were open—*wide open.*

He followed his authoritative woman down the hall, catching up with her as her foot hit the first step downward. Roaring his best he-man roar, he scooped her up aggressively and threw her over his shoulder.

"Muze! What are you doing?" she squealed.

"Establishing my dominance," he mock-growled, giving her a slap on her derrière. He expected argument or perhaps hands beating his backside in return. What he wasn't prepared for was her howl of laughter.

"This isn't dominance, you cave-creature…"

Hmph. Smart woman, realizing he'd never be a cave-*man*.

"…this is strong-arm tactics."

Dumuzi grinned because it sounded like Veronica was enjoying herself.

"And now you've thrown down the gauntlet," she snickered, wiggling her behind—which was mere inches from his face—provocatively. "I'm a master at this, Dumuzi," she chortled. "You'll never come out on top."

"Sweetheart, you'll be begging for me to be on top before I'm finished with you."

"Oh, you did not just call me sweetheart? You will pay for that, mister…"

The banter continued all the way down the stairs and into the kitchen where he allowed her—still ass-up, over his shoulder—to snag a couple of bagels before heading to the now too familiar meeting room, setting her on her feet only before they entered.

In the collective gods' first four hundred years in the compound, they'd used the room perhaps once a month. Now, it had become a multiple-times a day occurrence. *Figures*. Just when he had better things to do.

"Thank you all for coming…again." Marduk, the asshole, actually smirked over at him as they found a spot on the wall that wasn't occupied. "I'm sure I didn't interrupt anything important."

Oh, he was *so* going to pay.

"As you can see, Marla and Jeremiah are back with us."

Dumuzi felt Veronica wedge herself firmly behind him, peering out at what was probably a very odd sight. Despite her sexual dominance, she really was fairly timid, he could see how she might be freaked. How often did one have a full-sized male lion in the house? It was a good thing Sienna, Riley, and the feisty Frank hadn't been invited to the meeting. Sienna, for one, would be all over the fierce feline with multiple questions and eager hands. Dumuzi wasn't sure how Jeremiah would take that.

The vegetation god smiled and stroked Verrie's arm reassuringly, but she still kept herself partially hidden. In this situation, it wasn't a case of like mother like daughter.

Marduk continued, "Nergal has also rejoined us."

In Dumuzi's opinion, the king looked a little worse for wear at having to flip back and forth between realms so many times in the past few days…or it might be fatigue from dealing with his very pregnant queen.

Jake and his group of agents strode through the open door with Matthew in their midst. "Okay, Marduk. I think we're all here," Jake nodded. Dumuzi knew he meant with the exception of Shamash and Lahar who were probably, at the moment, knee deep in ancient ruins.

"Marla, would you like to take charge of the meeting?" Marduk sat down and gave the room over to the Feline Operations Agent.

"Thank you, god." Marla's Slavic accent was easier to bear, now they all knew she was on their side. "Since getting communication from enemy, Ridhwan, and finding he thinks prisoner he holds is Queen of Nergal." She inclined her head toward the king but speared Matthew with a quelling look when he gasped at that news. "Oh yes, frumos baiat, I see they have not told you. Our Bel is smart one, yes? She is taken and makes herself more valuable to Ridhwan, posing as wife to Underworld ruler."

Dumuzi explained briefly to Veronica. *Ridhwan is a new enemy, and while trying to kidnap Sham and Quinn for the purposes of fulfilling some fucked up prophecy, he ended up taking Matthew's mate, Beletseri.*

Muze wondered at Marla's familiarity with Matthew. She had called him a handsome boy, if his language skills weren't rusty, then tagged Bel with a possessive "our." Was there more to the trio's connection than everyone knew? Marla had been held by the pair for a short while a few weeks back. He'd be quite interested to find out what occurred within that short amount of time.

"We confiscated laptop of Quinn and have received more…instruction…for return to us of fake queen. First, we know Ridhwan wishes to trade for me—because of hate—and cat god Shamash and goddess Quinn for prophecy." She gave a truncated quote of said prediction. "It is written that cat-goddess will be born and will join forces with full cat god. That couple will be salvation of all."

Marla explained her position once again, "We cat shifters believe it true, and Ridhwan also believes. His interest, to gain control of realms by seizing Shamash and Quinn, two he thinks are named in prophecy. Bad cat shifter believe if he rules rulers, he is ultimate power. And why does he want me?" She shrugged unemotionally. "Me, he will kill."

"So, what are these new instructions?" Marduk asked, ignoring the prediction of her demise.

"Here, things get tricky," Marla nodded pointedly. "King Nergal is supposed to bring us to designated swap area, trade us for would-be queen, and is done. Ridhwan has three strong cat friends. We each have personal thug-guard while Ridhwan uses special power to transport us one by one to lair. All done. End of story. He owns cat god and goddess. He rules world."

"You've come up with a plan?" Marduk asked.

Marla shook her head. "We at first think we all go directly to Ridhwan's secret place to make trade and use special necklace to bring invisible, undetectable god with us to defeat him. Now is not possible. We meet at neutral location, and god cannot travel as quickly as Ridhwan from meeting point to lair."

Dumuzi quickly told Veronica, *Gods give off a distinct energy whether visible or invisible. We have a necklace which blocks that. The problem is gods have to travel, albeit quickly, from place to place. Ridhwan has a special ability to make any trip instantly. So, with a remote location involved, no god—even with the necklace—will be able to follow.*

"That doesn't mean I can't go," Dorian, the resident warlock spoke up. Dumuzi felt Veronica shiver behind him. Why the dark, magic one had that effect on women, he didn't know.

"My invisible energy is undetectable, and I should be able to follow Ridhwan easily. Furthermore, I can transport one other being with me who can wear the necklace." His eyes went around the room, assessing who should accompany him.

Jeremiah the lion's imperative roar cut through the room. All eyes turned to Quinn for translation. She complied in her evolving god-headspeak. *He say that make three of you.* Quinn was yet to be fully fluent in mind-talk, but she got more proficient all the time. *He travel instant and invisible as well, and his feline scent will blend with Ridhwan's other cats. Make him undetectable.*

"That's all very well," Marduk interjected. "But about the ones Ridhwan wants? We know Sham will go, but we're taking it for granted Quinn will agree to be included." The thunder god looked at Shamash's goddess. "You don't have to go if you don't want to. We can find another way."

Hah. Try stop me, the bold little pixie postured. *Where Sham go, I follow. No need to change plan.*

Marduk nodded, convinced by her conviction and was just about to bang the proverbial gavel for dismissal when Candy cleared her throat. The thunder god raised his brows.

"I know we should be done here, so forgive me for asking," Candy interjected, standing up and facing the crowd. "But why exactly are we all warm and fuzzy, running to rescue Bel now? If I'm not mistaken, she's the bitch who's been making our lives a misery, holding goddesses against their will,"—she looked at Dani-Lee—"and torturing agents."

Nobody needed that reminder of what had been done to Ken.

This time Nergal answered. "That's a fair question," he exhaled a deep sigh, "and I'll try to answer as honestly as possible."

Did the big deity look pained?

"I'm afraid when it comes right down to it, I might have been partially responsible for making her into the woman she's become." This time he turned and spoke directly to Matthew who had been listening avidly to all that had gone on. "It seems I was guilty of exploiting her before she turned on us, sequestering her away from any semblance of a real life…for millennia. She was very good at her job, and because of that, I saw her as having only one use. Even when she tried to, uh, convince me otherwise, I chose to brush her off. Hence, she was vastly overworked, completely ignored,"—he gave each and every god a cold stare. He wasn't about to take the personal rejection of Bel all on his own shoulders—"and eventually, I accused her of a crime which subsequently I find she did not commit."

Nergal's baby was killed in his crib, and it was thought Bel was the murderess…which she was not. Dumuzi told Veronica.

"Furthermore," Nergal kept on, "it has been ascertained the goddess Beletseri is now with child, and despite the other crimes for which she will still stand trial, her young godling should not suffer."

Matthew listened silently to this, head down, gripping his hands into tight fists.

"Okay," Candy snarked. "Long-winded much? You could have saved your breath. You would have had me at 'preggers' if you'd thrown it out first…your wordliness."

The king's lips curled up at Enlil's wife. There was no denying it. The irreverent goddess/agent could get away with murder where the royal was concerned. The two had a stare-down.

Dumuzi swore if the pair weren't married to others…

"Fine then," Marduk spoke into the awkward silence. "It's decided then. The only thing left to do is draw straws to see which one of us piggy-backs with Dorian." He looked around at all the eager faces. Adventures had been hard to come by until recently, and all the immortals craved action in any form. "But just a reminder, we are on hold until Sham gets back from his fact-finding mission in Mesopotamia with Lahar. Marla, will you be able to put Ridhwan off for a while?" he questioned.

Marla gave her signature shrug again. "He has not indicated timetable for trade. We will stall…" The FO agent's words broke down into nothing more than a buzz in Dumuzi's head as Archie nudged up against him. At the same time he registered the clenching of his stomach that was the precursor to a transformation. *Bloody hell.* The fucking demons were getting ready to push him right now? Hadn't this full moon already caused three separate episodes?

Otherworldly screeching filled his brain. He attempted to take deep breaths through his nostrils while alerting his friends. "Marduk! Changing," he growled. "Find Sienna. Protect Veronica. The demons are…making contact."

The last was no more than a howl, but he hadn't lost consciousness yet. "Lock me away. Quickly."

Archie was at his side, whining. He reached down a hand and felt the dog's soft tongue licking his wrist.

Wait. Why was he still tacitly aware? Normally, when he reached this point, he was a goner. And voices taunted *him*, but Veronica stood still, unaffected.

Gaddawah degga? Who is the monster? he heard.

Dumuzi struggled to answer. *Uggel e gun gaddawah nugta. I am a god, not a monster. Gralt geh ech dubt glah e tat. Leave her or I will kill you.*

A part of Dumuzi, still rational, communicated with the fiends from hell. How was that possible? Had his monster picked up their language from years of listening to them? It had to be the answer, but why, if he had been aware of them all this time in his alternate form, hadn't they been able to contact him?

Now, not only was he linked up to them, his semi-changed persona had him certain the demons were leaving Veronica and Sienna alone this time. *Veronica.* She stood next to him. He felt her, and the foolish woman had a strong hold on the arm Archie wasn't licking. She needed to run, or…maybe not. He hadn't hurt her last night, and he felt her now, knew her now. He was all…different.

I'm here. He heard her words and understood them.

We're all here, Marduk's voice penetrated as well.

Dumuzi looked around the room, and through a thick green haze, he made out the faces that ringed him. He could name each one. Still, his hackles were up as he tasted potential danger on his tongue.

Voices back, he warned.

That's right, Muze. We're hearing them through you. We need to find them. Keep them engaged. Dumuzi nodded his big, heavy head. His head. He blinked.

Wow, he'd never been aware of it before, but his monster's cranium was damned large and weighted.

Degga bah glah? Dumuzi asked. *Who are you?*

Ut nught dwigg ent. Do not seek us.

Muze was dimly aware that Dagon...or was it Nergal...was now interpreting for the group.

Uggla ga tat dubt. We will kill the goddess.

Dumuzi howled. *Glah bah dubt gol. You are the ones who will be killed,* he promised. *Ga beh bagga-glah, Gaddawah-Uggel tat ned-paggech. When we find you, the god-monster will make you pay.*

Apparently, that scared them. The connection was severed.

Dumuzi's mind, unfettered by demons went strangely quiet. He stood in the meeting room. He knew he was the monster. A terrifying grip twisted around his heart. What would his monster do now? It always took him hours to come down from his altered state. Should he be confined...or let loose in the woods to run it off? Dumuzi realized he was scared of this new awareness.

Marduk? His voice was a plea to the god who always had the answers. He was floundering and needed guidance. But it was Veronica's voice he heard first, requiring something different of Marduk...of his friends.

"What do you all do when you change into your other selves? What helps get you back to normal?"

"We usually go kick the shit out of somebody...or each other." Anshar sounded pleased.

The answer was something Dumuzi heard and expected. He'd helped them all through their alter-egos.

"What...?" Verrie hesitated. "Isn't that crazy? Don't you get hurt?"

LJ Vickery

Dumuzi looked toward the all-sky god and not only was the jokester grinning from ear to ear, but if his green miasma wasn't playing tricks on him, there was a definite snout emerging from the middle of the other god's face. *Well, hello and hell, yeah.*

Want to meet a serpent in the gym? Anshar growled, his fangs gleaming as they descended.

Or maybe two? Dagon's dorsal fins were not far behind, and the dark serpent looked downright gleeful at the thought of joining the fight. *I always fancy a little mud-wrestling.*

"Really?" Veronica's voice rose beside him. "This is your answer? To go beat the shit out of each other?"

Dumuzi thought he should be feeling a bit ashamed in front of Veronica, but mostly a delicious blood-lust began to wash over him. He quickly forgot about propriety and rumbled pleasurably, deep in his chest in answer to the serpents calls.

"I guess I have your opinion," she snorted and un-twined her hand from his...vines.

The goddesses stuck up for the way of the immortals. "Don't knock it girl, until you've watched the show." Glory came over and hooked her elbow through Verrie's. "Hot gods, hot monsters. Oh, yes. Totally lickable. There's nothing like a good knock-down-drag-out to take the tension off and ramp libidos up. Come on," she urged, pulling Verrie through the door. "Quickly now. Or all the good seats will be taken."

Dumuzi stretched to his full eight-foot height. *Oh. This was good.* There had never been a time in his life where he could remember feeling so anticipatory...so in tune with himself. Meeting his monster like this, acknowledging his other half was like finding a part of himself that had always been lost. It felt damned good, and as he settled into the sensations, he seemed to gain even more control. It was a heady awareness.

Green tendrils shot to the ceiling in lush celebration, and Dumuzi laughed...actually laughed...as the spirals came cascading back down toward Anshar and Dagon to begin poking relentlessly at the duo. In reply, they looked extremely annoyed. *Hah.* His coils had a sense of humor.

The beings in the room who had yet to file out thought this was hilarious, and bets were placed to see if money could be made on who would come out on top. Marduk one-upped the pot, telling the gods only the ones who bet on the winner would be entered into the "go-see-Ridhwan" lottery. It added to the general, overall reckless enthusiasm.

What a billing, thought Muze who was still amazed his mind remained his. *Serpents vs. Mud-monster.* GWF. Gods Wrestling Federation and this was the Saturday Morning Slam.

Within minutes, everyone amassed in the huge gym which encompassed the entire middle of the compound. Weight equipment was quickly moved and mats rearranged. Dumuzi noticed—he actually noticed—Nergal had called his wife Ereshkigal up from hell for the festivities. It had become an actual event.

He turned his green, murky eyes around the room and found Veronica. She wasn't looking exactly happy, but she wasn't scowling either. He postured and pulsated in her direction like an egotistical boggy-body-builder and won a small twist of her lips. *Shit.* He was ready to win this thing. It sure beat his normal being out-of-control rampaging. If he could continue to keep himself from running amok, he was going to seriously kick some serpent ass.

Enlil set himself up as referee, going over rules that had no meaning to Dumuzi, probably not to the snarling serpents either. The wind god had barely moved his tender flesh out of the way when fang met fang, and claw met claw. The battle was on.

The twin cousins tried tag-teaming him for a while—one sitting out while the other took him on—but they quickly gave up on that as Dumuzi dominated, using all the peripheral growth on one arm to encircle his victim while the other pummeled the helpless sea-creature. His opponents swiftly came to the conclusion two on one was a much better strategy.

In the end, they still didn't stand a chance. Dumuzi just had too many moving parts, and serpents were…well, serpents, and better suited to water than land. Since both Anshar and Dagon were stubborn 'til the end, neither would call uncle, and Enlil finally had to step in to end the match.

Well. Almost.

Dagon attempted to land one last slashing blow to Dumuzi's mid-section, amidst the hisses from the disgruntled audience, but his arc was deflected by Anshar—who, oddly enough had put money on Muze to win—and the errant claw dug a nasty furrow down the arm of the hapless referee.

So much for the match ending.

Enlil, enraged, turned bull and went after Dagon. Not to be left out, one by one, all the other gods morphed into their various bodies, plowing into the fray, and a fully joyous free-for-all was born.

Dumuzi, remembering his earlier cock-blocking vendetta against Marduk, ardently took on the thunder god, and managed a few good roundhouses before being clocked in the head by a giant polar bear.

As he went down, he caught Nergal pouting imploringly to his wife, who gave him a mock-mournful nod of her head. With a whoop, the king dove in with relish to join the fun.

An hour later, all bashed and bruised when their bodies came back to normal, the group chuckled and wheezed. For Dumuzi—relaxed but not out-of-it for the very first time with his brothers—life had never been so sweet.

Chapter Eighteen

"Well, that was amusing." Veronica stood over Dumuzi whose body draped across a portion of the long kitchen table, twitching while she dabbed at a particularly deep cut on his back. Similar large physiques were strewn in other positions throughout the room, being cared for by their goddesses, but despite the blood and gashes, the combatants all looked extremely satisfied.

Cretins. Veronica bit her lip to keep from smiling.

"That was so cool." Sienna bounced around the room on her toes. "Did you see them all, Mom?"

Yes, she'd seen them, and it had been an unbelievable sight, but she didn't want to add to Sienna's excitement.

"And Dumuzi...wasn't he the coolest of all?" she gushed.

Far from grossing her daughter out, it seemed the swamp-monster intrigued the hell out of Si. That got a semi-upside-down high five from her patient, along with a *"Hell, yeah."*

And Riley was on board as well.

"Totes, Si. He was awesome, but did you check out the king? Oh my God...or I guess you say oh my gods around here, don't you? But really. Sienna, have you ever seen anyone so huge...or cut? Those luscious abs…and his ass. I wanted to bite those muscles when his loincloth slipped up, and I got a good look."

"Enough, Riley." Aunt Frank's voice put an end to the musing about Nergal's rear quarters which was probably for the best as all the immortals in the kitchen were getting a huge kick out of the girl's vivid descriptions.

"Ahn't theah any noahmal guys in this damned house?" Frank moaned. "How ah we evah gonna go back teh ah regulah lives aftah this?"

Marduk, getting treated for a broken nose by his lovely wife Tess, spoke up although stuffily. "Don'd worry aboud dad," he winced. "We hab do make you forged all ob dis before we led you go."

Verrie couldn't hold back her laugh now, and neither could anyone else listening. Between Frank's Boston accent and the thunder god's broken nose inflections, the two were a hilarious duo. Marduk glared around the room, but it did him little good.

"Please, can I *YouTube* this?" Anshar begged.

"No," the chorus of immortal voices sang out in response.

"Ouch," Anshar cried, not because he'd been shut down, but because Lenore yanked a glass splinter from his leg where he'd crashed through the one and only window in the gym, a transom that ran the length of the room but was up…twelve feet. That he'd been thrown that high was beyond impossible, but they'd all seen Dumuzi's monster accomplish the feat.

Damn. Verrie shivered as she ran a hand over her god's well-defined lats. He was one strong pile of lumber and wasn't she looking forward to building a playground out of him later…or climbing to the top of his woodpile…or any number of other really bad metaphors that currently sowed seeds in her lustful mind. *Yumm.* Fun with plant life.

"Mom…Mom."

Verrie came back with a start to an incredulous Sienna who glared at her with hands planted on slender hips. "I asked if you'd let me and Riles take self-defense lessons from Enlil. He offered, but you were too busy drooling over Muze's back to hear," she accused.

"Geez, Si. Give your mom a break." Riley smacked her friend playfully in the head. "She hasn't had a boyfriend since the stone age…and that was your dad who completely sucked ass if you don't mind me saying."

"Yeah, well what about Aunt Frank? Huh? When was the last time she had a boyfriend?"

"Are you shitting me? Gram's a player," Riley scoffed. "She has guys after her all the time."

"Okay, girls. Enough." Verrie shut their verbal parlay right down. "You're just embarrassing us," she grumbled. "And, yeah, fine. Get some self-defense lessons," she said absently.

Verrie felt skewered by the stone age comment, imagining a big red "L" in the middle of her forehead, but what really had her shocked and in schoolmarm mode was catching sight of her normally easygoing friend's face. Frank had turned a mortified shade of red and gaped like a landed trout. And was that…what the hell? Had Ishkur just thrown off a compress Dr. Dani applied and stomped out of the room? Verrie wasn't the only one to notice.

"Whadtha fug is going od?" Marduk spit some blood into the bucket his wife kindly held.

Veronica wished she knew how to answer the god's question. She risked a discreet glance at Frankie and earned a small, curt shake of the head for her troubles. She'd have to catch up with her friend later when there was no rapt audience.

"The window is repaired." Dorian waltzed into the room, tugging on starched, white cuffs that showed the proper half inch below his well-cut black leather jacket. One would never know he had wholeheartedly been part of the earlier brawl. More surprising, his dark, dangerous visage—one that discouraged familiarity—held no menace for her daughter.

"Did you use magic?" she asked him breathlessly, moving close to look up into his coolly handsome face. "Can I see you do something?"

Far from disgruntled, the warlock bowed and presented Si with a blood red rose he plucked from the air.

"Oh my god, that was so *cray*," she squealed, using youthful vernacular.

Verrie felt the need to step in. "I apologize for my daughter, Mr…." Shit. What had she been told his last name was when they'd been introduced?

"Call me Dorian, Ms. Foxie, and I shall call you Verrie." —it wasn't a request— "But please don't worry about your charming daughter's exuberance. I was an adjunct professor at a Massachusetts college some years ago and am used to dealing with young women a good deal sassier than she." He sent his black eyes searching the room for his wife Addie-May who got pink around the cheeks and actually stuck her tongue out at her handsome husband.

"That's so romantic," Sienna sighed, her eyes not missing the heated exchange between the pair. When Dorian snapped his fingers and the couple disappeared, she nearly swooned. "Holy shit. Forget the romantic thing. Those two are smokin' hot."

Dorian must have left an explosion of testosterone in the room when he evaporated because a quick egress by gods and goddesses rapidly took place. Hell, Verrie felt it, and by the change in Dumuzi's breathing under her ministrative hands, her future mate did too. But how was she going to leave with her daughter looking on?

"Riley, Sienna? What say we go have a look-see in the cellah? These guys have dungeons ya know." Frank couldn't have said anything to spark Si's imagination faster.

"I heard about them." Sienna clapped her hands. "I've been dying to look. Can we, Mom? Marduk?" she looked imploringly at them both for permission.

The thunder god was no fool. He gave Verrie a commanding look that positively screamed "go fuck your man," and put his stamp of approval on the girls' trip to the bottom-most floor.

"Go hab fun." The boss-man flinched as Dani put a quick stitch in the slice at the top of his nose. "Jake should be dowed dare pudding Maddew away agaid, but dake a couble ob da agends wid you do be on da sape side."

Verrie heard him call out in his head. *Dunce, tell Flick and Gramps to accompany our human girls to the cellars. Have them get a nice long tour of every level, starting with the dungeon.* The god's head voice was amusingly normal in juxtaposition to his damaged-nose speech. He ran a tongue over his split lip and sent a speculative glance toward Frank before adding, *And don't forget the garages. I'm sure they'd all like to see Ishkur's stable of bikes.*

Funny, Marduk had picked up on the tension between Frank and Ishkur too.

Verrie looked down at her god, who'd turned, propped himself up, and eyed her like she was so much fertilizer. Luckily, Frank had made quick work of clearing out the girls. The ground was clear to have her way with Dumuzi. Thank you, Frank.

You're welcome.

What? No way. That sneaky bitch. When had Frank clued in to hear head-speak? Why had she hidden it? Verrie looked at the stragglers who remained in the kitchen, and not one of them seemed to have heard her buddy. *Huh.* So her friend already had mad skills—better than Verrie's—and could select and direct her god-talk. *Shit.*

You suck, Verrie sent back, acerbically.

"Who sucks?" Muze looked up, bemused at her nasty tone.

She became flustered. "No one, nothing. Forget I said anything," she tried to cover. "I was just thinking to myself, and it got away."

"Oookay." Her god didn't look convinced. It was time for distraction until she could get with Frank and find out what the fuck? It wouldn't be a hardship. Dumuzi was a major diversion who had eluded her for too long. She ran her hands over his bare chest, reached a puckered brown nipple and gave it a firm tweak.

"Uhh." The breath left his body in one quick exhalation. She lowered her head to kiss the affected nub and swirled her warm tongue over his interested protrusion while he cupped the back of her head. "Back to my room?" he questioned through clenched teeth.

Verrie lifted her face to look into deep green eyes. "Lead the way," she purred.

He moved her gently aside, leaped to his feet and bent at the waist, throwing his shoulder into her midsection to stand with her hanging over his back...again. Verrie sighed.

"This is just so you remember who's in charge." He patted her ass.

She could almost feel his impish grin. "Dream on, sport," she threw back, but her brain scrambled. Could she regain control? Did she want to? The rational part of her knew her need to orchestrate in the bedroom was because—since her parents died—her sanity hinged on directing every possible aspect of her life. That had only escalated when she'd found herself at the mercy of the demon voices.

One of the first psychiatrists she'd ever seen had said something to her that stuck. "Try to enjoy sex. You can't feel too crazy if you're busy concentrating on your libido. Orgasm has always been a great distraction from things that ail a troubled soul."

Verrie had embraced that, much to the confusion of Dwight Dickhead...who had always been more than happy with once a month sex. She also began taking total control in the bedroom while making their physical forays more frequent. It had been an okay arrangement. She found she liked being on top, both literally and figuratively, and her dominant side had been born.

Now the question was, faced with a real man…real god, who had hearty desires and by every indication a healthy sex drive, would she call the shots? Would she still want to?

Verrie reached down and pinched Dumuzi's fine ass and loved his little stutter-step. *Uh, huh. Yup.* She would—at least, some of the time.

"You're not going to make this easy, are you?" Dumuzi questioned, teasingly. "Why don't you give up and submit to my godly superiority like a good mate?" He ran a hand up her leg to the juncture of her thighs…not going the last half inch…which admittedly, would have felt damned nice. Despite his admirable attempt at distraction, Verrie noted the curiosity in his voice.

"Me-thinks the gentleman doth protest too much," she beamed, liking their battle. "Why don't you concede I'm going to call all the shots? I'll go easier on you if you're a good boy and don't give me grief," she volleyed.

They reached his bedroom door, and he kicked it open with verve even though it hadn't been repaired from Lenore's assault earlier. Still, Verrie liked the sound of his masculine display and sighed appreciatively.

"The only fight we'll have is any you put up while I strip you naked." His eyes glittered above hers as he dropped her onto the bed. He quickly unzipped and wrenched down his pants, kicking them away.

Gods. Gloriously naked.

"And once your clothes are gone, I'm going to hold your legs open while I eat your succulent pussy, and tongue you until you scream for me to bring you to orgasm. Then I'm going to pull back and plunge this cock"—he unashamedly grabbed his enormous girth, so Verrie had no doubt as to which cock he meant—"deep inside you and hold it completely still until you beg for it, long and loud enough for the whole house to hear. At that point, I'll relent and move inside you until you come stronger and harder than you've ever climaxed before."

The picture he drew was so vivid in Verrie's head, she misplaced her ability to speak and clearly lost this round of dominance. Then why did she feel like the winner?

He stood over her, a chiseled god carved from earth's elements, ready to tear down every wall she'd ever erected, and dammit, all she could do was lick her dry bottom lip and nod her assent. There was not a doubt in her mind Dumuzi would deliver on every one of his promises, and she waved the white flag. For once, she was going to lay back and enjoy the ride.

"Good," he nodded at her acquiescence. His fangs popped out the slightest bit. "I like thhhat." He gave a roguish lisp then joined her on the bed, on his knees. He bent, and using his extended canines, took a grip on the material at her neck and ripped her shirt right down the middle.

Cool air tickled her belly, but Verrie only had seconds to register that before one claw came up and snicked through the front of her bra, severing the halves and laying her swollen B-cup handfuls open for his perusal. Her pink nipples beaded, and she moaned when he dragged a long claw across first one tip, then the other.

"Pretty," he whispered.

She arched her back when he withdrew his touch.

"Soon," he rasped, and with the same ease, he hooked his long barb into the waistband of her jeans, tugging to rent the cloth in two.

"Green panties." His eyes grew warmer as he raked his gaze over her exposed skin and the tiny hipsters of which he clearly approved. Verrie could feel the moist heat coming off him in waves as he took her in like a lush oasis.

"Too bad they won't last long." While one hand pulled the remnants of her pants from her legs, the other tore her panties away, tossing the material aside until she lay completely bare to him. "So beautiful." One tendril escaped from his wrist and wended its way down to part the small strip of hair that covered her most sensitive spot.

Verrie gasped. So deliberate…so alive.

He pulled back with a snap. "Now, that's not the agenda we discussed," he teased. With forceful hands, he moved quickly to push her knees to her chest, pressing them to the sides, parting her completely and exposing her creamy, damp core for his perusal. "That's what I want."

He leaned in and holding her still, dipped his head down and swiped his tongue across her pussy. Verrie moaned. It felt so damned good, and it had been so long. Perversely, she remembered he said he would deny her orgasm, so she reached for it quickly before he became aware she could go over in an instant. But something must have given her away because he backed off, taking his talented tongue with him.

"No coming without my permission." With each distinct syllable, he tapped a smart staccato slap on her cunt. "*If* I'm quoting you, correctly," he chuckled.

Ooh. She squirmed. He'd definitely done this take-charge business before even though he'd let her have the upper hand earlier. So the question remained, how had she managed to get herself a wonderfully dominant, nasty boy who could also play the submissive? *Damned good luck.*

He leaned down and lapped her again, this time circling her clit to delve lightly into her crevice.

She squirmed and panted. "Deeper, Dumuzi. Please." She was so close, it wouldn't take but a second.

He pulled his head back again, and she growled.

"You want deep, Veronica?" he asked. "Do you remember what I said would happen next?" He let go of one knee in order to take himself in hand again.

Verrie could do nothing but watch in fascination as he moved his cock closer and closer to her weeping cunt. She quivered, she jerked. If he didn't put it in soon, she was going to burst into flames.

She felt the soft, smooth head draw through the space between her nether lips. He moved the bulbous tip up and down to gather moistness, and as she went to draw a breath, he thrust into her with one amazing lunge.

"Oh gods," she screamed. Verrie had no chance of stopping her cry. His huge, hot prick stretched her wide and filled her up. Tears of joy came to her eyes. *Shit.* It had been so long.

Dumuzi stilled above her.

"Did I hurt you?" he asked, his voice full of concern as he looked down at her, alarmed at the moisture in her gaze. He gritted his words out around a clenched jaw.

She dropped her hands to his hard, smooth ass, and pulled him tighter. "Not even close," she said smokily. Every nerve ending in her cunt sparked and zinged. She savored every inner twitch and moaned. "Just happy. You feel so damned good."

The tension he held left his face. "So do you, sweetness. But you need to get vocal, fast. Because I'm here to stay until you beg me to take charge, loud enough for everyone to hear."

Verrie couldn't help the smile that touched her lips as she swiveled her ass, relishing the way she could move under him to hit all the right spots. "Uh, Muze? There's only one problem with your plan," she lifted her head up and nipped at his lower lip, giddy over his penetration. "I'm going to come whether you move or not." She could already feel the ripples threading through her channel which made it damned hard to speak, but she forced the words to come. "The only one you're denying is yourself." She hooked her heels over his massive thighs and tipped her pelvis. "So, you might as well join me. I'm not waiting." She arched even higher. "Come with me," she keened.

His cock drew back and plunged deep again... and again. Internal spasms took over, and she clenched around him in ecstasy, her cries of completion moaned into his ear. When she felt him erupt seconds later, her inner muscles gripped and milked him. He roared his satisfaction right alongside her.

It took forever for Verrie to calm the wild pulse in her pussy which seemed to have a life of its own, but Dumuzi didn't seem to be complaining. Every time her muscles re-clenched, he gave an attentive manipulation of his talented equipment which stroked the echoes of her orgasm. He raised his head and stared deeply into her eyes, clearly enjoying the tremors of their after-sex, letting her know with a satisfied smile.

When the shocks finally died out, he gently kissed the end of her nose. She closed her eyes, and he kissed her lids, then brushed the finest of caresses across her parted mouth.

"Veronica?" he said, softly. She almost didn't hear him, she was so sated and near to sleep.

"Hmm?" she thought she answered. Maybe she did.

"I give in. Partially."

Verrie was pretty certain he'd spoken. She wrinkled her nose. *Yeah.* What had he said?

He continued, "Did you hear me? You win…but I win, too."

There it was again. Some lovely declaration. She nodded. If whatever it was made him happy, it made her happy, too.

She sighed and slipped into a warm, welcoming darkness.

Chapter Nineteen

Beletseri was furious. Not with Ridhwan, although he was a total douchebag, but with herself. She lifted up off the cave floor and wiped a hand across her mouth. *What the hell*? Bel despised weakness of any kind, and here she couldn't even control her own body. She felt tired and sick. The goddess didn't want to make excuses for herself, but it had to be the food her shifter-captors were feeding her.

She supposed it was her own fault. She refused to touch the raw meat that was the staple of their diet—Ridhwan allowed no fires for cooking. Therefore, she was relegated to bugs and fruit for her sustenance and could barely choke down the large cockroaches. She kicked dirt over the hole that held the spewed remnants of this morning's wiggling protein. If she couldn't adjust and start keeping the horrible food in her stomach, she'd have no chance of escape.

Godsdamned jungle. Bel walked to the opening of her prison cave. As always, it was guarded by two male cats. She pushed her long, limp hair from her face where the bedraggled locks seemed to constantly be damp with sweat. Ridhawan had better show his fucking face today. She needed a bath in the small river that ran next to the shifter settlement, and since her escape attempt, she wasn't allowed to go without his

211

express permission. Even then, she had to be accompanied by three shifter females and kept on a tethered line so she couldn't run again.

During her weeks of confinement, Bel had used her time wisely and done a thorough reconnaissance. She ascertained, early on, that the small village was under some kind of protective shield which made it undetectable to outsiders. But she also recognized, from the resident's comings and goings, it was not *completely* impregnable against egress. That was a useful bit of information. People, animals, even bugs—shudder—came and went, she just had to figure out how.

She also knew, from keeping a careful watch, how the rotation of guards worked—where they were at what times of day, and how many were employed. Ridhwan's warnings her god-like ability to mist in and out and her head-communications were both useless as long she was within one hundred yards of him was always in the back of her mind.

The day she attempted her escape, now two weeks past, she'd waited until the powerful black leopard shifter was nowhere to be seen, and the guards were at a point farthest from the river. She had permission to bathe that day and had demanded her rights at a time that seemed optimum. After splashing about for long minutes in a non-threatening way, she gathered her fortitude and made a run for it. It hadn't taken much strength to escape her female keepers—she was a goddess after all.

Her breakout had begun well. As soon as she was away, she quickly reached the barrier around the little cat world which she'd attempted to breach. *Attempted* being the keyword. The evil laughter of Ridhwan's right-hand men as they emerged from the jungle foliage still echoed in her head. Her egress had been blocked somehow, and she'd been quickly surrounded. Still, Beletseri didn't go down without a fight.

Fools that they were, they maintained human form to try to stop her, and before they smartened up, she had the satisfaction of snapping one opponent's leg with a particularly well-placed kick. Unfortunately, her superior reign was short-lived. Quickly realizing their disadvantage, they morphed from their vulnerable bodies into cats. They were no gods, but they were large and powerful when turned…too powerful for one goddess. Bel was pounced upon, bitten, clawed, and otherwise tormented in her naked state. She was subsequently dragged back to her cave and tossed onto the dirt floor like so much garbage.

She remembered the anger and fury that had eaten away at her as she paced her small area of confinement. Ridhwan had played a deliberate game of cat and mouse with her, the prick. He'd known she would try to escape and had purposely neglected to tell her his powers extended to his three deputies. She wondered, when he'd finally been apprised of her attempted escape, how hard he'd laughed…if the bastard even had a sense of humor.

Bel had been left without clothing—but had healed rapidly, thanks to her immortal blood—to stew in her own thoughts for a full day before Ridhwan joined her in the cave. She still recalled every humiliating syllable he'd uttered.

"Big breasts," he'd sneered. "Useless bags. I prefer my women sleek." He'd walked around her in a slow circle. "Ass overly plump and skin too white. What could the king possibly see in you? Chances are we haven't heard from him because he's moved on to finer...and younger territory."

Bel held her tongue with difficulty. If Ridhwan had actually contacted the king—instead of Marla as Bel had requested—Nergal hadn't answered because he was too busy laughing *his* ass off. Of course, she'd lied. She'd had to say she was queen to make herself more valuable to Ridhwan, possibly winning time for her real mate, Matthew, to come to her rescue.

Nergal, of course, hated her guts and would relish the fact she was out of the way...and out of the lives of all the gods she'd tried to best.

Bringing her mind back to the present, Bel looked out over the peaceful scene of cat-shifter females sweeping out their meager huts where a tumble of kittens frolicked and basked in the sun. What could this group possibly gain by following Ridhwan, by attempting to lure Shamash to their enclave? She hated not having those answers, but there was one thing she did know. The longer it took to hear from Marla or Matthew about a deal to set her free, the more she worried her gamble hadn't paid off.

Movement to her right caught her eye. *Ah.* Here was the cat-alyst for all her negative thoughts. Ridhwan, tall, ebony, asshole-ish...and looking svelte in white linen trousers with a matching tank that showed off all the luscious muscles in his upper torso. Who dared look like that? And did he think it would impress her?

Perversely, Bel hoped—as he neared—she stunk to high heaven.

"Ridhwan, darling." She attempted a sarcastic purr, but it came out snarky at best. "I've missed you." She continued in the same vein, hoping to disguise the weakness that continued to wash over her. "Not that I've had time to give you much thought," she fake pouted. "I've had so many things to keep me occupied, rearranging rocks, decorating,"—with puke, but she wouldn't tell him that— "maintaining correspondence…" She stepped back when he entered and indicated the hash marks on the wall she'd been making. Twenty-six days. She looked down at her wasted body. Another twenty-six and she'd be a walking skeleton. She brought her eyes back to her host and her eyebrows raised.

"My, we don't look pleased this morning." She smirked at his extra-dark visage. The prick was ridiculously serious most of the time, but his current glower was a new low. Just another thing to hate about him. Nobody said bad-guys had to be humorless. Take Matthew for instance—she trapped the sigh in her chest that threatened to escape. *No*. It would do no good to think of her god now. Now was when she had to be on her toes.

"We've had a slight setback," he growled, and she was momentarily without words. It was unlike him to share his plans. The only thing he told her was she was to be used as leverage—swapped for Shamash. Bel wondered what kind of setback Ridhwan referred to.

"Something I need to be concerned about?" Bel tried to keep her voice light.

"Yes and no." Now, he actually looked worried. Did that bode well or ill for her? "Your husband agreed to a swap." He paced. "You were to be returned in exchange for the god Shamash, Quinn, and Marla. We had everything set except for the timing of the transaction. Now…" He turned with a roar and punched the wall where her markers adorned the rock. Bel held herself very still. If he attempted to take his anger out on her depleted body, she wasn't sure she could take it.

Bel quietly backed up a couple of steps. "Now?" she urged as gently as possible.

"Now two wild-cards have been thrown into my plans."

"Wild-cards?" Bel carefully led him, hoping to hear more.

"Cat-goddesses." Ridhwan exploded. "Fucking cat-goddesses. I've been watching their line as well as a few others for centuries, making sure they all remained minor players. But now? What happens the minute I think I have the prophecy beat? A pair of trivial, diluted bloods surface to join forces with gods." His silver eyes flashed. "Which raises the maddening possibility that Shamash and Quinn are not the ones I want."

"Want for what?" Now Beletseri's curiosity overcame her illness. She found herself moving closer to the black-leopard shifter.

"To fulfill the prophecy," he spouted. "So, now I need to demand two more in my swap for you which I'm sure your husband will enjoy, immensely…especially since he is most assuredly under pressure from the Blue Hills group as it is. He isn't going to take my added request lightly, and I may be pushing his limits." Ridhwan paced again. "The last thing I want to do is rile him to the point where he feels his only option is to oppose me and declare war."

Yes. That *would* be a bloody mess...*if* the one Ridhwan was dealing with was Nergal. Which it couldn't possibly be. Bel knew the asshole had to be negotiating with Marla and Matthew because the real king of the Underworld wouldn't lift a finger for her.

Knowing Matthew was in charge, she wanted to assure her jailer a couple of extra, mostly-mortal "exchangees" wouldn't make a damned bit of difference to her mate, but she needed to approach it delicately.

"Don't be looking for cat-astrophes where there may be none," she soothed. "The thing my husband wants most is for me to be returned, intact and *unharmed*." She emphasized the last because Ridhwan seemed to have enjoyed her beating by his captains, and she didn't want a repeat of that scenario now that she was unwell. "Perhaps if I wrote him a note...texted him..." If she could just get her hands on a phone...

Ridhwan looked at her speculatively. "You might be onto something." He stroked his chin. "But not a text. A visual missive. You'll need to be cleaned up, of course, but if we can make a video and send it..."

"...to Marla and my husband," Bel prompted. The last thing she needed was her sorry ass being broadcast to anyone else. If Nergal or the other gods got a hold of it, she'd probably become *YouTube*'s number one hit in the immortal realms. Her lips twisted wryly. She was just *that* well liked.

"Yes, yes, of course," he said with an unmindful wave of his hand. Beletseri could tell his brain had begun racing onto unknown tangents. "It will certainly buy us the time we need."

"The time you need for what?" Bel couldn't help asking.

"None of your fucking business." His head jerked up, and he growled.

Ta-da. Bel curled her lip. Just like that, the Ridhwan she knew and hated magically reappeared.

"Don't think you can manipulate me, bitch, because instead of a nice loving video, your husband might just start receiving body parts," he sneered. "I bet that would get his attention."

"Yes," Bel replied coldly, "and would also foment the war you are so loathe to call down upon yourself. So, I'd watch it if I were you."

Without warning, the vicious cat reached out and backhanded her across the face, sending her spinning around, stumbling to her knees in the dirt. When she cleared her dizzy head, she turned a hate-filled glare toward him and regarded him coldly from beneath a curtain of greasy hair.

Was that a look of shock that passed over his features? If so, it was quickly changed into one of disgust. He grunted.

"You're a mess. You need to eat. I want you looking healthy when we send your image to Nergal." He walked to the cave opening with determined strides, calling to enlist help.

Huh. She must look pretty bad.

"You," he yelled out to the left. "Take this woman to the river and make sure she and her clothes are cleaned. And you," his yowl carried even farther as he gave orders to another group farther off, "travel to the marketplace east of here and find food the goddess can keep in her stomach. If I so much as catch another whiff of vomit in this cave, I will hold you personally responsible." There was a whimpering answer, and Bel nearly laughed. Good luck to that hapless feline. Even the thought of good food had Bel's stomach roiling again.

The walk to the river didn't take long, but the muggy, tropical air actually worked toward clearing her head. She went over what she'd gleaned—what Ridhwan had let slip— again.

One: There was some kind of prophecy, something the black-leopard wanted to fulfill in order to take control. Two: To that end, he thought he needed Shamash and Quinn, a cat-god and a cat-goddess, but Three: Now, he wasn't sure and needed to eliminate the possibility it might be one of two other cat-females who would make his wishes come true. Four and most importantly: Ridhwan must still be in contact with Marla and Matthew because her ass was still viable as a trade.

A wave of dizziness swept over Bel, and she stumbled over a root. One of the female cat-amounts grabbed her arm, not unkindly until she regained her equilibrium. *Shit*. She was going downhill fast. Bel really hoped Ridhwan would get things moving. Otherwise, there wasn't going to be much of her to rescue.

Chapter Twenty

"Mom, do I really have to go back to school?"

Verrie rolled her eyes. They'd been over this a dozen times with her daughter firmly of the belief finishing the last two weeks of her junior year was a complete waste of time. In Verrie's opinion, it was bad enough the girls had missed the two days after their eventful weekend.

"Absolutely. You have finals. And besides, what am I going to write to your principal? 'Please excuse Sienna's absence. She's been haunted by demons and is being watched over by a group of gods. Hope you have a nice summer?' Geeze Si, it's bad enough I had to lie to your father and tell him you're staying with me at Frank's house until school's out and you travel with me back to Colorado."

"She has a couple of good points, Si," Riley giggled. "Besides, going to school could be really fun. We'll have invisible bodyguards the whole time we're there, and if we don't know the answers to something on our exams…"

"Hold that thought, Riley-Ann Dewalters." Verrie noticed Frank's voice had reverted back to a not-so-thick Boston accent as it would when she was calm. "If I catch you cheating, I'll make sure you take the whole friggin' junior year ovah. You got me?"

Riley ducked her head and sent a "We'll see" look toward Sienna.

Verrie thought the bodyguard thing was pretty funny—odd but funny. Frank, as well as the girls, would have their own invisible escorts. The gods had made it very clear a deity or two would be sticking with each of them for every moment they were outside the Blue Hills property. The immortals were taking no chances anything would happen to Sienna, Riley, or Frank, and for that, Verrie was thankful.

She was also delighted at how things were working out between her and Dumuzi. They'd discovered sexual playtime was their new favorite way to spend the day...*and* all hours of the dusk and dawn while sleeping the nights away like the dead. It was a kick to find out Muze liked to fuck in a well-lit room, just like her. Dwight had been an under-cover-of darkness type. She liked to use nights for snoozing and recharging her batteries, and so did Muze. And speaking of recharging, Verrie wondered how she was still standing? She stifled a giggle.

The girls had spent their past few days of "compound" time training with a very patient Enlil who was determined they learn to protect themselves against not only humans but gods and other immortals. They'd discovered all other-worldly beings had a life force, much like a heart, which when compromised would render them dead or debilitated. It was a huge secret with which to be trusted, but it looked like they were all going to be a part of the god's lives, so these were secrets they needed to know.

It amused Verrie that Frank also took part in the fighting sessions. After having watched for the first half day, her friend developed the utmost respect for Enlil, who she said was tough but sensitive to the girls, and joined in. The prospect of getting older and living in the city by herself after Riley flew the nest was a major factor convincing her to get physically tough.

As for Verrie? She'd taken some lessons from Dumuzi, but they had quickly devolved into sex-play. She snickered. Even though she'd learned the most vulnerable places on her mate's body, she wasn't sure the knowledge of those particular spots would help in a fight.

And speaking of mates, the house had begun to buzz with plans about an amulet ceremony for her and Dumuzi to take place the day before a huge celebration of the summer solstice that had been on the god's docket for quite some time. The events were only a week away which seemed rushed, but once Dumuzi explained the whole "gods have to find their *Chosen*" thing to her, she understood the need for haste.

Verrie took her leave of the girls and Frank as they prepared for yet another workout. Dumuzi was off doing some reconnaissance with a few of the gods in a part of Malaysia where Marla thought the rogue leopard shifter might be hiding. So, Verrie went out to the stone veranda at the back of the house and sank into a deeply cushioned chair, turning her face up to the sun.

She hadn't had any down-time to think before this, but now that she did, her biggest fear reared its ugly head. Something was bothering Dumuzi. She feared he was having second thoughts on her being "the one." And really, how *could* he be sure? It was true he'd turned visible for her, but if she understood god-rules correctly, that could mean they had some blood-connection thing. It didn't necessarily mean she was his forever woman. It bothered her that every time a conversation about their impending ceremony popped up, Muze seemed to grow quiet and tense, quickly changing the subject. Verrie could put it down to one of two things. Pre-wedding jitters…or a change of heart.

She needed to know more about what made a *Chosen,* to ascertain if she had anything to fear. And a couple potential fountains of information arrived on the patio just as she'd hoped. Emesh and Douglas walked hand in hand toward her. They'd just come in from an overnight, long-distance haul. Douglas was a trucker, and Emesh had taken to riding along with him for company. The two enormous, hot males were all about the love, so who better to give her the skinny.

Emesh flopped down into one cushy—and luckily sturdy—lounge chair. "I'm beat." He ran a hand over his magnificent bald head, his ebony skin shiny with sweat. "And it's too hot out here. Who's responsible?" he smirked and blinked amorous eyes at his partner.

"That would be the god of summer. Oh. You, Emesh," Douglas replied, teasing his heated partner.

Verrie begged to differ. Not about the source of heat but the cause. Douglas, in skin-tight jeans that emphasized his bite-able ass was probably the one provoking the heated sheen on Emesh and the surrounding area.

Verrie sighed. She hated to break the mood between the two. It was pretty obvious they were both tired…in the kind of way that would have them sexually engaged in a matter of minutes. *So, no.* It wasn't time for a heart to heart. It was actually time for her to exit, stage left.

"I'll leave you gentlemen to the patio," she offered, rising from her seat.

"Oh. Don't think you have to go on our account." The look that zinged from Emesh to Douglas was even more heated than before and gave lie to the god's words.

"Are you kidding? I'm going inside before I accidentally get burned," she laughed. "Enjoy your…sunbathing." She walked through the French doors, and with an afterthought, turned. "Do you want me to lock…" Verrie shook her head. Engaged in the most sinful kiss, the pair had already begun to mist out. *Oh my gods.* Could they really "do it" while invisible, or were they just going elsewhere to continue their tryst. Verrie wasn't sure she wanted to know. The last thing she needed to imagine were invisible couples fucking like bunnies as she walked through one of the vast rooms. *Huh.* Another question to add to her list.

It seemed like everyone was busy with one thing or another. Absu was in the kitchen, giving cooking lessons to little Maity who seemed to have more food on herself than anywhere else, but the pair were having a lot of fun. When she asked where his wife Charlie was, Absu told her a bunch of the ladies had gone to the mall for a day of shopping and spa-ing. Great. That explained the lack of goddesses.

Verrie wandered around aimlessly for a while, picking up knick-knacks and running her fingers over some fine, soft leather furniture. Who would have thought she could be bored in a multi-level house filled with immortals? Wait. Multi-level. Her eyes took on a knowing gleam. *Oh, hell yes.* She knew exactly where to go.

Verrie strode assuredly to the elevator, and when its silent doors opened, she pushed the button for the dungeons. She'd promised Matthew a "talking to," and now was a perfect time. She'd see what his troubles were all about, then pump the god for information that might shed light on her own personal woes—win-win.

She was met at the bottom floor by a couple of the blue-guys who were currently guarding the egress. Verrie hadn't been formally introduced to the group and tried to tamp down her curiosity over their azure tones while stating her business.

"Hi, I'm Verrie. We may or may not have met already." Shit. Did all blue guys look alike? "I'm interested in talking to Matthew…the prisoner. I'm sure Jake said it was okay."

"Cerulen." A short bald individual came forward from behind the other two and stuck out his hand.

Okay. He looked completely different from the elevator sentries. She took his proffered palm and was surprised to find it warm—another preconception debunked. They weren't as cold as they looked. "And this is Scobalt and Berylm," he continued. Scobalt, Verrie confirmed, was a deeper blue than his friends, and Berylm was more highly muscled than the others. She'd remember them next time around.

"Jake didn't mention the prisoner was to have guests," Cerulen's charmingly accented voice cut into her thoughts. "And the agent is not in residence at the moment."

Verrie was aware Jake and Candy as well as Ken were DEA agents and flipped back and forth between their east coast home and their west coast job. Since they were commuting god-style, it only took them half an hour to get to and from California, but still, she didn't want them to bother Jake.

"Is there anyone else you can ask?" She put a small push on her words that often worked toward getting her own way. It was funny. Small things she'd always been able to do—like down deep knowing if someone was good or bad, and pushing people's minds to make them amenable to her wishes—had always puzzled her. Now, she knew her small amount of god's-blood was responsible for her "powers", and she felt less guilty using them.

"No need to give me a nudge," Cerulen grinned.

Shit. He could feel that?

"I'm already in touch with our head of security, Razure who has a direct line to Jake. We should have you an answer in…wait." He got that look. The one that meant he was talking on another level. When his eyes refocused, he smiled. "Jake says it's okay as long as you don't get too close."

"Thanks." Verrie let out her held breath. "And thank Razure and Jake, too," she added. The little man bowed and swept a hand down the hallway.

"If you would follow me," he said.

Matthew was already standing at his bars, having obviously heard their conversation with his superior god-hearing. But the dungeon was so echo-y, Verrie momentarily wondered how she was going to keep her questioning private from the blue men. Matthew answered that question quickly enough.

They can't hear us if we talk in our heads. They can only communicate with their own kind that way. I'm assuming there's something you'd like to keep secret from them? In answer to her raised eyebrows he shrugged. *I don't get many casual visitors.*

"I think it would be a good idea to speak out loud, *for most of our conversation,"* Verrie amended in head-talk. "And FYI, I'm not very good at keeping things private from the immortal residents. But your situation is well known to everyone here except me." She turned and nodded a quick thank you to Berylm who came up behind her with a chair. Verrie took a seat and settled in.

"So tell me. When did your idea of god-dom and the other immortals' conception of such head in different directions?" Verrie thought it was a good question and watched as the almost too handsome blond pondered. *Yes.* Almost too handsome. Thank the gods for the placement of his eyes or good women everywhere would have been throwing themselves at his feet.

"You have me wrong, Verrie. I can call you Verrie, can't I?" he added charmingly.

"Of course." She inclined her head for him to continue.

"I'm a newly made god, less than a year in this incarnation. The goddess Beletseri… my lovely wife"—had those too close together eyes teared up—"chose me several months ago and turned me into an immortal." He paused to regroup, clearly overcome with emotion. "We're really still in our honeymoon period, and I'm having some difficulty being apart from her," he apologized.

"I'm sorry." And Verrie was surprised to find out she meant it. Apparently, love even for bad-guys made her sappy. Verrie wanted more of the story and pushed

Matthew a bit to explain. "I understand she's been kidnapped, but I'm not certain how that was accomplished."

"We were at the circus looking for...trouble." The big god shrugged. "Bel was in the wrong place at the wrong time. Ridhwan was poised, prepared to abduct Shamash and Quinn but ended up with my wife instead."

Verrie nodded. "I understand the pair of you have long been a thorn in the side of the gods who reside here."

Matthew straightened up. "If you're asking if I aligned with Bel to make their lives a hell, then yes, I'll admit to that."

"But why?" Verrie asked.

"Because they all contributed toward making her lonely and miserable for thousands of years." His lips hardened. "You heard your exemplary group must find their mates before September fifteenth, or they get sent back to hell?"

Verrie nodded tersely.

"Well, it was our goal to hold...not kill...any one of the women who were to be their *Chosen* before they were able to undergo the amulet ceremony. That way, they'd have to go back to the Underworld. Where they belong." Matthew folded his arms across his massive chest.

"But to what end?" Verrie questioned again. "What did you expect to accomplish if you managed to be successful?"

"Suffering," Matthew spat. "Suffering for all the arrogant assholes above." He stood up and paced his cage. "You have no idea. And truthfully, neither did I

228

until I was mated and could feel what my Bel felt—the amount of torment she suffered at their hands. The hurtful words they carelessly flung at her. It amounted to nothing less than bullying. She wasn't good enough…smart enough…*godly* enough for them to waste time with her. She needed friends, and what did she get? Nothing. An existence devoid of happiness…and love. You've seen people here on earth spend their lives without it and know how bitter they become. Imagine going thousands of years without one single friend or lover. Is it any wonder Bel looked toward under-gods and demons for fulfillment? I should be jealous and angry she took Nedu, the gate-keeper of the north as a lover, but in fact, it's just the opposite. I am grateful to him for giving Bel just one small scrap of tenderness."

Verrie was torn. Should she be the one to set Matthew straight about Nedu? She'd been at the meeting where Nergal had declared the gate-keeper in league with demons. Verrie weighed it carefully and felt it was best to fill Matthew in. She switched to head-speak, concentrating on Matthew alone, and hoping she wasn't broadcasting to all the gods..

I want you to take a deep breath and sit down, she told him. *And it's important you maintain a calm visage no matter how much the information I'm about to impart angers you.* When he didn't answer she prodded. *Do I have your promise?*

You do, Matthew finally answered, somewhat reluctantly, and sat.

Fine. I'll make it as succinct as possible. When Nergal interrogated Nedu, he found that Bel was not responsible for the death of his child. Nedu was. Not only that, but the gate-keeper had been working with a group of demons and someone much higher up—or lower down—for many years before meeting Beletseri. Here she paused to take a deep breath. *That someone ordered Nedu to befriend your wife. To manipulate her. Feeding her hatred of Marduk's group until they convinced her to do everything she could to bring them to heel, have them stripped of powers. This continued right down to the current plan of trying to kidnap Chosen to make sure the gods get sent back to hell.*

Verrie sat and watched the play of emotions tighten Matthew's face into a mask of fury. She waited patiently until his jaw unclenched and his fists eased into flatness on his knees. She gave a huff of relief. It had been the right decision to tell him. She could read it in his demeanor without even using her magic touching ability. If one of his "enemy" gods had told him, he never would have believed it. As it was, he believed her.

Who is it? This kingpin? He stood and gritted the words out of his head.

"They don't know yet," Verrie replied, whispering this time. "There is much investigating being done with some faction who Nergal calls "glowies" attempting to locate the group of demons with whom Nedu had his long association."

"Tell Marduk to let me free." Matthew's eyes glittered dangerously. "I would help locate the fiends…after I have eviscerated Nedu."

"Your revenge against that individual will be unnecessary," Verrie told him. "Nergal's interrogation left the man's mind little more than a cracked shell for a short period of time. The king doubts whether the minor god will be able to do much more than drool for the next few weeks."

"Then I owe the king a huge debt," Matthew sneered. "But I would also help him locate the one who controlled the gate-keeper."

"Well, that's not up to me." Verrie had given Matthew a lot to think about, but now she was anxious for some answers of her own. Yet, how to change the subject? "You'll need to speak with Marduk and Nergal. They may see reason if you show them the passion you've shown to me…and speaking of passion…"

Matthew's brows went up. "We weren't," he said, "speaking of passion." He looked Verrie up and down. "Ah. I see. You've given me everything you know, and now you want something in return. Am I correct?"

"Not unless you're willing." She felt the color move up into her face. "And it's nothing I can't find out from some of the other gods or goddesses. I just thought since we're here, alone…"

"That I would fill in some gaps in your god-education. Is that it?" Surprisingly, his tone turned almost kind.

"There are things Dumuzi hasn't explained. Things that might be…bothering him."

Matthew sat back down and looked at Verrie, long and hard. "I'm not sure you have anything to worry about. When a pair is meant to be mated, any doubts about love and forever-ness take a back seat."

"But that's my point," Verrie began before glancing over at the blue men and switching to head speak, feeling like she was acing the conversation-privacy thing. *How does Dumuzi know we're meant to be mated? I'm not having any doubts on my end, but he seems more unsure the closer we get to our ceremony.*

Matthew gave her what could only be an encouraging smile. *Don't worry. Dumuzi knows you belong to him and vice versa. The minute his amulet lit up for you, your combined fates were sealed.*

Amulet? Verrie knew she looked stupefied. *You mean his life-giving force? What does that have to do with anything?*

Now Matthew looked a little less sure of himself. As a matter of fact, he looked decidedly uncomfortable. *Umm. You know... When a god meets his true Chosen, his amulet lights up. He hasn't...he didn't...*

"No. He hasn't, and he didn't." Verrie leaped up out of her chair, startling both Matthew and the guards. "Lighting up, huh? He never said a word. And because this hasn't happened, I'm probably not 'the one'?" she spouted the last sarcastically. "Well, how about that? It looks like he's been feeding me a line," she snapped, "and to what end?" She sent Matthew a scathing look that wasn't meant for him. "You can bet I'm damned well going to find out...right before I kill him."

She stalked down the hallway, quietly ranting. *Gods-damn prick.* Dumuzi knew all along he had to light up. And he hadn't. He'd been keeping that little gem away from her...and why? For sex? She couldn't imagine that. She'd shown him her willingness even before the talk of mating ceremonies.

The god had some explaining to do...and fast. And he also better hope she hadn't learned too much about his vulnerable bits during her brief self-defense lessons. If she had, he was in serious trouble.

Chapter Twenty-one

Dumuzi and the other gods returned from the jungle with only mosquito bites and sweaty balls for their troubles. The area Marla thought might hide Ridhwan had simply been an enclave of real cats...not shifters.

The whole time he'd been gone, all he could think about was getting back to Verrie. And...*yeah*. How his amulet had not yet lit up for her yet. How was that possible? In the short time they'd known each other, she had become everything to him. Their physical attraction, right from the start, had damned near bowled him over. And the lightness and joy she brought to every other aspect of their togetherness was downright amazing for a woman who had faced so much adversity.

She teased, she joked, she was brilliant in her knowledge of the human psyche. And when she'd playfully yet thoughtfully analyzed his years of holding himself in a stoned-like stupor, she'd nailed his condition on the head...and he hadn't yet told her the most fucked up part. She'd have a field day with that one.

He'd fallen for her. That was for sure. He couldn't imagine moving on in life without her or her sassy daughter or her quirky friends—to go back to his empty existence where his only trusted confidante was Archie. No thank you.

To those ends, it was time to seek some advice.

Marduk? Where are you, brother?

In command central, taking a turn monitoring computers and surveillance while Sham and Lahar are gone, he answered.

Do you have a minute to talk? Dumuzi didn't pause. He was already headed in Marduk's direction. Their designated leader never said no when one of his household had problems to discuss.

Absolutely. I was starting to go cross-eyed here, anyway.

Dumuzi heard the thunder god chuckle. Not surprising. Marduk was a man of careful planning and succinct action, not a techno-geek-god. He'd probably rather he was back in hell than in mainframe purgatory.

Dumuzi entered the computer room to see Marduk with his feet propped up on a desk filled with keyboards, motherboards, and wires. A partially eaten sandwich, a cup with coffee dregs, and a large plate of cookies—compliments of Absu and Maity no doubt—were perched next to his calves.

If Lahar could see the boss now, the logical god would have a meltdown. Nobody did "feet up" on Lahar's desk, and food was strictly forbidden. Dumuzi gave a mental shrug. Not his problem. Marduk lived by his own rules, and Lahar wouldn't find out from him.

Marduk saw him eyeballing the food. "Have a cookie," he encouraged, snagging another for himself and leaning back in his seat. "And tell me what's stuck up your ass?"

Ah, yes. The thunder god had a colorful way with words. Dumuzi figured he might just as well get down to it.

"It's about me and Verrie." He took the offered dessert and put it in his mouth. He knew it was good, but it tasted like so much cardboard in his spit-dry mouth. "As you probably figured, we've, uh, been together a bunch of times by now."

"Yeah," Marduk smirked. "The noises coming from your room kind of gave that away."

Dumuzi chose to ignore that and plowed ahead. "But my amulet hasn't lit up for her yet." He knew he mumbled and ran the words together, but by Marduk's suddenly stiff posture, the boss understood.

The thunder god brought his feet down and placed them on the floor, righting his chair in the process. He put his cookie back on the plate and stared hard at Dumuzi. "You're sure?" he asked, keeping the angst out of his voice, for which Muze was thankful.

"I'm sure," the veggie-god confirmed. "And it's not like there's anything wrong between us." Now that Dumuzi had begun, he couldn't seem to stop even if the shit he spewed fell into the category of "over-share."

"The sex is fantastic. She's hot and ready all the time, and I'm surprised I'm not a walking dry-husk with the amount of ejaculate I've gushed in the past couple of days." He ran a hand through his long red hair. "And when we're not fucking, we're talking…for hours or laughing at something we both find mutually ridiculous. I feel like she's in my head and under my skin, and Verrie says she feels the same way. So what's the problem? Shouldn't I be lit up all over the place by now?" Dumuzi couldn't keep to his feet a moment longer. He sank down to the edge of the desk and sent pleading eyes to Marduk. Please, please, please let something reassuring come out of his boss's mouth.

Marduk stayed silent for a long time, and Dumuzi began to despair before figuring out the thunder god was touching base, internally, with his wife. Muze felt his shoulders relax a bit. Between Tess and Marduk, an answer had to be found.

When Muze noticed a tiny upturn in Marduk's mouth, he gripped his hands on the desk beneath him. Dare he hope that they'd come up with something?

"My wife wants to know if, in all of your dialoguing, either one of you has mentioned the "L" word."

"What? Love?" Dumuzi looked dumbfounded. "Well, yeah...uh, no... But..." he spluttered, "it isn't necessary. She knows how I feel about her, and I know how she feels about me...so... The actual words haven't been said yet...but..." He rubbed the spot between his eyebrows and grimaced. "Do you think that's it? Could it be that easy?" His heart leaped. Maybe it could. He jumped to his feet. "I'm going to go find her right now." He headed for the door.

"You're welcome," Marduk called out sarcastically.

"Yeah," Muze chuckled excitedly over his shoulder. "Thank your wife for me." He picked up his pace to a jog, trying to focus on where in the house Verrie might be. *Kitchen...no. Bedroom...blank. Gym...aha. Gym.* He honed in on the multiple voices emanating from that room, and even though he didn't hear his mate, that's where she had to be. Sienna, Riley, and Frank were practicing with Enlil, and if he was

236

lucky, Veronica would have shed some of her inhibitions and be working out as well.

Rather than barge in through the main doors, Muze thought to go the long way around and slip in the back. That way he could stand behind a stack of unused equipment and watch without being seen, keeping Veronica from feeling self-conscious. He skirted the big center room and slid in through the small door off the three-season porch.

Huh. There was a god already hidden, watching, and Muze felt a smile brush his lips. Damned if it wasn't Ishkur.

Hey, buddy, Dumuzi spoke silently and put a hand on the other god's shoulder.

Ishkur, when he turned, looked guilty as hell.

What the…? No way. Had he been eyeing Verrie? It couldn't be… *Fuck.* What if Ishkur was the one to light up for her?

She's mine, Muze bawled, going balistic. *You can't have her. I don't care if you light up and I don't. I'll kill you before I let you touch her.* His core hardened to dead-wood, and vines wound viciously from his arms and legs, reaching for…strangling Ishkur. Let the god use his fire against him. He'd fight him to the death if need be.

Muze. Stop. I'm not here for Verrie. Ishkur tugged on his vines. *Do you hear me? I. Am. Not. Here. For. Verrie.* The words, gritted out tersely, got through, but Dumuzi wasn't sure what they meant. If the prick wasn't watching Veronica, who did he have eyes on? With the small vestige of control left to him before he totally snapped, Muze growled out his question.

Who are you watching?

Frank, you bonehead. Now call off the tendrils, or they'll be kindling.

Frank? Dumuzi's greenery shriveled and retreated, and though he was left swampy, his brain began functioning more fully. *You mean, Frank, Frank? As in Verrie's aunt and Riley's grandmother?*

Yeah. That's right. And fuck you. Ishkur sounded anything but pleased, brushing himself off and straightening his clothes.

Dumuzi stood back and blinked. He didn't know what to think. Nor was he quite sure why the god of fire would be hiding his interest.

Why are you hiding, then? Dumuzi was beginning to regain his body. It was the fastest transformation he'd ever undergone, and oddly, he'd been completely aware the entire time he was vegitated. What a difference since Verrie had entered his life.

Because I'm an ass, and I've already done the marrying a non-Chosen human once, and I don't want to repeat the process, even if I do find the lady attractive.

Have you…kissed her?

Yeah. And it was fun, but not earthshattering, and I didn't light up, so it's nothing but hormones. Nothing. If you fucking tell anybody, I'll turn you into a bonfire.

I won't tell anybody if you won't rat me out. Dumuzi thought he owed Ishkur an explanation. *The reason I went so jungle-like on your ass is I haven't lit for my woman yet.*

No shit? Ishkur's ire was diverted. *But you know she's the one, right?* He didn't wait for an answer. *What am I saying? Of course, she is, or you wouldn't have lost it so badly.*

Muze knew he must look pathetic. He was half god, half vine-man, and one hundred percent unsure of himself with Veronica. He began speaking out loud. "I was just about to go tell her I love her," he admitted to Ishkur. "I had a talk with Marduk. He and Tess figured maybe I haven't lit yet because I haven't said it."

"Well *you're* a dick, aren't you?"

"Hey," Muze gave Ishkur a dark look. "You're one to talk."

"Okay, so we're both dicks, me for kind of leading Frank on," Ishkur admitted, then shrugged his shoulders. "But Frank is not my *Chosen*." He paused. "So what do you think? You gonna go tell Verrie now?"

"I…"

"Hey boys." The giddy voices wafted up from the driveway which disappeared into a lower floor garage and was carved into the gully behind them. "What's up?" The group called out. The goddesses were loaded down with shopping bags, and more than one of them was sporting big hair. They'd really done it up at the mall.

The ladies misted out and misted back in next to the pair of gods. Candy, Lenore, Holly, Glory, Charlie, Quinn, and Addie-May, all looked very pleased with themselves.

"Where's Verrie?" Lenore asked. "We have some things for her." A waggle of the platinum blonde's eyebrows told Dumuzi what would be in the small pink bag Lenore dangled in front of him. He sighed. There would be no chance for him to declare his love with such a huge audience. He sucked back in the last of his vegetation and conceded defeat. His poetic soul was going to have to wait until shopping had been discussed.

"She's in the gym with Enlil, Frankie, and the girls," he disclosed.

"Great." Glory hooked her arm into his, and Charlie snagged Ishkur. "Let's go." Given no choice, the two gods were led back into the sunroom and through the small door to the gym. This time there was no escaping detection by the sparring crew, the incoming chatter reverberating off the walls.

Candy sped across the gym and threw herself at Enlil, hugging him fiercely, then scooped a foot behind his knees and sent him tumbling backward to the mat. Riley and Sienna squealed, and Frank looked put out.

"We've been tryin' to do that all aftahnoon," she groused. "I guess it's a goddess thing."

Amidst all the clamor and prattle, Dumuzi sought out and found Veronica's eyes, only to find her glaring at him with undisguised anger. *Shit*. What had he done? Last he'd seen her, they'd had multiple-orgasm sex against his shower wall before he took off for the Malaysian Peninsula. What could possibly have happened since?

"Dumuzi," her voice rang out, loud and pissed across the room.

"Veronica?" He raised his brows and tried to relay with a sour look if she had a problem, airing it in front of everyone wasn't his normal practice. Surely, what she had to say could wait.

"You fucking asshole."

Or not. Dumuzi steeled himself for what was to come.

"Were you going to tell me, or were you just going to keep screwing me until you got tired of me and kicked me out?"

Dumuzi was blindsided, and so was everyone else in the suddenly quiet room. He couldn't help but notice the shocked look on Sienna's face. For Veronica to go off without regard to her daughter, the issue had to be huge.

"Do you want to explain what you mean?" He tried to keep his voice calm and even. "I have no plans to kick you out. We're going to be mated in a week, remember?"

"Is that with or without your fucking amulet lighting up?" she asked, arms folded across her heaving chest.

Oh shit. She'd found out about the damned amulet before he could get to her. What was he supposed to do now?

"I was going to tell you—" he began, but she cut him off.

"Yeah? Well, don't bother. The fun's over buster. It seems I don't have what it takes to light you up, and you were too much of a coward to tell me. So, rather than leaving me waiting at the altar, I quit right now." She looked over at her daughter. "Come on, Si. Let's pack up and get out of here."

"Wait, you can't do that." Dumuzi still wasn't a hundred percent certain why he hadn't lit up, but he sure as shit knew he wanted her to stay. "I love you." He went for broke, and when his amulet didn't light, he spread his hands toward her in supplication. "I love you," he shouted as she continued to walk away.

And damn. *It wasn't working.* What the hell was he going to do now? He couldn't live without her.

"Save it, Dumuzi." Veronica spun and her eyes filled. His heart nearly split in two. She didn't believe him.

Fuck. He'd said the words, and his body didn't believe him, either. Was this how it was going to end? His guts turned over, and he felt like he was going to be sick.

Muze was so busy trying not to puke as he watched Verrie and her group stride from the room, he barely noticed Quinn frantically gesturing between him and his departing mate.

He didn't want help. Didn't want any interference. What good could Quinn do? Dumuzi threw up a mind-barrier so none of the gods and goddesses could talk to him, try to tell him his business. Quinn, knowing this, grew more pissed off and moved her hands a million miles an hour in front of his face. She could gesticulate all she wanted. He didn't know sign language.

What he did know, was that he needed to go think. *Alone.* Muze whistled for Archie and stalked out the back door, his dog at his heels.

Chapter Twenty-two

He was twenty minutes and two miles into the woods before Flick, the DEA agent, caught up with him at a full run.

"Cripes, Muze. Can you frigging slow down?"

The god vaguely registered the human who had to be crazy to bust ass coming after him. First off, the run had left the guy sweaty and gasping for breath. Second, if Dumuzi lost it and turned swamp-monster, they wouldn't so much as find a chromosome left of the godsdamned idiot.

Dumuzi turned to face the agent. "What do you want, Flick? And make it quick. I'm not feeling patient…if you catch my meaning."

Flick blanched but didn't back down. Muze heard the pounding of feet on leaves heading their way and gave the agent props. He wasn't so stupid as to have come out alone.

Scobalt, a deeper blue than usual from his run, came up beside Flick and put a hand to the agent's shoulder. "You should have waited for me," he said, and the heated look that passed between the two totally pissed Dumuzi off.

"You're shitting me, right?" He raised his head and arms and spit the words to the heavens. "Every frigging person in this place can find a partner but me? What the

243

fuck do you want me to do?" He watched his two pursuers blink twice at each other, and Scobalt's hand fell away.

"Uh, I'm not sure what you're talking about," Flick's voice came out rough. "But we're here because of Quinn. She says she has something to show you. That it's important. Didn't you see how upset she was before you took off?"

Muze snorted. "How could I miss it? She was right up in my face with her hands, but I can't read that language."

"Well, I can." Flick's sister had been born deaf, and he was proficient in signing. "She was telling you to stop acting like a big pussy...and that's a prime compliment from a cat goddess. She said something about the love coming off you in waves whatever that means. You know how she's always been able to tune into things the rest of us can't, tapping into that enhanced other senses thing that a lot of deaf people have? Well, hers seemed to have been working overtime, and our normally timid Quinn has flipped out. She's gone to confront Verrie, and she wants you back at the compound like, right now."

"Fuck that," Dumuzi turned to go, but Scobalt's voice stopped him.

"Are you going to give up on your lady just because she protests a little much?" he asked softly with a compelling Teutonic lilt. "Sometimes, you have to fight for what you want."

Just who was the blue guy talking to here? Muze thought, seeing Scobalt's fingers twitch unconsciously in Flick's direction.

"You can't expect love to simply fall in your lap. If you have a true mate, and it takes some time to get things right, the rewards will be even sweeter. Work things out, Dumuzi. Don't let past fears drive you away."

Okay. So, the words fit for him and Verrie, but Muze was no dummy. They were also aimed at the agent who shifted from foot to foot, looking anywhere but at Scobalt.

Damn. Even if he fixed his own shit, whatever barrier existed between these two guys was way out of his league. Gay relationships were miles away from his expertise. He tried to picture himself orchestrating a blue on caramel kiss between the Latino and the Lauernley but…not happening. The best he could do would be to drop a word to Emesh and Douglas. The male mated pair could be a lot more help than him. *Hell.* What did he know about love of any variety? Jack-shit if his present situation was any indication.

"Fine." Dumuzi turned his feet back toward the house. "I'll come back with you, but don't expect Veronica to cave. Once she makes up her mind to something…" He pictured her taking charge in many of the recent sexual adventures they'd had, and the thought made him groan. It wasn't fair a woman so right for him couldn't be his mate. He was beginning to see the dilemma Ishkur found himself in, only the exact opposite. And like his old friend, he needed to get himself under control.

"You know what?" He whipped around to face Flick and Scobalt. "You're right. I'm not letting her go without a battle." Dumuzi stood up a little straighter and walked a little faster. "Fuck the amulet thing. I won't live without Veronica." And he knew he wouldn't. If Muze underwent the amulet ceremony with Verrie, and she was not his true *Chosen,* then the half amulet—which was removed from him to be implanted in her shoulder—would not light. A phantom half would not regenerate in him, and he would die. As simple as that, but Dumuzi refused to dwell on the possibility. Veronica *was* his *Chosen.* End of story.

****

Verrie threw things into a suitcase she'd purloined from the same fucking closet where she and Dumuzi had met for their first encounter. It hadn't made her feel all warm and fuzzy when grabbing the bag, remembering what had happened in that lovely dark space. *Shit no.* It made her tears come even faster.

She ignored the imperative knocking at her door.

Damn him. Damn Dumuzi. Why hadn't he been honest? She'd fallen for him…hard…and even worse, she'd fallen for the whole "mine for eternity" line of bullshit—hook, line, and sinker. If he'd wanted to play, hell, why hadn't he just said so? Verrie had been completely and irrevocably attracted to the god. It wouldn't have been so bad being his plaything without the whole amulet bullshit.

And what the fuck was up with the gods and amulets thing, anyway? Why couldn't the all-powerful immortals just marry whomever they wanted and say screw it to the powers who made the rules? Verrie would have been happy spending a normal life-span of time with Dumuzi. Forty years together sounded damned good in lieu of where they stood now—which was nowhere.

Verrie ignored the pounding on her door for a little longer but eventually, couldn't stand it. It had to be Sienna who was furious with her for quote "giving up" on the best thing that had ever happened. She did not expect to see Quinn when she yanked open the door.

"Quinn. Hi, umm…" Verrie looked up and down the hall, expecting to see more faces, but it was strangely quiet. "I'd invite you in, but I'm kind of busy right now. Packing to leave and all." She gestured behind herself. Verrie wasn't about to pretend everything was okay, then slink away in the night like a bad date.

Important thing. Quinn said in god-speak and thrust a small pink bag into Verrie's fluttering hands, not giving credence to Veronica's declaration but stalking right past her into the room.

"What? I don't understand." She realized her words had been aimed at the back of Quinn's head, so were useless, but she was hesitant to use head-talk because she still had a hard time directing it to just one person; her time with Matthew a possible anomaly. She laid a hand on Quinn's shoulder and turned her around.

"What's the bag for?" she asked, holding the small thing up and jiggling it in the air.

New bra. You put it on. Quinn's face was unsmiling and resolute. She crossed determined arms over her small chest and glared at Verrie, daring her to disagree. Verrie was no pushover and took the challenge.

"I'm not putting on a bra for whatever fucked up purpose you immortals have in mind, nor am I pausing in my bid to get out of this madhouse." She dropped the bag between them. It landed with a soft thunk on the carpet. "You can donate this to charity."

Don't piss me off, Quinn replied, having that phrase down pat. *This for your own good. You thank me soon.*

"The only thank-you you'll get is a nice little note in the mail, saying 'Much obliged for the good food and taking such special care of Sienna.' That's it. Now out you go." Verrie swept her hand in the direction of the door, only to have it caught with a...handful of claws? Oh, hell no. This wasn't happening.

Small whiskers popped out from Quinn's cute little cheeks while her nose flattened and flexed. Verrie's mouth fell open as she was soft-pawed back toward her bed.

No use fighting. Quinn smiled, pushing. Two sharp canines glistened, making Verrie more amenable to listening.

Damn. What was with these shifters and their fangs? Absently, she wondered if Dr. Dani doubled as a dentist.

The backs of her knees hit the mattress, and she toppled like a tree. "You should be nicer to me, you know," Verrie told Quinn. "I'm related to your husband, and I might...I could..." she wasn't able to finish the thought. Verrie had been about to speculate she might be able to get her inner cat on, but that was too crazy to contemplate.

Apparently, Quinn disagreed.

What? Turn to pussy? She grinned in a very feline-like way. *I count on it once you are goddess. I need another female to prowl with.*

Verrie groaned. "You guys are all so messed up." She tried to sit up on the bed, but Quinn pushed her back down, playfully if Verrie was not mistaken. *Great.* Now they were acting out a cat and mouse thing. "Okay, fine. What do you want me to do?"

First, get out of shirt. Quinn reached down with a sharp claw and in one swipe popped all the front closing buttons. Verrie's shirt gaped open.

Uh-uh. There was no way this petite little kitty was going to undress her without getting a fight. Verrie narrowed her eyes, then went limp as if to comply, but in one swift move rolled to the end of the bed where she sprang up, landing lightly on her feet. "Don't mess with me," she hissed—ah shit. She hissed.

The cat who was still half goddess laughed in Verrie's head. *You are going down.*

The cat chick had turned nuts on her. Veronica needed help, and with a house full of gods, someone was bound to come to her aid, but she was too afraid she'd get Dumuzi. *Dammit all.*

"Listen, I know I can't fight you. You're a leopard for shits and giggles and a goddess in real life. Just back the fuck out of the door, and we'll call this quits."

Pick bag up off floor and put bra on. I not leave until you do.

Verrie weighed the options. She didn't have any. She hated being told what to do, but she was fresh out of ideas.

Fine, she grunted at Quinn-cat. *But there will be a reckoning, and it may involve collars and leashes.* Verrie thought she might have heard a purr as she retrieved the hated bag, but by the time she stood up,

Quinn's puss was impassive. Who said poker was for dogs.

Verrie skinned out of her ruined shirt, and popped the front closure to her leopard print bra. *Yeah*. Suck that up, kitty. Leopard print. She pulled the bright, white demi from the bag. Cute. Push-em-up half-sees so the tops of her pink nipples were on display. And Quinn wanted this why? She looped it over her arms, hooked the back closure and arranged her nipples to be on center. If she was going to flaunt them, they might as well be picture perfect.

"Your next move, puss," she stood back and waited.

Throw on robe and lose pants, Quinn ordered.

"I'm not sure what you have in mind." Verrie dropped her jeans and bent to give a purposely full view of her very average behind while rummaging in the packed case for her robe. "But if it involves your husband, I'm not feeling it. You, on the other hand, if you're looking for a little change of pace, will need to lose the dominant species shit. I have a control issue, and I like to be in charge."

Much I might like that, Quinn laughed, *this about you, not me. Put robe on and move it. We have places to be, people to meet.*

"This isn't funny, you know." Until that moment, Verrie had still been thinking she could outmaneuver Quinn and skedaddle. But seriously? People to meet? In her new white nipples-up underwire? Verrie donned her robe over the bra and scant panties and swept out the door.

"Where to?" She was so screwed.

Quinn grabbed her hand which thankfully had gone back to fingernails and tugged her down the stairs. At that moment, the door opened below, and Dumuzi was escorted in by Flick and Scobalt, looking as reluctant as Verrie felt. *Okay.* So this was some elaborate intervention, a ruse to get the two of them back together. Verrie got it. Sexy underwear…hot god. Maybe they were going to be thrown into that dungeon room together to work out their differences? *Damn.* Why did that thought have moisture pooling between her legs? She scowled for effect while walking down the last few steps, hoping to just get the supposed "fix" over with.

Oh goody. An audience. While she'd been descending and Muze entering, an immortal contingent of a half-dozen or more had gathered to hold witness to whatever humiliation Quinn had cooked up.

Closet, the cat-goddess barked now that she was no longer a cat.

What? She wanted them to revisit the spot of their first make-out session? That was just cruel.

"Quinn. Cut it out. Right now. Veronica isn't interested. She's made that perfectly clear." Dumuzi's face was devoid of emotion.

"Me?" Verrie wanted to wipe the nonchalance right off his handsome mug. "You're the one who doesn't light up for me and wasn't man enough to tell me about it."

He winced.

Good. That's what she wanted…so why did it make her feel like a mean bitch?

Into closet. Now. Quinn wasn't messing around. *And if you don't make quick, you have more audience*

251

than just me. Some gods here would pay money to front row seat for what I have planned.

No thanks, Quinn. Anshar's voice cut through immortal-silence. *I don't need to see Muze's sorry ass. And if we so much as glance at his naked woman, we'd end up strangled by invasive vegetation in our beds tonight. No. We're all good.* He spoke for the entire crew. *Do what you have to do.*

Quinn gave him a nod and pulled Verrie toward the closet with one hand while backwardly signing to Flick with the other. Verrie supposed she told the agent to entice Dumuzi to the small cloakroom because without turning, she felt the big god on her heels.

Flick left them at the door, and the unlikely trio went in to have the portal closed behind them…which thrust them into the dark. *Well. Nearly.* Verrie could see in the almost zero light conditions, and she knew the immortals could, too, so now what? It was Quinn's game.

Verrie, drop robe, Quinn ordered. Verrie sighed. She wasn't going to fight. It wasn't as if Dumuzi hadn't seen everything already. She undid her sash and let the silky material drop to her feet. Standing in just her small panties and her new, sinful bra actually had her pulse quickening, just a bit.

Dumuzi, forgive me, you undress, quickly too. Quinn sounded a little more hesitant this time, and Verrie had those suspicions confirmed when the kitty added. *If Sham get back…don't you tell my husband this because if finds out, someone be dead-meat. Probably be you, Muze.*

Verrie's first thought was she'd be long gone by the time Sham got back, but Muze apparently took the threat seriously. He shucked his jeans. Verrie's tongue stuck to the roof of her mouth as his delectable man-parts came into view, and she had to give herself a shake and remind herself why she was walking out that door as soon as Quinn's little game was over. Dumuzi might be drool-worthy and funny and smart, but dammit he'd scammed her. Eternal mate indeed. Temporary bed-mate was more like it. Still…

So what you did on first day, in closet? Quinn asked, a little breathlessly.

Well, duh. What did she think they'd been doing? Checking out the hangers?

Muze answered. *I lifted her up by her ass, and she wrapped her legs around my waist.* His voice was raspy and deep.

Veronica played along because…*okay.* It was a turn-on remembering.

But I tweaked both your nipples on the way up if you recall.

Do it, Quinn ordered, shakily, and the pair complied. Both women witnessed Dumuzi's body tense as he lifted and Verrie's nails plucked the god's brown nubs as she twined herself around him.

Bless her, Quinn still had the presence of mind to ask what occurred next. *And then?*

Well, we kissed, Muze answered.

A blistering heat began to build where her panties barely masked the hard bit of Dumuzi that lay between them. Her lips met his, and he groaned, kissing her back. Verrie cut it short. She was getting too carried away.

What next? Quinn prodded.

Then I stood back and helped him strip, Verrie said, shakily. *But since he's got his clothes off, I think the next bit involved me touching his...cock, then...using my tongue on him.* Verrie reluctantly slid down his body and stood a few feet back, legs shaking.

All while I did this, Dumuzi added smokily, putting both hands behind his head and locking his fingers.

Oh yeah. I'd forgotten that part, Verrie wet her lips, already tasting him without yet putting him in her mouth.

More, do. If Quinn's voice got any huskier, Verrie swore she'd be asking the girl to join them. As Verrie dropped to her knees and brought one finger up to spread the lovely moisture around the tip of his cock, that funny lighting thing she remembered happened again. The one she vaguely recalled from their first trip into the closet. A couple of the hanging jackets to their left took on a bit of a ghostly glow. *Weird.*

She tipped her head forward and swiped his velvety head with her tongue. What the...? Her stark white bra lit up like...like she was some kind of black-light poster.

Thank gods, Quinn breathed.

Verrie spoke shakily. "Wait. What's happening?"

Dumuzi brought his hands down from in back of his head and brought one palm low to cup her glowing, white-clad breast. "I don't know. It's...compelling," he admitted. "I'm drawn to it."

Verrie tried to tamp down her hysterical, nervous laugh. "No shit, Muze. Any excuse to touch my boobs."

"No. That's not what I meant." He ignored her sarcasm. "Something strange is happening here." He turned troubled eyes to Quinn. "Did you make this happen? Do you know what it's about?"

I know, but I not make happen. You do. You ever heard photosynthesis, Muze?

Uh, duh. Of course, but what does that have to do with anything? He looked confused.

You, Verrie? Quinn asked.

Sure. It's where a plant stores energy from the sun, Verrie supplied.

Right, Quinn breathed out. *Then attracts bees…pollinators…Chosen.* She emphasized the last word, and Verrie's brain chimed with a huge "ding-ding," we have a winner, at the exact same moment the blank look left Muze's face. His head-voice burst forth with the knowledge.

Oh my gods. I don't light up like the other guys, he gulped. *My amulet is glowing for you…it has been the whole time. But it can only be seen as ultraviolet light, in darkness with white things.*

And of course his room was all done in dark, masculine colors, and they'd mostly "trysted" during the day. They'd been their own worst enemies.

Muze turned fully to Quinn. *How…why…Quinn, you are a genius.* He picked her up in an enormous embrace and swung her around the confined space. She sputtered and squirmed.

Okay, Muze. I get it. You happy. But you also naked with enormous…thing pressed into my stomach. My pretty sure Sham tear you limb from limb if he catches whiff of your scent on me.

Dumuzi dropped her like a hot coal.

Verrie remained on her knees in shock. *He lights up for me,* she said to no one in particular. Her eyes focused on Muze's thighs. *You light up for me.* She reached out and touched his abdomen, reverently, then reached to find his hand. *How did you know, Quinn?*

Mad eyesight skills, she coughed, trying to avoid Muze's massive, evident prowess as his male parts bobbed and weaved from happiness. *I always capable of seeing more spectrums than other people. Just didn't know come in handy for this.*

Verrie looked up at Muze, and Muze gazed down into her eyes. She slowly rose to her feet and they moved into each other's embrace, barely hearing Quinn's parting words. *Leave you two now to...kiss and make up. I explain things to everybody, and, uh, yeah. Well. Bye now.*

The door snicked open and clicked shut.

There was no one in the world but Dumuzi.

Chapter Twenty-three

"Now, where were we." Dumuzi nuzzled Verrie's neck and inhaled her perfect pipevine scent. "If I'm not mistaken, we were attempting a reenactment here," he teased cheekily.

"Reenactment," Verrie murmured blankly, clearly enjoying the feel of his lips nipping their way down the column of her throat. He moved back up to skim lightly across her full mouth.

"Yes, ma'am." Muze jogged her memory, "We're recalling things that happened in the closet that day before Marduk distracted us."

Veronica finally burst out laughing. "Of course, we are. And if memory serves, my mouth was just about to get busy." She gave his chest a playful shove. "Muze, if you want me to suck your cock, you should just say so."

"Oh, is that where we were?" he asked innocently. "Oh, yeah, that and…something else as well." He grinned at her in the tiny room which presently looking like a giant black-light poster. "If I recall…I might have been positioned something like this." Muze backed up and put both hands behind his head.

"Ah, now I remember," Verrie grinned. "I do believe you're right. So, remind me of something else." This time it was Verrie who moved toward Muze, going on tiptoe to capture his bottom lip between her teeth and give a sharp nip before she moved back. "In this little scenario, did I have all my clothes on…or off?" She was practically naked as it was, in her do-nothing bra and panties, but he needed her fully unclothed.

"I think you were just about to remove everything," he told her with conviction even though he knew it wasn't true. She might disagree, but would she comply?

"You're a bad boy for telling a fib," Verrie chastised and didn't remove the damnable last scraps of her clothing. Instead, she walked around behind him and ran a soft hand over one quivering ass cheek. "You know what bad boys get for their naughty thoughts, don't you?"

Without warning, she landed a hard, stinging swat to his backside that surprised the hell out of him…but damned if a moan didn't burst from his throat—that and his cock grew exponentially harder. *Gods.* She'd ramped up her dominance game, and who would have figured an ass-smack would turn him on? He swallowed. Perhaps everything Verrie did had the capacity to arouse him.

"You liked that," she purred, peeking around to take a look at his cock while running her nails across his lower back. "Well, we can't give one cheek all the attention and have the other feeling left out, can we?"

Dumuzi waited, holding his breath as she ducked back, steeling himself for the next slap, but it didn't come. She was a damned minx, making him wait…anticipate. And shit if it wasn't working. The longer Verrie held back, the more he wanted the sharp blow. He growled.

"Impatient?" Verrie tormented. She snaked one arm to the front of him and wrapped her fingers around his ultra-stiff rod. "Perhaps a little squeeze to remind you who's in charge."

As his mind took in this new development and his focus became centered on her hot little hand tightly gripping his cock, she hauled back with the other palm and slapped side number two. *Damn.* His penis leaped under her fingers. This was freaking hot. He'd gotten wind of some spanking scuttlebutt from a couple of his buddies, but he'd never known it would be like this.

Dumuzi growled. *Okay.* Tease time was over because he needed some action. "Bra and panties off, Veronica," he demanded through clenched teeth. "I need to be buried deep in your pussy right the hell now."

She dropped her stroking hand, but not to remove her remaining clothing. Verrie crossed her arms over her very fine chest.

"What the hell?" he managed to grind out, not happy with the way that had gone.

"You're taking over." Veronica paradoxically went from dominatrix to pouty vixen. And in a fucking blink with a lick up the edge of his chest into the fringe of his armpit, she turned the tables once again. "Who's calling the shots here... mate?"

"Not mated yet," Dumuzi conceded. "But okay, how about this for a compromise? Here's what you get to do. Order me to fuck you, right now, and I won't lower my hands." Muze clenched his fists above his head.

"That might work," Veronica's voice oozed sex appeal as she reached back for the clasp on her bra and unhooked it. *Yes.* The material fell away from her beautiful breasts, and Muze licked his lips. He wanted those nipples in his mouth ASAP, but when he loosened his hands and moved toward her...

"Uh-uh." She waggled a finger, backing up as much as she could in the confined space. "You want to fuck me? You promised to stand there. No touching."

Shit. This was worse torture than waiting for that ass-slap. It was difficult to think straight, but he forced himself to plug his brain back into the socket his prick seemed to have stolen. He attempted reason. Reason told him—because the mother of all orgasms was currently building in his balls—he should go without touching...for a short time if he could stand it.

His little flirt must have felt his acquiescence because she trotted out all her womanly wiles.

She began by running her hands up her sides to lift both breasts in his direction. She hefted their glorious weight—weight he wanted under his own palms—then spent what seemed like forever rolling her pink nipples between her thumbs and forefingers, continuing to drive him mad.

Just when he thought he couldn't take any more, she turned her back to him, looked over her shoulder with lids at half mast, and hooked her fingers into the top of her leopard skin panties. She lowered them half an inch.

Yeah. More. More.

"Nope. Not yet," she wrinkled her nose in a very fresh way. "First, I want to know how we're going to do it?"

"How we're...what?" Again his brain went to mush.

"How are we going to do it?" she repeated, a dirty-girl look on her face. "Should you bend me over that stack of suitcases or maybe press me up against the wall? Should we make a pile of coats on the floor with you on the bottom, and I can climb on?"

She wasn't actually tapping her mouth with her finger, was she? Wasting precious time, pondering the perfect position?

Dumuzi couldn't stand it any longer. He'd been very patient, but now he lost it. Veronica was his *Chosen,* and with that fact established, he needed to possess her in the fastest and deepest way possible. And thanks to her teasing, it would probably be very fast.

"That's it, Veronica. No more bullshit." He brought his hands down and closed the two feet that separated them in one stride. He grabbed both sides of her panties and yanking outward, shredded them to nothing. Verrie didn't even look surprised. Gods, he loved how she baited him.

Standing tall and pulling her close, his prick became happily cradled against the warm smoothness of her belly, his balls tickled by her downy nest of pubic hair. Dumuzi groaned, wedging his hand between them and swiping a finger through her pussy crease. Ahh. His mate was completely ready for him. Feeling and smelling her arousal did him in.

Shifting slightly, he grabbed both globes of her ass and lifted her easily to the proper height. His hips split her in two and with one swift move and a single gasp from Verrie which he swallowed into his own mouth, she was speared—impaled deeply on his cock—then shoved back against the wall. Gods, she felt so damned good…so tight around him. It was all he could do to hold his immortal strength in check. He suddenly became scared at the depth of his need. He was a god, and she was not yet a goddess. He had to pull back…lighten things up before he hurt her.

"So, I guess it's the wall," she interrupted his thoughts with a rasping chuckle, letting him know she was more than fine.

Still, he was concerned with his indelicate handling. "Are you okay? Am I being too rough?" Muze focused on her face which showed only joy.

"Better than okay," she hummed back at him, going in for a quick, deep kiss and rotating her hips. "What about you?"

"I think I'm going a little unglued and crazy here," he answered, warning her, but also scooping her higher, halting her motion and positioning himself to angle deeper into her hot spot with renewed vigor.

She keened at the new trajectory. "Oh gods, Muze. Don't let me stop you."

Verrie dug her nails frantically into his shoulders, and the sharp little bites snapped what was left of his self-control. He found himself thrusting and thrusting to the accompaniment of her voice in his head screaming, *Yes. Yes.* He couldn't have held back if he wanted to, and restraint was the last thing on his intrepid mate's mind.

The world outside him and Verrie—outside the strangely illuminated closet—ceased to exist. He moved a hand between them and parting her hair, found her clit and pinched. She screamed into his ear, and it was the biggest fucking turn on he could imagine.

Verrie grabbed at his head and demanded his mouth. When he gave it, she forced his lips apart and thrust her tongue deep. When his joined the battle, she sucked it into her mouth and held him captive, demanding the same dance from his tongue as his dick performed in her pussy. Dumuzi was more than happy to oblige.

Oh shit, Muze, she trilled in his head. *I'm going to come.*

He didn't need to be told. He could feel the tightening in her channel, the extra rush of wetness that preceded her orgasm. His own juices gathered, poised in his balls with screaming impatience. She needed to let go first...she needed...*Ahh.* Her contractions grabbed onto his cock, thirstily milking, and with her cunt's unwitting permission, Dumuzi opened his floodgates to burst cum up inside of her with an explosion unprecedented in his long life.

He had to fight to keep his feet, his emitted sperm suddenly rendering him as helpless as Sampson's cut hair, but unlike the emasculated Sampson, Muze quickly recovered and felt like the most powerful being on earth. He wanted to shout, to yell, to proclaim to the world he'd found his woman.

Yeah, we know, was the reply from a highly amused Anshar. *All of us do. You guys should be more careful to use your filters. Not that it wasn't amusing, but I'm afraid Sienna may be scarred for life and the rest of us? Well...we'll all be in our rooms by the time you two get cleaned up and come out of the closet. Oh, and did I mention, that now, as well as the sign-up sheet for the naughty room in the basement, the girls are going to put one outside the coat closet?* The sky god's snickering filtered away, along with the after-tremors of Verrie's orgasm.

Dumuzi looked down at his lover. How was she going to take their inadvertent PDA?

Her face screwed up and turned red, but before he could get words started that would calm her down, Verrie began chuckling. Her chuckle turned to a chortle, and her chortle to a big, roiling belly laugh. Muze felt the vibrations all the way down to his still embedded cock…and it was most pleasant.

"Oh, dear," she finally wound down to a snicker. "I'm going to have to do some serious damage control with my daughter." Tears from laughter left tracks down her lovely, flushed face. Muze kissed the wet trails.

"It seems to me she'll take it all in stride. Neither you nor your friend Frank seems to have brought your girls up with anything but honesty and a healthy love of life—with all that entails. I'm sure she's already processed it and let it go." Muze decided Verrie might need a little extra reassurance. "Besides, if I know the women of the household, they head-blocked the girls from the worst, once they got wind of what we were doing."

"Still…to have everybody listen…" Verrie's face turned a lovely shade of ultra-violet pink.

It was Dumuzi's turn to laugh out loud. "Oh, please. Do you know how many couplings I've been witness to since the guys started finding their *Chosen?* Something about you fated ladies has us forgetting our boundaries and leaving our good sense on the floor next to our discarded jeans. Please, do not think twice about this." He kissed the top of her head and reluctantly slid out of her body, thinking quickly, retrieving a scarf from a shelf above his head to deal with "fall out."

Verrie looked down while he mopped them up, her shoulders shaking again. "I hope that wasn't anyone's favorite?" she laughed. "You've gotten some of your...photosynthesis...on it."

Sure enough, Muze looked down, and spots of light-up ejaculate dotted the material. He grinned at Verrie. "We could have saved ourselves a lot of trouble if we'd just had night-time sex like normal people. It would have put the whole amulet fear to bed before it even got started."

"That's true," she giggled back, feeling young and carefree for the first time in years. "And we would have found out about your awesome new glow-in-the-dark paint earlier, too. Do you think we should bottle it?"

Dumuzi snarled and put a hard kiss on her mouth for her cheekiness, but her playful words gave him ideas about various ways he might be decorating her body in the future.

Chapter Twenty-four

Once Verrie got over her embarrassment of having nearly-public sex—and with the help of some hilarious stories from the Goddess League—she was able to ascertain Sienna hadn't heard anything that would require therapy. Life was settling into a nice pattern. The girls were happily escorted to school each day, and Frank was accompanied to work, kicking and complaining, but her complaints were overridden by the gods—better safe than sorry.

Verrie and Dumuzi were having scads of fun vying for dominance in their relationship, sexually as well as intellectually, finding that switching off on the partner-in-charge was more titillating than having it all one way or the other.

The uncertainty pervading the household was due to waiting for word from Sham and Lahar. The pair still weren't back from their ancient history crawl, and it looked like—although the gods couldn't hold off the summer solstice—the amulet ceremony might have to be postponed. This caused a great deal of worry for Dumuzi who wanted Verrie to be a full-fledged goddess during the next cycle of the moon when the voices would return.

To that end, he'd done a lot of thinking, and Veronica knew he'd come to a decision with which she would be displeased. When she woke up one morning, and her mate-to-be was not wrapped around her, but pacing back and forth outside on their balcony, she knew his decision had been finalized.

Verrie got up and slipped a robe over her shoulders, quietly pushing the slider open.

"Hey." She moved easily behind her big man and threaded her arms around his middle, pressing her nose to his back, inhaling his woodsy scent. "What's got you up and out of bed so early?"

He reached for her forearm. "It's time we act instead of react," he said cryptically. "We need to go see Marduk…and Nergal." He turned in her arms and rested his chin on top of her sleep-tousled hair. "I have an idea how to take care of your demon voices before they hit again."

"Why do I know I'm not going to like what you're about to suggest?" Verrie's gut tightened. The gods were all used to Underworld intrigue, violence, and demons, but she'd led a pacifistic lifestyle and wasn't sure she could agree with the "might makes right" attitude her new housemates espoused. And she was certain that's what Dumuzi had in mind. "Are you going to tell me what's up your beanstalk or make me wait?" she attempted to lighten his worries.

"I think you should wait so you can weigh in with your opinions after hearing everyone else's. If I tell you now, you're just going to try to dissuade me."

That sounded regrettably ominous, but Verrie could see by the set of Dumuzi's jaw, his mind was made up. He wouldn't tell her, no matter how much she coerced or threatened. She moved away from his warm body reluctantly and took his hand to draw him back inside.

"Then let's get dressed. The sooner we get this over with, the sooner we can get back to important things like…sex." And that was the truth. She couldn't hide it and didn't want to. Verrie was so voracious for her man, copulation was never far from her mind…or his either, thankfully.

"If what I have planned works, everything will be solved, and I'll never have to let you out of bed again." He reached up under the bottom of her robe and palmed one warm globe. "Except to eat," he teased, nipping at the soft lobe of her ear. "We'll need to keep up our strength."

Verrie almost let go of her anxiousness with his deliberate attempt at misdirection, but when Muze's god-voice made a general announcement, she ended up stiffening and pulling away.

Marduk and anyone else who's interested in hearing a strategy I've conceived, join me in the meeting room in ten minutes. And Marduk, can you call Nergal to attend as well as Lavarette?

This better be good, Muze. Marduk's grumpy voice came back. *Girin finally slept through the night last night, and Tess and I were full of energy this morning…if you catch my drift.*

Dumuzi laughed, *Hah. Serves you right for all the meetings you've called on me at inopportune moments. Sucks to be you. Sorry Tess,* he sincerely tagged on.

Don't fret, the goddess came back. *If this is about solving Verrie and Sienna's problems, I'm on board. You shouldn't have to consider the sexual needs of an old married couple while you're trying to launch your own lives together.* She spoke both from the heart and tongue-in-cheek at the same time.

There was more distinct mumbling and grumbling from all quarters at Dumuzi's request, but the one bit of communication totally unexpected came from the glowie, Lavarette.

I'm, uh, already on-premise, Marduk, her little voice replied. *So, there's no need to have Nergal try to locate me.*

That got a major response of "Oohs and Hmms" from the household at large, but no one seemed to have an actual handle on why Lavarette was already at the compound. If Verrie wasn't mistaken, the glowie—whom she had yet to meet—was in for some major interrogation by the Goddess League.

Okay, everyone, you heard Muze. Ten minutes. Marduk cut off the on-air speculation.

Verrie and Muze hit the shower, but unfortunately, there was no time for play. It was a quick in and out...and not the good kind.

The final tally in the conference room, when taken, was a quorum minus eight. Among the missing were Sham and Lahar who were still in the middle east, Dagon and Enten who had accompanied the girls to school, and Absu who'd gone with Frank—excited to pick up a few ideas for food from around the North End where Frank worked.

The big news of the morning, causing lots of raised eyebrows and open mouths, was Lavarette easing through the door quietly behind King Waylon of the Lauernley...holding his hand.

It was apparent Waylon's blue entourage was aware of what was going on between their king and the glowie and felt quite protective. They had formed an impenetrable ring around the pair which spoke of something more than a wish to keep the gossipy goddesses from approaching.

Verrie was astonished getting her first look at a glowie. She didn't know what she expected, but it was nothing like the lovely sight Lavarette made. Slight and ethereal, the waifish female was white with a blue cast, had enormous dark eyes, and was completely bald. There was something very sexy about her, and it was quite clear why Waylon would be smitten. He postured arrogantly when the Underworld king began to speak to the fey being.

"So this is where you've been 'vacationing,'" Nergal broke the flood of quiet speculation dousing the room. "I had no idea you were even acquainted with the Lauernley, other than when the battle was waged below."

We had to rescue Kulla a few weeks back, Dumuzi let Verrie know.

Nergal turned harsh eyes to the blue royal. "You're treating my head of security well, I hope, King Waylon?" There was no mistaking the warning behind Nergal's words. He clearly cautioned Waylon not to toy with Lavarette, or the Underworld would bring forth great wrath.

"In answer to that, I'll just say she might not be your head of security much longer," Waylon responded smoothly. "I'd start taking resumes if I were you."

Wow, Verrie thought. It was quite clear Waylon wasn't talking about an alternative job offer, but what was up with Lavarette's sourpuss at his announcement?

Trouble in paradise already? Verrie could commiserate. These alpha types didn't make loving them very easy.

"Congratulations then." Nergal didn't look convinced.

"Lavarette, Waylon, I'm sure the two of you will be very happy," Marduk truncated the conversation. Was that a pissed off light suffusing the little glowie's body? If so, it was the loveliest form of anger Verrie had ever seen.

Marduk redirected everyone's attention again, "And now, down to business."

Gods and goddesses found seats while Dumuzi gave a reassuring squeeze to Veronica's hand and strode to the front of the room. He looked at all the sleepy faces.

"I'm sorry to drag you out of bed so early, but I had a thought that kept me up most of the night, and I figured I'd share." He paused and looked at Verrie. "You all know the last time Veronica called to the demons, you were unable to find the cretins. The closest you came was ascertaining they weren't in Nergal's home territory." He stood straighter, and his brown eyes took on a greener tinge. "Now, because I was somehow connected to Verrie's ancestors, thousands of years ago…"

"Because of a drunken bet made at Aham-nishi's Inn one night," Shamash's amused voice cut into Dumuzi's speech as the cat-god and Lahar appeared in the room, dusty and tired.

Dumuzi's eyes widened, suitably confused. "Hello to you, too." He shook his head. "Do you want to run that by me again?"

"In a minute," Sham coughed. "Anybody able to rustle up some food and water before we get started?" He made an open-lipped grimace as if ridding his mouth of centuries worth of grit. He looked around, not seeing the god who usually fed them. "Shit. No Absu? Who's going to make food?"

His wife rushed gleefully to his side and gave him a fierce hug.

Leftover veal parm, she assured him. *It'll only take a sec.* She gave Charlie a look, and the pair popped out, then poofed back in a few heartbeats, one goddess holding two plates of cold Italian, and the other proffering giant mugs of iced water.

"Ah. Angels." Shamash moved to take the offerings and put a sandy kiss on his mate's mouth. She didn't seem to mind the added element to their lip-lock. The gods eventually broke away and sat down to eat…with gusto.

While the returning pair shoveled in food, inconsequential chatter started up around the room. Soon, it was like the boisterous group had forgotten all about business as the air filled with quips and laughter. Dumuzi put an end to that.

"Guys. Are you going to fill us in or just fill yourselves?" he roared over the clamor. The room went silent.

Verrie shot him a look. The two god-travelers had just spent the last week and a half in the desert, gathering information to help her. She didn't want her mate to appear ungrateful.

"Eat first. We can wait," she assured the duo.

"No. No. I get it," Sham smiled at Dumuzi. "We can talk and eat at the same time. My mouth can do

272

food while my brain takes care of conversation." He switched to head-talk.

Sorry, Muze. I won't keep you in suspense. Funny thing, history. It turns out we were a bunch of drunken sots in our old days, Shamash smirked. *You can't believe the shit we uncovered in the ruins of the temple of the gods. Luckily, the remains of our lives are buried deep underground and in a place where it will never be discovered by archaeologists even with the advanced satellite imaging they use to find buried building and roads.*

We, on the other hand, continued Lahar, *were able to hone in on the remaining half-life of god-forged isotopes to eventually locate the exact spot we were looking for. It took a lot of digging—through millennia of good gossip—and when our own cluster-fuck is solved, Sham and I have an ark-load of juicy tales to share. But for now…*

For now, Shamash took over, *you're never going to believe how this whole thing got started.* His face turned serious. *First let me say, we found census records in the old city hall building, and both of the twins that I, uh, got to know…*he looked apologetically to Quinn…*Arwi and Abi, we think, gave birth nine months after my little…episode with them in 256 BC.*

"Both of them…you think," Verrie stated. *Wow.* So it was a given. Her family and Franks, together for centuries, were really related.

Yeah. It sure looks like it. But get this. The only twin's child recorded was Arwi's. Two days later, however, at the exact time that Abi's baby would have arrived, the birth records for the household indicate a servant girl gave birth. There was total silence in the room as everyone waited for Sham to continue. *Just a little too much of a coincidence, don't you think, especially since the sisters kept diaries showing they raised both babies.*

Clearly, he'd made up his mind the second child was Abi's. Verrie concurred.

We searched forward in time for as many generations as were recorded on buried cuneiform...

"How come you didn't bring back some tablets?" Kulla asked. "It would have been nice to handle some real communication for nostalgia's sake."

We thought about it, Sham answered, *but figured the gods in charge had gone to so much trouble burying them, they might be pissed if we snatched some. And on top of all the other shit going on, we don't need to bring overgods down on our asses.*

Everyone dipped their heads in agreement. Low profile was definitely to their advantage.

Anyway, after the stone records, we went to more current archives. What we found didn't surprise us. The female descendants of Arwi and the line springing from the supposed servant never parted ways. Arwi's descendants were linked to Abi's from that first birth onward. To this day, the lines have remained together.

"My mother and Frank," Verrie confirmed. "Me and Nancy, Si and Riles."

Relatives, for sure, Sham confirmed. *Not just friends. When we get the results of the DNA test on you guys, not just the Enlil sniff, we can be certain baby number two was Abi's. The child was simply designated as a servant's in the records.*

"But why?" Glory asked the question which had been about to spring from Verrie's lips.

Most likely to save face. Now Sham looked uncomfortable. *Records were forged to make it look like I wed Arwi.* He glanced at his mate, Quinn, reassuringly. *But that's impossible because I had already been pulled to hell by that time. Obviously, Arwi's family looked for me and was told I wouldn't be back, so they felt safe with the lie. Abi, on the other hand, would have produced an illegitimate child. Therefore, the need for subterfuge.*

"The good news to all this as I see it," Marduk qualified, "is whoever is behind the demons attempt to drive Verrie and her ancestors mad never knew of the second child from Shamash's loins, and therefore, the voices only went after one paternal line."

"And that had to have begun in 239 BC when Arwi's child was seventeen because that's when I had *my* first demon episode," Dumuzi finished.

Now back to that. Shamash had that shit-eating grin on again. *The defining moment which got Muze involved actually occurred before the twins figured out they were pregnant, and when I was still busy celebrating my great victory in court that had freed their uncle. It was mere days before the factions I opposed framed me and had me sent to hell.* He shrugged. *So, here's the story. I met up with my good buddy Muze one night in Aham-nishi's Inn.*

"That sounds like a really shifty place, along the lines of the Mos-Eisley Cantina in *Star Wars*," Candy smirked.

"You've got the picture," Dumuzi said with a nod. "I remember *going* there a good many times, but I never remember getting home."

Well apparently neither of us remembered this particular episode, Shamash concurred, *and if you hadn't insisted—as evidenced by some accompanying documentation—we draw things up legally after you lost our bet, none of this,* Sham waved a hand between Muze and Verrie, *would have happened.*

"So tell us already." Anshar loved a good wager. "Don't leave anything out."

Oh, I won't, Sham grinned. *I especially won't leave out the instigator of the wager.* The god narrowed his cat-eyes at Anshar, and the sky god lost all his color.

"Me?" he yelped.

Right in one, Sham nodded, shoveling more of the parmesan into his mouth. *Now, do you want me to tell it or not?*

Anshar nodded reluctantly.

This is all according to an eyewitness account that was included as a codicil to Muze's signed instrument. It seems, on the night in question, the three of us were stumbling drunk, and I began making claims—bragging I could tell truth from fiction, no matter the source. He cleared his virtual throat. *You have to understand, I was young and still high from the biggest court case of my career. But Muze...Muze was even younger and stupider, and Anshar, never bright to being with, was there to egg him on.*

That earned Shamash a one fingered salute which he ignored. *So, when I made my self-important statement, our dear sky-god friend took Dumuzi off for yet another drink, and they discussed the terms of a possible wager. A wager the gods on high took note of.*

Sham took a big swallow of water, and before he drained the glass, his wife misted out and back in, carrying another for her cat-man. He put the finishing touches on his food and sighed appreciably.

"Now, for those of you who don't quite understand how it is for an immortal, let me tell you time is all relative amongst the gods, and according to the whims of the higher powers, it can be very loosely construed. Those who are a rung ahead of us on the power scale can foresee a lot of what will happen and like to think past is present and present is future. They've always sounded like your current day quantum physics guys, only a little more arrogant."

Verrie, with a few of the others, looked suitably puzzled but remained patient despite their ignorance.

"So, when Dumuzi finally came back to me and challenged me with a statement—with a little help from Anshar—I was tasked to determine whether what he told me was true or false. Apparently, I got a rather confused look on my face. I was purported to mumble something about 'from a human perspective or something higher?' but eventually, I made my decision and spit out the verdict."

"So, what was Muze's statement? And what was the verdict?" Huxley had been very quiet, but Verrie had been told he'd been the butt of a life-changing god-fuck before, so he seemed extra curious.

"Wait. Wait. I remember." Anshar's face lit up with the biggest shit-eating grin Verrie had ever seen.

"You do?" Lenore elbowed him in the ribs. "You fucker. I should nail your ass for messing with people's lives the way you do," she warned. "No more wagers for you." She shook a finger under her mate's nose. "Do you hear me?"

"Yes, sweet thing," he assuaged, but truly he didn't look the least bit repentant.

"So, anyway," Sham cut in, not letting Anshar have the spotlight. "Muze's big truth or untruth was: *I know what it's like to, uh, be between the legs of someone who is related to you.*"

Clearly, he cleaned up the language for the room full of listeners.

"Now, I had to know that was a crock of shit because all my female relatives were happily married, and I was well aware Muze wasn't hitting on the males, so I must have been about to call bullshit when it's said I hesitated. I looked like I might be about to pass out or be sick or something. I had to have been wondering if the upper gods—who gave me the power of veracity— were taking note of the happenings, and construing the truth in their own way.

"But I must have dismissed my intuition because when I finally came to a decision, I called the conjecture false. Dumuzi, who should have known better than to test me with such a simple premise, to begin with, easily conceded, and I won the wager...or so I thought."

"What were the stakes?" Now Nergal was rapt.

"If I lost, which I didn't think I had, I promised to give one of my female relations to Muze for his eternal pleasure. If Muze lost, he was to pledge his life and devotion to protecting my bloodlines from cruel and unusual harm."

That brought the assemblage to a total still point. Complete silence encompassed the room as Sham's revelation was digested. Nergal was the first to speak again.

"So, from this drunken agreement, because Muze lost, from that point on, he became the champion for all the ladies of your blood who suffered from the demon voices." The king paused, letting that sink in. "And because the overgods are so bored and devious, they took Sham's ruling as only partially correct because indeed, Dumuzi is currently sleeping with Verrie which to them, at the time, was something of which they were already aware."

Verrie followed his reasoning, albeit slowly.

Sham tipped his head in agreement. "That they did. To make a neat, little, closed loop, they made good on my bet and gave one female relation, Verrie, to Muze for his eternal pleasure." Sham finished with a flourish of his glass in the happy couple's direction.

"So both of you were correct…or *became* correct." Verrie was having a hard time following it all, but it seemed to work for the gods who were nodding sagely. She was just relieved the mystery of why Dumuzi reacted to her episodes had been solved. Apparently, Muze felt the same way.

"So, now that my protective instincts have boiled down to a drunken bet, we only have to find out why the demons haunt the descendants of Arwi and Sham."

"Which, if I'm not mistaken, was the reason you called this meeting in the first place," Marduk reminded the swamp-god.

"Correct." Now Dumuzi's eyes lit up in a dangerous way. "We need Verrie to talk to the demons again."

"But we've already tried that," Kulla intervened. "And a bunch of us searched while she did and couldn't come up with their location."

"That's because you weren't the women's protector." Dumuzi's eyes glowed. "And now that I know a legally binding document found in the hall of gods proclaims me as such, I'm even more certain my plan will succeed."

"And what is your plan?" Marduk clearly wanted it stated even though everyone in the room had already figured it out. Even Verrie, who'd been a little slow on the uptake, knew what Dumuzi was about to propose. She shivered, awaiting his pronouncement.

"Easy pickings, guys. When Veronica calls the demons again, *I* will be the one going into the depths of hell to search out the voices and put an end to this bullshit."

Chapter Twenty-five

Dumuzi saw the narrow-eyed glance Veronica sent his way. He'd known she wouldn't be pleased about his trip to hell, but really…who better? Once he was in the demons' realm, his protective reactions would kick in, he'd turn swamp monster, and consequently, kick some demon ass. It had occurred to him, of course, he might need back up.

"Lavarette," he honed in on the thoughtful, highly intelligent face of the glowie he'd invited to attend. "I know this is a lot to ask, but I was hoping you and a contingent of your security forces could join me. You know the terrain, and you work better than most in Underworld conditions."

"No fucking way," King Waylon snapped, immediately squashing Dumuzi's request. "I will not have her placed in danger with unknown demons in an unsecured location."

Dead quiet met his declaration. Lavarette crossed her arms over her chest while spearing Waylon with narrowed eyes.

Dumuzi stifled a groan. Waylon did *not* just say that. Even the swamp monster would have known better than to undermine a powerful woman's initiative

There was a lot of uncomfortable shuffling amongst the gods. Man, was the blue guy out of touch with how things worked for females—whether human, goddess, or glowie. The king was in huge trouble. Dumuzi took a step back and waited for the shit to fly.

"Excuse me?" Lavarette's voice flowed like warm honey from her throat as she faced Waylon with the deceptively innocuous question. "Did you just answer for me?"

The king looked down his haughty nose…and blinked, suddenly, seeming not so sure. "Uh, yes," he managed after a strangled cough. "I may have overstepped, but I feel there is no need for you to accompany the god when he has so many other, more powerful friends at his disposal."

Yipes. What a masochist. Dumuzi almost smacked his temple. The king had done it again.

Anshar was happy to take advantage with quiet bets ricocheting around the room in head-speak only the gods and goddesses could hear. Lenore didn't even try to stop him although she'd previously ripped him up and down for placing wagers. The *Chosens'* eyes were gleaming—waiting, anticipating…no, *expecting* a smack-down.

"More powerful?" Lavarette repeated, still flowing honey, but this time barbed with stingers. "Do you recall the nature of my job for King Nergal?" Lavarette's nose reached only to Waylon's sternum, but suddenly, she was the most formidable presence in the room.

"Why yes, my dear," Waylon placed both hands on the glowie's shoulders, still not seeing the danger. "You are the head of his security team." He seemed to have found his footing as he answered.

"That's correct." She inclined her head, never taking her eyes off her large, blue target. "And do you have any idea what that entails?" she asked, maintaining a mild give and take with an amazing amount of control.

"I assume it means you monitor his computer systems for problems, perhaps dispatch forces to take care of any bothersome issues that might arise." Waylon shrugged. "I know you dabbled with your sword during the battle to rescue the god, Kulla."

Apparently, everyone but the hapless blue king felt the chill coming off the normally warm being. They all watched the clusterfuck unfurl as he dug his own hell, deeper and deeper.

"You know, my dear," he added, "I have a head of security back in my home valley."

Lavarette's eyes widened in what Muze could see was mock surprise. "Oh? You don't say. And here I thought Razure was your head of security."

"My sweet girl," King Waylon laughed. "Razure is a warrior. He is the head of my security *forces*," he proclaimed loftily. "It's an entirely different thing."

Dumuzi and everyone else knew Lavarette had handled more than her fair share of physical combat in hell when rescuing first Dagon, then Kulla. The blue king didn't know of Dagon's extraction and seemed to have wiped Lavarette's heroics with Kulla from his mind.

She'd set him straight.

Without taking her eyes from the royal, Lavarette called over her shoulder. "Raze?"

Just that use of the tall guy's nickname should have told Waylon something was brewing...that the two were well acquainted. "Tell your king what we did last night while he was on video conference with his home."

That got the king looking askance—jealousy if Muze was any judge.

"Your lordship," Razure stood tall and cleared his throat, but refused to look directly at his ruler. It was obvious he'd never crossed his boss before and wasn't comfortable starting now. He remained respectful. "Ms. Lavarette and I were sparring in the gym."

The king's brows came together, and he became thoughtful, letting go of whatever suspicion had clouded his face. "A good way to remain fit," he allowed, clearly not quite happy the two were interacting but relieved, nonetheless. "I hope you were careful with her, Razure."

The top guard couldn't hold back a snort. "Yeah...I mean, yes, sir. I was careful," he agreed, before adding snarkily, "careful to remain alert."

"Alert?" Waylon looked suitably confused. "To what ends? I fail to see any danger to you or Lavarette in Marduk's household."

Geeze. Dumuzi's and a dozen other heads shook. The king was particularly thick.

"Sweetness." Butter would have melted in Lavarette's mouth as she addressed Waylon. Her liquid tones as she reached up and wrapped her hands behind the huge king's head lulled the giant man. She stood on tiptoe and put her lips to his ear. "Raze didn't mean he was looking for resident hostiles," she crooned.

"What then?" The royal bent so to better accommodate the glowie.

"Silly. He was protecting himself from friendly fire."

"Friendly…"

Lavarette brought her head sharply into contact with the king's cranium, stopping anything else coming from his mouth. His head snapped back, then rocked forward, dropping so when the glowie lifted her skull, she caught him a hard clip under his chin.

The blue gargantuan staggered backward and crashed against the wall. Everyone who had been behind him moved quickly away, fully aware what was about to happen. The toppling tree had plenty of room to fall, and when he did, Dumuzi bit back the urge to yell "timberrrr" because the king looked cross-eyed, but pissed off enough to start a fire with Muze's tendrils.

But speaking of pissed off…

"Don't mess with me, Waylon." Lavarette glared down at him. "I'm the king's Champion in the Underworld. If you're interested in me, don't think you're going to take that away from me or forget who I am for a single moment."

"Bravo, Lavarette. Well done." Nergal stood up and clapped. He'd clearly known from their first meeting how fierce the petite glowie was, and there hadn't been any hesitation on his part before naming her as his Champion. He let the full extent of his amusement show on his face. Dumuzi thought him very brave, but perhaps Nergal—being a king himself—had some kind of immunity to royal retribution. Still, Muze wondered how it would go between the two kings after that PDA…public display of aggression.

Lavarette was another who didn't seem intimidated.

"So, Dumuzi, you were saying?" The glowie turned to him and continued the conversation as if Waylon had never interceded.

"Umm," the swamp god coughed and regrouped. "I asked if you and a contingent of your warriors would like to accompany me to hunt down these rogue demons."

"And the answer to that is yes, I'd be more than happy to watch your back." She swept imperious eyes to the Lauernley king who was picking himself up off the floor.

There was a growl as Waylon looked menacingly in Lavarette's direction. He took a quick step toward her.

She quickly and smartly finished up. "You can fill me in on all the details later. Eeep!" The air left her body as the king lunged, lifted, and threw her up over his shoulder. Her head hung down, and she gave the entire room a cheeky, upside-down smile and a final wave of her adorable, little three-fingered hand before being hauled from the room.

"Will she be alright?" Verrie asked, looking horrified.

"Hell, yeah," Lenore answered, fanning herself. "She'll be more than okay. Did you see the look on Waylon's face? Who wouldn't want to be Lavarette right now?" There was a spate of lustful agreement and half-lidded sighs from the rest of the women in the room.

"Really? You know, you guys, nothing in this house is normal," Verrie groused. But Muze noticed her nipples had hardened beneath her t-shirt in response to the show of power that had just unfolded. "Dammit.

What have I gotten myself into?" Veronica breathed out but held up a quick hand. "And don't anybody answer that," she ordered. "It was purely rhetorical."

Laughter came from every being in the room, breaking the sexual tension, and the meeting was resumed.

"Let's get back to business." Was that a tear of laughter Marduk wiped from the corner of his eye? "Muze. Take control of this discussion, would you? If that's at all possible."

"My pleasure, boss." Dumuzi looked around the room. "Now that we've established I'll be going with a back-up glowie contingency, would anyone else care to join me? The more, the merrier."

"I'd be interested," King Nergal replied, and he wasn't alone. Almost every hand went up around the room.

The royal asked the next question. "Do you have any idea how much Underworld territory you'd like to cover?"

"I've been thinking about that," Muze mused. "I'm going to make a leap here and look at things historically." Everyone quieted, settling down to listen. "When I was in Mesopotamia, I had my episodes off and on from 239BC until I was taken to the Underworld in 17AD." He tried not to look at Veronica. This was the first time he'd mentioned his descent to hell in her presence.

"Once I was in Nergal's realm, I stopped suffering from the changes, and as you all recall, I didn't have any in Merrymount either. So my thought is, perhaps I was too far away from Verrie's ancestors to detect their distress?"

"Or there was no distress to detect. My ancestors might have been too far away from the demons to hear them." Verrie jumped up out of her seat, clearly excited. "I think I've already told you. When I lived in Boston, I was full of the voices, every month, but once I moved to Colorado…nothing. Nada. Zip."

"Okay," Marduk broke in. "What if we assume both situations? In order for the demons to get the upper hand, Verrie's people had to be within a certain proximity to hear them. And Muze had to be near to the women in order to effect his change."

"I'll take this a step further," Nergal supplied. "The demons must have made a move from a position near Sumer when Verrie's ancestors left the area. In order to orchestrate their harassment there, they needed to be in the nether-world below the Hellenic Trench. But when the ancestors of Arwi moved, they clearly followed. It makes sense. From what you've shown on your timeline, Verrie's family moved from Sumer to England. At that time, maybe they were still privy to the voices or maybe not. But for a certainty, Muze wasn't. He was in Merrymount and incident free. But when Verrie's people moved to Boston in 1820…"

"I started having my episodes again," Dumuzi confirmed. "The women or the demons may have been too far away in England, but Boston was on my doorstep."

"I'm going to put in another guess." Nergal leaned back in his chair and stroked his square jaw. "I'm going to say these demons are currently hiding out and operating in the part of hell that lies under the Atlantic Ocean below the Laurentian Abyss." He named an underwater valley off the coast of Canada. "The only other possibility would be the Puerto Rico Trench, but that doesn't feel right. Not only is it a few hundred miles too far, but Manungal rules there. She's always been a hard-ass and known for keeping bad elements in check."

Dumuzi looked thoughtful. "So the Laurentian Abyss it is. How do we get there?"

"It shouldn't be too difficult to transport the group that needs to go." Nergal grimaced. "The real problem will be how to deal with Galla."

There were groans all around the room.

Fucking Galla, thought Dumuzi.

"Okay, I'll bite." Verrie had it right to look worried. "Who's Galla?"

Nergal answered, "He's a deposed Babylonian demon who—last these gods saw him," Nergal leveled his gaze at the squirming immortals, "was most likely eating the flesh and drinking the blood of any hapless mortal who got in his way."

Dumuzi watched Verrie screw up her face. "Really," she exclaimed. "Then why does this…thing…get to be in charge of an area of hell?"

"Because, my dear, his daddy is none other than the devil himself—Beelzebub, The Prince of Darkness. And when the overgods were tired of Galla's antics on earth, they delicately negotiated with Mr. Supreme-nastiness to send his son below. The offshoot was, in order to rid the earth of him, Galla was made into a god." Nergal looked like he smelled something bad as he finished. "He was subsequently given dominion over the portion of Underworld we've mentioned."

Nergal plucked at his bronze armbands. Dumuzi had hardly ever seen the deity look so disgusted.

"Technically, I'm Galla's boss. He and I have maintained a…working relationship…for a good many years. He's always invited to my little soirées and I to his. But only to keep the peace and not rattle his father. I've always refrained from poking my nose too far into his business. For that reason, he might not take lightly, me asking if a party can infiltrate his territory to hunt down and destroy some of his creatures. Creatures who could easily resemble what he once was."

Dumuzi understood the problem. And it sucked.

"That's not saying I won't attempt it." Nergal held up a hand, straightened, and gave Verrie a nod. "We can't have any little godlings you and Muze produce being harassed by Underworld scum, now can we? And that's what we're talking about here. You being at the mercy of some lowlife, demon trash. No," he got to his feet and thrust his chin in the air, "that isn't going to happen on my watch.

"Let me run all this by Ereshkigal. Historically, she's had an easier time dealing with Galla. I'm certain she'll come up with a diplomatic way to approach him," the king assured. "In the meantime, let me know when plans for your summer solstice celebration—and, of course, the amulet ceremony—are complete. The queen and I wouldn't think of missing them even if she is unusually large for this juncture of her pregnancy."

The king eyeballed Dr. Dani who had repeatedly refused to give over the possibility of multiple-fetal-formations. The doctor simply smiled beatifically at the king.

"Fine. Keep playing it that way," he pursed his lips at Dani. "Good day, all. I'll get back to you as soon as

I've been in touch with Galla." Nergal misted out, and the room let out a collective held breath.

It had been a mind-blowing morning.

Dumuzi wasn't sure what anyone else had planned, but he was rung out. It was only ten a.m., but he was going back to bed—he eyed his mate—for more than one reason. He tugged on her hand, giving her a suggestive twitch of his mouth, and with a few curt goodbyes, they left the room.

****

Really? Muze growled.

It was getting old, how jarring Marduk's voice had become. One orgasm away from giving Verrie a promised trifecta, the thunder god pontificated again. At least this time, nobody had to get dressed. The communication was done head-style.

Nergal just got back to me, Marduk's voice broadcast. I*t seems, with very little cajoling from Eresh—and a great deal of wine—Galla has not only acquiesced to our request but has intimated he will be more than happy to allow god-intervention toward whatever demons are responsible. Apparently, there is a group in his domain that has been out of hand for centuries and has succeeded in shutting down his attempts to police their area of Hell. And by police, Nergal believes Galla means extort. It seems, the demon-turned-god likes payment from his 'subjects,' and this particular group has continuously thwarted his demands, using some kind of protective energy with which Galla is unfamiliar. If we can solve this problem for him, we have his permission to remove those we think are responsible for obstructing him and bring them back to Nergal's realm for questioning.*

He paused before continuing. *Anyone who is interested...and not pregnant*—he said this because several of the goddesses were currently knocked-up and feeling like it didn't preclude them from helping to deal with bad guys—*should meet Nergal and Ereshkigal in the foyer in twenty minutes to be transported to hell.*

Dumuzi placed a kiss on the end of Verrie's nose. "That's me, babe." He couldn't keep the excitement out of his voice. "Don't hold lunch."

Chapter Twenty-six

Beletseri was abruptly awakened by rough hands. *Gods-dammit*. She'd had a particularly puke-y night and sleep had just overtaken her.

"What the fuck time is it?" she spewed grumpily, wrenching her shoulder away from a suddenly harsh grasp. It had to be one or two in the morning.

"Shut up and get to your feet." It was Ridhwan's voice.

"Don't tell me it's time for my video debut," Bel scathed, remaining on the ground and remembering Ridhwan had said he was going to send a visual message of her to…hopefully, Marla and Matthew. "I'm not exactly looking my best right now."

"Idiot." Ridhwan seethed. "That's not what brought me here in the middle of the night." He kicked her in anger. "There's something going on in hell, and I'm sure it has something to do with your husband's search for you."

Why he thought that, he wasn't letting on.

"You have to be hidden in case he's found a way to come for you, and I have to go take care of business before all of my plans are ruined." He grabbed Bel and yanked her up.

"Exactly where am I going?" the goddess asked, moving out of his anger-zone and absently brushing off the small, night-time crawly things that always lurked and nestled next to her warmth while she slept. The insects which had bothered her tremendously during her first few weeks of captivity now garnered little interest.

"If your husband infiltrates our hideaway, the first place he and his people will look for you is in this cave or a hut here in our main sanctuary area. We need you away from this central location with your scent and trail obliterated," he growled. "There is a hidden grotto inside our westernmost boundary. You will be rubbed with cat pheromones and taken there."

"Great. A bath in kitty-pee. I can't wait," Bel grimaced. How many more indignities would she have to suffer before Matthew found her?

Ridhwan yowled to the big shifter who had been guarding her door. *Funny.* She hadn't seen his *other* two right-paw lieutenants in several days. She had no time to think on that as Ridhwan thrust her into the currently present, tremendous tabby's hands.

"Make haste and don't let her out of the grotto until I return," Ridhwan ordered his guarding puma. "There is something I should have taken care of as soon as those other cat goddesses were discovered by the gods. I hope it's not too late." He poofed out in a high snit.

"Raaa-ow," snarked Bel. "Someone's got his tail in a kink." She jerked her arm out of her bodyguard's big paw and gave him a stare full of distaste. "You may show me the litter box, and the way to this grotto, but no touching, or I'll have my husband de-claw you the minute he arrives." Bel didn't have to repeat her warning. She was herded from the cave, but happily, even during her...spraying, there was no direct touching.

Bel, walking through the dense underbrush, breathed in the fresh, night air. Although the jungle remained thick and acrid, and her own scent was now anything but pleasant, the cloying aspect of the cave and its surrounding terrain was missing. Perhaps she'd been doing things all wrong. Would it behoove her to stay up all night and sleep during the uncomfortable heat of the day? It might make a difference to whatever was ailing her. She'd have to ask her captors if that was possible, but weren't kitties mostly nocturnal? Perhaps they'd changed their schedules to keep an eye on her, and the shift would benefit them all.

Roots and rocks marred the overgrown pathway, but Bel's goddess vision spotted most of them, keeping her from tumbling indelicately to the ground. She snorted to herself. One thing was certain. When she finally got out of this vermin-ridden jungle, she was never going outside again. As lonely as the Underworld had been, she pined for her old apartment where everything was comfortably familiar. She wondered if there wasn't a small plot of Hellish real estate somewhere down below she and Matthew could eventually call their own. Bel sighed. If her whole deceptive debacle got back to Nergal, Bel had no doubt her idea of a small plot and the king's interpretation of such would be worlds apart.

After being thrust into a cool grotto, the next hour was uneventful. Bel remained on edge, but didn't know what she waited for. Ridhwan had mentioned the possibility of her husband showing up because of some fracas in Hell. Maybe that's why she felt so alert although it wouldn't be *her* husband coming to the rescue, now would it?

Bel tried to stay positive. She could hope for a coup where her god would come charging in with Marla and Jeremiah as cavalry to the rescue. Now that would be a happy event. And the timing couldn't be any better. Ridhwan was in Hell, and two of his butt-sniffers were absent.

Bel bit one of her previously elegant nails which was now severely length-challenged. Top-most on her mind? Why had Ridhwan gone to Hell? It seriously bugged her, but those musings were doing no good. Instead, she should be planning what to do if escape-time presented itself.

Bel's eyes drifted around the vine-covered grotto where she'd been taken. She had earlier walked the perimeter and knew the back wall of her enclosure was integrated with the energy barrier system Ridhwan had erected. The two side walls were impenetrable due to thick vines and thorns, and the front was guarded by one overgrown tom.

She'd spent weeks studying the comings and goings of her captors after her one and only unsuccessful attempt at escape and was well aware either Ridhwan or one of his key-three had to put their body through the invisible barrier in order to hold it open for others to pass. She'd thought previously everyone—and everything—could just walk through it, but she had been mistaken. She would not be caught with another such misstep.

She let her mind work through various scenarios. It was dark, and her viney prison was smack dab at the farthest boundary of the cat-world. If she could overpower her sentry and drag his body… No. That was out of the question. She was too sick and weak to overwhelm him. Even if her goddess powers returned full-blast, she would still have had a tough time against the huge shifter. Better to regain her strength or wait for…

What was that? Her senses went into overdrive. Was that a rustling in the brush? She watched her guard straighten up, suddenly on alert. He heard it too. Could it be… Bel watched the trees anxiously for a moment, then her shoulders fell.

Shit. Of course not.

The hulking cat relaxed too, laughed, and picked up a large rock. He threw it toward the noise. The white, lumbering shape of an enormous moonrat took a direct hit, then skittered around the small clearing confused before running back across the jungle floor to disappear into the undergrowth. Fucking rodents.

The second time the noise occurred, Bel barely looked up. Neither did her guard until a strangled cry a short distance away split the night.

What the…? Definitely cat and most certainly anguished.

Her babysitter drew forth a lethal-looking knife, walking several paces into the undergrowth. Bel tiptoed forward and stood, poised at the entrance, listening. She wished she understood their damned cat language. She'd give anything to know what the pair were yowling back and forth.

Wait. Over the caterwauling. Was that a human voice? *Female?* Was it Ridhwan yelling? Had he brought back a human from his trip to hell? A goddess? There was only one way to find out, and she risked nothing to try. Bel figured out early on although Ridhwan knew gods communicated by head—and he could throw up interference to block it—he was completely unable to hear immortal head-speak.

Is there a goddess out there? Bel queried.

Yes. No. I mean sort-of. Who am I speaking to?

Before Bel could quite get her mind around that or begin to place the voice, she focused into the dark and saw her own watchman dragging one of Ridhwan's other top-cats out of the jungle with an arm clamped around his middle. His other was locked around the body of a small, squirming female. A third person or cat unknown, walked behind them, sporting a lethal posture.

Quinn? Bel asked of the ether, then shook her head even before she got her answer. It couldn't be Sham's mate unless the new goddess had passed a crash course in god-speak. Last Bel knew, the deaf *Chosen* could speak it, but not fluently enough for the nuance that had been in the little sampling Bel had just received.

No. It's not Quinn, came the answer, amidst angry huffs and puffs. The group was so close now, Bel forced herself to be patient. She took a few steps back and took stock. There certainly was a lot of kicking and swearing going on. Whoever was being taken captive, the female didn't take her manhandling lightly. But fight as she may, she wasn't able to shake off the shifter. So it wasn't an *actual* goddess. No female deity—except for Bel in her emaciated condition—was that weak. This was all very strange. Head speak without goddess cred? Nothing added up.

"Let me go, you fucker." The language was certainly heartening to Bel. She'd gotten sick and tired of the simpering female cats surrounding Ridhwan, they were all a bunch of spineless pussies.

298

But this approaching bundle of anger? This could be good. At best, it would be another person who could help Bel to escape. At worst, the woman would break the infinite boredom. Bel would have a new and interesting playmate to keep her diverted. And for those reasons, Bel stepped forward to intervene. She couldn't have them damaging the best thing that had happened to her since she'd ended up in the godsforsaken hole.

"Give her to me," Bel ordered the cat with an attempt to conjure her once-commanding voice. "Attend to your kitty-friend before he expires. It looks like he needs some serious help." Bel certainly hoped so.

A small, writhing body was thrown her way, and thank gods, whoever it was caught herself before plowing into Bel. The impact would have sent the goddess crashing to the ground. Instead, Bel held out a hand to steady the projectile-being.

"Get your hands off me," the scrapper yelled, and Bel backed off.

"Okay, I don't have to be told twice." The goddess put both palms up, face out. "I'm captive here too," she said out loud.

But they can't hear or speak our language in their heads. Bel took a long sniff and filled her nose with the other's energy. *But how is it you can? You're not a goddess.*

Who wants to know? Large dark eyes, framed in a pale face surrounded by long ebony hair, blinked suspiciously in her direction.

The name is Beletseri, Bel offered. As far as she knew, it would mean nothing to whoever this was

Oh my gods, the female cried. *Matthew's Beletseri?* Bel's guest dropped hard to her butt in what looked to be shock.

Bel, also knocked for a loop, recovered first. Crouching low, her heart beat faster. *That's me. How do you know Matthew? Who are you?*

Instead of answering, the new captive looked around. *Shit. That means we're in the jungle somewhere. Somewhere they can't find us.* She shook her head, panicking. *Man, am I screwed.*

Bel moved forward and took hold of the girl's shoulders. The goddess needed answers before shock set in.

Tell me who you are, and why you're here?

The girl blinked twice.

My name is Riley. And I'm pretty sure they took me by mistake.

Chapter Twenty-seven

Verrie sat in the kitchen, fretting about Dumuzi being in hell. She poured her third cup of tea and sat, joining several goddesses who were also brooding about their men. Jake, Douglas, and Dorian, who had stayed behind, were keeping them company, doing a lot of smirking at the women's fussing when a faint call came in.

Immortals…school… It was Dagon's voice. Two words, then…silence. Verrie leaped to her feet as Tess tried to contact the god again, unsuccessfully, then attempted Enten, also with no luck.

"Sienna. Riley," Verrie cried, suffused with panic but not knowing what to do. Her eyes darted this way and that to goddesses who were suddenly checking holsters and grabbing carving knives out of drawers. They were wasting no time.

"What's going on?" Dorian grabbed Tess's wrist as her fingers closed around a meat-cleaver. The warlock couldn't tune to head-talk and needed to be brought up to speed, quickly.

"Call from Dagon," Tess barked. "From the school grounds. He was cut off, and now, there's no reply. We need to move. Fast."

Dorian was gone in an instant. He'd be first on the scene because of his ability to transfer from place to place instantly. The rest of the immortals had to travel god-style, but they would be on site in less than five minutes.

Candy took a hard hold of Verrie's arm. "You stay here. I'll keep you plugged into my brain every second we're gone, so you'll know what's happening." The goddess turned and noticed Glory was grabbing a lethal looking screwdriver from the junk drawer. "And oh no you don't," she raised her voice shrilly. "You will stay here with Verrie," she ordered. "There's no way we're explaining to Enten why his extremely pregnant wife put herself in danger."

"But my husband…"

"…will be fine," Candy pointed a finger at the goddess. "Unless you're there to distract him." She was half-way misted when she snapped one more order. "And call Absu." The god was with Frank. "Tell him we have trouble and to get his charge home right now…and to watch his ass."

Charlie negated the need for Glory to head-connect after Candy completely disappeared. "Don't bother, Glory. I'm going to Absu in case the shit hits the fan for him, too, but don't worry you guys. Between the two of us, we'll have Frank back in no time." She disappeared without another word, and the kitchen went suddenly quiet.

Verrie found herself in the embrace of Glory—as hard as that was around the enormous mound of the goddesses stomach—but the contact was comforting.

"They have to be fine." Verrie tried like mad to hold back her tears. "Dagon and Enten wouldn't let anything happen to the girls." Glory continued to stroke her back but didn't answer. The goddess stifled a groan. Surely that wasn't good.

It seemed like the longest five minutes of Verrie's life, waiting for Candy to get to the scene and connect back. In the meantime, she heard Glory mind-calling Ereshkigal in Hell to get help reaching the guys who had gone to confront the demons in Galla's realm. There was no way for the goddess to contact the Blue Hill contingency by conventional means. On earth, they used satellite dishes and towers to transmit their head signals over long distances. There were no such conveniences down below. The best Glory could do was contact the queen who had the power of communication within all Hell's realms. Ereshkigal would alert Marduk and company. The gods, accompanied by Nergal, needed to know there was an emergency at home

After a minute or two of trying, the goddess made a frustrated noise. "I can't seem to reach her," Glory worried. "Perhaps she's visiting her sister…" At that extremely opportune moment, Anna walked into the room, looking for Jake.

"Wow. It's a ghost town around here. Has anybody seen my husband?" she asked, wiping the sweat off of her face with her shoulder.

"You don't know?" Glory's mouth dropped open.

"Know what?" Clearly, Anna hadn't been privy to the activity taking place. Verrie noted the work-out clothes, then spied the ear-buds draped around the goddesses neck.

"You've been cranking the tunes again." The pregnant goddess shook her head but wasted no time filling Anna in. "There was a call from the school grounds. Dagon was just able to let us know there was trouble. Everyone took off except us." Glory snapped her fingers. "We were just trying to reach your sister, Eresh, so she can let the guys in Hell know something's up. But she's not answering. I'm thinking she might be up above, visiting Ish-Din or your father."

The situation was instantly clear to the savvy goddess. "I'll find her." Anna quickly downed a glass of water that had been abandoned on the counter and disappeared. Verrie didn't know what to make of that and must have looked confused because Glory explained.

"Anna is half-sister to Eresh and Ish-Din. Their father is the old king, Shulmanu, and Anna's the newfound illegitimate sibling. Luckily, that still makes her blood to an Overworld being which means she's allowed up there when we're not. If Eresh is visiting, Anna will find her."

"Okay…" Verrie's bewildered reply was cut off by Candy's voice.

We're here you guys. Dagon's hurt, we don't know how badly yet, Holly is checking. Enten's down too and not moving. Dani's going to him. It looks like he's on top of someone.

There was the sound of scrambling.

It's Sienna. Verrie, it's Si. She looks fine. Candy's tone changed. *Glory, you hold on girl. Enten's out, and it looks like he's hurt pretty badly. But Dr. Dani's got him, and he's breathing.*

A pause followed. Verrie's gut twisted in knots.

I've got Sienna in my arms, Verrie. She's scared…with a few bumps and bruises. It looks like

Enten pushed her down and shielded her from whatever got to him.

Verrie had no right to feel so relieved with a wide-eyed Glory next to her, wringing her hands over her husband's condition. She was poised to ask more about Enten's injuries when another inquiry came through.

What about Riley?

They all heard the question, and it hadn't come from a voice the immortals had ever heard in their heads—Verrie knew right away it belonged to Frank. Candy immediately imparted the news Verrie had been about to ask for.

Riley's gone, Frank. Whoever did this...they took her.

Verrie slumped into her chair. Her head dropped to her hands. It was too much to take. Because of her and Sienna, they'd put their best friends...*no*, their closest relatives in danger.

Verrie could only marvel at the strength in Frank's reply when it came. *Absu and Charlie are bringing me back to the compound,* she stated. *We'll discuss how we're going to get Riley when I return.*

In the midst of all the horror, Verrie noticed there was not a trace of a Boston accent in Frank's god-talk. It was funny how Verrie's mind under siege could fixate on something so mundane instead of fully processing the rest of the fucked-up shit happening. But she wasn't given the option to space out for very long.

Tess arrived back at the kitchen, all business. "Come on," she poked Verrie's arm. "We need to take a couple of cars and pick up our wounded. And we need to make it fast. Dr. Dani says the guys are both losing a lot of blood."

"Why the car? Why not poof them back here?" Verrie questioned.

"When there are severe injuries, going invisible isn't an option."

The goddess turned at Glory's anguished cry and gave her the most irrefutable and assured look that was possible. "Severe, but not enough to kill them, Glory, do you feel me? Nobody's dying. But they need immediate care." She looked back at Verrie. "So, let's go."

The goddess went to a pegboard by the doorway, snagged two key rings and tossed one over. "You know where the school is."

Verrie nodded and followed Tess out the back door.

What about bystanders, gawkers? Glory's voice followed in the wind. *What if someone has called 911? We can't let them be taken to a hospital.*

The goddesses are on it, Tess assured her. *They're busy wiping minds left and right. Candy is really good at it, in case you've forgotten.*

Good. That's right. Glory's panicked voice calmed down a little. *Just get Enten home to me, safely. I'll go up to the infirmary and make sure everything's ready for Dani when they get back.*

Excellent, Tess replied. *ETA will be approximately forty-five minutes.*

Verrie drove as fast as the speed limit would allow...plus eight. In Boston, that was what urban myth allowed as the "won't get stopped" overage. She hoped—all the way—the geeks who had put that shit together were correct.

When Verrie finally came upon the scene, it was surreal. There was blood everywhere, a contingent of goddesses propped Sienna up, and another surrounded the two downed gods. But the most fucked-up thing were pedestrians who strolled around the carnage as if nothing was amiss.

Verrie couldn't imagine the amount of power it took to keep all the would-be witnesses from…witnessing, but the intense and painful scowl on Candy's face told the tale. And the effort was taking its toll. Verrie wasn't sure how much longer the petite agent's brain could hold back so many. The sooner they got the gods loaded into the vehicles, the better.

Tess's vehicle beat Verrie's there by a few minutes…clearly, the goddess was not as constrained by speed limits as Verrie. Jake and Douglas already had Enten halfway to her car, carrying him as gently as possible.

Verrie ran to Sienna and gathered her shaking daughter into her arms.

"Mom, I…"

"Shhh… Quiet now, Si. Let's get these guys taken care of, then we'll talk." She stroked her daughter's hair. "Everything will be okay. Don't worry. They'll find Riley. I give you my word. They're gods after all."

Sienna gave a little hitch of her shoulders to show she'd heard her mother but seemed content otherwise to keep her face buried in Verrie's chest.

Damn. Verrie hoped she could deliver on the promise she'd just made.

Addie-May and Obedience transported Dagon a little more creatively. Being witches, they used skills Verrie hadn't seen before. They'd conjured a wheeled gurney to appear under the ebony-haired god which Holly now pushed toward the car Verrie had driven.

"Careful." Verrie, who had Sienna in tow as she made her way to the driver's side heard Holly warn the witches as they got Dagon to the vehicle. "Ease him in slowly. His right arm is nearly severed, and we want to try to save it. Otherwise, he'll have to regenerate, and that will take a lot of time and pain."

Shit, she sure was calm for someone whose mate was nearly in pieces. Her brow *had* creased as she said it, but Verrie knew there was an unspoken relief the injury hadn't been to his left side. A blow to his amulet could have been fatal.

As the witches facilitated Dagon's airborne move into her car, Verrie looked over to where Jake and Douglas finished placing Enten into Tess'. The cold god's back was a bloody mess, and they'd laid him across the rear seat on his stomach.

Verrie knew the most worrisome aspect of both god's injuries was that neither was currently awake. Dani said it was due to massive blood loss, and if that was the case, the sooner they got the pair back to the Blue Hills to receive banked blood, the better.

On the trip home, Verrie didn't even try to obey the speed limit. If she got stopped this time, she had Holly with her who hadn't left her injured husband's side. The goddess wouldn't hesitate to mind-blank anybody who tried to stop them. Still, the trip seemed to take forever. Verrie couldn't help but send repeated, worried glances toward her daughter. Sienna looked to be in shock, and Verrie couldn't blame her…even without knowing the details of what had occurred.

As they drove around the circular drive and up to the front door of the compound, Verrie saw Glory—and the other women who had misted on ahead—standing outside, waiting.

Dani wasted no time employing all hands to bring the injured pair up to the infirmary, but having received that help, shooed all but the wives from the room. The ousted women joined Verrie and Sienna back in the kitchen within minutes of arriving home. Jake had a determined look on his face as he approached her daughter.

"Sienna, you need to focus." Jake hovered over Verrie where she stood, hugging her daughter. "We need to know exactly what happened."

"Jake, don't you think…" Verrie had been about to ask the agent/god to cut her daughter some slack, but Sienna shook her head at her mother.

"No, Mom, I need to tell him. If I can help them find Riley, they need to hear it."

"That's right, Sienna. Good girl." Jake pulled out a chair and eased her away from Verrie. He directed the girl gently onto the seat, then called over his shoulder. "Hey. Somebody? Anybody? How about some orange juice?"

A glass appeared instantly at Sienna's elbow, compliments of one of the witches. Verrie would have laughed under any other circumstances. Witch tricks, Federal Agent tricks. *Oh yeah.* Jake was good. A little playing nice, a little gentle coercion. His training sure showed with the orange juice. Textbook precautions to get her daughter's blood sugar level back under control.

He let her have a long sip.

"Now, why don't you tell us the details?"

Verrie watched Sienna take a second gulp from her glass, then draw in a deep breath. She didn't hesitate. "The last bell rang, and we'd planned to meet by the steps at the side of the building—the ones by the library."

Verrie nodded. She knew the spot.

"Enten was with me, Riley and Dagon were already outside, across the street on the grass by the sidewalk. The minute we separated from the crowd and started to cross the street, I heard Dagon yell a warning to Enten. He said, 'Behind you.' I looked up and saw a blurry figure moving toward them, too, going really fast. The next thing I knew, Enten threw himself on me and we went down."

Tears leaked from the corners of Sienna's eyes as she struggled to keep her voice even.

"I knew something bad was happening to him because his body kept jerking on top of me...and...and he was making horrible groaning noises in my ear, but he also kept telling me I was safe, he wasn't going to move, and wouldn't let them get me."

Now her daughter was outright sobbing.

"I looked over at his hand, the one I could see with my face turned to the left, and he'd...he'd frozen it to the ground so he couldn't be moved." Sienna threw herself from the chair to wrap herself around her mother knees. "He wasn't just *being* hurt, Mom. He was hurting himself too...to protect me. His hand was bleeding so badly where he kept it anchored."

"Hush, baby, hush, it's okay. He was doing what he could. He's the god of winter, you know, and I'm certain his hands are used to that kind of punishment.

Jake?" Verrie appealed to the agent for some additional words to calm her daughter.

"Hell, yeah, Sienna. Don't worry about Enten. I gather he's had frostbite a million times in his life. And besides, gods heal extra fast. His hand is probably completely fine by now."

Verrie noticed he didn't say anything about the horrific injuries to the god's back.

"Now, more about this blur you saw," Jake prompted, turning Si's mind back to the unresolved issues at hand. "Can you tell me anything about it? Take your time. Think hard."

Sienna grew still before rising into her mother's embrace. "Well" She wiped her eyes, attempting to pull herself back together. "While Enten had me down, I could see a little of what was going on across the sidewalk, and I know this will sound kind of strange, but it looked like the…thing attacking Dagon and Riley was…it seemed almost like a…like a… No. I was probably just imagining things."

"Come on, Sienna. Really?" Jake laughed. "You're in a house full of gods who morph into hell knows what, and you're wondering about some other strange creature that shows up? And remember…this is also Boston we're talking about," Jake's voice joked, but calmed too, in an irreverent way.

Si responded, "Yeah, you're right." The girl swallowed hard and dared try to name what she'd seen. "The blur looked like a big black cat."

Si brought her eyes to Jake's to gauge his reaction.

Verrie caught her breath. She'd been at the meeting, listening to the gods talk about their enemy Ridhwan, but Sienna hadn't. Sienna knew about

Beletseri but didn't know a cat-shifter held the goddess. It had to be the same man, and Jake knew it as well.

"I believe you, Sienna," Jake nodded.

Verrie's daughter sat up straighter with the substantiation and let her hold on her mother drop.

She drew a breath and continued, "Dagon tried to pull Riley behind him with one arm while holding off this blurry cat with the other." She paused. "I saw…" Sienna grew suddenly pale but pushed away Verrie's hands that shot out once again to support her. "No. Let me finish." She squared her shoulders. "I saw the cat-guy…slice through Dagon's arm, then as…blood started going everywhere, the thing grabbed Riles and disappeared."

"Disappeared," Jake reiterated. "And that was it?" His calm tone lent strength to Sienna.

"Yes. Uh, no actually." She scowled. "If I didn't imagine it, the whole weird blur thing got kind-of… bigger before it went away." Her forehead creased. "I'm not sure how to describe it. Before it disintegrated, it grew or looked…heavier." Her fortitude gave out with that last recollection, and Sienna sank back down in her chair. She looked wiped. "Will any of that help?" She worried her bottom lip, unusually pale.

"I'm sure it will. Especially when we call Marla and Jeremiah," Jake assured her.

Sienna had met the unlikely pair who were currently trolling the vast forests of Malaysia for signs of Ridhwan, and Verrie instantly thought the same thing as everyone else in the room if the head-buzz was any indication. Because Marla was a cat-shifter, and Jeremiah was a full-time cat, the FO—or feline operations agents—had to be able to help.

"Remember," Jake continued. "They do the popping from spot-to-spot thing gods aren't able to do, so they'll know better how it works," he ended on a positive note.

"Like my husband," Addie-May interjected and looked around the kitchen. "Dorian?" She peered around the goddesses and the big bodies—agents and Lauernley—who had crowded into the room while the discussion had been underway.

"Sweetheart?" Addie's voice took on a confusing note. "Wait. Has anybody seen my husband," she attempted to joke. "Big guy. Dark. Always looks like he's ready to take someone's head off?"

By the end of her little speech, she looked worried. Then she lost all her color.

"Shit." She turned to Sienna. "A large blur left the scene," she stated. "Bigger than the one that came in."

Sienna nodded her head. Verrie knew where this was going.

The witch slumped back against the refrigerator for support. "Well. Now we know—for better or for worse—what happened. Si's big-ass blur included one extremely tenacious warlock."

Chapter Twenty-Eight

Marduk insisted Muze take a back seat for the hell-raid. It was the only way he would allow the monster-changer to come along. He feared if Dumuzi was given any power in a possible take-down, they'd have no demons left to question when the dust settled.

The thunder god looked at the group assembled behind him and grimaced as he tried, once again, to push through the invisible barrier they'd run into. "I knew it was too easy," Marduk groused. "Why would Galla seal off this section of his domain? He has to know this is against all Underworld rules."

They stood, puzzling things out when King Nergal rounded a group of rocks and trotted up to the group, adjusting his loincloth. All eyes turned to him, and he abbreviated his stride.

"What? A god can't take a piss?" he groused and looked around at the halted party. "Why have you stopped?"

"If you could hold your coffee better, you would've known we hit some kind of force-field." Marduk rolled his eyes. "You'd better call Galla and tell him to let us pass."

It was Nergal's time to eye-roll. "Seriously? You think some two-bit demon-turned-god gets to dictate where I can and cannot go?" Gleaming white teeth showed in an arrogant smile. One that would have had lesser beings falling to their knees. Marduk wasn't one.

"Okay, your greatness. If you're so powerful, do your thing." The thunder god stood back and crossed his arms over his chest. "Let me guess. It's Ali Baba Open Sesame," he smirked sarcastically.

"Funny god, but you're warm." Nergal walked close to the barrier and extended both arms as if in supplication. Marduk and his men watched with equal parts skepticism and awe as two of the god's tattooed runes—one on Nergal's right forearm, the other on his left pectoral—began to glow and dance.

"What the…?" Marduk's mouth dropped as energy arced between the king and the impedance. There was a white pulse like the flash of a camera, and the barrier trembled, shimmered like the surface of a pond that had been gently disturbed by a dipping dragonfly, then calmed. Nergal lost his glow and lowered his arms.

"After you, gentlemen," the king mugged. "Open Sesame."

Marduk bit his tongue and refused to respond. The royal was far too smug for the thunder god to acknowledge the feat. Unfortunately for Nergal's big head, Anshar had no such compulsion.

"What did you do?" The sky god practically attacked the king's arm. "What was that?"

Nergal had only to look down his nose imperiously, and Anshar backed off.

Marduk screwed up his mouth. *Giant prick* was obviously enjoying the hell out of this.

"How is it that all this time," Nergal posed, "I've penetrated the barrier you erected around your abode, and you've never inquired how?" he smirked, "Did you think it was magic?"

Shit, Marduk thought. He'd never given it a thought. *Fine.* Let the king act all superior. Marduk wasn't about to ask.

Again, Anshar went for the bait. "Tell us how you do it," the blond god cajoled, playing right into Nergal's already inflated sense of self.

"Fine. If you insist." The king gave the entire group a sniff and swept a hand across his tattooed body. "I'm surprised none of you have queried about my ink before."

Right. Marduk scoffed silently. As if Nergal had ever been a warm, share-gossip-and-secrets kind of ruler. When they'd been sequestered in hell, he'd been a royal prick, and since the advent of their "friendship," after they'd all made up and played nice, they'd had too many other things to worry about.

"Well, we're asking now," Enlil interjected testily.

Nergal was less likely to play with the wind god's head than with Anshar's, and Marduk could tell Enlil the bull was impatient to move on. *Bravo.*

Nergal sighed and let the ego-trip slide. "When I was inducted as king of the Underworld, I was given control over the minor kings and realms here below," he explained. "The old king, Shalmanu was smart. He had dealt with the vanity of these lesser gods a time or two and found they all liked to hide things from him— goods that should be taxed, purloined belongings from other kingdoms—so he devised a key system to unlock any door…any obstacle."

He looked down at his pervasive scroll-work.

"As a wedding gift to me, my father-in-law had me tattooed with the same access codes he used, his residing on a group of stone tablets." He stroked the two tattoos which had just lit up. "Mine are much easier to carry around," he grinned. "I'm not sure exactly how they accomplish their goal, but when I approach the unbreachable, I simply open my energy in that direction, and one or more of these runes light up. They never fail me in my forays to otherwise forbidden places. As you can see, it's a handy little tool." He swept an arm forward. "So, now you know my secret. After you, gentlemen." He gestured down the long hallway.

Marduk acknowledged to himself he was impressed, but he wouldn't tell the king that.

The thunder god knew they were getting close to a goal of sorts when a dire stench met their noses. Marduk sent a discreet glance to Shamash to keep an eye on Dumuzi. The rotten smell might send him over the edge, and they didn't need any slaughters here today. They needed answers. The thunder god held a finger to his lips and urged the group quietly forward.

"Pssst. Boss."

Marduk waved a hand behind him at whoever had spoken and continued to move forward in a crouch. WTF? All his gods knew better than to talk right now. He was incredulous that one of them would breach protocol when the urgent plea repeated in head-speak.

Marduk. Please stop.

Really? Marduk made an angry face no one could see. He didn't want to cease his forward momentum, dammit, but the voice belonged to Lahar, and the god of logic would never... *What? Wait.* Lahar was supposed to be invisible when not around the three currently in the compound who turned him solid. That made no sense.

Lahar? Did you just speak?

"Duh." Lahar's voice smacked him out loud again, albeit quietly, before switching back to stealth. *Which is why we need to stop, Marduk. As logically as I can surmise, Douglas, Glory, or Quinn have to be nearby. If that's the case, we need to find out why.*

I'll ask, Marduk growled. He opened a wider communication channel. *Douglas? Glory? Quinn?* The deaf mate to Shamash still wasn't completely up on all god-speak yet but would recognize her name when spoken. Marduk waited. There was no answer. *Shit, Lahar. Head back the way we came. See if you can find them.*

The curious group paused, watching Lahar head back down the hallway. Not ten feet away he lost his corporeality. Marduk's blood ran cold. He watched as Lahar turned around and came back into a physical body. *Fuck.* That could only mean one thing. One of their three immortals in question was…up ahead. Where the demons lived. But how had the slimy bastards gotten their hands on one of them?

Sham? Emesh? Marduk appealed to the two gods whose mates were part of the equation and received a shake of their heads.

I'm not feeling Quinn, Shamash stated with an anxious shrug.

I'm not getting Douglas's energy either. Emesh looked equally confused.

That leaves Glory, but with her babies due within the month, I can't imagine she'd be anywhere but the

318

compound. Marduk was frozen with indecision…which was very unlike him. But pregnant goddesses were their lifeblood, and he hesitated to make a wrong move if indeed Glory had been taken.

Nergal, with a highly pregnant wife of his own, reacted in a more territorial way and growled before taking over.

There's only one way to find out. His face turned hard, and his jaw set in a tense line. *We move in. Now.* He was about to take the lead when Marduk shook off the dread which held him immobile. He put out a hand to stop the king.

It's okay. I've got this. He signaled, and the group was on the move again.

Marduk came to the end of the long corridor they'd been following and inched his way toward the doorway. It opened into a large chamber where light from a fire breached the darkness that was the gods' cover, and demon chatter filtered into their ears.

Marduk hugged the wall and dared a quick look into the cavernous space before pulling back.

There are a dozen or more demons sitting in the center of the room but no sentries. They've acted without interference for so long, they obviously feel safe, he reflected. *The entire group is congregated around a fire, fifty feet to my right at two o'clock.* Marduk looked back to where Dumuzi struggled, having a hard time staying in god-form.

Muze. If you can't keep it under control, you'll have to leave.

No. I'm good, the swamp god growled and hitched a few tendrils back up his sleeves.

Okay. Marduk signaled, giving orders. *On three, we storm them but no killing. Dead demons don't talk, and we need answers for what they've been doing.*

Marduk received nods of agreement.

On my count. Three…two…one. The group burst into the room, and all hell broke loose. Just not the kind they'd imagined. As they entered at a run, they saw a dark, cloaked figure twenty paces behind the demon group take surprised note of the gods. He lobbed something into the center of the fire then disappeared in a raging, snarling hissy-fit.

Before Marduk or any of the gods had a chance to move another inch whatever had been tossed into the fire detonated in an enormous explosion that sent them all crashing back against the far wall, driven from their feet by the horrendous and unexpected concussion.

Being gods, they were only down for a few seconds, but when they made it back to their feet, the scene of devastation and carnage became instantly apparent. There wasn't a living hell-spawn left. Vile smelling demon parts, along with small scattered fires filled the vast room. Marduk stomped out the one by his left foot and wiped something that looked suspiciously like brains off the front of his shirt. Gods-dammit, what had just happened?

"Did anybody see who that was?" Marduk growled, flicking sticky gray matter off his fingers. He noticed a shocked look pass over Shamash's face. "What?"

"No. It can't be." The salvation god shook his head. "It makes no sense." His face hardened. "Or it makes perfect sense." Shamash got a hold of himself and turned to Marduk.

"It was difficult to see the intruder, but my nose got a full profile, and I'd trust it anywhere. My olfactory senses are never mistaken. The shadowy figure who just blew up our enclave of answers? That was none other than our newest enemy, Ridhwan."

Marduk tried to process that startling revelation, but as the shell-shock cleared, he became immediately panicked. "Glory." His eyes darted around the room, hoping not to see anything that looked remotely humanoid.

"All remains are demon," Lahar assured his boss. The logic god had already done a quick scan of the room, not for a moment forgetting the whys and wherefores of his body being corporeal. "If they have her, she wasn't in this room."

"Okay. Spread out," Marduk told his gods. "If Glory's here, we need to find her, and if not," he sent a raised eyebrow toward Lahar, "we need to figure out what's giving our friend his body."

It was soon discovered there were so many pathways and mazes off of the main room, it was impossible to do a thorough search. Marduk brought all his men back together to form a better plan of attack for this conundrum.

"Lahar, since you're the only one who pops in and out from embodied to invisible, you need to be our canary in the coal mine."

Lahar nodded, obviously following Marduk's reasoning, but Nergal wasn't familiar with the saying.

"What does a canary have to do with our forays?" the king asked.

"It's a human saying," Marduk educated him. "It simply means a canary will be susceptible to poisons in a mine, becoming the first to succumb. Since Lahar is the one going from solid to mist, we need to use him to search one egress at a time. Lahar will lead the way, and as soon as he turns invisible, that tunnel becomes meaningless. The team turns around, marks that passage as a no-go, and attempts the next."

"Very methodical approach. I like it," Nergal agreed. "But it does mean we could be here for a while, and I myself... Wait. I'm getting something from my wife. Probably a request for ice cream. If you'll just excuse me for one moment."

Marduk, already keyed up and beside himself thinking of Glory, attuned to the king's rigidity as he turned his back.

"What is it?" the thunder god asked when Nergal faced him again. His voice was so worried, everyone riveted to what the royal would say.

"I've had communication from Ereshkigal. Your compound has been in touch with her. Dagon and Enten ran into trouble at the girls' school." He cleared his throat, and Marduk knew it was very bad news.

"Dagon and Enten are both badly injured and the girl, Riley, has been taken."

"Ridhwan." The name was spit like an expletive from Dumuzi's mouth.

"I think you're correct, Muze." He turned an anguished face back to the king. "Can you ask her if Glory, Quinn, and Douglas are okay?" He closed his eyes, waiting for the answer. It took several minutes of relay time.

"All well, and all at the house." Nergal sighed along with everyone else, and a rejuvenated Marduk snapped into command mode. "Lahar, that puts a different spin on why you're corporeal. Stay here with Enlil, Anshar, Ninurta, Kulla, and Ishkur to find out why the hell you have a body."

"Not me," Ishkur interjected. "I'm coming to help look for Riley."

Marduk was puzzled at Ishkur's diffidence, but he wouldn't deny the older god. Ishkur never asked for anything. It was obviously important and no skin off his nose to substitute gods. "Fine. Huxley, you stay here below. Keep me informed if you find anything. Nergal?" He didn't pause to look before misting. "Get the rest of us back home."

Chapter Twenty-Nine

Dumuzi popped into the kitchen along with the other gods and immediately took in the devastated faces and postures around the room. He went swiftly to Veronica and Sienna, wrapping them in his big arms, attempting to impart comfort.

Frank paced, her face white and tense, and Muze noted she didn't hesitate for a moment when Ishkur went to her and gathered her in a tight embrace. She sank into his arms, burying her head in his chest. It took about two strokes of his hands on her back before Muze saw her shoulders begin to heave with sobs. He drew his eyes away, it was just too painful. Clearly, the two had something going between them, but now was not the time to ask.

"Jake, fill me in." Marduk took charge in a way that gave energy to the previously lethargic room.

"Two cat shifters arrived at school today, just after the final bell rang. Dagon and Riley were already out on the street. Enten and Sienna were on the way to meet them. The cats blindsided Dagon and Riley. They pretty nearly tore his arm off and snatched her. Another one came at Enten, but with a warning cry from Dagon, he was able to throw his body over Sienna and protect her. He's sporting some pretty deep claw gashes in his back. Even if Si hadn't seen the shapes and known them to be cats, Doc Dani would have been able to tell the damage had been done by feline."

"So, now Ridhwan has Bel and Riley too, the bastard," Dumuzi cursed. He was puzzled though. He couldn't for the life of him figure out why Jake had delivered that speech with a tiny lilt of hopefulness embedded. He didn't have to wait long to find out.

"Here's the good news," the agent imparted. "When Dagon called us, Dorian was right here, and he immediately went to the scene. He arrived easily five minutes before us. It was apparently just enough time for him to hitch a ride with the cats."

"You're shitting me?" Marduk's face went from bleak to expectant. "He trailed them? You're sure?"

Jake nodded. "Sienna saw the size of the cat-energy coming onto the scene and the size of it going out. The departure definitely contained our warlock. The problem is, he doesn't head-talk, so we can't find out where he is or what's happening. Against our wishes, Addie-May has gone looking for him. She headed to the Malay peninsula by herself to try to hunt him down."

"Shit. I'll call Marla. She and Jeremiah are there, scouting." Marduk pulled his cell phone from his pocket. Dumuzi saw the look of self-disgust on the thunder god's face. He was clearly kicking himself for not giving anyone else a way to contact the FO agent which might have had them on top of things sooner. But nobody blamed the thunder god. Who knew the connection would be necessary?

"Marla? Marduk," he began. "We have a situation." He plowed right on, not allowing the agent to speak. "Riley, one of the young girls here? She's been kidnapped by Ridhwan's men, and Dorian is in pursuit. He will have followed them with the same skills you have to attach to someone's energy. If he's in Ridhwan's hidden enclave, you probably won't find him, but his wife might be able to. Right now, she's in your neighborhood, scouring the countryside. Use any means necessary to try to locate her, then combine your powers to try to come up with that asshole who has our people."

Marduk paused, listening.

"Yeah… Right… Okay. Keep in touch." He closed his phone.

"Marla knows someone…a witch who she's worked with before. She's going to try to contact her to find Addie-May." He ran a hand back through his long, dark hair. "This is really getting out of hand with the number of factions involved."

"Who cares? If it means keeping Ridhwan from his goal…which is, I assume, to rule over all realms and beings." Jake threw out some decent logic in the absence of Lahar. "And if I'm not mistaken, that includes humans, witches, gods, cats, and whoever else is out there. So, there should be no foul in calling in all factions to bring him down."

"He's right, Marduk. As a matter of fact, shouldn't we contact the Grand Council of Immortal Beings?" Dumuzi pondered. "The more fire-power we have, the easier it will be to thwart the bastard. It seems to me he's been working under the radar for far too long."

"You may be right, Muze," Marduk nodded. "Nergal, you're a member of the council. What do you think?"

The king answered without hesitation. "I think they're not going to care about the fate of one human girl when all the immortal worlds are threatened. If we let them in on this now, they're going to go in with guns blazing. They'll probably—in order to contain the threat—blow the Malay Peninsula clean off the map and be damned for human collateral damage." The king frowned. "So, Muze, to answer your question, we may have to bring the council in eventually, but now is not the time."

"Sound advice." Marduk saw the devastated look on Frank's face as she'd come up from Ishkur's chest when Nergal declared Riley's life of little import to the council. He was definitely not playing with that fire unless all else failed.

"Okay. Everybody try to chill. Right now, I'm headed to the infirmary to see how Dagon and Enten are faring. Muze, I want you to come with me," Marduk issued the order, and Dumuzi obeyed. Marduk misted out with Muze following on foot, only a minute behind.

When he reached the room, Marduk had already conferred with Dani, and it looked like both Dagon and Enten were starting to stir. Muze didn't intrude toward their bedsides where the two wives were keeping vigil over their gods, but Marduk gave a smiling squeeze to the doctor's arm before approaching Muze's spot on the wall to talk.

"They're going to be fine," Marduk assured him. "Now, tell me what's going on with Ishkur and Frank."

Dumuzi was surprised this was on Marduk's agenda. In the scheme of things, possible mates were not the priority that came to mind, but the thunder god had always been good at multi-tasking.

"I'm, uh, not at liberty to discuss that, under penalty of having a motorcycle blow up underneath my ass next time I go for a ride."

Ishkur was in sole charge of vehicle maintenance in the basement garages.

"But I will tell you we don't have a *Chosen* situation here."

"Too bad." Marduk scowled. "I needed a little good news. And speaking of which, Dani says Dagon's arm knit back into place without any problems so he won't have to try to regenerate."

"That's a happy thing for all of us," Dumuzi agreed, walking with Marduk toward Dagon's bed where the god looked suddenly lucid. "Nobody wants to hear a whiny serpent for weeks on end."

"Fuck you, Muze," Dagon groused. *Yup.* He was back in working order, but also trying to get out of bed.

"Cut the shit, Dagon," Marduk pushed him back down, gently. "Doc Dani says you'll be laid up for a few days."

"Screw that," the god hissed. "I let the bastards get Riley, and I'm going to remedy my mistake. I failed her, Marduk."

Were those tears in Dagon's eyes? Dumuzi thought so. He knew how Dagon felt. He'd failed one person or another all of his long life.

"You didn't fail her," Marduk assured Dagon. "You were blindsided. There was nothing you could do, and still, you didn't let them get all they wanted. Thanks to you fighting so hard and taking some huge abuse, Enten was able to get his body over Sienna to protect her. Without your involvement, we would have lost two girls instead of one."

328

"He's right, Dagon," Enten's weak voice came from the other bed, and Muze turned.

"Ah. Enten's back in the house. The ice-man cometh," Dumuzi teased.

"That's what she said," Enten bantered back, and Muze knew the *winter* god would be fine. Nothing proclaimed a god's fitness better than sex jokes.

"So what do we do now?" Enten questioned.

"Dani?" Marduk asked. "Is it okay if I call everybody up here? Will it tax the guys too much?"

"I don't think so," the doctor speculated. "I'm pretty sure not knowing what's going on will do them more harm than a briefing. Just keep it short," she advised.

"Got it." Marduk switched to brain-chat. *Everyone to the infirmary in a quiet and orderly fashion, please.*

One by one, everybody showed up. Blue guys walked, gods misted, and humans came on foot. As quickly as possible, Marduk filled the injured in that Dorian had followed Riley. Then he told an incredulous audience, those who hadn't gone to hell, what they'd found down there, and how they now knew the whole demon-voice, kidnap-Bel, get-hands-on-Sham-and-Quinn things were all related…with Ridhwan as the lynchpin.

Nergal, on premise, had clearly, by this time, given things a lot of thought to the situation and shared what he'd pieced together. "So, this shifter fellow, Ridhwan is very patient. If I'm not mistaken, he's been waiting and working steadily on the damned prophecy for several thousand years. His greed to gain jurisdiction over every living being in Heaven, Earth, and Hell by getting Sham and a cat-goddess under his control has been long in the planning."

Dumuzi, along with the others in the room remained quiet.

"I'm going to go out on a limb here to make some informed speculations," the king continued. "I figure he's been smart as well as patient. I think he's been watching Sham for a very long time, knowing he was the cat-god in the aforementioned prediction."

There were nods of agreement.

"When Sham procreated in ancient Mesopotamia, our industrious friend enlisted the help of some demons and started harassing Sham's bloodline…at least the one of which they were aware."

"Why didn't Ridhwan just take Arwi's child?" Dumuzi puzzled.

"Perhaps because Sham had been relegated to Hell by the time that child was born, and Ridhwan, knowing he couldn't do anything with half of the equation, bided his time until Sham was back on earth."

"So, when Sham came top-side in the sixteen hundreds, why didn't Ridhwan take my ancestors then?" It was Veronica who asked this time.

"I have a feeling your family had moved one too many times by then, and although the demons were still able to enter your heads, I don't believe they could locate you, physically. Ridhwan had fucked up, relying on the demons who aren't the smartest, so eventually, he had to concoct another plan.

"Marla and Jeremiah mentioned in the 1940s that blood was being banked at hospitals, and Ridhwan began finding women who had god blood," Marduk interjected. "That's when he tried to start making baby cat-goddesses of his own."

"Correct," Nergal concurred. "If he'd known where Verrie's family was, he wouldn't have gone to that trouble. He would have taken any family member who was alive at that time." The king looked around at all the rapt faces and kept hypothesizing.

"Which leaves us with what's happening now." He enumerated, "One—Ridhwan fathers Quinn. Two—Quinn meets Sham and puts the Blue Hills compound on the radar. Three—Ridhwan and his buddies watch the house when, voila, Sienna and Verrie show up, and Four—Ridhwan, probably both thrilled and confused, suddenly has two more females who may or may not be involved in the prophecy. Remember, it didn't say the cat-god and cat-goddess had to be mated to each other, just that the coming together of the pair would make the fated divination come true…as in becoming acquainted, not necessarily having sex."

"Geez, this is all so screwed up," Sienna cried, saying what everyone else was thinking.

"Yes, it is," Marduk agreed. "But he's a twisted fuck, and there's no telling the extent of what and who he thinks to manipulate. I agree with all of Nergal's conjecture. And I'll add that Sienna was probably the target for kidnapping today, but the cats got a whiff of Riley who has the same markers in her blood, and they grabbed her instead."

"My thoughts exactly," Nergal concurred. "And on the hierarchy of command, I think the minute Sham was sent to Hell from ancient Mesopotamia, Ridhwan enlisted the help of our traitorous gate-keeper, Nedu. I…extracted from Nedu that he was in league with a group of rogue demons, and I'm going to make the connection those were the ones we raided today."

Nobody argued.

"Nedu also manipulated Beletseri who was ripe for outside alliances because of her unhappiness. Bel—thinking she was working to feather her own nest—helped forge the documents with Eresh that led Sham earthward again. Ridhwan would have orchestrated this to have access to Sham's future cat-goddess." He gave a wry twist to his mouth. "Then he had Bel sneak in a clause that would bring Sham back to hell in the future so they could easily get their demon claws on him."

It was a lot to take in, but Muze saw the truth in all of it.

Nergal looked very pleased with himself. Most other's just had their mouths hanging open. There were a few holes in the theories the king had put forth, but with luck, they'd be filled in if the group could get the upper hand and capture crafty Ridhwan

To that end, Dumuzi hoped they'd hear from the warlock, Dorian, sometime soon.

"Now, if you don't mind, Eresh is telling me, repeatedly, your gods left in Hell need me. Probably for a lift home. I'll be back in a flash."

Nergal disappeared while everyone stood around, digesting the cluster-fuck that was Ridhwan. Dumuzi had to hand it to the black leopard, he'd played things pretty well up until this point. But what he hadn't planned for was Sham having some pretty powerful friends backing him up. Hopefully, it would be the arrogant bastard's downfall.

Everyone was just about to call it an exhausting afternoon and retire to rooms to await word when word *came*…of a sort. Nergal gave the call out on all head-channels even though he spoke to Marduk directly.

Marduk. You wondered what made Lahar visible down here?

If Muze wasn't mistaken, there was a note of dumbfoundedness in the king's voice.

Yeah, Nergal. What have you found? Marduk's face set stoically to receive another spate of bad news.

We've found the source, he supplied cryptically.

And? Marduk sounded put out. Why was the king prolonging the suspense?

And I'd get your guest houses ready if I were you, he told them with clear dismay. *We've found a prison camp.*

Muze heard the shock in the almost-always-under control king's voice as he filled them in.

There are seventeen women down here, ranging in age from late thirties to mid-eighties. A handful of them have been here for nearly seven decades.

There was dead silence around the room before the king continued.

I'm sending word to Mamitu and Rephaim to join you before they arrive.

Mamitu was a kind and benevolent women's advocate judge, and Rephaim was a women's counselor. Both immortal.

We're going to need them in order to proceed and not scare the prisoners. Some of the ladies are pretty…fragile.

By the time Marduk had the wherewithal to answer, Dani had already head-mustered the goddesses to empty the second guest house for the women's arrival.

"Have them sent right to the cottage," Dani told Marduk. "I'll establish barriers, so no light comes in through the windows."

Clearly, her thought process covered all necessary bases at break-neck speed. After years in hell, sunlight would be devastating to the women.

"I'll have a raft of medical equipment at the ready over there." She pointed to the group of gods. "And I don't care who does it, but make sure the refrigerator and cupboards are well stocked in the cottage."

She misted out quickly, figuring her orders would be followed.

Deferring to his medically trained better, Marduk obeyed without question.

Dani says take them right to cottage number two, he told Nergal. *We'll have everything ready.*

Dumuzi mulled it all over while he emptied groceries from a shelf into a bag.

There were two more, very fucked-up questions. How did these women fit into Ridhwan's twisted scheme? For there was no doubt this was more of the evil cat's doing. And who, from the group down below, was Lahar's relative or *Chosen*?

Chapter Thirty

Bel and Riley stood blinking at each other in the dark. The girl hadn't gone into shock like Beletseri figured, but had, instead, recovered nicely after a short minute of silence. Bel was hardly prepared for what she said next.

You let them think you're the queen, Ereshkigal, the girl cracked. *Pretty smart thinking.*

Bel breathed out slowly. *Okay.* Where was this headed? The goddess was cautious. *So you know Marla,* she fished. *And that's how you know Matthew?* Bel felt momentary elation. Yes. The two had to be working together for her release.

Yup. I know Marla, and Jeremiah, and Matthew. She looked closely at Bel's face then started speaking again. *I also know all the gods and goddesses at the Blue Hills. And I know King Nergal and Ereshkigal too.*

Bel stumbled backward as if slapped. She went down onto the leaves. When she was able to respond, she did so shakily. *Do they…are they…*

The girl Riley looked to be mulling over her answer to the truncated questions. She finally sighed and moved forward to stroke Bel on her arm. A strangely comforting touch.

Yeah. They all know. Matthew got captured and taken back to the compound by Marla. He's been in the dungeon ever since, yelling his lungs out for you at all hours.

At Bel's open mouth she continued. *But don't worry. I think things are going to go in your favor now.*

What do you mean? Bel could barely draw breath. She couldn't believe her old boss, or for that matter, any of the gods she'd screwed over were worrying about her.

Nergal's on board with pretending you're his wife so they can get you out of here. I guess there will be some kind of trial when you get home, but Marla and a few of the goddesses are speaking up on your behalf. It might not be so bad. Riley looked around. *Certainly not as bad as this fucking place.* She shivered.

Bel felt like she'd been smacked in the gut and wished wounded cat-man would shut the fuck up as he continued to howl in pain. Some silence would be good to get her head around what the girl had said.

"Can you puh-lease take the caterwauling someplace else?" Bel yelled. "Some of us are trying to get some sleep."

She and Riley glanced outside as some discussion took place between her guard and the uninjured newcomer. Then their guard, the biggest of the cats, picked the hurt one up and stalked away. The recruit stationed himself outside their hidey-hole and took up position as their substitute sentry.

"Well, at least things are a little quieter now." Bel needed time to process Riley's take on things in the Blue Hills. To that end, the goddess indicated a bunch of leaves she'd gathered into a pile. It was small but would have to do as a sleeping spot for both of them.

"We really should try to bunk down. Morning will come fast." She hoped the girl wasn't critter-phobic.

"Uh. No thanks." The girl looked at Bel askance. "You need the sleep way more than me, and that pile's not big enough for two. Damn. It's probably been pretty tough being here with the extra worry you have. I can't imagine trying to get weird food to stay down even with a normal constitution," she prattled. "I had a friend who couldn't keep anything in her stomach for weeks. She had to rely solely on prenatals."

"Prenatals?" Bel had never heard that term before. Was there a thing available that would settle her constantly churning stomach?

"Yeah, you know. For your..." Riley looked at the sentry and got a cagey and knowing look on her face. *Oh, yeah. They're not supposed to know.*

Now Bel was really confused. *Not supposed to know what?* she asked.

You don't have to pretend with me. Everybody at the compound has heard, and Matthew is ecstatic...when he's not screaming for everyone to come rescue you.

Young lady. Bel gave her best, strictest face. She hated being in the dark. She hated, even more, when the darkness had to do with her. *Explain this very minute exactly what you're talking about.*

Riley looked at her incredulously. *Duh. Your pregnancy, of course.*

My... It was a good thing that Bel was sitting, or she would have fallen over. Her head spun, and what the fuck? Part of her knew instantly Riley was correct. But the other part? *Oh no.* This could so not be right.

What makes you think I'm pregnant?

I have ears, you know, Riley smirked. *It was Marla who told everybody about it. Those cat shifters have great noses, and I think she whiffed some hormonal thing on you before you got snatched.*

My gods. I'm pregnant. Bel started to laugh. *I haven't been sick all this time, I've been gestating.* Her laughter turned edgy as she thought back to all her "symptoms." *I should have known.* She shook her head. *I'm such an idiot.*

Wait. You didn't know? Now it was Riley's turn to look bewildered. *You're a grownup.* She threw up her hands. *How could you not know?*

Bel's laughter was spiraling out of hand. And much to her chagrin, she couldn't seem to stop. It had taken on a certain hysteria, and she could see worry reflected in the girl's eyes. When tears began streaming down her cheeks, she knew she was screwed. Bel couldn't stop thinking about a baby…her baby…and captivity…and Matthew. It was all suddenly too much.

A stirring outside their vine enclosure had Bel vaguely knowing the guard approached, obviously to find out what was wrong. Her laughter grew louder. *Dammit.* She had to get a grip. She didn't need another back-hand that might…oh, hell no.

Bel slammed her mouth shut. She decided right then and there she wasn't going to be tossed around anymore. *No way.* She had a baby inside her who needed protecting. No more fucking hysterics.

"What's the problem in here?" their jailer stalked in and asked. "As if I give a shit." His eyes were cold. "Shut the hell up, or I'll do it for you."

"That won't be necessary," Bel clipped, biting back her emotions and wiping her eyes. "We…"

She was about to finish her apology when something beyond their grotto caught her eye. *Shit*. Reinforcements? One cat was bad news, but two were worse. She'd had her share of torment at the hands of Ridhwan's commanders, and even pregnant, she'd weathered it. But she doubted whether the tender human could withstand their rough treatment. She scrambled to her feet, grabbed Riley up and thrust the girl behind her. "Call off your friends. We're going to settle down now and go to sleep. I promise we won't make any more noise."

"My friends?" The guy looked suitably confused before a large, disembodied rock came down on the sentinel's head from behind. He fell to his knees, struggled to get up, but was pushed back to the ground…by nothing Bel could see. He grabbed at this throat clawing and gasping for breath.

Bel looked carefully for the cause but saw only shadows in the trees. She didn't know what was going on.

As she puzzled, the cat's eyes rolled back in his head, and he slumped, lifeless, face-first into the dirt. Bel was no fool. She wasn't about to waste a gods-given, perfectly good opportunity. She grabbed Riley's hand.

"Let's go." she cried. Paying attention only to the horrified girl who looked at the unmoving body at their feet, she urged her to move. Bel tugged and got forward momentum. Then ran up against a solid wall of hard flesh.

"Ah, shit. Never mind." Not bothering to glance at the new threat, she pushed Riley behind her again, steeling herself for the cuff she knew would be coming.

It didn't.

"Dorian?" Riley's voice squeaked high and excited from behind her. "I'm so happy to see you. How did you get here?"

"Dorian?" Bel repeated numbly. "As in the warlock Dorian?"

She looked up. Way up. Which was unusual for a goddess who was five-foot-eleven.

She'd never before had the pleasure of a formal introduction to the dark, powerful entity who'd joined forces with the Blue Hill gods, but damn. He gave off some highly dangerous vibes. She backed away slowly...very slowly.

The girl behind her had no such trepidation. She moved quickly around Bel and wrapped her sweet little human arms around the big guy's waist.

"Oh my god, I'm so glad you're here. We're safe."

"For the moment, and only if we move quickly," Dorian said in a low, controlled voice. "I came in on the energy of the cats as they moved through the barrier, and we'll leave the same way. We'll use this one's body to open it up to us again, but we need to do it without alerting all the guards."

Beletseri found her tongue now there was action afoot and dropped right into scheming mode. "All the sentries except this one and the pair who were just here are simple cat-shifters with plenty of strength but no powers. Between the two of us, we should be able to overwhelm them if they become aware. What we don't need is the very bad cat you came in with getting wind of what's happening. He travels like you do which means if he hears anything, he'll be on us. Next to Ridhwan—who thank the gods is not here—that puss is the nastiest alpha in the sandbox, and if he shows up, we'll have a hell of a fight on our hands."

Dorian nodded at her in quiet acknowledgment and silently hoisted the downed panther's body up over one shoulder. "I've already taken out the two border guards who were behind your pen. If we go quickly, there's no reason anyone will even know we're leaving. Come on, Riley. You'll have plenty of time to give in to emotion when we get you home."

Bel looked over and watched the shivers beginning to move over the girl's body in waves. She slung an arm around her shoulders and pulled her forward.

"We're all in this together, right, brave girl? And seriously? What better company could you have than a pregnant goddess and an arrogant warlock?" She looked up and saw an amused spark in Dorian's eyes before he turned and walked away. She drew Riley along at her side, cajoling her and matching the large male's steps.

The barrier had an odd shimmer which alerted residents when they were about to come in contact with it. Dorian approached purposely. By slinging the shifter's lifeless body across the divide, the force field would be deactivated, and they'd be free. *Sort of.* Because what would they do once they were in the jungle?

"Warlock, what's the plan once we cross over," Bel whispered.

"I am able to take one person with me when I dissipate," he told her. "Of course, that will be Riley. You will have to mist out in the way of gods and find your way home. I understand the trip is two-and-a-half hours long for your kind."

"Fine, but I'll have to be one hundred yards from here to make it happen because of Ridhwan's barrier spells. Damn. It's a good thing I've suddenly found new strength," Bel lied. She wasn't about to tell him that in her depleted state, she'd be lucky to make the needed dash to one hundred yards. And if by some miracle she did and was able to dissipate, her trip home would take a damned long time.

But she wasn't about to complain...nor balk at having to turn herself in to be held captive with Matthew. *If* by some miracle she made it.

Bel let herself have hope. Her husband's embrace was so close she could almost taste it...and its flavor was a lot better than raw beetles.

Dorian took one look back at both women, signaled, then flung the body across the barrier. Just like that, a doorway opened.

Bel gave a sigh of relief. *Almost there.*

Dorian gestured for Riley to go first, and...fuck. An alarm immediately sounded.

"Shit," Dorian clipped out, pushing both of the women through the opening. "There must have been additional security protocols I didn't anticipate."

Guards began streaming through the woods, amassing behind them.

"We need to move," the warlock growled.

Bel gasped as the head-cat—the abusive bastard—suddenly appeared in front of them. He made to grab Riley.

"Oh no, you don't." The goddess was quicker.

She sent a leg up and landed a strong kick on the shifter's wrist, sending his arm up into the air. Bel followed up with every last bit of her goddess strength, landing a punch at the kitty, mid-chest. His body flew fifteen feet away, and he seemed momentarily dazed.

Bel turned to the warlock. "Dorian. Grab Riley and go. You've got about ten seconds before he's back on his feet."

"But what about you?" Riley was the one who asked.

Clearly, the sweet child didn't know the history between Bel the immortals. None of them would give a damn she was left behind.

"Don't worry about me. I'll hold him off until you get away. Then I'll do my thing. No problem" She stalked forward. Maybe she could land a foot to this guy's gut while he lay prone, then make her escape. *Yeah. Right.* And pregnant pigs fly.

The male had already morphed into a badass cat and bunched his haunches for a spring.

Bel frantically turned to the pair who seemed to hesitate. "Go," she screamed.

Dorian gave her a look. He knew as well as she did there was no way she would make it.

"Good luck, Bel." He gave her a quick bow, seized Riley's arm…and they were gone.

Chapter Thirty-one

"Gram, we can't just leave her there."

Verrie watched the ineffectual comforting Frank attempted to impart to her granddaughter. Riley remained incensed Bel had been left behind. She'd accepted all the hugs and tears shed for her homecoming but hadn't let go of her incredulous anger.

Riles turned to Dorian whose wife Addie-May clung to his arm, having returned from her futile search to find her husband already at home.

"Bel didn't get away," the girl spat, but asked for final confirmation. "Did she?" Riley skewered Dorian with a demanding look.

He didn't even think to condescend. "No. There was no way in her depleted state she would have been able to get by the cat and make it one hundred yards," the warlock answered honestly.

Riley turned to Marduk. "Now that we know where she is in Malaysia, you're just going to leave her there? She's really sick, you know. She looks awful. I could tell even in the dark. There were bruises on her face and arms from getting knocked around. They'll beat her worse now because she helped me get away. She could lose her baby." Tears leaked out of Riley's eyes.

Verrie saw Marduk raise his brows at Dorian. The warlock gave a helpless shrug but confirmed Riley's assessment. "She looked quite ill, and yes, there were signs of abuse…some old, some new."

"And this business about Bel helping you two get away?" Marduk questioned Dorian regarding the testimonial Riley had delivered earlier.

"It was odd that is certain. But Bel *did* attack the cat-man when he made a grab for Riley and kept him away long enough for us to depart," Dorian admitted.

"She also got between me and our guard earlier when the guy was pissed off. She was protecting me." Riley's mouth set firmly even as tears continued to drop. "You have to do something," she snapped. "You're gods, and witches, and…blue guys. You know where this asshole's hideout is now. Just go back and get her."

"It's not that easy, Riley," Shamash spoke up. "They have a barrier that holds us out. Ridhwan could sit inside and pick us off, one by one. Don't think that with his years of studying gods, he doesn't know exactly where our vulnerable spots are."

"So you're just going to give up? Leave her there? You're supposed to be the good guys." Sienna moved to Riley's side and looked just as pissed off as her friend.

"I didn't say we're giving up," Marduk attempted to soothe the girls. "But right now, we're in the process of dealing with a group of women he's kept prisoner for a lot longer than Bel. We're moving them into our cottages. It's a delicate process."

That was certainly true, Verrie thought. At the moment, Dani-Lee was taking charge of the females with help from Mamitu and Rephaim, the two women's advocates Nergal had recommended.

"Well, I for one don't want anybody making trips outside the compound until Verrie and I have mated," Dumuzi spoke into the uncomfortable silence, surprising everyone by looking extremely fierce. A shiver of lust went down her spine. This strong god was the man she'd marry and live with for the rest of eternity. *Hell, yeah.* She felt like she needed to howl…in a good way.

But wait. Why was he in such a hurry to get them mated?

"What's your rush, Muze?" she asked, rubbing his back to calm him.

"With all this talk and evidence of imprisoned women, I want to make sure when we rescue Bel…"

Verrie noted the surprised look on Riley's face.

"Yeah, Riley," he assured the girl. "Have no doubt, we'll be doing that as soon as the big-wigs here hash out a decent plan. Anyway, before I leave, I want to make sure Verrie's a goddess, so if the shit hits the fan, she can have advantages immortals have over enemies. I want her to have super-strength and agility…"

"And you want to have crazy god-sex with her ASAP," Lenore smirked. "We get it, Muze."

Verrie was in the dark about what "crazy god-sex" might mean. Because…hadn't they already done that? Her face must have looked perplexed because Lenore took pity.

"Don't worry. I'll fill you in soon, girlfriend, just not in front of the impressionable youngsters."

Muze glanced hopefully at the thunder god.

Marduk appeared thoughtful and spoke to his wife, Tess. "All this hoopla means no summer solstice celebration." He stroked his chin. "I suppose that can't be helped. How fast do you think we can get a mating ceremony underway?"

"How fast do you want it?" Tess replied, looking at the clock.

It was barely five o'clock. Verrie blinked. How in the world could so much have happened in the two-and-a-half hours since school let out?

"Well," Marduk pondered. "The time difference between here and Malaysia is thirteen hours. Their day is..?"

Verrie was damned confused. What did Malaysia have to do with a mating ceremony?

"Sunrise at seven—in just one hour—and sunset at seven-thirty," Lahar supplied, giving over the information but looking discombobulated and far less logical than she'd ever seen him.

Verrie wasn't surprised. He had to be preoccupied with his visibility which they now knew was somehow connected to the women refugees. But he still hadn't lost his intelligent edge. Verrie knew few others who would be able to do calculations in the face of a possible eternal mate nearby.

"Thank you, Lahar. I'd like to arrive with a full contingent of gods tomorrow night by six p.m., their time. If I calculate in for just under two hours of god-travel time…" Marduk started mumbling.

"We need to leave here at three in the morning," Lahar answered again, not waiting for his boss to do the math.

Verrie had confirmation Lahar was in no way compromised, knowing his future might rest right around the corner.

Tess laughed, "Okay, come on, ladies. We have an amulet ceremony to accomplish." The goddess began herding women from the room. "Eight o'clock in the chambers below," she tossed back at her husband. "Don't be late."

Marduk chuckled at his feisty wife. "Wouldn't think of it. And while you fuss with the mate-to-be, we'll be working out a plan of attack to rescue Bel."

Verrie and the girls—along with Frank—were drawn off by a group of extremely enthusiastic women. She didn't know what made her heart pound faster—in three hours she'd be mating with Dumuzi or in ten, he'd be on his way to embark on a very dangerous mission.

If she'd had an opportunity to ponder, she might have panicked. As it was, she was caught up in a tide of waxing, oiling, and hair styling which the Goddess League would not be denied.

A number of them had gone on to procure special food for the banquet afterward while still others lit the "thousands of candles in the ceremonial spaces."

Sienna, Frank, and Riley stood and gaped a lot, except when they were shown the glorious silk gowns they would be wearing. That even perked up the introspective Riley long enough for a fashion show that had Verrie sighing. The girls were really growing up.

Her own robes were plain and made from a rough spun linen. Lenore, a fountain of information continuously flowing from her lips, told her she and Muze would be dressed simply to show elaborate trappings had nothing to do with their love for one another.

Verrie had been momentarily left alone to breathe and was nearly ready for her trip to the basement halls when a cacophony of angry voices outside her bedroom made her pause as she finished securing her robe.

"No. You can't go in." Lenore's raised tones told Verrie Muze must be attempting to see her. Was he having second thoughts? She moved quickly to her door and pulled it open.

"Lenore. It's okay. If Dumuzi needs to see me, it must be important." Her gut clenched. She looked at her god, standing in his homespun loincloth and nothing else. He was flipping gorgeous. And the love shining from his eyes was more than she'd ever hoped for.

So, forget it. If he was getting cold feet, she wasn't going to let him back out now. No way could she live without him. She wondered if the ceremony would "take" if his friends bound and dragged him to the altar.

"Um. Are you going to ask me in?" He looked decidedly uncomfortable.

"Of course." She swept back from the door and issued him an invitation with her hand. He entered and began to pace.

Verrie couldn't stand it. She strode toward him, put a hand to his chest and halted his progress. "What is it?" she asked.

He took her forearms in a tight grasp. She could feel tremors. This was not good. "Verrie, there's something I haven't told you."

Oh my gods. Could he have another wife? Wives? Was he gay? Terminally ill? Verrie went through a long, rapid list and dismissed them all. She was just going to have to pry it out of him.

"Sit. Right now and tell me." She pushed him onto the bed. He went without a fight. "We have a delicate

349

timetable here, so you better spill," she told him, combating her fears with practicality.

"I know. And I should have told you this before." He ran a hand through his hair which lay in messy, red tangles. Clearly, he'd been worrying for a while.

"This might be a deal breaker for you." His troubled eyes met hers.

A little of Verrie's chest pain eased. *Okay*. He wasn't the one putting a stop to things. He thought *she* might.

"Just spit it out, love." The use of the endearment clearly undid him. He dropped from the bed to his knees, landing at her feet to hug her around the legs.

"I killed my family," he cried out.

Verrie went blank. It was the last thing she expected to hear from him.

"Excuse me?" she said confusedly.

"Well...I would have killed them if they'd been human," he repeated. "Which is the same thing as killing them. And that's why I was relegated to hell."

She quickly regained her equilibrium. Clearly, it wasn't all cut and dried like he'd just laid it out. He wouldn't have been allowed a second chance by Nergal and company if he was a cold-hearted murderer. Nor would this wonderful group of gods embrace him as a brother if he had committed such a heinous crime.

"Why don't we sit back here on your bed, and I'll try to explain." His pained expression tore at her heart.

Verrie drew Dumuzi up from the floor and settled them both on the mattress. Pulling him close to her side, she waited for him to begin.

"It was 17 AD."—Verrie had heard that date before—"I had turned into my swamp monster, but this time, I wasn't able to get myself away from home like I always had before."

His eyes focused on the wall opposite them, and Verrie knew he was seeing back in time.

"Along with the anger and destruction I display now when the change takes over, in the early days, my episodes included deluging any area surrounding me. I turned land to swamp."

Okay. That made sense. He was god of swamps and vegetation after all. She patted his hand, and he continued.

"That particular day, my mother, my father, and my sister were in the house with me when I changed. Because of me being out of control, our home got sucked underground, under a deep layer of mud."

Verrie found herself holding her breath. She could almost feel the wetness that would have come up over his loved ones' noses, smothering them. She took a deep haul of air into her lungs, shaking it off. She needed to keep listening.

"Of course, my family are gods. And as you've been made aware, only complete blood-loss over a prolonged period, total incineration, or irreparable harm to our amulets can kill us. Which means my family didn't die, but they were really dirty. And angry. And worried enough for their future, they had me sentenced and sent to hell."

Verrie was stunned. She sat perfectly still, digesting what Dumuzi had said. His broken voice brought her back to awareness.

"I completely understand if you want to call things off. I never want to do anything that will harm you or Sienna. But I can't give you that. I…"

Verrie cut him off. She was so angry she could barely get the words out. "Of all the fucked up, bitchy things a family could do to you." she railed. "How dare they?"

She saw Muze shake his head, clearly not understanding, but Verrie was on a roll.

"They sent their own child to hell…for a condition you had no control over? Hadn't they heard of doctors…of…of…exorcisms…or whatever the hell else was used at that time, for gods' sake? Ooh," Verrie fumed. "Are they still alive and well somewhere?"

Dumuzi nodded, wide-eyed.

"Well then, just wait 'til I meet them. They'll get a piece of *my* mind. Send you to hell, indeed. They are so *not* welcome to meet their grandchildren when we have them."

"Grandchildren?" Dumuzi's voice sounded thin but hopeful.

"Of course," Verrie came out of her tirade and blinked. "You didn't think I could look at the cute little godlings around here and not want one of our own, did you?"

"You mean…us…kids…you'll still mate with me? Even after what I've told you?"

Verrie took Muze's face between her hands and put a very succinct kiss on his mouth.

"Damn right, my love. You would never, ever hurt me or Sienna. I know that," she told him. "And if you do start to get out of hand—which I seriously doubt—first line of defense, Archie, will alert us. And if that isn't enough, the gods and goddesses around here will keep you in order."

She beamed into his astonished face and couldn't resist teasing. "And if all of that doesn't work," she tipped closer and gave his earlobe a sharp nip. "I'll be a goddess, remember? And I'll kick your sorry ass...after I make sure—with whatever means I have at *hand*—it's a lovely shade of red."

Bingo. Dumuzi's mind was off his confession and on to bigger and better things as evidenced by the impressive tent lifting his loincloth. Verrie reached a hand under and gave his equipment a squeeze. *Yes.* These gods knew how to dress down, commando style.

"Now, go." Verrie shooed him off the bed. "We don't want to keep our friends waiting. And the sooner we finish with this amulet bullshit, the quicker we can get down to more interesting things." She looked at his twitching loincloth again.

"Have I told you I love you?" Dumuzi grinned—even if it was a toothy, growly, swamp-monstery kind of smile—letting all his feelings show in his eyes.

"Yes, you have." She got up and gave him a push in the direction of the door. "And I expect you to show me just how much, later."

"It's a date." He resisted her shove long enough to pull her into his arms and lay a heavy-duty kiss on her mouth, one that shook her down to her bare feet. Verrie nearly swooned. *Hell, yeah.*

Feeling an incredible tingle throughout her body with his kiss, she marveled at what the goddesses told her. Apparently, directly after the amulet placement, she'd be more lustful than she'd ever been before...in her life. Was that fucking possible? As it was, from

Muze's kiss alone, she was going to have to mop up before she went downstairs.

The door clicked behind her god as he finally departed. Verrie did her finals in the bathroom before being met outside the door by a group of gleeful females. Her hands shook. It was time. The gaggle made its way to the basement—all the way past the door with the sign-up sheet outside she'd yet to explore, past Matthew who gallantly told her how beautiful she looked, and down a long corridor which seemed to slant deeper into the earth. When she reached their destination, her breath caught.

The room was beyond description. It exuded an ancient aura that couldn't be real—the house had been built only hundreds of years before, not thousands—and yet Verrie felt she'd been transported back to what she imagined resembled an ancient Mesopotamian temple.

There were candles everywhere and writing on the walls in unrecognizable script. Carvings had been made on the floor, the altar, and stone artifacts displayed on columns around the sides of the room. She thought she spied a few that resembled some of the gods…yes…there was Enlil, for sure.

Verrie was led to the front where an altar stone had been raised at a slant, and while the assemblage sighed, she was gently put into place with her back against its coldness. Once she was alone and the women sat in their seats, she heard a soft chanting coming from outside the room. Her eyes focused on the doorway, and one by one the gods—decked in the finest of raiments set off by shining gold armbands and torques—moved down the aisle and into the room.

When the group paused at the altar, Dumuzi came forward and positioned himself next to her, putting his back to the other half of the slab. He picked up her hand and kissed it. The chanting ceased, and Marduk looked suddenly befuddled.

"Uh, Muze? Who did you pick as best man?"

There was no hesitation. "I want Shamash to do the honors," he said in a strong, clear voice. "He made it possible for me to take this lovely woman as my *Chosen.*"

Shamash stepped forward and took a lethal-looking knife from Marduk's outstretched hand. "It will be my honor," the cat god replied reverently.

The room seemed to hold its breath as the first slice was made in Dumuzi's flesh. The skin of his shoulder was peeled back, and Sham made short work of the muscle layer that flexed below. Verrie could feel Muze flinch and watched as a twist of leather was put between his teeth which he bit with ferocity. She found a similar one being urged upon her, and took it in her mouth, hoping when her time came to undergo Dani's knife, she would be as brave as her fine god.

Dumuzi held her gaze as the doctor began, making similar cuts in Verrie's shoulder. She couldn't help it. Her eyes filled with tears at the fiery pain that tore through her, but as soon as the half amulet was taken from Dumuzi and placed in her body, a different kind of burning took hold.

Verrie's hand squeezed her mate's, and their fingers re-twined. Just that small amount of stimulation had her pussy clenching with need. She sensed her shoulder accepting Muze into her life and closing up. Somewhere outside of her, she heard cheering.

The transfer had clearly been a success, but she hadn't been worried. All she could feel was the heat of Dumuzi as he pressed into her side. He lifted their combined hands and kissed her knuckles, brushing over one of her nipples on the way up.

Verrie cried out.

The explosion between her legs came on fast and hard, the spasms overtaking her before she even knew what hit. The orgasm had been so strong, it sapped the energy from her legs. She had to bite the leather hard so she wouldn't scream. *Oh my gods.* Her eyes felt like they were rolling back in her head. Had she just had the most incredible climax of her life from that small touch to her nipple? In front of all of these people?

When her head stopped spinning, she heard their voices.

"Time to clear out everybody, unless we want a different kind of show." It was Candy's smart mouth in the doorway, ushering everyone clear. "Let's go folks. Move it or risk an x-rated documentary on the mating habits of immortals."

At that point, Verrie ceased to care. She trusted Candy would clear the room. She turned to her mate and pressed herself up against him where he stood, back still to the rock.

She slithered down his body, spitting the leather out on the way, lifting his loincloth, and pressing her cheek to his hard shaft. "Do you have any last words," she said huskily, "because I'm about to suck you dry."

Dumuzi groaned and lost his mouthpiece. "How about a promise that once you're through, I'm going to fuck you until you scream my name."

"I'll go with that," Verrie said, opening her lips and sliding them over the velvet soft head of his luscious pink cock.

She didn't hesitate. His length went down her throat, and she exerted a pressure on his cock she didn't know was possible. If her mouth wasn't full, she would have smiled. *Ah. Goddess lips.* Stronger and more able to accommodate her well-hung husband. She groaned around his girth. Gods, he tasted good. She worked up his length, then swiped a saucy tongue over the moisture seeping from his tip. *Heavenly.* She closed her eyes and savored. When he would have moved, she pushed him back. Oh, no. She was in charge here…and this immortal strength thing was awesome.

"Stay right there," she growled and lowered her mouth again.

Within seconds he found a rhythm that had him rocking his hips, moving gently in and out of her mouth.

She popped loose for a second. "Don't hold back," she gasped, taking him fully down her throat again.

That's when he let go of his restraint. Both hands came up behind her head, one threading through her hair as he fucked her mouth, thrusting into it with abandon.

Yes. Verrie had always loved giving blow-jobs, but now her enhanced skills brought the experience to a whole new level. She could taste, she could feel, and her tongue was everywhere as he sought his release.

When it finally came, her man roared as the eruption moved up from his balls, past her sensitive lips, to burst forth from his cock into her throat. She swallowed it all, licking him, squeezing him for every last drop. When she finished, he put his hands under her armpits and raised her to her feet.

"That was…indescribable," he told her, dipping to her mouth. Verrie felt so naughty as he tasted himself on her tongue. It fueled more of her own wetness which had spread until she was slick with wanting.

"I can feel your pussy without touching," Dumuzi told her, incredulously. "I was told the connection between us would be infinite."

Verrie could barely nod her head. That's why the blow-job had been so good. She'd been feeling it right along with Muze.

"Now we're going to see what fucking is like," he promised, placing his hands under her ass and hiking her up high. He spun them around and placed Verrie's back against the altar. Her linen rucked up around her waist. "Gotta love these robes," he panted. Without preamble, he surged into her waiting cunt.

Verrie screamed, "Yes." She wrapped her legs around him as tightly as she could, linking her ankles behind his back, driving her heels into his ass. "Fuck me, Muze," she wailed.

And he obliged.

He became a pile-driver, pistoning into her depths, bending his knees and tilting his prick up inside to hit her hot spot, over and over again. It felt so good, so strong, so commanding. And it certainly didn't take long. Verrie found herself reaching for the peak, tensing every muscle inside herself until that final punch, that pinnacle. She shouted her release and clutched his cock with her inner muscles until she was sure he'd be rendered immobile. But his god strength carried him on to a half dozen more thrusts, until he too attained that ultimate height and emptied into her with long, hard spurts.

They stood there afterward, wrapped around each other, dazed. Muze rested his forehead on hers until his breathing came back under control.

"Wow"

"Double wow," Verrie agreed. She looked up into his eyes and saw laughter lurking just below the surface.

"What?"

Muze let his monster smile out. "Wanna do it again?"

Epilogue

The banquet long over and travel having taken place, the group of gods moved silently through the jungle. At the last minute, before leaving the compound, Marduk had taken pity on Matthew and brought him along under penalty of much pain if the god didn't agree to stay with them. They'd added to their party minutes ago, meeting up with Marla and Jeremiah.

Oddly, Matthew had integrated himself into the group so well, any outsider looking on would never know he was—or had once been—the enemy.

Dumuzi noticed Dagon stayed next to Bel's mate in an almost protective manner. Well, the two of them *had* worked together at one time.

His mind came back to present when Marduk rendering a warning. *We're almost upon them.*

All Muze's concentration was focused, just like everyone else's, on finding Bel's energy and extracting her without injury. Riley and Dorian had said the goddess was weak, but they were hoping she still had enough fight in her to advocate for herself if the need arose.

All right, Nergal. Marduk instructed. *Do your thing.*

The king stepped forward and raised his hands toward the barrier in front of them. Two runes, one on his forearm and the other on his chest began to glow…the same two, Muze noted, that had glowed in hell when they entered the demon's lair. Clearly, Ridhwan had been responsible for both as they contained this, his telltale signature.

Within seconds the shields were down. The rescue party stormed across the fallen barrier and into the clearing to be met inside by…nothing.

Well, almost nothing.

There were a number of cowering women, children, and old men hunkered closely in the center of the settlement. But that was all.

No guards, no Ridhwan…and no Bel.

The camp had been close to abandoned, recently and hastily.

The adrenaline running through the group dropped to render them speechless.

All except Matthew, who refused to believe his eyes. "Noooo," his anguished cry split the dusk.

The rest of the immortals quietly regrouped to discuss their next move.